COTTONMOUTH

Center Point
Large Print

Also by Sean Lynch and available from
Center Point Large Print:

Death Rattle

**This Large Print Book carries the
Seal of Approval of N.A.V.H.**

COTTONMOUTH
THE GUNS OF SAMUEL PRITCHARD

SEAN LYNCH

CENTER POINT LARGE PRINT
THORNDIKE, MAINE

This Center Point Large Print edition
is published in the year 2020 by arrangement with
Kensington Publishing Corp.

Copyright © 2020 by Sean Lynch.

The text of this Large Print edition is unabridged.
In other aspects, this book may vary
from the original edition.
Printed in the United States of America
on permanent paper.
Set in 16-point Times New Roman type.

ISBN: 978-1-64358-608-3

The Library of Congress has cataloged this record
under Library of Congress Control Number: 2020930524

This book is dedicated to the cowboy in all of us.

COTTONMOUTH

CHAPTER 1

Sarpy County, Nebraska, five miles east of Papillion
March 1874

The reverend reined his wagon to a halt. Four men on horseback were blocking the road ahead. All were wearing town suits and bowlers, and he'd never seen any of them before. They were also wearing revolvers in shoulder holsters, which were plainly visible under their open riding jackets.

"Top of the mornin' to you, Reverend Hoskins," the oldest of the riders said. He tipped his hat.

"Do I know you gentlemen?" Reverend Hoskins said.

"No," the man said. "But we know you. You're Charles Hoskins, the pastor of the Baptist church in town. We know your family, too. Sitting next to you is your wife, Mary, your daughter, Maura, and your wee little son, Charles junior."

"How, exactly, do you know all this?" Hoskins asked.

"Why," the man said, "you're famous, Reverend. Your sermons are all the rage. They're right popular with the railroad laborers in these parts. Especially the ones where you call for all

9

the workers to band together, hold out for more money, and strike iffen they don't get what they want from Brody's railroad company. Those sermons are real barn burners, so I'm told."

"Now I know who you are," Hoskins said, making no effort to hide his contempt. "You're Quincy Agency men, aren't you? Cottonmouth Quincy sent you to intimidate me into silence and to stamp down the poor, abused, souls being worked like slaves by John Brody."

"It's true," the man confirmed, "we're employed by the Quincy Detective Agency. And as a matter of fact, we did come here to persuade you to temper your sermons to a tone more sympathetic to Mr. Brody's interests. By the way, Mr. Quincy certainly wouldn't appreciate being called Cottonmouth by the likes of you."

"I didn't give him that name," Hoskins retorted. "Quincy earned it himself by slithering around like a serpent, hiding like a thief, peering into keyholes like a rat, and doing John Brody's bidding."

"You surely have a right hostile notion of Mr. Quincy's character," the man said, "for a man of God. I thought all you preachers were supposed to be the forgivin' type?"

"Quincy doesn't need my forgiveness," Hoskins said. "If he wants to save his soul, he needs to repent his wicked ways and stop helping Brody wage war on his poor workers."

"I'll be sure and tell him you said that," the man said. The men with him chuckled.

"Charles," Mary said in a hushed whisper to her husband, "turn us around." The fear was plain on her face and clear in her voice. "We need to leave. Now." She pulled Maura, who was twelve, and Charles junior, who was six, closer.

"I'll not be buffaloed by Cottonmouth Quincy's hired thugs," Hoskins declared. "You're blocking our way," he said to the riders. "Yield the road and let us pass."

"I don't suppose you're going to voluntarily agree to stop sermonizin' against the railroad," the man said, "and stirrin' up all the workin' folks, are you?"

"I certainly am not."

"Mr. Quincy figured you was gonna say that," the man said, drawing his revolver. He nodded to his men, who also drew theirs.

One of the riders guided his horse close enough to the team pulling Hoskins's wagon to seize the harness. Mary stifled a scream and covered both her children's eyes as they huddled together.

"Step down outta that rig, Reverend," the man ordered, "and bring your family with you."

"We will not," Hoskins said. "I'm not afraid of your guns."

"Maybe not," the man said, aiming his Remington at Mary Hoskins and cocking the hammer back, "but I'll wager your wife is."

11

"All right," Hoskins said, clambering out of the buggy. "Don't shoot." He helped his wife and children disembark.

As soon as the Hoskinses left the wagon, the Quincy men dismounted. One climbed into the driver's seat the reverend vacated.

Hoskins stood protectively in front of his family. It did him no good. The leader holstered his pistol, nodded again, and another of the men clubbed the reverend in the kidney with the butt of his gun. The thin pastor fell gasping to all fours. Mary Hoskins began to cry, along with both of her children.

"Today we're gonna preach you a sermon," the leader said, "and it ain't even Sunday. The topic of this sermon is wrath and retribution. Put your right hand under the wagon wheel."

"What?"

The man kicked Hoskins in the ribs, dropping him from all fours to his stomach. "You heard me, Reverend. Put your hand under the wheel."

"Please," Reverend Hoskins pleaded. "Don't do this."

"Either your hand goes under that wheel, or your daughter's head. Which'll it be?"

The terrified Hoskins hesitated. The leader gave another silent signal, and one of the men roughly snatched twelve-year-old Maura from her mother's arms. Another simultaneously grabbed Mary and Charles junior by the hair and held them in place.

Maura was dragged, also by her hair, screaming and flailing in terror, and forced to the ground with her head under one of the wagon's rear wheels. The Quincy man in the wagon's seat held up his whip, awaiting the order to start the team of horses.

"No!" Reverend Hoskins said. "Let my daughter go." He crawled to the wagon on his belly and extended his right hand under the front wheel.

The leader gestured to release the girl. Maura Hoskins scrambled to her feet and ran sobbing into her mother's arms. Then the leader nodded a final time, and his man in the wagon cracked the whip.

The wagon lurched forward. Reverend Hoskins cried out in agony as his hand was crushed. His wife sank weeping to her knees, bringing her children with her.

The leader halted the wagon. He walked over to where the reverend lay cradling his mangled hand.

"Are you gonna continue to rile up workers against Mr. Brody and his railroad?"

"N-no," Reverend Hoskins sputtered.

"That's good," the man said. "Because Mr. Quincy gave specific orders about what we're to do if we catch wind of you givin' any more sermons incitin' unrest against the Brody Railroad Company. We'll be back, and what happened today will seem like a church social. We'll burn your church down, Reverend, with you and every one of your flock in it. Then we'll end your wife and daughter in their own beds and shoot your son dead on your doorstep. Do you understand?"

"I understand," Hoskins said.

The Quincy men holstered their revolvers and remounted their horses. "Don't you make us come back," the man admonished, "you hear?"

"I won't," Hoskins said weakly. "You'll have no more trouble from me."

"I reckoned as much," the man said. He shouted, "Cottonmouth Quincy sends his regards," over his shoulder as he and his three companions rode off.

CHAPTER 2

Atherton, Missouri
April 1874

"I thought I'd find you here," Ditch Clemson said as he entered the marshal's office. His lifelong friend, Marshal Samuel Pritchard, was seated inside at his desk. He was assembling the components of a chair he'd crafted himself.

Ditch put his hands on his hips and shook his head. "It's almost noon," he said, "and the train from Saint Louis is due to arrive any minute."

"So?" Pritchard said without looking up.

"So?" Ditch mimicked, making no effort to conceal the exasperation in his voice. "You know that European feller, Count Strobl, is gonna be on the train."

"So?" Pritchard repeated.

"All the newspapers are writin' about how Strobl got himself kicked out of his own country on account of dueling. He's reputed to be exiled royalty, and one of the deadliest shots east of the Mississippi."

"Why should I care?" Pritchard asked.

"You should care," Ditch said, "because he's been bragging to every reporter who'll listen that he's gunning for you."

15

"Keep your shirt on," Pritchard said, looking up from the partially assembled chair. "Why would this Strobl fella be on the prod for me? I don't know him from General Lee."

"Evidently, he knows you," Ditch said, "at least by reputation. You're tellin' me you ain't a little worried?"

"Nah," Pritchard said. "What's worryin' get you? Anyhow, I'm almost finished puttin' the last leg on my chair. I'll be along in a minute."

"Sometimes a little worryin' can keep you alive. What am I supposed to tell your sister, Idelle, after you get shot to pieces sittin' at your desk, covered in sawdust, fiddlin' with a wooden chair?"

"You worry too much," Pritchard grinned, fitting the final leg into the seat. He placed the chair on the floor, sat in it, and smiled in satisfaction. "After all we've been through together, do you reckon I'm gonna let a fancy-pants, foreign duelist put a hole in me?"

Pritchard stood to his full six-and-a-half-foot height and smiled down at his medium-sized friend. "Besides," he said, "I have no choice but to make my own office chair. The old one is too small. The only way I can get furniture big enough to fit me is to make it myself."

"I just don't want to see you get shot again," Ditch said, looking up at the towering marshal. "Neither does Idelle. She is the mayor, after all.

16

She's insisting on going to the station herself to meet this Count Strobl. She plans to ask him not to provoke you. She doesn't want to see anybody get hurt."

"Sometimes," Pritchard said, "people get hurt. That's a fact. Occasionally it can be prevented, other times it can't. More often than not, it's their own damned fault. Idelle ought to know that as well as anyone. You, too."

"I reckon so," Ditch agreed.

Samuel Pritchard and David "Ditch" Clemson had grown up as friends, neighbors, and blood brothers in rural Atherton. Teenagers when the Civil War began, they fled as partners after Pritchard's father was murdered, his family's property and lumber business were stolen, and his mother was forced to marry the man who'd orchestrated it all: Atherton's corrupt mayor, Burnell Shipley. Young Pritchard was shot in the head, presumed dead, and buried in an unmarked grave.

That was when his fiercely loyal friend, Ditch Clemson, dug him up and found him still clinging to life.

After his resurrection, and bearing a telltale gunshot scar on his forehead over his right eye, Pritchard assumed the alias "Joe Atherton" to protect what was left of his family. Departing Missouri, the boys enlisted in the Confederate army as guerillas in Arkansas. After a series of harrowing escapades, Pritchard and Ditch, no longer boys, survived the war and parted ways.

Ditch, a skilled horseman, had grown weary of war and killing. He went farther south and sought his fortune in Texas. Within a few years he flourished as a rancher and cattleman.

Pritchard chose a different path, also in Texas; he joined the Texas Rangers. Over the next ten years he blazed a trail, in gun smoke and blood, throughout the Republic of Texas and the New Mexico and Arizona Territories. "Smokin' Joe" Atherton, as he became known, earned his nickname for his propensity to send those who challenged him to "smoke in hell." He also earned a well-deserved reputation as the fastest, and most lethal, gunman on the frontier.

Last summer, fate brought Pritchard and Ditch together once more. The duo joined forces on a cattle drive and ended up back in their hometown. There they courageously faced down Burnell Shipley and his crew of murderous lawmen, but not before Pritchard's mother was killed and his younger sister, Idelle, was taken hostage. The two heroic young Missourians, neither yet thirty years old, eliminated the mayor, cleaned out his crooked gunmen, rescued Idelle, and freed the town of Atherton from the yoke of abuse and corruption that characterized Burnell Shipley's decades-long reign.

In the nine months since their epic battle in the

streets of Atherton, the town, finally out from under the shadow of Shipley's iron-fisted rule, once again prospered. Ditch and Idelle, fulfilling her childhood wish, got engaged.

Ironically, with Burnell Shipley's death and the passing of their mother, Idelle and Samuel Pritchard inherited the vast wealth of Atherton's lucrative lumber, cattle, and merchandizing enterprises once controlled exclusively by Shipley.

Pritchard, however, refused any part of the abundant inheritance. He left his share of the money, and the running of Atherton, in his younger sister's capable hands, comforted in the knowledge that Ditch, his most trusted friend, was at her side. As a result of Pritchard's reticence, Idelle found herself in the unique and unexpected position of being the wealthiest person in Jackson County, Missouri. And until the special elections coming up in June, she was also the acting mayor of Atherton.

Pritchard contented himself with putting to rest the alias Smokin' Joe Atherton, and the role of Ranger, gunfighter, and man-killer that had made him a legend under that infamous title.

Meanwhile Ditch, at Idelle's insistence, announced his candidacy for mayor to fill the vacancy created by Burnell Shipley's abrupt demise. She knew he had the temperament, business acumen, and ethical foundation to lead Atherton out of the trauma the community had endured throughout the war, and at Shipley's filthy hands.

At Ditch's, Idelle's, and the town council's prodding, Pritchard had taken on the job of town marshal. He had also, reluctantly, allowed himself to be nominated as a candidate for Jackson County sheriff and grudgingly accepted the position of acting sheriff until the election.

"Are you comin' with me to the train station," Ditch asked impatiently, "or ain't ya?"

Pritchard brushed off the sawdust from his button-front shirt and belted on his pair of .45 Colt revolvers. He topped his blond hair, which was closely cropped at the sides and back but long enough on top to mostly cover the bullet-hole scar on his forehead, with his Stetson.

"Let's go welcome the count," he said to Ditch, gesturing toward the door. "I'd hate to keep royalty waiting."

CHAPTER 3

It was overcast, chilly, and threatening rain when Pritchard and Ditch reached the depot. A sizable crowd, larger than the usual group of townspeople meeting the afternoon train, had assembled at the station. Both men surmised the extra gaggle of spectators were connected to the impending confrontation between the mysterious European passenger and Atherton's town marshal. The train slowly came to a halt in a cloud of hissing steam.

Idelle waved to them from across the station. When they met, she gave her brother and fiancé a hug. Like Pritchard, she had blond hair and crystal blue eyes. But unlike her colossal, raw-boned, and muscular brother, Idelle was petite and delicate of feature.

"There's talk all over town of a showdown," she said, glancing around at the people milling excitedly about. "All these folks have come to watch you and that Count Strobl fellow shoot each other to pieces."

"They'll likely be disappointed," Pritchard said.

"Please be careful," Idelle said. "I read in the *Kansas City Enterprise* that Count Strobl has already killed four men in duels since coming to America; one of them with a sword. They say he killed over a dozen more in Europe."

"Hell," Ditch grunted, "Samuel's killed more'n that in one afternoon." Pritchard elbowed his friend.

"This isn't a joke," Idelle said. "According to the article, Strobl's a professional duelist. Which means somebody's put up money to have you killed."

"You're jumping to conclusions," Pritchard said calmly. "Maybe this Strobl feller's just passin' through?"

"Who are you kidding?" Idelle said. "Atherton's only a small town on the rail line to Kansas City from Saint Louis. There's no reason for him to get off the train here, other than you. And why would he brag to all those reporters about wanting to challenge you if he wasn't on the prod?"

"I don't know the answers to those questions," Pritchard said to his sister, "but gettin' worked up over things that ain't yet occurred makes no sense. Give me a chance to meet this Count Strobl. Who knows? Maybe he's a swell feller."

"And maybe he'll shoot you on sight," Idelle said drily.

"Folks are unloading," Ditch remarked, pointing to the passenger cars. They scanned the people as they got off. The crowd's eyes were on Marshal Pritchard, over a full head taller than anyone else at the station, as the passengers began to disembark. Pritchard's, Ditch's, and

22

Idelle's eyes searched for the mysterious Count Strobl.

"Who is she?" Ditch whistled as a woman stepped off the train.

A number of women had already disembarked, but this particular female stood out dramatically from the rest. She looked to be in her early to mid-thirties, was of slightly less than average height, and possessed a remarkably beautiful face. In addition to extraordinary green eyes, she had pale skin, freckles, flaming red hair tucked under her bonnet, and a strikingly buxom figure.

Another feature that distinguished this woman from others in the crowd was the elegant, and clearly expensive, dress, hat, and matching parasol she sported. Such elaborate feminine attire might have been commonplace in New Orleans or Saint Louis, but was in stark contrast to what women in Atherton typically wore. In addition to its cost, the woman's dress was very formfitting and exposed a great deal of her prominent bust.

The woman seemed aware that many of the men, and more than a few jealous women, had taken notice of her.

"Never seen her before," Pritchard said.

"Would have remembered if I had," Ditch said. "I can't tell if she's on the outside of that dress tryin' to get in, or the inside tryin' to get out."

"Put your jaws back into place," Idelle said,

pinching Ditch until he winced. "You two clods act like you've never seen a girl before."

"I've seen plenty of girls," Pritchard said, "but none like her. She's built like a burlap bag full of bobcats."

The red-haired woman's gaze stopped when it met Pritchard's. She stared at him through emerald eyes. After a moment's evaluation, she turned abruptly on her heels and headed toward the luggage car.

"Wonder what brings someone like her to Atherton?" Ditch said.

"Never you mind, Ditch Clemson," Idelle said.

CHAPTER 4

Count Strobl wasn't hard to spot. A slender man, six feet tall and perhaps a decade older than Pritchard's twenty-eight years, stepped from the train. He wore a fur hat, a monocle, a sculpted Vandyke, calfskin gloves, a half cape, and knee-high riding boots under tailored jodhpurs. Other than an ornately engraved, gold-handled walking stick, no sign of a weapon was visible on his person. He walked with the signature arrogance of the nobility class and paid no attention to the gawkers pursuing him. At his heels was a large, burly, hard-faced man with Germanic features, wearing a thick coat and laboring under a bulky trunk and heavy suitcase.

When Strobl noticed Pritchard, he momentarily removed his monocle and appraised the tall lawman with an expression of disdain. Then he replaced the lens and strode purposefully over.

"You are Joe Atherton, I presume?" Strobl said in an Austrian accent.

"Nobody here by that name," Pritchard said. "I'm Marshal Samuel Pritchard."

"Ah," Strobl said. "I recall reading about how you abandoned your title and traded it for another. A cowardly act, if you ask me. No matter. You are Atherton, I am certain of it. You're younger than

25

I expected, but you are indeed him. I suspect, under your chapeau, one would find a scar in the shape of a pistol ball, would they not?"

"And you are?"

"Count Florian Strobl," he said, nodding his head and clicking his heels. "Of the Vienna Strobls."

"This here's Ditch Clemson," Pritchard said, gesturing to his friend with his thumb, "of the Missouri Clemsons. The lady with him is my sister, Idelle Pritchard. She's Atherton's acting mayor."

Strobl snorted derisively at Ditch and Idelle.

"What brings you to our fair town?" Pritchard asked.

"Calling this pigsty 'fair' is wishful thinking, Marshal. Once you have beheld the Roman Colosseum or the Acropolis, a cesspool like Atherton is hardly worthy of note."

"I've heard it said beauty is in the eye of the beholder," Pritchard said. "And you ain't answered my question."

"Speaking of beauty," Strobl said, turning his attention to Idelle and continuing to ignore Pritchard's query, "I daresay, I didn't expect to find so magnificent a creature in such a deplorable locale."

Ditch stepped in front of Idelle and scowled.

"I read in the newspaper you've come to Atherton to challenge my brother to a duel?"

Idelle said, ignoring the count's compliment. "Is this true?"

"Of course," Strobl replied. "I would not otherwise travel all the way from Chicago to this inconsequential village without purpose. Your immense brother, who is called 'Smoking Joe' by many, possesses a reputation as the most fearsome warrior in the Americas. He is what is known in my country as 'big game.' I intend to make him my trophy."

The crowd surrounding the two men went wide-eyed and silent. Anticipation dotted their eager faces.

"If I'm supposed to be flattered," Pritchard said, "I ain't. And I told you already, my name ain't Atherton. It's Pritchard."

"Atherton or Pritchard, it makes no difference," Strobl said dismissively. "In either case, you are nothing but an untitled serf." He returned his focus back to Idelle.

"Once my business with your brother is finished, mademoiselle," Strobl continued, "I could be persuaded, if you were to ask me politely, to clear your palate of the bumpkin you must be so weary of bedding and allow you the privilege of sampling the bedside manners of Austrian royalty." He raised a monocled eyebrow at Ditch. "But only if you bathe, first."

Ditch let go of Idelle's hand and began to move forward with his fists clenched. Pritchard cut him off and stepped between his friend and the count. Idelle also restrained Ditch, putting her arms around her fiancé.

"A wise move, mademoiselle," Strobl said to her. "Leash your dog, lest it be whipped."

"I get what you're doing," Pritchard said. "You've got some notion of European dueling etiquette you're trying to foist on me by insulting my sister and friend. You want me to take offense and insult you back. Then you can claim your honor has been besmirched, or some such nonsense, and challenge me to a duel. Is that right?"

Strobl gave a haughty nod in reply.

Pritchard casually tipped his hat back, revealing the scar on his forehead, and looked down at Count Strobl. "It won't work. You ain't gonna provoke me."

"This remains to be seen," Strobl said. "I see you are wearing a pair of pistols. I have noticed that in America, unlike the more civilized parts of Europe, men wear their weapons openly, like Christmas ornaments. This is yet another sign of your primitive country's status as a nation of uncultured rubes. Are those guns merely for decoration, or can you use them?"

"He can use 'em, all right," Ditch retorted. "He killed more men than the pox."

Pritchard held up a hand to quiet his friend.

"We abide by the law in this town," Pritchard

said to Strobl, "and I'm the law. I shoot people only when my life, or somebody else's, is on the line and I can't avoid it. I don't kill over insults, participate in duels, nor allow them to be fought in our streets. I don't give a whit how things are done in Vienna, Austria. For as long as you're here in Atherton, Missouri, you'll behave, and obey our laws, or find yourself arrested and locked up."

"I'm impressed with your ability to think and speak so coherently," Strobl said with a smirk. "By your appearance, Joe Atherton, I expected you to be hanging from a tree by your tail, peeling a banana with your feet, and incapable of rational thought."

"I'm pleased to have exceeded your expectations," Pritchard said with an easy smile. "And that's the third time I've told you I'm not Joe Atherton."

"I care little for what you call yourself," Strobl said, lifting his chin. He deliberately elevated his accented voice for all in the crowd to hear. "Nor do I care for your petty laws or idle threats. You, Atherton, are an oafish cur and a craven coward. You will not rise to the defense of your own sister's honor, which proves both your cowardice and her status as a strumpet. I hereby, in front of all these witnesses, challenge you to a duel. Your effeminate spinelessness is an affront to my masculine sensibilities, and I am justifiably offended. Therefore, I demand satisfaction and insist you meet me on the field of honor."

Strobl removed the glove from his right hand with an elaborate gesture and reached out to slap Pritchard's face with it. The crowd gasped.

Pritchard easily blocked the dainty blow and punched Count Strobl square in the face with his massive fist. The European was rendered instantly unconscious and fell like a dropped sack of grain.

Strobl's heavy-shouldered servant cursed in Austrian German, dropped the luggage, and thrust a hand inside his coat.

"Don't do it," Pritchard admonished him. People standing nearby scattered.

Ignoring the warning, Count Strobl's servant clumsily withdrew a Gasser Army Service revolver and began to bring it to bear on Pritchard. He never got a chance to pull the weapon's double-action trigger.

Almost faster than the eye could follow, Pritchard drew one of his Colts and fired. The .45 caliber bullet struck his would-be killer directly in the center of his forehead. He was dead before he hit the ground.

Across the platform, two men who'd disembarked from the train watched the deadly encounter unfold with interest. One, a stout, middle-aged man in a derby hat and striped suit, put a cigar to his lips. His companion was younger, taller, leaner, and clad in a dark suit and wide-brimmed, black, Boss of the Plains Stetson. He wore a U.S. Army Smith & Wesson Model 3, chambered in .44 S&W American, in a cross-draw holster.

"Who's the pistoleer?" the older man asked.

"He's the town marshal," the younger man answered, lighting his companion's cigar.

"You don't usually see men that big move that fast," the older man said around his cigar. "He's maybe the fastest I've seen, and I've seen a few. How come I've never heard of him before?"

"You have heard of him," the younger man said, "you just don't know it. He made a name for himself as a Texas Ranger under the moniker 'Joe Atherton.'"

The older man's eyebrows lifted. "You're joking with me, right?"

"That's him," the younger man acknowledged.

"You're telling me," the older man said incredulously, "that Smokin' Joe Atherton is Atherton's town marshal?"

"He goes by the name Pritchard now, but that's him, all right. His sister is Idelle Pritchard, the mayor."

"This might be a problem," the older man said, his brow furrowing.

"No, it ain't," the younger man said.

31

CHAPTER 5

"Good morning, Your Highness," Pritchard announced as he unlocked the cell door. "Time for breakfast. You don't want to stand before Judge Pearson on an empty stomach, do you?"

Count Florian Strobl sat shakily up from his bunk and looked blearily at the tall marshal looming over him. His appearance was markedly different from the arrogant European nobleman who'd stepped off the train the day before. Both of his eyes were black, swollen nearly shut, and a thick plaster bandage was pasted across the bridge of his swollen nose. His hair was disheveled, and his expensively tailored suit wrinkled from being slept in all night in a jail cell.

"It is about time I spoke with someone in genuine authority," Strobl said in a now heavily nasal, Austrian accent. "I wish to lodge a complaint about the barbaric manner in which someone of my station has been treated."

"If you're referring to the accommodations," Pritchard said, "save your breath. Atherton's only got one jail. We treat every prisoner alike, whether they're kings or peasants."

The count's broken nose had been set the previous afternoon by Atherton's only physician, Dr. Mauldin, after Pritchard carried the unconscious Austrian over his shoulder to the lockup. The town's undertaker, Simon Tilley, took custody of Strobl's servant's remains.

"Don't just stand there gawkin', Tater," Pritchard told his deputy. "Serve the prisoner his breakfast."

"Here you go, Your Majesty," Tater said, stepping forward and bowing. He extended the tray of food to Count Strobl. "Sorry I was caught flat-footed," he apologized. "It's just that I ain't never met no Eu-rope-ean royalty before."

Toby "Tater" Jessup was Marshal Pritchard's only deputy. He was a jovial, rotund, and hardworking fellow in his forties who'd earned his nickname due to the shape of his physique and his widely known affinity for all things edible, especially baked potatoes. His previous occupation had been the town handyman, and he occasionally filled in at the livery on days when the stable manager wasn't feeling well. More of a jailer, clerk, and janitor than a law enforcer, he didn't even carry a gun. But he was the only person in town who wanted the job of deputy town marshal after Pritchard and Ditch killed all the previous town marshals and county deputies during their battle to wrest control of Atherton from Shipley and his band of crooked lawmen.

Not that many deputies were needed. In the nine months since Pritchard took over the job of town marshal and acting county sheriff, crime in Jackson County had plummeted.

"What is this filth?" Strobl said, lifting the cloth and examining the contents of the tray.

"Biscuits and gravy," Tater said proudly, "with fresh coffee and strawberry preserves from the diner across the street. Mrs. Dady Perkins runs the place, and she makes the best biscuits this side of—"

"You expect me to eat such slop?" Strobl cut Tater off in midsentence. He upended the tray from the deputy's grasp and sent the meal crashing to the floor. "Such a meal may be suitable to the rubes who inhabit this revolting dung heap, but not for the tastes of Count Strobl."

Tater stepped back, aghast. Pritchard wasn't sure if his deputy was upset because he'd had the tray smacked from his hands or because a perfectly good breakfast lay ruined at his feet.

Pritchard stepped into the cell. "Get the bucket and mop," he told his deputy. "The count's going to need it."

"I don't mind cleaning it up," Tater said. "It'll only take me a minute."

"Do as I say," Pritchard said to his deputy. To the count, he said, "Looks like you'll be going hungry this morning."

In response, Strobl spat on the floor at Pritchard's feet.

"Forget the mop," Pritchard called over his shoulder. "Just bring the bucket."

"But how's he gonna clean up all that mess on the floor without a mop?" Tater protested.

"He's going to use his coat," Pritchard replied.

"I will do no such thing," Strobl said indignantly.

"You most certainly will," Pritchard said. "I don't know how it's done in Austria, but here in Missouri we clean up our own messes. You have three seconds to strip off your fancy coat and get to moppin', and two of 'em have already expired."

"If I refuse?" Strobl said, raising his chin in defiance.

"Then I'll mop up the mess with your hair."

"You wouldn't dare."

"You seem to have a problem with your geography," Pritchard said, taking a step forward.

"Geography?" Strobl said, the first inklings of fear beginning to color his face.

"You keep forgettin' you ain't in Austria anymore. What's it going to be, Your Highness? Your coat, or your scalp?"

Count Strobl stood in the courtroom with as much dignity as a man with two black eyes, a broken nose, and clad in a coat covered in biscuit crumbs, gravy, coffee, and strawberries could muster. His monocle hung from a cord around his neck, because both of his eyes were too swollen to support it.

Sitting behind the bench was the Honorable Justice Eugene Pearson, formerly of Jefferson City. Governor Woodson had dispatched the judge to Atherton from the capital to oversee the upcoming elections and to help restore law and order in the vacuum of authority created in the wake of the removal-by-force of the Shipley faction. Pearson had served honorably on the side of the Union during the war, possessed a no-nonsense demeanor, and had a reputation for being a fair magistrate, if hard as an Iowa winter.

"How do you answer the charges against you?" Judge Pearson asked.

"Charges?" Strobl said incredulously. "Against me? If there are charges to be leveled, they should be directed at Marshal Joe Atherton."

"I already explained to the prisoner, Your Honor," Pritchard shrugged, "several times, that I ain't Joe Atherton anymore."

The judge nodded. "The court has recognized the unique circumstances surrounding Marshal Pritchard's previous use of the alias 'Joe Atherton.' It should also be noted that under that name, Marshal Pritchard was cited for heroism by both the governors of Missouri and the Republic of Texas, as well as the governors of the territories of New Mexico and Arizona."

"I do not recognize any of those petty authorities," Strobl scoffed. "If they are not of royal lineage, certified by the crowned heads of Europe, they hold no sway over me or my affairs."

"I'll ask you again," Judge Pearson said to

Strobl. "How do you plead to the charges against you?"

"As you can clearly see," Count Strobl began, ignoring the question and pointing to his face, "I have been insulted, assaulted, and humiliated by this gigantic ogre without provocation. All this occurred after my valet was murdered in cold blood by cowardly assassination. I am of noble birth and have been unlawfully persecuted by those beneath my station, which includes you. I demand immediate reparation, an apology, and the right to challenge my persecutor, Joe Atherton, on the field of honor."

"That was quite a mouthful," Judge Pearson said to Strobl. "I'll just assume you plead *not guilty*. How's that?"

"Of course I am not guilty," Strobl said. "Did I not just say this?"

"I've spoken to the marshal here, and about two dozen witnesses to what transpired at the train depot yesterday," the judge went on. "I'm prepared to render my verdict."

"Do what you must," Strobl said, "but do it quickly. I grow weary of this nonsense. I have endured quite enough abuse at the hands of oafish bumpkins passing themselves off as government officials and arbiters of the law."

"It is the ruling of this court, based on an overwhelming abundance of evidence, that you, Count Florian Strobl, came to the town of

Atherton for the express purpose of challenging our town marshal to an illegal duel. When the marshal refused your provocations, you attempted to assault him, at which time he defended himself in a manner consistent with every able-bodied, red-blooded man in Jackson County; he whomped you one in the snoot. Your employee then tried to pull a pistol on the town marshal, which was both his folly and his end, seeing as how Marshal Pritchard happens to be the fastest gun this side of perdition."

"Preposterous," Strobl muttered. "What you claim are the ravings of a deluded mind."

"You are hereby found guilty of provoking a duel and assaulting an officer of the law. The fine is fifty dollars for each charge, along with a twenty-dollar fine to cover the burial expenses for your manservant, whose death is ruled as self-defense."

"I will not accept the ridiculous ruling of this kangaroo court," Strobl said. "And I will pay no such fines."

"Suit yourself," the judge said. "It's thirty days in jail for each charge, with another thirty tacked on to cover the undertaker's expenses. And one more thing; the guns in your luggage, as well as the sword-cane you were carrying, are hereby confiscated until you leave Atherton. I won't have you challenging any more of our citizens to duels once you get out of jail. Court adjourned."

"This is not justice!" Count Strobl yelled as Pritchard led him from the courtroom. "This is nothing but the whim of a vulgar peasant in a black robe!"

"You're wrong about that," Judge Pearson answered. "If I'd wanted to indulge my whim, I'd let Marshal Pritchard duel with you. Then we'd all be happily rid of your uppity carcass."

CHAPTER 6

"The place is packed," Ditch remarked to Pritchard.

"Too bad the building ain't completed yet," Pritchard said. "It'd be a bit warmer inside if the roof was finally done."

Pritchard and Ditch were inside Atherton's partially completed town hall, amid a bustling crowd of townspeople.

Construction on the new town hall began the previous autumn, but the onset of the Missouri winter had delayed progress considerably. Now that spring had arrived, the work resumed with renewed vigor.

The large, four-story structure had enough of a frame in place to support four walls, and the big furnace shipped in by rail from Chicago was operational. The roof, however, was only halfway completed, and a canvas tarpaulin covered most of the open portion. There was, of course, no furniture installed yet, so the citizens of Atherton had to content themselves with standing during their town meeting.

Prior to Mayor Burnell Shipley's death, there had been no need for a meeting hall. Shipley ran the town single-handedly from his office in the Atherton Arms Hotel, or the Sidewinder Saloon across the street, both of which he owned, and found little use for either a town council or a place for them to meet. Shipley felt a town hall was unnecessary since he neither required, nor desired, input from Atherton's citizens.

For the past fifteen years, when elections were held at all, they were conducted in secret. The ballot boxes were guarded, and the ballots counted, by Sheriff Horace Foster and his deputies, all bought and paid for by Shipley.

In the wake of Shipley's demise, an audit of his assets and finances was conducted by Judge Pearson. These assets now legally belonged to Idelle and Pritchard, though Pritchard deferred any claim. Several hundred thousand dollars in gold, silver, and currency were discovered, as well as the deeds to most of the property within Atherton and in surrounding Jackson County.

Idelle, as the heir and acting mayor, deposited the funds in the Wells Fargo Bank in Kansas City. With Judge Pearson's help, she set about returning the money and property confiscated by Shipley before, during, and after the war to their rightful owners. In many cases, these properties had to be deeded to the owner's next of kin because their original owners, like Pritchard and Idelle's father, had been murdered by Shipley and his men.

Despite her efforts to return as much stolen land and money as possible, Idelle still found herself in control of most of the cash, much of the town, and significant landholdings within the county. This was because the rightful owners had fled, were deceased, or could not be located.

With this in mind, Idelle began sprucing up Atherton. She felt that if she couldn't return to the rightful owners the money and land that Shipley had stolen, she could at least use them to improve the community at large.

The first thing Idelle did, as Atherton's new acting mayor, was dramatically lower the local taxes. The elimination of the usury and unlawful levies imposed by Shipley on every business and property owner in Jackson County was celebrated with relief and gratitude.

The next thing Idelle did, with Ditch's assistance, was commission an architect and construction firm from Kansas City to build a town hall and a new, multiroom school building to replace the town's cramped, weathered, two-room schoolhouse. With her own funds as collateral, she provided low-interest loans to Atherton's several religious congregations for the purpose of repairing, expanding, and updating their churches.

Since Atherton already had a thriving lumber mill and a ready, willing, and able labor force, these new civic projects were welcomed with gusto. Idelle also tasked crews with fixing sidewalks, installing streetlamps, and properly fencing off and landscaping the town's cemetery, which had hitherto been only a wooded hill overlooking Atherton. A park was designed and created, in the center of town, replete with a bandstand, gazebo, and benches.

Finally, at Pritchard's request, the old marshal's office, which had been little more than a shack with only one, dungeonlike, cell, was replaced. The previous marshal, Elton Stacy, had little use for a jail, since most of the offenders he or his deputy marshals arrested were either run out of town, shot, or summarily hanged. The old marshal's office was torn down and rebuilt in brick, with a single reinforced window, a siege door, and an eight-celled, iron-barred jail. In the back was a small private room with a cot where Pritchard slept.

Pritchard refused to stay at the Atherton Arms. More than a decade as a horse soldier and Texas Ranger instilled in him deeply Spartan habits, and left him largely eschewing material possessions. He owned his guns, horse, and a few clothes, and had no interest in owning property. Had a room not been built for him in the marshal's office, he would have slept in the livery stable with his horse, Rusty.

As a teenager Pritchard fled Atherton on the big Morgan, who'd been broken and trained by Ditch and his father. Rusty carried Pritchard faithfully throughout the war, during almost ten years as a

Texas Ranger, and brought him safely back home to Missouri with Ditch.

Idelle was in the process of rebuilding their family's stately home on the land where it once stood, a few miles outside Atherton, before being burned to the ground by Burnell Shipley a decade before. The property was adjacent to the Clemsons' horse ranch. She hoped to live there with Ditch after their June wedding, once the house was completed. It was on that plot of land that Pritchard and Idelle buried their mother, Dovie, alongside their father. Pritchard and Ditch put him into the ground the day he was lynched.

"This town meeting is called to order," Judge Pearson proclaimed, banging his gavel on a plank stretched between two barrels. Seated next to him was Acting Mayor Idelle Pritchard and the town council. Few heard the judge, and the crowd continued to chatter and murmur. Pearson gave Pritchard a signal.

"Pipe down!" Pritchard commanded in his booming voice. "We've got a meetin' to commence!" The room grew silent.

"The first order of business is to announce the date for the upcoming elections for mayor and county sheriff," Judge Pearson began.

"What's wrong with keeping Mayor Idelle?" a woman asked.

"Nothing," Judge Pearson answered, "except that Idelle has withdrawn her name from consideration." Groans of protest erupted from the crowd.

"While it has been my privilege and honor to serve you good folks, and the town of Atherton," Idelle said, "it was never my desire to be mayor. I took the job to help restore order. Also to try and give back, as best I could, what Burnell Shipley took from all of us. I don't want to be mayor. I want to go back to teaching school."

"The town of Atherton couldn't have asked for a better leader to guide us out of the troubles of our past," Judge Pearson said. "I think we would all agree that since Idelle took over the reins, Atherton is night-and-day different from before. This very building we're meeting in stands as testament."

Applause broke out, with plenty of whistles and cheers.

"As you may remember from last month's town meeting," the judge went on, "the governor's office in Jefferson City has authorized an election and designated me to monitor the proceedings. The vote will be held here at the town hall during the first week of June."

"That's less than two months away," someone in the crowd called out.

"That is correct," the judge said. "We must close out the nominations tonight, so we can get on with the campaigning and prepare for the election. So far, we have only Dave Clemson on the ballot for mayor—"

"Hurray for Ditch!" a voice cried out. "Ditch for mayor!" another joined in.

"—and Samuel Pritchard," Pearson continued, "our appointed town marshal, on the ballot for sheriff."

"Smokin' Joe for sheriff!" a man's voice blurted. The crowd exploded in rebel yells and cheers.

"Simmer down," the judge said, pounding his gavel on the plank to restore order. "The town recognizes that 'Smokin' Joe' is an alias which once referred to Marshal Pritchard but is no longer to be used. Let's all respect the man who was so instrumental in giving us back our home and address him as he wishes to be addressed."

"We could call him 'Smokin' Sam,'" another townsman chirped. The crowd devolved into laughter.

"You've gotta admit," Ditch grinned at Pritchard, "it's kinda got a ring to it."

"Would you care to respond to the citizenry," Judge Pearson asked Pritchard, "on the topic of your name?"

"Like many of you," Pritchard addressed the townsfolk, "I had to do things during the war to survive, and to protect my family, that I ain't especially proud of. One of those things was take a name not my own. Also, like many of you, I want to put those times behind me. If you'll allow me to do that, and serve you as Sheriff Samuel

Pritchard, instead of Joe Atherton, I promise I won't let you down. Thank you."

If the applause and cheers were raucous before, they were cacophonous now. It took a full minute before Judge Pearson was able to quiet the crowd again.

"If there are no further nominations for mayor or sheriff," the judge said, "I will close out the nominating process." He raised his gavel.

"One moment, Your Honor," a man spoke from the back of the room. All eyes turned toward the speaker.

"I wish to nominate myself," the man said, "for the position of mayor."

He was the middle-aged, stocky, well-dressed man in the derby hat who'd arrived on the train the day before, along with another passenger now standing beside him. This second man was younger, taller, leaner, and clad in a dark suit, black hat, and cross-draw pistol.

"And who might you be?" Judge Pearson asked.

"My name is Benedict Houseman," the man said, "attorney-at-law. I'm formerly a resident of Saint Louis, and currently a resident of Atherton. And I hereby nominate this man," he gestured to his tall companion with his cigar, "Jack Stearns, for the position of sheriff of Jackson County."

CHAPTER 7

After the town meeting, Pritchard, Idelle, and Ditch strolled to the restaurant inside the Atherton Arms Hotel for dinner. Since Idelle took possession of the hotel, the facility had been renovated, the prostitutes and crooked gamblers evicted, and the kitchen staff replaced with a competent chef and crew who actually knew how to cook. The trio enjoyed a decent steak dinner, which Pritchard and Ditch washed down with an excellent, locally brewed beer.

"Who's this Houseman character?" Idelle asked.

"Don't know," Ditch said. "Never heard of him."

"Me, either," Pritchard said. "Nor that Stearns fellow. He damn sure ain't no attorney nor politician."

"What do you mean?" Idelle said.

"He's a gun hand," Ditch answered for Pritchard. "Ain't no doubt about it."

"A gunfighter?" Idelle put down her fork. "How can you tell?"

"They ain't hard to identify," Pritchard said, "iffen you know what to look for."

"I don't see how they can waltz in on the noon train as strangers one day and then run for office the next," Ditch said over his beer. "Doesn't seem right."

"Maybe not," Idelle said, "but it's legal. Judge Pearson told me both men filed papers with the post office yesterday, as soon as they got off the train, to declare their residences at the Atherton Arms Hotel. They also registered to vote in Jackson County. As residents of Atherton, regardless of how little time they've been here, they're now eligible to become candidates for public office."

"Did the judge tell you anything else?" Ditch asked.

"He said he was curious," Idelle said. "He told me he was familiar with most lawyers in Missouri, but had never heard of this Benedict Houseman fellow. Said he was going to send off a telegram to Jefferson City to find out what he could about him from his contacts in the capital."

"That gives me an idea," Ditch said. "I'll speak with John Babbit tomorrow." Babbit was the editor and publisher of Atherton's weekly newspaper, the *Athertonian*.

"Houseman said he hailed from Saint Louis," Ditch continued. "Maybe John can check with his sources there and come up with something on those two fellers?"

"Good idea," Idelle said.

"Seems kinda odd, doesn't it?" Ditch said. "A couple of strangers nobody ever heard of, comin' into town and offerin' themselves up as candidates to run things in Atherton? Mighty odd, if you ask me."

"Not so much," Pritchard said. "Atherton has a reputation as a wealthy town. After we took down Shipley, word spread around that the old boss was gone and a young schoolteacher was acting as mayor in his place. I'm sure all that money Idelle deposited in the Wells Fargo Bank in Kansas City had more than a little to do with it. Anyhow, it ain't surprising to me someone would try to move in and take over."

"I didn't see my parents die," Idelle declared, "and nearly get killed myself, along with my brother and fiancé, to sit idly by while another crooked carpetbagger swoops in and takes over our hometown."

"Take it easy," Pritchard said to her. "Ain't nobody gonna take anything from the Pritchards; not ever again. We were just kids when Pa was murdered, and when . . . what happened to Ma. We ain't kids no more. Anybody who tries to hurt us, or take what's ours, is gonna regret the day they was birthed. You have my oath on that."

"Pritchard speaks for me, too," Ditch said. "I may not be the fastest gun on the frontier, like your brother, but I hit what I aim at. I won't let any harm come to you, Idelle. I swear it."

Idelle reached across the table and took her brother and fiancé's hands.

"How could a girl get so lucky?" she said.

"My question exactly," a voice said from behind her.

The trio looked up to find the green-eyed, ginger-haired woman from the train station standing beside their table. She was wearing a cleavage-enhancing, burgundy-colored dress and looked even more stunning, up close, than she had at the rail depot the day before. Pritchard and Ditch stood.

"I apologize for the intrusion, Mayor Pritchard," the woman said, "but I understand you're the owner of the Sidewinder Saloon?"

The Sidewinder Saloon, situated across the town square from the Atherton Arms Hotel, was once Atherton's main watering hole, gambling hall, and bordello. The Sidewinder was also Burnell Shipley's home away from home and had been the unofficial headquarters for his gang of corrupt town marshals and county deputies. Since inheriting the bar, Idelle had closed it down. The two-story building currently sat idle.

"I am the owner of the building which used to be called the Sidewinder," Idelle said as Pritchard and Ditch stood up. "And who might you be?"

"My name is Eudora Chilton," the woman said, "recently of Memphis."

Idelle made the introductions. "This is my fiancé, David Clemson," she said, "and my brother, Marshal—"

"—Pritchard," Eudora finished. "I know. I watched him gun down a man at the train station yesterday, shortly after my arrival. I must say, this town surely knows how to welcome a lady with a bang."

"That man pulled a pistol on the marshal," Ditch said defensively, "and was about to shoot him. He was also given fair warning. You say, 'gun down' as if he was murdered."

"I didn't mean to imply any wrongdoing by the marshal," Eudora said demurely. "I merely stated I witnessed a man's death at the end of the marshal's revolver."

"I'm sorry if my actions offended you," Pritchard said with a wry grin. "I'm sometimes prone to thoughtlessly puttin' my survival above my manners."

"No apology necessary," Eudora replied, grinning herself and directing her green eyes directly at Pritchard's blue ones. "It wasn't the first time I've witnessed a man shot."

"Seen a few gunfights, have you?" Pritchard said.

"More than I care to admit," she said. "Although I must also admit, the efficiency with which you dispatched your opponent was impressive. Most of the shooting fracases I've glimpsed were rather messy affairs, with innocent bystanders often the unintended targets. May I join you?"

Idelle had no choice but to offer the newcomer

a chair at their table. "What's your interest in the Sidewinder?" she asked, once they all were seated.

"I'll lay my cards bare," Eudora said. "I'm looking to reopen the Sidewinder."

"You want to buy a defunct tavern?" Ditch asked.

"I know the saloon business," Eudora said. "I've worked in drinking establishments in Little Rock, Oklahoma City, Denver, Dallas, and Memphis. Through my endeavors, I have accumulated more than enough money to invest in my own establishment. I've decided I want to do it here."

"Why open a saloon in Atherton?" Idelle asked. "Why not open a tavern in a big city, where you can make more money?"

"It's true I can make more profit in a bigger town," Eudora said. "But with a bigger town comes bigger headaches. In a larger town or city, I'd have to pay off crooked lawmen and politicians to stay in business, which I don't like. What I do like is a place like Atherton. It's small but flourishing. From what I've heard, Miss Pritchard, you're an honest woman. So is your brother. Here in Atherton I can run an honest business without interference from crooked officials."

"Atherton has been getting along fine without the Sidewinder Saloon for almost ten months,"

Idelle said. "What makes you think we want to open it back up?"

Eudora smiled. "You are certainly young," she said, "but you're no fool, Mayor Pritchard. I'm sure you're aware that men will drink, and gamble, and consort with women, whether you try to stop them or not. Sooner or later, whether it's me or someone else, a saloon is going to reopen here in Atherton. With me in charge, you'll get a cooperative, law-abiding, business owner who won't water down the liquor, run a crooked table, or employ unclean girls. I want to live in this town, so I won't do anything to soil it. Can you honestly say the same for anyone else who might open up a watering hole here?"

"She makes a good point," Ditch said. "The lumber- and cattlemen have been complaining somethin' fierce about having no place to wet their whistles since the Sidewinder shut down."

Idelle gave him a stern look. "What's wrong with the hotel bar?" she asked. "They can still get a drink here."

"You really want your fancy hotel lobby filled with saw-dusted mill workers and dirt-covered cowboys every night?" Eudora asked. "Working men want a place to drink, not sip."

"I'll have to think about it," Idelle said.

"Of course," Eudora said, rising to her feet. Pritchard and Ditch once again stood. "I wouldn't expect your answer tonight. Please know that

I will pay whatever price you deem fair. I'm staying at this hotel and will await your reply to my offer. It was a pleasure meeting you, and I thank you for your time and consideration."

Eudora Chilton made her exit. Most of the men in the restaurant and bar, Pritchard and Ditch included, stared at the extremely shapely redhead as she departed.

"That's one bold woman," Ditch said.

"It wasn't her attitude I was noticin'," Pritchard said. Idelle wrinkled her nose at him.

No sooner had Eudora left, than Benedict Houseman and Jack Stearns entered the lobby. They stopped at the registration desk to acquire their room keys before noticing Pritchard, Ditch, and Idelle in the restaurant. The two men approached as the threesome stood up to leave. Pritchard and Stearns made eye contact as Houseman extended his hand to Idelle.

"Good evening," Houseman said, tipping his hat. "Allow me to introduce myself. I'm—"

"I know who you are," Idelle interrupted him, ignoring the outstretched hand. "I heard you announce your candidacy for mayor at the town meeting."

"Is there something wrong with that?"

"I'm not sure," Idelle said. "I don't know anything about you. No one in Atherton does. You only arrived yesterday."

"In that case," Houseman said, "I look forward

55

to getting to know you and the rest of the citizens of Atherton once I'm in office."

"Getting a little ahead of yourself, aren't you?" Ditch said. "Last I checked, you have to win an election to become mayor."

"That's merely a formality, son," Houseman said.

"That remains to be seen," Ditch said. "By the way, only my father, who's deceased, gets to call me *son*."

"Is that a fact?" Houseman grinned.

"It is," Ditch said. "Don't do it again."

"You're rather a feisty fellow," Houseman said, his grin widening. "I believe I'm going to enjoy our political contest."

"What about you, Marshal?" Stearns addressed Pritchard. "Are you feisty, too?"

"Not me," Pritchard said. "I'm the easygoin' type."

"I saw for myself just how easygoing you are," Stearns said, "yesterday at the train station. I watched you ease a man into an early grave."

"Sometimes," Pritchard said, "a man practically asks to get shot."

"On that point, Marshal, we agree."

"I think we've had enough conversation for one evening," Houseman said, stepping between Stearns and Pritchard and once again tipping his hat to Idelle. "My associate and I will bid you all good night." He turned to Ditch. "Best of luck in the upcoming election campaign."

Houseman ushered Stearns toward the stairs. The taller man walked away from Pritchard backward and kept his eyes riveted on the big lawman as he went. He also kept his right hand free.

"I don't like him," Idelle said, once they'd gone.

"Which one?" Ditch asked.

"Both," she said.

CHAPTER 8

"Good mornin', Marshal," Tater said as Pritchard emerged from his private room in back of the jail. "Sleep well?"

"I did," Pritchard replied, scratching his jaw. Tater already had the stove fueled and burning, and the smell of coffee brewing filled the office. A tray containing breakfast for Count Strobl was on Pritchard's desk.

"You want I should feed the prisoner now?" Tater asked.

"Just a minute," Pritchard answered with a yawn. "Let me wake up His Highness before you open the cell door. I'd hate to have a repeat of yesterday's mess."

"Waste of good biscuits and gravy," Tater said, "iffen you ask me."

"Rise and shine, Your Lordship," Pritchard said. He clanged on the cell's bars with the key ring. "Breakfast is served."

Strobl lowered the blanket and peeked out from under it, blinking up at Pritchard. He looked even worse than the day before. He was unshaven, disheveled, and it took several long seconds for him to come out of his slumber and realize where he was.

"Here's your morning chow," Pritchard said. "You might want to eat while it's still hot."

Strobl slowly sat up and ran his hands through his cowlicked hair. "Did anyone ever tell you, Marshal Pritchard, that you are an exceptionally annoying man?"

"Yep," Pritchard answered. "But only once."

"What's on the menu today?" Strobl asked. "Besides misery?"

"Flapjacks and bacon," Tater said, patting his ample stomach. "Already had mine at the diner, when I picked yours up."

"Why am I not surprised?" Strobl muttered.

"I'm going to open the cell door now," Pritchard said, "and Deputy Jessup is going to hand you that tray of food. You've got eighty-eight days left on your sentence. If you don't want the rest of your meals to be served in a bucket, you'll behave and eat like a civilized person. If you make a mess of my jail again, I'll make a mess of you. Do we have an understanding?"

"You will get no more trouble from me," Strobl said wearily. "I recognize that in here I am a caged lamb among brutish wolves."

Pritchard unlocked the cell door and Tater handed over the tray of food. Strobl sat on his bunk and surveyed his meal.

"You will soon find out," Strobl said, "that it is you, Marshal Pritchard, who are the lamb surrounded by wolves."

"Is that supposed to frighten me?" Pritchard said, relocking the cell door.

"Bullets don't care whether you are afraid or not," Strobl said. "My only regret is being trapped in here and unable to stake my rightful claim on the prize."

"What's he babblin' on about?" Tater asked.

"Pay him no mind," Pritchard said, buttoning his shirt. "Maybe His Royal Highness will be less grumpy after he eats?"

"I hope so," Tater said. "I sure don't want to hear a bunch of gripin' out of him all day for the next three months. The way he talks, with that funny accent, gives me a headache. Him always complainin's only gonna make it worse."

"I'm goin' across the street for my own breakfast," Pritchard said. "Mind the store while I'm gone, will you?"

"Sure, Marshal," Tater said. "You mind if I try out your new chair?"

"Help yourself," Pritchard said, buckling on his revolvers and grabbing his hat. "I'll make another one for you in a couple of days. Anybody needs me, send 'em over to the diner."

Pritchard left the marshal's office and was strolling across the street when he was hailed by Ronnie Babbit, the ten-year-old son of news-paperman John Babbit. Ronnie was delivering the weekly paper to the businesses along the main street.

"Coupla fellas were looking for you, Marshal. They asked me where to find you?"

"Who were they?"

"Don't know," Ronnie said. "They rode into town just now and put up their horses at the livery."

"What'd they look like?"

"Like saddle tramps. One had on a big fur hat and coat, and the other was wearing a duster and chaps. They didn't smell too good. I think they'd been ridin' awhile. I told 'em where your office was. I didn't do anything wrong, did I?"

"Of course not," Pritchard said. "Run along and deliver your papers."

Pritchard resumed his walk to the diner and had just reached the opposite sidewalk when a voice called out from behind him.

"Joe Atherton!"

Pritchard instantly dropped and rolled. The shotgun blast aimed at his back tore out a chunk of the diner's glass-topped door where he'd been standing.

As Pritchard came up out of the roll, he pivoted 180 degrees and drew his right-hand pistol. Facing him, in the middle of the street, were two men standing side by side. One, wearing a fur trapper's hat and a buffalo-skin coat, was wielding a double-barreled shotgun. The other, in a duster and Stetson, aimed a Colt Cavalry model in his direction.

Pritchard stepped sideways as he fired, simultaneously drawing his left-handed Colt. He watched as the man in the buffalo-skin coat staggered to one knee, broke open the shotgun, extracted the empty shells, and began to reload. He knew he'd hit him in the gut, but buffalo hide was thick and tough, and pistol bullets passing through could be slowed considerably.

Pritchard took cover behind a post, turning his body to minimize his exposure, as a bullet fired by the man in the duster thwacked against it. Pritchard returned fire with his left-handed gun. He was gratified to see his adversary drop his revolver and topple onto his back.

Buffalo-skin closed his shotgun and stood up. Pritchard took careful aim and shot him in the face, just as he raised the weapon. Like his companion he tumbled backward, reflexively firing the shotgun into the dirt at his feet as he fell.

Pritchard covered the downed men with his revolvers as he approached them. People came tentatively out of the various businesses and advanced on the scene.

Pritchard needn't have worried. Buffalo-skin was dead, his eyes staring unblinkingly into the morning sun. The man in the duster had been hit in the throat. He was still alive and had both hands clasped around his neck, as if strangling himself, in a futile attempt to stem the geyser of blood spouting from the wound. After a few seconds of sputtering his death rattle faded, and he expired.

"Is everybody all right?" Pritchard called out, holstering his left-hand Colt and reloading the other. "How about in the diner?"

"I'll need a new door," Dady Perkins answered, wiping her brow with flour-covered hands. "Nobody inside was hit, thank heavens."

"Who were they, Marshal?" Wynn Samples asked. He was the proprietor of the general store. "Did you know them?"

Pritchard holstered his recharged right-hand gun and drew his left-side Colt. As he extracted the empty case and reloaded, he knelt and looked into the dead men's faces.

"I have no idea who they were," he said. "Never seen either of 'em before in my life."

Benedict Houseman and Jack Stearns emerged from the diner, donning their hats and coats as they came out.

"Witnessed the whole thing from inside the restaurant," Houseman said. He reached into a pocket for a cigar. "Nicely done, Marshal. I'm gratified to see you're uninjured." He lit the cigar. "Would've been a shame for you to be out of the sheriff's race before it began."

"I'm touched by your concern for my well-being," Pritchard said. He reholstered his gun.

"Like I said last night," Stearns commented, "for such an easygoing man, Marshal, you certainly know how to ease a fellow into a grave. In this case, two fellows."

"I'm easygoing, all right," Pritchard said. "Easygoing as hell."

CHAPTER 9

"Are there any other witnesses who have something they wish to offer this inquest?" Judge Pearson asked.

It was a little before noon, and the judge had temporarily evicted the construction workers laboring away on the town hall. He was once again seated at his makeshift bench, with Pritchard standing before him. In the gallery was a collection of townsfolk, including Acting Mayor Idelle Pritchard and Ditch Clemson.

In response to the judge's query, the group of people in the under-construction town hall looked at one another, shrugged, and shook their heads as one. Most had been spectators to the gunfight and had already related what they'd witnessed.

"I have something to say," Benedict Houseman spoke up.

"Go ahead," Judge Pearson said.

"I'd like to note for the record," Houseman began, "that, if anything, Smokin' Joe Atherton's—er, excuse me, Marshal Pritchard's—reputation as a pistoleer is understated. He was set upon by two armed men, in broad daylight, who tried to back-shoot him in the middle of the street. The marshal had no choice but to defend himself. His quick action in dispatching that pair of cowardly murderers not only saved his own life, but undoubtedly prevented injury or death to any number of innocent bystanders. I believe Marshal Pritchard should be absolved of any charges in their righteous deaths and cited for his courageous service. The good citizens of Atherton can sleep well, safe in the knowledge that the law enforcement officer acting as guardian of their town is so capable of carrying out his sworn duties."

The people in the hall began to clap their approval.

"What's Houseman up to?" Ditch whispered to Idelle. "Practicing for his upcoming mayoral campaign, perhaps?"

"I'm not sure," she said. "I agree with what he said, but I don't like the idea of him saying it. I don't trust him, Ditch. He's got something up his sleeve."

"I'm with you on that," Ditch agreed.

The judge rapped his gavel for silence. "I was getting to that part," he said. "It is the ruling of this court, after hearing all pertinent evidence, that the actions of Marshal Pritchard were both lawful and appropriate. The deaths of the two men who tried to do him in were justified. This court is adjourned."

People patted Pritchard on the back and shook his hand as they filed out of the courtroom. Judge Pearson signaled for the construction foreman to round up his crew and resume their work. Within minutes, only Judge Pearson, Pritchard, Ditch, and Idelle remained.

"You have any idea who those two gunmen were?" the judge asked Pritchard.

"I wish I did," Pritchard said. "I can't recall ever seeing either of them before."

"Are you sure?" Ditch asked. "Between the war, and all those years rangerin', you put down an awful lot of men that needed puttin' down. Who knows how many folks connected to some of those notches might still carry a grudge."

"That may be true," Pritchard said, "but I'm sure if I'd seen those fellers before I'd remember."

"It doesn't matter," Idelle said. "Neither one of them can tell us anything about their motives now. Forgive me for changing the topic, but am I the only one uncomfortable with Houseman's rousing speech on my brother's behalf?"

"For a guy whose sidekick wants to take your job," Ditch said to Pritchard, "he surely was complimentary."

"I don't know what it means," Judge Pearson said, "but I'd keep an eye on him. That slick-looking associate of his, too."

"Way ahead of you," Ditch said. "I already spoke to John Babbit. He's sending out inquiries by telegram to some of his fellow newspapermen in Omaha, Kansas City, Saint Louis, and even

66

Chicago. He hopes to have something on Houseman or Stearns, if that's their real names, in a couple of days."

"Which reminds me," Judge Pearson said, doffing his robe. "I've got a telegram to send myself. We'll see if the governor's office has any information about Mr. Houseman or Mr. Stearns. I'll let you know what, if anything, I find out. Good afternoon."

As Pritchard, Ditch, and Idelle walked out of the town hall into the uncommonly warm April afternoon, they were confronted by Eudora Chilton. She wore a flattering blue dress, which, like last night's attire, accented her prominent cleavage. She held open a parasol in gloved hands.

"I heard about what happened," she said to Pritchard. She collapsed the parasol, lowered it to her side, and stepped in close to him. She looked up at him through her hypnotic green eyes. "I'm pleased to see you're alive and unhurt."

"I share your sentiment," Pritchard said.

"You have a very dangerous job, Marshal," she went on. "Since I arrived in town, you've nearly been killed twice and killed three men in less than three days."

"Two of 'em he dropped before breakfast," Ditch pointed out. Idelle discreetly kicked him in the ankle.

"Some might consider that bad luck," Eudora said.

"You're not implying that your arrival, Miss Chilton, has somehow brought me misfortune?" Pritchard asked, a hint of a smile cracking his lips.

"Most of the men I've known haven't considered me unlucky," Eudora said, batting her eyes.

"I'll bet," Idelle said. It was Ditch's turn to covertly kick her.

"I didn't realize Atherton was such a violent place," Eudora said, turning to Idelle.

"It's not, usually," Idelle said. "It's mostly hard-working, God-fearing folks and their families, living peaceably amongst one another. Which is how we'd like to keep it."

"Who wouldn't?" Eudora said. "Which is the reason I sought you out, Mayor Pritchard. It occurred to me I was quite forward last night, imposing myself during your supper uninvited. I'd like the opportunity to make it up to you. Please allow me to host you three at dinner, tonight in the hotel, as my guests. We can get to know each other better. I'll be happy to answer any questions you may have about me or my offer to buy the Sidewinder."

"I'm not sure I'll be avail—"

"What can it hurt?" Eudora cut off Idelle before she could refuse the invitation. "At the very least you'll get a free meal, and who knows? Perhaps we'll become friends."

"Very well," Idelle said, reluctantly accepting. "Ditch and I would be delighted to dine with you."

"How about you, Marshal?" Eudora stepped in even closer. Her breasts pressed hard against his abdomen. "A man of your size must enjoy eating."

"I generally don't turn down free meals," Pritchard admitted. "Especially if the company is as charming as yours promises to be. Count me in."

"Excellent," Eudora exclaimed, unleashing a smile of her own. "It's settled, then. We'll meet in the hotel lobby at seven. Good afternoon."

She turned on her heels, put up her parasol, and walked away, daring Pritchard and Ditch not to stare at the sway of her hips as she departed.

"Better watch out, Pritchard," Ditch whistled. "I think she's got her eye on you."

"It ain't her eyes he should be watching out for," Idelle said.

CHAPTER 10

Ditch met Pritchard at the undertaker's office, where the marshal was going through the pockets of the clothing belonging to the two men he'd shot earlier that morning. The undertaker, Simon Tilley, was a skeletal man in his sixties only a couple of inches shorter than Pritchard. He was busy measuring his two newest customers for boxes, which his adult son Seth made in the woodshop behind the mortuary. It was where Pritchard had obtained most of the components for his new wooden office chair.

The man in the buffalo-skin coat had a fatal gunshot wound just above his upper lip and another one in his lower abdomen, as Pritchard suspected. He had no identifying papers on his person and only a plug of chewing tobacco, a skinning knife, and fourteen dollars stuffed in his boot.

Pritchard fared little better with the man in the duster. Besides his belt and holster, and a bag of tobacco and some rolling papers, all he had were eleven dollars and a small silver frame holding a picture of a plain-looking woman with a sad smile.

"Find anything on their horses which could help us identify either of these hombres?" Pritchard asked Ditch.

"Nope," Ditch replied. "I found blankets, clothing, and some food, but that's all I could come up with. It looks like both of 'em were living out of their saddles."

"Who's gonna pay for their boxes and holes, Marshal?" Tilley asked.

"I'm takin' the fourteen dollars," Pritchard said, "to pay for the replacement of Dady Perkins's front door. You can keep the other eleven, and whatever you can get for their guns, saddles, and horses. That ought to more than cover your time and expenses."

"It will indeed," Tilley said, "but you might as well give me the fourteen dollars, too. Seth's the one who's gonna be fixin' the diner's front door."

"You're right," Pritchard said, handing over the cash. "I plumb forgot."

"Speakin' of forking over money," Ditch said, "Mr. Samples down at the mercantile told me to tell you he's got a parcel for you that just came in on the train."

"Let's go," Pritchard said to Ditch. "I've been waitin' for that package to arrive."

When Ditch and Pritchard entered the general store, the proprietor, Wynn Samples, waved them a greeting.

"I hear tell you've got somethin' for me?" Pritchard said.

"I do," Samples said. He was an honest, good-natured, and well-liked family man who

Idelle put in charge of Atherton's lucrative retail establishment after inheriting it from Burnell Shipley. The previous proprietor, Oliver Manning, was an old skinflint and Shipley lackey whose duplicity, though not criminal, played a role in her mother's death. At Idelle's insistence, Pritchard ran him out of town when she became acting mayor.

Samples came out from under the counter with a horizontal box wrapped in brown paper. "Here it is," he said with a grin. "All the way from Connecticut."

Pritchard unwrapped the box to reveal a brand-new Winchester Model 1873 repeating rifle. Ditch whistled.

"She's the newest rifle Winchester makes," Samples said as Pritchard hefted it. "It's supposed to be their finest yet. First one I've had here in the store. Sports a steel receiver, instead of brass like the Yellow Boy or Henry, to better handle that newfangled .44-40 cartridge. Holds fifteen of 'em."

"That's only a couple less than our Henrys," Ditch commented. "You can still load on Sunday and shoot all week."

"You got the ammunition for it?" Pritchard asked.

"A whole case for you," Samples replied, "and five extra cases for me to keep in stock here in the store. Once it gets around that you favor this model, I've got a feeling I'm going to be selling a few more rifles. I've already ordered a dozen to keep in stock."

"Put me down for one of 'em now," Ditch said. "If I'd known you were gettin' a new Winchester, I'd have got one, too. Why didn't you tell me?"

"I figured I'd test it out first myself," Pritchard said. "Didn't want you to spend your money unless the gun was worth it."

"I'm certainly fond of my Henry," Ditch admitted, "but if this new Winchester is as good as Wynn says, and good enough for you, it's good enough for me."

"How much do I owe you?" Pritchard asked.

"It ain't cheap, Marshal. It's fifty dollars for the rifle, and another ten for the case of ammunition."

Pritchard put the cash on the counter and shook Wynn Samples's hand. Though he'd declined his portion of the wealth once belonging to Burnell Shipley, as well as his share of the hefty proceeds from Ditch's infamous cattle drive to Abilene from Texas, Pritchard was no pauper.

Pritchard had accumulated a savings of over $13,000. Some was accrued as wages, but most was earned in reward bounty collected during his tenure as a Texas Ranger. He'd originally intended to use the money to buy a ranch and build a home for his beloved bride, Caroline, somewhere near Austin, where her folks hailed from.

That was before her death at the hands of outlaw Winston Boone and his son. Most of Pritchard's money now rested in the Kansas City branch of the Wells Fargo Bank, although he hoped that might soon change. It was Idelle's intention, with the help of Judge Pearson's influence, to eventually convince Wells Fargo to open a branch in Atherton.

"C'mon, Ditch," Pritchard said, tucking the carton of cartridges under one arm and hefting the rifle with the other. "Let's drop this stuff off at the jail and get ourselves some lunch. I missed my breakfast, remember?"

"I can always eat," Ditch said, following on Pritchard's heels.

"Let me know how the new Winchester shoots," Samples called after them.

"Will do," Pritchard answered over his shoulder.

When they arrived at the jail, Tater was fit to be tied. Not only had he been holed up inside the marshal's office all day with Count Strobl, and missed all the action with Pritchard's big gunfight, which was the talk of the town, he also missed his midday meal.

"It's about time you returned," he scolded Pritchard. "A feller could starve to death in the length of time it takes for you to come waltzin' back. And if that ain't enough to frazzle my nerves, I had to hear about your shootin' fracas from Dady Perkins when she brought over the prisoner's lunch. When I heard the shots, I just knew you had to be mixed up in it. I was plumb worried sick about you. I thought you might've been killed, till I was told you wasn't. It's enough to give a feller the vapors."

"If by the 'vapors,'" Strobl said from inside his cell, "your deputy was referring to his frequent bouts of flatulence, then indeed he was vexed by your absence. I've known Belgian draft horses to break less wind."

"Whyn't you go piss up a rope, Your Highness?" Tater shot back. "I happen to have a sensitive stomach. Besides, you already got fed. I didn't."

Tater turned back to Pritchard. "I must say, Marshal, if he's royalty, I'd hate to see how the common folk act where's he's from. All he's done since you left is whine and complain. I've known newborn babies who don't whimper as much."

"I'm sorry, Tater," Pritchard said. "I apologize for leaving you here by yourself for so long. It's been a hectic morning." He handed his deputy a silver dollar. "Why don't you get yourself over to the diner and rustle up something to settle your stomach?"

Tater's eyes got big when he saw the silver dollar. "You want your change back?"

"Hell, no," Pritchard said. "I want you to eat hearty. Get goin'."

Once Tater departed, Pritchard set the rifle and ammunition on the desk, removed his hat, and plopped heavily in his new chair. Ditch took a seat in his old one.

"Looks like our own lunch is gonna be delayed," Ditch said.

"Don't wait on me," Pritchard told him. "Go eat. I'll get something when Tater comes back."

"I've got a better idea," Ditch said. "I'll head over to the diner, fetch us both some grub, and tote it back here where we can eat together. How's that sound?"

"Truth be told," Pritchard said, "it sounds mighty good. I'm famished." Ditch nodded and made his exit.

"I overheard talk about your violent encounter this morning," Strobl said from across the office. "Did I not say earlier that you would soon be the hunted one?"

"As a matter of fact," Pritchard said, turning in his chair to face the count, "you did. Just what exactly did you mean by that?"

"This is something for me to know," Strobl said smugly, "and for you to find out."

CHAPTER 11

Stearns had just finished cleaning his Smith & Wesson .44 when the knock on his hotel room door sounded. The weapon lay unloaded and disassembled on the dressing table. He drew the .32 caliber Smith & Wesson Model 2 from its shoulder holster, cocked the hammer, and pointed it at the door.

"Who is it?" he asked.

"It's me," Houseman's voice answered from the other side of the door.

"Come in," Stearns said. He continued to point the revolver.

When Houseman entered and saw the pistol leveled at his head, he abruptly halted in the doorway. His eyes bugged, his jaw dropped, and the unlit cigar fell from his mouth to the floor. He slowly raised his hands.

"Why are you pointing a gun at me?"

Stearns lowered the hammer and returned the compact revolver to its underarm sheath. "To put you on notice not to enter my room unannounced."

"You could have simply asked," Houseman said, letting out his breath and stooping to pick up his cigar. He closed the door behind him.

"The gun makes the point better," Stearns said, "and saves me words."

"Can't argue that," Houseman said, lighting his cigar. "We need to talk."

"What about?"

"What do you mean, 'What about'? You know exactly what I'm referring to. The Marshal Pritchard situation, that's what. He gunned down two men this morning without even breaking a sweat. It changes things."

"It changes nothing," Stearns said. He finished wiping down the individual components of his revolver with an oiled cloth and began to reassemble it.

"How can you say that?"

"Those two half-wits deserved what they got, taking someone like the marshal on in the open the way they did. They must have figured since they were double his number, they were twice as deadly. It cost them dearly."

"You knew Pritchard was Atherton all along, didn't you? Before we arrived in town? Even before I hired you?"

"I suspected it," Stearns confessed. "Read a newspaper article before Christmas that said Atherton had taken up town marshaling under a new name somewhere up north. I thought it was an odd coincidence the marshal here was named after the town he worked in. Wasn't sure it was Atherton until I saw him at the station when we arrived. He sorta stands out."

"You've met him before?"

"Not personally," he said. "I saw him gun a man down in Texas, not long after the war."

"You could've told me."

"Told you what? My suspicions?" Stearns shook his head. "No point in making a fuss until I was sure."

"His presence here in Atherton doesn't concern you?" Houseman asked.

"Not yet," Stearns said. "Why should it?"

"Because the marshal's no fool and he's damn good with his guns, that's why. What if he finds out what we've got planned and comes gunning for us?"

"Don't worry, Benedict," Stearns said. He began inserting .44 cartridges into his gun's cylinder, one by one. "He ain't gonna find out nothin'. Besides, pretty soon Marshal Pritchard's going to have his hands full just stayin' alive."

"What's that supposed to mean?"

"Let's just say," Stearns said, putting in the final cartridge and snapping the top-break revolver's cylinder back into place, "the town of Atherton is about to host some out-of-town visitors, and leave it at that."

CHAPTER 12

When Pritchard met Ditch and Idelle at the steps of the Atherton Arms it wasn't yet sunset, but it was well after the majority of businesses had buttoned up and most of the town's working folks had retired to their homes.

Pritchard spent the afternoon in his room in the jail, cleaning his revolvers and his new Winchester rifle, which was packed and shipped in grease. He also, as was his daily habit, practiced with his guns.

Ever since he'd been bound, placed on his knees, and shot in the head with a pistol, Pritchard swore he'd never again allow a gun to be pointed at him without the ability to shoot back. He was only a teenager then, and it was the morning after his father was murdered. It was also the day after he killed his first man.

Since that fateful day, Pritchard always kept a brace of pistols within instant reach.

In the days, weeks, months, and years that followed, as a soldier and Texas Ranger, Pritchard killed too many men to remember. A crack rifle shot as a boy, he discovered as a Confederate horseback guerilla that at close range pistols often proved more effective than rifles. He also learned that having two guns was faster than reloading.

As a result of these and other lessons learned in the crucible of mortal combat, he trained himself to shoot equally well with either hand.

Pritchard's daily practice regimen consisted of at least twenty minutes of drawing and dry-firing his unloaded guns, taking aim at a coin affixed to the wall in his room. He was deliberate about his training, and at least once a week rode Rusty out of town into the country and conducted the same practice regimen with live ammunition.

Ditch, who'd grown up with Pritchard and been with him from the beginning of his introduction to the martial use of the one-handed gun, had witnessed Pritchard's daily practice routine countless times. He was the only person, besides Pritchard, who knew the secret of his friend's phenomenal speed and accuracy with revolvers: years of focus, effort, and discipline. Everyone else who'd witnessed Pritchard's extraordinary skill as a pistoleer was either dead or believed he possessed a Herculean, natural aptitude imbued by either God or the devil. Few would have guessed it was merely consistent training, coupled with religious practice and hard work.

After practice and cleaning his weapons, Pritchard used what was left of the afternoon to polish his boots, belt, and holsters. He also got in a shave, haircut, and a bath at the barbershop. While Tater went across the street to the diner to obtain Count Strobl's evening meal, Pritchard ironed his only white shirt and put on a string tie.

Pritchard belted on his pistols, and was pinning on his star, when Tater returned carrying the prisoner's supper.

"Jumpin' July jackrabbits, Marshal Pritchard!" Tater exclaimed when he saw Pritchard. "Why're you all duded up? You goin' to a weddin', or a funeral?"

"Just having dinner at the hotel, Tater," Pritchard said, "with Ditch and Idelle."

"You sure it's just them two you're gonna be dinin' with?" Tater grinned. "I saw you talkin' in the street earlier today with that red-haired vixen who came into town on the train."

"She might be in attendance," Pritchard admitted. "That don't give you cause to draw inferences, you nosy old coot."

"I ain't drawin' no inferences, Marshal," Tater said innocently. "I just ain't never seen you get a haircut and a bath on the same day, and certainly not before eatin' a meal with Ditch and your sister. Today you done both."

Pritchard pulled down Tater's hat over his eyes. "I can't get nothin' by you, can I?" he laughed.

"If you two imbeciles are both finished with your juvenile banter," Count Strobl said from within his cell, "I await my dinner."

"What's an *imbecile?*" Tater asked.

"He just called us stupid," Pritchard said.

"That's mighty rude," Tater said, squinting

at Strobl. "Tell me, Your Lordship, iffen I'm so stupid, how's come I'm on the outside, and you're on the inside, of that there cage?"

"Doesn't seem too sage to me," Pritchard added, "insulting the man whose job it is to feed you before he actually feeds you."

"I'll say," Tater said. "I knowed a feller once who insulted the waiter at a chophouse in Kansas City while he was orderin' his dinner. Guess what was in his stew when it was finally brung to his table?"

"I don't want to know," Strobl said, rolling his eyes, "but I am certain you will tell me anyway."

"You guessed it," Tater said triumphantly. "Beef and boogers."

"I have suddenly," Strobl said, his accented voice dripping with sarcasm, "just lost my appetite."

"That's too bad, Your Highness," Tater said. "Your dinner tonight was meat loaf, taters with gravy, and baked beans. It's as good a batch of meat loaf as Dady's ever made. I already sampled some, myself."

"This fact does not bewilder me," Strobl said. "Frankly, I'm surprised my own dinner made it to the jail uneaten."

"You sure you don't want your supper?" Tater asked.

"Positive," Strobl said, slumping to his bunk and putting his face in his hands.

"Can't let a good meal like this go to waste," Tater said, stuffing a napkin into his collar.

Pritchard made his exit, leaving a gleeful Tater devouring his second dinner of the evening, and went off to meet Ditch and his sister.

"Look who's got himself dressed up," Ditch said to Idelle as Pritchard greeted them. "I'm starting to suspect our town marshal is trying to impress someone."

Idelle leaned in and sniffed. "You're right," she said. "He took a bath, too. It's a bad sign."

"Can't a feller clean himself up once in a while?"

"That question," Ditch said, "is mighty comical comin' from a man who'd rather sleep on the prairie, or in the stable with his horse."

"It surely is," Idelle said. "I've got my eye on you, big brother." The trio entered the hotel and made their way across the lobby to the restaurant.

"You two act like I'm gonna marry the woman," Pritchard said. "Hell, I never saw her before yesterday, and only just met her last night. Just how gullible do you think I am?"

"Do you really want me to answer that?" Idelle said.

"I can handle myself," he insisted.

"You can handle yourself with your fists," Ditch began, "and certainly with your guns. Your heart, my friend, is another thing altogether. You haven't encountered a critter like Eudora Chilton before. She's a helluva lot of woman. I'd watch out, iffen I was you."

"He's right," Idelle continued. "She's out of your league. Not to mention, at least five years older than you. And by the looks of her, she's been around some. Who knows how many men have sampled her charms?"

"Legions," a feminine voice said from behind them. "I've been with so many paramours I keep a corral in my bedroom to park their horses."

They turned and found Eudora Chilton had again walked up unnoticed behind them. Idelle's face instantly went crimson. Ditch suppressed a grin. Pritchard didn't.

She was wearing her hair up and was clad in an elegant, shoulderless, low-cut, blue dress. She also wore a radiant smile. Every man in the place was staring at her.

"I'm so sorry, Miss Chilton," Idelle said, "I didn't realize—"

"Forget it," Eudora cut off her apology. "In your shoes, I'd think the same of me. I believe it's admirable how you look out for your brother. He's lucky to have a sister who is so forthright. Shall we be seated?"

A waiter led them to a reserved table with candles already lit. "I took the liberty of ordering wine," Eudora said as Pritchard pulled out her chair.

"I only drink whiskey and beer," Pritchard said. "Me, too," agreed Ditch.

"That just means more wine for Idelle and me," Eudora said. The waiter, familiar with Ditch and Pritchard, had already taken the liberty of placing a shot of rye and a beer for each man on the table.

"I've never had wine before," Idelle said. "Nor drank anything with alcohol in it."

"That's perfect," Eudora said, pouring a glass of red wine for Idelle and herself. "Then this shall be a night of firsts." She raised her glass. "Here's to new friends."

Pritchard and Ditch raised their shot glasses, and Idelle timidly raised her wineglass. Her cheeks were still red with embarrassment. They all clinked their glasses together and drank.

"It tastes sweet and sour at the same time," Idelle said, puckering her lips. "Mama told me that about wine once. Now I know what she meant."

"Your mother is an insightful woman," Eudora said. "Will I get to meet her?"

"She's dead," Ditch spoke up, to spare Idelle from having to answer. He knew the topic of her mother's death was still raw with his fiancée. "She passed last summer, here in town."

"She didn't pass," Idelle corrected him. Her eyes began to mist. "She was murdered, like our father, by the same evil man; Burnell Shipley."

"I'm sorry," Eudora said, "I didn't mean to—"

"No apology is necessary," Idelle said. "It is I who should beg your forgiveness, for the awful things I said about you earlier. My mother taught me better manners. I shamed her, and myself, when I spoke so thoughtlessly."

Eudora put her hand over Idelle's. "You have nothing to be ashamed about, and if your mother were here she couldn't be anything but proud of you. Any words spoken before are forgotten." She looked into the younger woman's eyes and smiled. "I meant what I said during our toast about making new friends. I want to be yours."

The waiter came and took their orders. Idelle chose chicken, Eudora veal, and Pritchard and Ditch slabs of rare beef.

"I must say," Eudora said, taking another sip of wine, "the Pritchard family has done well in Atherton. You're the mayor, your brother is the town marshal and sheriff, and your fiancé, a wealthy cattleman, I hear, is hoping to take over the mayor's job from you."

"We're doing all right," Idelle said. "But we're simply trying to put this town back together after a long, dark spell. We'd be a lot better off if the name Burnell Shipley had never graced the town of Atherton."

"I keep hearing his name," Eudora said. "I gather yours is not the only family whose loved ones he killed and whose property he plundered?"

"He was a vile man," Idelle said. "That's the best that can be said about him."

"I understand he's dead, is that right?"

"That's right," Ditch said, setting down his beer and wiping his lip on his sleeve. "Deader than Abraham Lincoln. He's buried up yonder, near the church cemetery overlooking the town. We wouldn't plant him alongside decent folk. I go up there every once in a while, after I've had a drink or two, and piss on his grave."

"Ditch!" Idelle said. "That's appalling!" She turned to Pritchard. "Did you know about this?"

"I go with him," Pritchard said. "We have pissin' contests over Shipley's marker."

Eudora laughed, while Idelle looked aghast. Eventually she started laughing, too.

"Tell us about yourself," Pritchard said to Eudora.

"Not much to tell," she said. "I was born and raised in Kansas. I got married young and was hoping to raise crops and children, like my parents. Then the war came along."

"The war," Pritchard said.

"That damn war," Ditch said.

"Like so many women," Eudora went on, "the war claimed my husband, but I didn't know it. After the surrender, I heard no word, so I went off in search of him. I discovered he'd died of eruptive fever while in captivity at Rock Island."

"It must have been very hard for you," Idelle said.

"Me, and everybody else," Eudora said. "You may remember the days after the surrender were particularly difficult for those who'd fought on the side of the Confederacy."

"I remember," Pritchard said.

"I wasn't much older than you are now, Idelle, when I found myself far from home, broke, and alone. I had only three things in my possession: my looks, my wits, and my will to survive. I found work in a Little Rock saloon. From there I moved up to different towns, and bigger and better saloons. By the time I got to Memphis, nearly ten years later, I'd learned the saloon business and made myself a pile of money."

"How'd you end up in Atherton?" Ditch asked.

"I'd grown tired of big cities. I missed the quiet life of my childhood. I packed my things and took the rail line from Memphis to Saint Louis. From there I intended to go to Kansas City, and on home to Kansas. But when I heard about Atherton, and learned there was no saloon in operation here, I couldn't help checking it out for myself."

"What did you hear?" Idelle asked.

"I struck up a conversation with a news-paperman who got on the train in Saint Louis. He evidently traveled frequently between there and Kansas City. He told me a little about Atherton and what had happened here last year. Somewhere in the conversation, he mentioned that the local saloon had been closed down. Fate took care of the rest."

"So, what do you think of our little town," Ditch asked, "now that you've seen it?"

"It's perfect."

"Do you really think you'd enjoy living in a place like Atherton after all your years in the big city?" Idelle asked.

"You have no idea," Eudora said, draining her glass. "All I want is to open a small saloon, settle down into running it, and spend my remaining days in peace and quiet."

"Here's to peace and quiet," Pritchard said, refilling Idelle's and Eudora's glasses and raising his beer.

"To peace and quiet," Ditch repeated, lifting his mug.

"Hear! Hear!" Eudora said, raising her wine-glass. Idelle followed suit, and once again four glasses clinked together as one.

CHAPTER 13

"That was a lovely meal," Eudora said. "Would you care to join me in the hotel bar for an after-dinner drink?"

"Why don't we have our drinks in the restaurant?" Idelle said. "It's more intimate here."

"Exactly why I want to go to the bar," Eudora said. "There's something I'd like you to see."

"We'd be glad to have a drink with you," Ditch said before Idelle could protest further.

The quartet was led to the hotel's small bar, which was heavily congested since it was the only place in town to buy a drink. Their waiter guided them through the elbow-to-elbow crowd in search of an open table, but none were available.

"Not being a drinker—" Idelle began, speaking loudly to be heard.

"—before tonight," Eudora cut in with a wink.

"—before tonight," Idelle agreed, "I guess I never really noticed how overcrowded the Atherton Arms' lounge can get in the evening."

"This little bar is packed every night," Ditch said. "There's no other place in town to wet your whistle."

"What this town needs," Eudora said, winking

at Idelle and offering a conspiratorial smile, "is a saloon."

"You've made your point," Idelle said with a laugh. "You win, Eudora. Not only are you charming, and make a very persuasive argument, you've made me realize I can't let my own personal reservations affect what the people want. I've decided to let you reopen the Sidewinder."

Pritchard smiled, and Ditch let out a rebel yell.

"You won't regret it," Eudora said. "Besides," she said, stepping in close to Pritchard and running a hand along his bicep, "I'm sure the marshal will keep me in line."

"This calls for a drink," Ditch said, scanning the throng for a waitress to no avail.

"I'll go to the bar," Pritchard offered. "You folks wait here."

Pritchard squeezed his massive frame through the congregation. "Two beers and two glasses of red wine," he said to the bartender, as he scrambled to fill drinks.

"It'll be a few minutes, Marshal," the harried bartender answered. "I'm a little behind."

"No hurry," Pritchard said.

"Why don't you let me buy you a drink, Marshal?" a voice said from behind Pritchard. He turned around and found a short, squat man wearing a tied-down holster facing him. Due to the teeming crowd, the man was very close. He suddenly tossed a shot of whiskey in Pritchard's face and went for his holstered revolver.

The instant Pritchard saw the man, whose expression and body language belied his intentions, he recognized the imminent threat. He also realized his short assailant had tossed the whiskey in an attempt to blind and distract him while he simultaneously drew his gun.

Pritchard turned his head just in time and caught the hurled liquid in the side of his face and neck instead of his eyes. In the same motion, he reached down with his left hand and snatched the long barrel of the man's Colt revolver as it cleared the holster. He sidestepped, and levered the seven-and-a-half-inch barrel toward the floor.

The revolver fired, and someone at the bar cried out. A split second later, Pritchard had his own Colt revolver out. Before his attacker could cock his weapon and fire again, Pritchard placed his own gun barrel under the man's chin, pointed upward, and fired.

The short gunman's hat, and a portion of the top of his head, flew off. He sank to the floor, dead before he arrived.

The twin gunshots silenced everyone in the room. With all eyes on him, Pritchard scanned the vicinity for any other threats. He holstered his gun only after being satisfied his attacker had no associates with him.

Pritchard set the gunman's revolver on the bar

and wrung his left hand, which was stinging from diverting the gun barrel as it discharged. A quick glance assured him there was no injury to his fingers other than a coating of powder soot.

"I'm hit," a man said. He held his calf, which seeped blood through his fingers, and allowed his two companions to lower him to the floor. All three looked to be cattlemen. Ditch elbowed his way toward them, with Idelle and Eudora appearing behind him.

"Samuel," Idelle said, rushing into her brother's arms. "Are you all right?"

"I'm okay," Pritchard said. He nudged the body at his feet with the toe of his boot. "Can't say the same for this feller."

"Thank heaven you're unhurt," Eudora said. "You sure know how to worry a gal."

"How bad is it?" Pritchard asked those attending to the injured patron.

"It don't look too bad," said one of the men examining the wound. "Just grazed him, really."

"I'm all right," the wounded man said, letting his friend bandage his leg with a bar towel. "Given how jam-packed it is in here, I guess we should count ourselves fortunate I'm the only injured bystander. Just my luck it had to be me."

"Could've been a lot worse," the bartender agreed. "Nice shootin', Marshal. Pluggin' him upward through the noggin likely saved somebody else a hole."

"Go get Dr. Mauldin," Pritchard ordered a patron. To another patron, he said, "Fetch Simon Tilley." To the bartender he said, "Get this injured man a bottle of whatever he's drinkin', on me. And while you're at it, pour a round for the house."

"The marshal's buyin'!" somebody called out. A series of hoots and yells erupted, and a mob of thirsty patrons charged the bar.

"Anybody know this guy?" Ditch asked, pointing to the dead man. "Any idea why he'd want to shoot the marshal?"

"Never seen him before," a bar patron said. "He ain't local," said another. "Not a clue," said a third.

"How about you, Marshal?" the wounded cattle buyer asked Pritchard. "Do you recognize him?"

"I've never laid eyes on him before," he answered.

"I know who he is," said Ditch.

"You do?" Pritchard said.

"I do," Ditch said.

"Who is he?"

"He's the fifth person who's come to Atherton in the last couple of days to put a bullet in you," Ditch answered.

"What are you implying?" Idelle asked.

"I ain't implyin' nothin'," Ditch said to her, "I'm flat-out sayin' it. The first two were that uppity Austrian count who wanted to provoke a duel, and his pistol-packin' servant. The third and fourth were those two saddle tramps who tried to back-shoot him this morning. And now this pint-sized pistoleer at the bar." He scratched his head. "I'm no college professor, but I think I'm beginnin' to detect a pattern."

"So am I," Pritchard said.

CHAPTER 14

"It is the decision of this court that the death of the aforementioned, and unidentified, gentleman currently occupying a table at Tilley's Mortuary was an unavoidable act of self-defense. Court is adjourned."

Judge Pearson banged his gavel on the plank-bench in the town hall, and the crowd slowly began to file out. Ditch, Idelle, and Eudora surrounded Pritchard. It was nearly midnight, and the judge was wearing his nightshirt under his robe.

Despite the lateness of the hour, Judge Pearson convened the death hearing immediately upon receiving word of the shooting. He wanted to obtain fresh statements from the witnesses, rather than have to hunt them all down the following morning.

"Two death hearings in one day," Pearson said to Pritchard as he rose from his seat, "and one the day before. That's got to be a record, Marshal, even for you."

"I'm just glad it wasn't my death you were presiding over," Pritchard said.

"Did you find anything out about your would-be murderer?" the judge asked.

"I went through his pockets at Tilley's," he said.

"Evidently he'd only been in town a few hours. He had a ticket stub from the Saint Louis train in his britches. He also had over one hundred dollars, so he wasn't broke. There was nothing else on him which would tell me his name or occupation."

"That ain't exactly true," Ditch said. "Tell the judge about the man's gun, Pritchard."

"What about his gun?" Judge Pearson said.

"His revolver, a Cavalry Colt .45," Pritchard said, "had the front sight filed off."

"So?" Pearson said.

"Occasionally," Pritchard explained, "a revolver's front sight blade will snag on the holster when it's coming out. Some who fancy themselves fast-draw artists will alter their shootin' irons by filing off the front sights. They believe it'll give 'em a faster pull."

"Does it?" Pearson asked.

"I never thought so," Pritchard said. "It ain't the gun which determines the speed of draw, it's the man slingin' it."

"That wasn't the only unusual feature on his revolver," Ditch said. "There were five notches carved into the grip."

"It sounds like he might have been a professional gunman," Judge Pearson said.

"It kinda looks that way," Pritchard admitted.

"In light of this evening's shooting incident," the judge said, "I'm beginning to agree with your suspicions about the motives of the two men who attacked you this morning, not to mention that eccentric European fellow residing in our jail."

"I hate to admit it," Pritchard said, "but signs point to all of them being guns-for-hire."

"I told Pritchard it was pattern," Ditch said.

"That would certainly explain the inordinate amount of gunplay in Atherton of late," the judge agreed. "Why do you suppose we suddenly have a glut of professional killers walking our streets?"

"You can't have guns-for-hire," Idelle said, "without somebody hiring them."

"But who?" Eudora said.

"Findin' that out might be harder than it sounds," Ditch said. "Samuel made a lot of enemies during the war, and even more as a Texas Ranger. Fact is, there could be dozens of people with a hankerin' to see him planted."

"One way or another," Pritchard said, "I'm going to find out. Perkins's Diner got shot to hell this morning, and luckily nobody was hurt. Tonight, some poor cowpoke mindin' his own business and having a beer took a bullet on account of me, and again, luckily was only grazed. Nobody's luck can hold out forever. The next innocent bystander near me when somebody makes a play for my hide might not be so fortunate."

"What do you plan to do?" Eudora asked.

"Tomorrow morning," he said, "Count Strobl

and I are going to have a little chat. I've got a feeling he might be able to provide some insight."

As most of the people left the courtroom, three newcomers entered. They were Benedict Houseman, Jack Stearns, and a pretty young brunette about Idelle's age.

"If I may impose on you for a moment, Your Honor," Houseman said to Judge Pearson. "I'd like to have a word with you."

"It's quite late," the judge said. "Can't it wait until tomorrow? We just finished a death inquest and I'm dog-tired. I want to go home and get into bed."

"It's an urgent legal matter," Houseman pressed. "I believe it best you're made aware of it tonight."

"Very well," Judge Pearson relented. He made no effort to hide his disdain. "What's so damned important that you're keeping me from my slumber?"

"I'd like to introduce you to someone," Houseman said, motioning to the young woman. She stepped forward.

"Surely, Mr. Houseman," the judge said, "social introductions could wait until morning?"

"Judge Pearson," Houseman went on, ignoring the judge's question, "may I present Miss Bonnie Shipley, formerly of Saint Louis."

Pritchard, Idelle, and Ditch looked at one another incredulously.

"Did you say her last name was Shipley?" Idelle asked.

"I did indeed," Houseman said. "Miss Shipley is the daughter of the late Burnell Shipley, and the rightful heir to all of his assets and estate. She's filed a claim in Jefferson City, challenging the inheritance. I'm representing her interests as legal counsel in the matter."

"You don't say," Judge Pearson said. He turned to Miss Shipley. "Allow me to introduce Acting Mayor Idelle Pritchard, her fiancé, Dave Clemson, Miss Eudora Chilton, and Marshal Pritchard. I'm not sure if you know it, ma'am, but the Pritchards have already been awarded Burnell Shipley's assets, most of which the court has already acknowledged he stole from them and other residents here in Atherton over a period of many years."

"Shipley's estate and assets are now formally in legal dispute," Houseman said. "The matter remains to be adjudicated."

"We'll see," Judge Pearson said.

"Indeed, we will," Houseman said. "With your permission, I would like to arrange a time to meet and discuss the issue?"

"Come by tomorrow at ten," Judge Pearson said.

"Very well," Houseman said. "I bid you good night."

"It was nice to meet all of you," Bonnie Shipley

said, without feeling. Idelle merely nodded, and Pritchard and Ditch tipped their hats. Houseman began to escort Miss Shipley toward the door. Jack Stearns lingered behind.

"Heard about your little pistol fracas in the hotel bar earlier," Stearns said to Pritchard. "It would seem interacting with you, despite your famous easygoing nature, can be a mite unhealthy?"

"Only for cowards and back-shooters who fancy themselves pistoleros," Pritchard said. He stared evenly at Stearns. "Regular folks, like you, Jack, got nothin' to worry about."

"I ain't worried, Marshal," Stearns said, resting his hand casually on the butt of his Smith & Wesson. "Not a bit."

CHAPTER 15

The streets were deserted as Pritchard walked Idelle, Eudora, and Ditch back to the Atherton Arms from the town hall.

"How do you like that?" Ditch said. "Burnell Shipley has a daughter?"

"If that's who she really is," Idelle said. "Don't you find it odd nobody's heard of her before? It's been more than nine months since Burnell's death, and it's not like there weren't plenty of newspaper stories announcing his demise. Why didn't she come forward right away, or when Judge Pearson got sent here by the governor to settle accounts last autumn?"

"It's mighty suspicious, all right," Ditch said. "The fact that she's bein' shepherded by that shady lawyer, Houseman, and his gun-totin' sidekick don't make it any less suspicious. Especially with them two makin' no secret of tryin' to take over this town by runnin' for mayor and sheriff."

"I suppose it's not impossible she's Burnell's offspring," Idelle said, "although I don't detect any physical resemblance. It's common knowledge he visited prostitutes in Kansas City and Saint Louis. Maybe he sired her with one of the painted ladies he frequented?"

"If she is Burnell Shipley's daughter," Eudora said, "and she wants to lay claim to property already awarded to you by the courts, she'll have to prove the relationship."

"How could she do that?" Idelle asked.

"I'm no lawyer," Eudora continued, "but I've bought and sold a few properties in my time and had my share of dealings with civil law. If this 'Bonnie Shipley,' or whatever her name really is, wants to successfully challenge you and Samuel in court she'll need to produce a birth certificate or witnesses who have special knowledge that'd be willing to testify under oath that she's his daughter."

"What do you mean by 'special knowledge'?"

"Someone like the doctor who delivered her, for example, who could testify that Burnell was in the room with the mother during the birth. Or someone who will testify that Burnell admitted she's his child. Or possibly a landlord who would testify that Burnell paid the mother and daughter's bills, such as room and board, over a period of time. In theory, there are any number of ways the relationship could be asserted."

"Sounds like the kind of testimony that could be bought," Ditch said, "iffen there was enough financial incentive."

"I was thinking the same thing," Eudora said. "I've seen it before, especially with mining claims. I've known dead-broke dirt-scratchers who were all alone in the world until they struck pay dirt. Then, all of a sudden, relatives they never knew they had crawled out of the woodwork like cockroaches, filing no end of claims on their fortunes."

"You're awfully quiet, Samuel," Idelle said. "Don't you have an opinion about this Bonnie Shipley situation?"

Pritchard wasn't paying attention to the conversation. He was busy scanning doorways, windows, and alleys as they walked, and didn't hear his sister's question.

"Aw, leave him alone," Ditch said. "He's had a rough day."

"That's right," Eudora said, reaching out and taking his hand. "You were almost killed today. Twice."

Pritchard deftly stepped around Eudora without breaking stride and switched her hand from his right to the left. Though an ambidextrous shooter, he was right-handed and wanted to keep his dominant arm free to draw.

"Don't tell me you don't have an opinion on the matter?" Idelle pressed her brother.

"My opinion of Bonnie Shipley, Benedict Houseman, and Jack Stearns," Pritchard said to Idelle, "doesn't matter a whit. This ain't the first time strangers tried to take what's ours. You forget, I watched Pa hanged and Ma forced into a marriage to save my life, only to be double-crossed after I was marched to the river and skull-shot."

"I didn't forget," she said solemnly.

"I don't know much about civil law," Pritchard continued, "or outlandish claims made by mysterious strangers. You should know by now, Idelle, that I ain't much for words. All I know is that anyone who tries to take what's ours again is gonna regret crossin' the Pritchard family. That's as certain as sunset."

They arrived at the Atherton Arms. Ditch and Idelle resided in separate rooms until the wedding, and their house was completed. Eudora was lodged at the hotel as well. Pritchard checked the lobby before they entered. After the day he'd experienced, he was taking no chances.

"Thank you for a lovely dinner," Eudora said to them.

"You're kidding?" Ditch said.

"Not at all," Eudora countered. "I enjoyed our time together."

"The gunfight and death inquest didn't detract from the evening's charm?" Idelle asked.

"Not in the slightest."

Idelle gave Eudora a hug. "I'm glad we got to know each other better."

"And I'm glad you let me strong-arm you into allowing me to open the Sidewinder."

"Let's have lunch tomorrow here at the hotel," Idelle suggested, "and work out the details."

"Consider it a date," Eudora said. Ditch tipped his hat and began to escort Idelle up the stairs.

"Hey, Ditch," Pritchard called after him. "In light of recent developments, it might be advisable for you to start packin' your pistol."

"I was thinking the same thing," Ditch said. "See you in the morning."

While Ditch was a fair hand with a revolver, he much preferred his Henry rifle when a gun was called for and generally didn't carry a sidearm. He did, however, own a custom, five-and-a-half-inch-barreled .45 Colt identical to Pritchard's twin revolvers. It was purchased from the same Abilene, Kansas, salesman Pritchard won his guns from in a shooting contest at the end of their cattle drive from Texas.

"Will you see me to my door?" Eudora asked Pritchard.

"I'd be honored," he said, extending his elbow.

They ascended the stairs and were soon at Eudora's room. She stood on her tiptoes, leaned in, and sniffed Pritchard's neck.

"You smell like whiskey," she said.

"I know," Pritchard said. "I wore my last drink."

"Would you care to come in for another?"

"I could be persuaded," he said.

"What would it take to persuade you?" she asked, looking up into his blue eyes through her green ones.

Pritchard lowered his mouth to hers. It started slow and tentative, but gradually grew in strength until he had one hand locked around her tiny waist and his other was filled with her flaming red hair. Eudora responded by putting both arms around his broad back. Her nails dug in, pulling him closer, and she returned the fierceness of his kiss.

Eudora forced herself from his embrace long enough to fumble with the lock and enter her hotel room. He closed the door behind them, and before his eyes could adjust to the darkness inside Eudora had slipped out of her dress. As Pritchard unbuckled his guns, she tore at the buttons on his shirt.

A frantic moment later they fell, naked, onto the bed together. Their subsequent coupling was frenetic, passionate, and incredibly intense, with each seemingly trying to consume the other. Just when it looked like they'd exhausted themselves, and their mutual rhythm appeared to subside, one, or the other, would increase the tempo to yet another fever pitch.

After collapsing, spent, into each other's arms and slumbering awhile, one would again revive the other and their raucous, carnal undertaking would resume. Their on-again, off-again, love-making continued for the remainder of the night, with neither Pritchard nor Eudora getting much sleep.

· · ·

Pritchard squinted at the sunlight filtering in through the curtains. Eudora was already awake, leaning over him on one elbow and tracing the bullet scars on his chest with her forefinger.

"Good morning," Eudora said. "Sleep well?"

"Actually," Pritchard said, rubbing his eyes, "I don't remember sleeping much at all."

"Me either," she smiled. "All I remember is being rode hard and put away wet."

"My apologies," Pritchard said, slowly sitting up. "It's been a while."

"Evidently," Eudora said, falling back into the spot Pritchard had just vacated. "Your enthusiasm was difficult to ignore. I feel like the busted bronc after a rodeo."

Seeing her naked for the first time in full light, Pritchard noticed Eudora was even more beautiful than he'd originally thought. Her skin was quite pale, and she was liberally spotted all over with freckles.

Eudora was also older than he'd thought. While she had a magnificent physique, with long, muscular legs, full hips, and a small waist beneath her full breasts, her lean face showed crow's-feet he'd not noticed before. He guessed, like most women, she concealed such irrelevant flaws with the artful application of makeup. He surmised she was at least thirty-five. This put her, at a minimum, seven years older than him.

"You held your own," Pritchard said with a grin, as he searched the floor for his trousers.

"I'm glad to hear you think so," she laughed. "It's been a while for me, too."

She watched him dress. "Tell me about Caroline," she said after a moment's silence.

"How did you know about her?"

"A newspaper article I read. It said she was murdered."

"She was," Pritchard said, buttoning his pants. "Two weeks before we were to be wed in Austin."

"Is it true you killed more than fifty men you held responsible for her death?"

"I wasn't counting," Pritchard said, sitting on the bed and pulling on his boots.

"You've killed a lot of men, haven't you?" she asked.

"Like I said, I wasn't counting."

"I've heard it said you killed dozens and dozens during the war, and even more as a Texas Ranger."

"Folks say a lot of things," Pritchard said, shrugging into his shirt. "What they say ain't always the truth."

"I read another newspaper story about a town in the New Mexico Territory called Magdalena. The author wrote that you killed another fifty men there. Is that the truth?"

"I was still a Texas Ranger, back then," Pritchard said, standing up, "and I had help."

He looked down at Eudora, lying naked on the bed below him. "You seem awfully interested in how many scalps I've collected," he said. "Any particular reason?"

"I've heard the myth of the man they call Smokin' Joe Atherton," she said. "Last night I sampled the man called Marshal Samuel Pritchard. I guess I wanted to see which one I liked better: the myth or the man?"

"And your verdict?" Pritchard said.

"The man," she said, pulling him back down to the bed.

CHAPTER 16

Count Strobl was snoring away in his cell when Pritchard arrived at the jail. Tater Jessup, always up with the roosters, was sitting at Pritchard's desk and sipping coffee. He was anxiously waiting for Pritchard to relieve him, so he could go across the street to the diner, pick up the prisoner's morning meal, and get his own breakfast.

"Mornin', Marshal," Tater greeted him. "It's after eight. You're later than usual."

"I had a busy night," Pritchard said.

"I heard. Folks're sayin' some fool tried to shoot you over at the hotel?"

"Something like that. Sorry I'm late, Tater. Go fetch your breakfast."

"Don't have to tell me twice," Tater said, eagerly rising to his feet. "Dady's makin' French toast and sausage this mornin'. I could smell it all the way from the livery."

After Tater departed, Pritchard went to his room. He stripped off his clothes, washed up, and gave himself a shave. He'd changed into a new set of dungarees and a fresh, button-front shirt. He was pinning on his badge when he heard the door open.

Pritchard belted on his revolvers as he walked

back into the office. Tater, out of breath, had come back without the tray of food for the prisoner. With him was John Babbit, Atherton's newspaperman, who was also red-faced and panting.

"You've got trouble a-comin', Marshal," Tater blurted. "Big trouble."

"He's right," Babbit said.

"Take it easy," Pritchard said. "What's all this about trouble?"

"John here says some men just got off the eight-forty from Kansas City," Tater said.

"Men get off the eight-forty every morning," Pritchard reminded him. "That ain't unusual."

"Not like these fellows," Babbit said. "These men aren't lumbermen or cattle buyers. I got a look at them myself."

"How'd they come to your attention?" Pritchard asked.

"They came to my son's attention first," Babbit said. "Ronnie was selling papers down at the station this morning, as usual. He said a tall, bearded man, dressed in black and wearing two guns, asked him where he could find Joe Atherton."

"What did Ronnie tell 'em?"

"He pretended like he didn't know the name, then he came and got me. I saw them, Samuel. There's five of them. The one Ronnie described is nearly as tall as you, but much thinner. He looks about forty and has a long beard. He's packin' two pistols, just like Ronnie said. He's with four other hard-looking men who're all carrying guns."

"They surely don't sound like beef buyers or lumberjacks," Pritchard agreed.

"You know anybody who fits that description, Marshal?" Tater asked.

"Maybe," Pritchard said. "You might be describing a fellow outta Topeka I once ran across when I was rangerin'. Calls himself Struthers."

"You mean Dingo Struthers?" Babbit said. "The bounty killer?"

"Could be him," Pritchard said. "He's tall and thin, wears two guns, and always used to travel about with a posse."

"As soon as I spotted them," Babbit went on, "I came running to warn you as fast as I could. Last I saw, they were moseying toward the jail. I spotted Tater in the diner, grabbed him, and we headed straight here."

Pritchard rubbed his chin. "Could be nothin'," he said. "But in light of all the gunplay going on lately, I think it's better to err on the side of caution."

"Caution will make little difference if Dingo Struthers is hunting your head," Count Strobl said from within his cell. Tater and Babbit's abrupt arrival had awakened him. "I've met Monsieur Struthers, in Chicago. He shares both your lack of manners and lust for violence. It would appear,

114

Marshal Atherton, your day of reckoning has come at last."

"Why does he always talk like he's readin' a bedtime story?" Tater asked.

"You and I," Strobl addressed Tater, "my portly prison-keeper, may well meet our own ends unless we reduce our immediate proximity to the marshal. I would suggest, Deputy Jessup, that you release me, abandon your post, and, as you Americans so colloquially say, 'head for the hills' with all haste."

"Shut up," Pritchard said to the count. "And how many times do I have to tell you, my name ain't Atherton?"

"What do you want me to do?" Babbit said.

"I'd be obliged," Pritchard began, as he unlocked his new Winchester rifle from the wall-mounted gun rack, "if you'd scoot over to the Atherton Arms as quick as you can and fetch Ditch. Tell him what's up, and that he might find his Henry rifle of use. Also, you might want to suggest he arrive by an indirect route."

"On my way," Babbit said, dashing out of the office.

"What about me?" Tater said, grabbing the double-barreled shotgun from the rack, breaking it open, and inserting two buckshot shells into its dual chambers.

"I want you to ford up here in the jail," Pritchard ordered, "and keep watch on the prisoner."

"But you'll need me," Tater protested, snapping the shotgun's action closed. "Even if Ditch gets here in time, it'll still be two against five. Let me come along with you, Marshal?"

"I'd be right honored to have you fightin' at my side," Pritchard said, putting a hand on Tater's shoulder. "And I ain't never gonna forget you offered. But I may need to move fast, which ain't your strong suit. Besides, you're more valuable in here. I've got a very important task for you."

"What task?" Tater said.

"If I don't come back—"

"One can only hope," Strobl interrupted from his cell.

"—I want you to remain here and guard the count."

"Guard the count?" Tater said, incredulous. "He ain't goin' anywhere. He's locked up."

"You heard me. These men might well be on the way to break Count Strobl out of jail. If they get past me, you're going to have to hold them off alone. Can you manage that?"

Pritchard didn't believe for an instant that the infamous bounty hunter Dean "Dingo" Struthers and his posse of professional gunmen had come to Atherton to spring Count Florian Strobl.

Despite his abundant luggage, elaborate wardrobe, and European pistols, Pritchard and Judge Pearson found less than twenty dollars in the Austrian's possession. For all his arrogant posturing about refusing to pay his fines on the grounds of principle, Count Strobl, if indeed actually a legitimate count with claim to royal lineage, was broke.

"I'll get 'er done," Tater said, puffing out his chest, setting his jowls, and gripping the shotgun with both hands. "You can count on me."

"I knew I could," Pritchard said.

"Do you expect me to believe that you're actually going to leave this blithering idiot here alone to protect me?" Count Strobl said indignantly. He stood leering through the bars, one black eye supporting his monocle. "The incompetent fool will probably shoot me by accident, if he doesn't shoot off his own foot first."

Pritchard suddenly drew one of his revolvers with his customary lightning speed. He leveled it at Strobl's face with the hammer back. "If you say one more word, Your Highness," he said, "I'll save Deputy Jessup the trouble and shoot you myself."

Count Strobl's eyes widened, his mouth gaped, and his monocle popped out, but he said nothing.

"You won't have to," Tater said. "Because if His Highness don't stop bumpin' his gums, I'm gonna hog-tie and bit-bridle him. That ought to keep him quiet."

"If I were you," Pritchard said to the count, "I'd say a prayer this ain't my last day. Because if I depart this earth, you might be leavin' right behind me."

"You can practically bet on it, Marshal," Tater said, scowling at the count. "Like His Highness said, this scattergun might just 'accidentally' go off. Iffen it does, it ain't gonna be my foot catchin' the buckshot. It'll be paintin' that jail cell with royal brains."

Pritchard lowered the hammer on his revolver to half-cock and extracted the empty case left over from the shooting in the bar at the Atherton Arms the previous night. He inserted two fresh cartridges into the Colt, loading the weapon to its full capacity of six rounds. He topped off his left-hand gun as well. Normally, his guns were carried loaded with only five bullets each.

Though the Colt Single Action Army had a six-shot capacity, gun-savvy folks knew to load the weapon with only five cartridges, opting to leave an empty chamber under the hammer. A round beneath the Colt's firing pin, even if the hammer was at half-cock, brought the potential for an unintentional discharge if the gun was dropped, or while jostling on horseback.

In this regard Pritchard preferred his venerable Remingtons, which had a feature allowing the hammer to rest on a notch milled between the cylinder holes. This permitted safe carry while fully loaded with six cartridges.

Yet despite the somewhat less safe design, Pritchard had to admit the handling characteristics and accuracy of his new Colt revolvers was unmatched, and superior even to his revered Remingtons. His months of daily practice with the guns had made the newer pistols almost extensions of his hands.

Nonetheless, after fully loading his Colt revolvers, he retrieved his old pair of 1863 Remington New Model Army revolvers from within an oiled cloth in his desk. They'd been a gift from Ditch after Caroline's death, and were cap-and-ball guns that had been converted by a Dallas gunsmith to fire metallic cartridges.

Pritchard loaded the Remingtons with six .44 caliber rounds each. He took extra care to ensure the hammers rested in the safety notches before stuffing one revolver into his belt at the front, and the other in back.

Next, Pritchard loaded his new Winchester rifle with fifteen of the newfangled .44-40 cartridges, regretting that he'd yet had an opportunity to try the weapon out. He left the chamber empty and stuffed his hip pockets with spare ammunition. The last thing he did was refill all his vacant gun belt loops with .45 cartridges for his two Colts.

"I can see 'em comin'," Tater said, squinting through the shutter-slats and bars of the jail's front, and only, window. "They're all the way down by the general store. I count five of 'em.

They're struttin' down the middle of the street like they own the town."

Pritchard peered through the window over Tater's shoulder. "That tall one is Struthers, all right," he said. "Two of the men with him are carryin' long arms, but I can't tell from this distance if they're rifles or shotguns. I'm going out to meet 'em."

Pritchard donned his hat and hefted his rifle. He levered the Winchester's action, chambering a round, and inserted a cartridge into the loading gate to top off the magazine.

"This jail's built of brick," Pritchard said to Tater, "with iron bars on the windows and a double-thick siege door. Lock up after I leave, and don't open for anybody until I get back."

"What if you don't come back?" Tater said. "What then?"

"Then I'll leave it to your discretion," Pritchard said.

"*Auf Wiedersehen*, Marshal," Count Strobl called after him. "I won't say it was a pleasure knowing you, but I will say it shall be a relief to be rid of you."

"We have a saying in this part of the country, Count Strobl," Pritchard said, as he opened the door. "Don't count your chickens before they're hatched."

CHAPTER 17

Pritchard heard the thick door's heavy bolt close behind him as he stepped out of the marshal's office onto the wooden sidewalk. He could see a group of four men, led by Dean "Dingo" Struthers, whom he easily recognized, making their way toward him in the center of the street. Pedestrians and shop patrons on both sides stopped and stared at the unusually tall, bearded man wearing a brace of pistols, and the quartet of gunmen behind him, as they made their way through Atherton.

Pritchard bootlegged the Winchester vertically behind his leg, hiding it from view. He discretely propped it, muzzle-up, behind one of two full rain barrels posted under the downspouts on either side of the jail's door.

"Howdy, Dingo," Pritchard called out as the men approached. Struthers and his men halted twenty yards from the jail. "Been a long time."

"Good mornin', Joe," Struthers replied in a gravelly voice.

"I don't use that handle anymore," Pritchard said. "Not since I gave up rangerin'. I go by my given name, now: Pritchard."

"I heard somethin' about that," Struthers said. "Gets a mite confusin', iffen you ask me, tryin' to figure out what to call you these days."

The men behind Struthers slowly began to spread out. A pair went on either side of him. All looked to be in their late thirties or early forties, and all wore tied-down pistols. One of the men, on Pritchard's left, carried a sawed-off shotgun loosely at his side. Another, on his right, cradled a Henry rifle in the crook of his arm.

"What brings you to Atherton, Dingo?"

"You do," Struthers said, turning his head to spit tobacco juice without taking his eyes off Pritchard.

"Did you miss me," Pritchard said, "or are you workin'?"

"I'm afraid I'm workin'," Struthers said.

"That's too bad," Pritchard said.

"I kinda think so, too," Struthers said. "Never had nothin' against you."

"Likewise," Pritchard said.

"You know where this is goin', don't you?"

"I do," Pritchard said. "What I don't know is *why*."

"Usual reason," Struthers said. "Money."

"Are you gettin' paid enough to die?" Pritchard asked.

"Mighty confident, ain't you?" Struthers said. "You're good with them pistols, no doubt about it. But you can't beat five guns. Nobody can."

"Don't have to worry about beatin' five," Pritchard said. "Just you."

"Me?" Struthers grinned, displaying blackened teeth.

"That's right. First one of your men twitches, you get shot directly."

"You'll be finished right after me."

"True," Pritchard said. "But you won't be any less dead."

Struthers gestured toward the throng of onlookers on both sides of the street, who were staring in rapt attention at the unfolding drama. "You really want to see all these folks you're sworn to protect get shot to hell and gone?"

"Not particularly," Pritchard admitted. "But if you think my concern for their safety is gonna allow you to shoot without me shootin' back, you're sorely mistaken."

"It seems," Struthers postulated, "we're at loggerheads. What do you reckon we ought to do about it?"

"I propose you and your crew turn around," Pritchard suggested, "go back to the station, and get on the next train out of Atherton. That way neither you, nor me, nor any of these innocent citizens have to catch a bullet."

"I'd surely like to," Struthers said, "but I can't. The money's too good."

"Don't suppose you'd mind tellin' me who put the price on my head?"

"I wouldn't mind at all," Struthers said. "But I can't."

"You can't," Pritchard said, "or you won't?"

"I can't," Struthers said. "Truth is, I don't rightly know."

"You don't know?"

"No idea," Struthers said, and went for his guns.

Sixty feet was too far to risk a headshot. Pritchard easily outdrew his opponent with both Colt revolvers and put two simultaneous shots straight through Struthers's middle. The big man dropped his guns and fell on his face. His four associates responded by bringing their own weapons into action.

Pritchard thumbed back the hammers and triggered his revolvers as rapidly as he'd ever fired, sending shot after shot at the four men still standing. He realized he wasn't shooting as accurately as he was accustomed to, due to the need to fire quickly. Even if he missed, he hoped the high volume of gunfire he was putting out would rattle his adversaries enough to prevent any of them from drawing a solid bead on him. At the same time as he rapid-fired, he backed up toward the cover of the rain barrel.

Bullets whizzed all around him, and he heard them thwack against the brick wall of the jail behind him. Pritchard also heard terrified screams, and sensed townspeople scurrying for cover.

He saw one of Struthers's men shooting at him with a pistol stagger to one knee. The gunman dropped his revolver and clutched his chest as Pritchard fired another shot into his torso. He sank to the ground and didn't move again.

Just as Pritchard's two Colts ran dry, the gunman with the shotgun raised his weapon. Pritchard looked straight down the twin eyes of its double barrels, waiting for the imminent blast. He dropped his empty revolvers and went for the two Remington .44s in his belt.

As he drew his second pair of revolvers he cringed, expecting the buckshot's impact. Even with his phenomenal speed and skill, he realized he'd never get the Remingtons up in time.

Suddenly the shotgunner dropped his scattergun and tumbled to the ground on his face. The .44 rimfire cartridge from Ditch's Henry rifle, fired from the rooftop of the general store, took him through his right eye.

Pritchard got behind the rain barrel just in time, as the gunman wielding his own Henry rifle began focusing his fire. Bullets steadily struck the barrel, releasing miniature streams of water gushing to the sidewalk.

Holstering the Remingtons, Pritchard grabbed the Winchester, which was already cocked. He waited for his opponent to lever the Henry's action between shots, then shouldered his rifle, took aim, and cut loose.

Pritchard was behind cover, but his target was in the open. He put four shots into the rifleman before he hit the ground, his Henry rifle falling into the dirt alongside him.

The last shot fired was from Ditch's rifle, which barked again from above. The remaining gunman dropped his empty pistol and was reaching for the Henry rifle belonging to his dead comrade, when the .44 slug entered the top of his skull.

Pritchard stood up from behind the barrel, his rifle at the ready, and started walking toward the five men lying in the street. He covered them as he advanced. The silence in the wake of the gunfight's abrupt conclusion was deafening.

"Oh my God," he heard a woman cry out, anguish in her voice. He looked up from the bodies long enough to see several people rush to someone lying on the sidewalk in front of the baked goods store.

"Jenny van der Linden's been hit!" a man declared. "Somebody fetch Doc Mauldin!"

Jenny was the fourteen-year-old daughter of Braam and Pearl van der Linden, who operated a bakery in town. She worked at her parents' business before and after school each day. The girl was unconscious and lay supine with a spreading red stain on the front of her dress. Her father gathered her in his arms as others restrained her hysterical mother.

Braam van der Linden headed off to Dr. Mauldin's office at a run with his wounded child and a tortured expression on his face. A group of townsfolk followed in support. Ronnie Babbit ran ahead to warn the doctor.

Many others hastened to the center of the street, where Pritchard stood over the downed gunmen. Idelle appeared, along with Eudora, and a moment later an out-of-breath Ditch came running up with his Henry rifle in hand.

Of the gunmen, three of four members of Struthers's posse were dead. The fourth, the pistoleer Pritchard shot twice in the chest with his Colts, was dying. The unmistakable sound of his death rattle announced his inevitable fate.

Struthers, however, was still alive. He lay on his side, curled into a fetal position with both hands tightly clutching his belly. Blood and tobacco juice flowed from his mouth.

"I'm gut-shot," he announced, stating the obvious. He strained to get the words out. "Fetch me a doctor."

Pritchard kicked him onto his back. Struthers gasped in agony. "I can't get you a doctor, you son of a bitch," he said, fury spreading over his face. "The town's only sawbones is attending to an innocent little girl who caught a bullet on account of your cowardice and greed."

Pritchard dropped his rifle, reached down with powerful hands, and pulled Struthers to his feet. Once he had the big man standing, he balled his fist and landed a mighty blow on the bounty hunter's jaw.

Struthers fell once more to the ground, this time out cold. Pritchard turned on his heels and headed for the jail. He strode with purpose, his face a mask of rage.

"Carry him to the jail and lock him up," Pritchard commanded over his shoulder. Several men instantly bent down to comply. No one wanted to challenge the marshal in his current state of mind.

Ditch collected Pritchard's rifle and his two discarded Colt revolvers. He, Idelle, and Eudora scurried after him.

"Open the door, Tater!" Pritchard boomed. The jail's door swung open, and he stormed inside past his wide-eyed deputy. He snatched the keys from his desk and was at Count Strobl's cell in two strides.

"I'm sorry to see you've survived, Marshal," Strobl said as Pritchard unlocked the cell door. "I had hoped for a different outcome."

Pritchard swung open the cell door and stood in the doorway facing the count.

"You said you knew why men have been coming to Atherton gunning for me," Pritchard said. His voice was even, flat, and in contrast to the flaming anger in his eyes.

"That is correct," Strobl said. "I also said that it was for me to know and you to find out."

"There's a little girl who caught a bullet because of a price on my head," Pritchard said. "I want to know who put it there."

"I'm sure you do," Strobl said, examining

his fingernails. "Incidentally, my breakfast is overdue. What do you intend to do about it?"

Pritchard grabbed the Austrian by the throat with both hands and lifted him entirely off the ground. Count Strobl's monocle dangled from its lanyard, his eyes bulged, his arms and legs flailed, and his expression changed from arrogant boredom into mortal terror.

"Tell me who put up the bounty," Pritchard said through his teeth, "or I'll tear your blue-blooded head clean offen your shoulders."

By now the office was filled with people. In addition to Tater, four townsmen entered, carrying the unconscious Struthers. Ditch, Idelle, and Eudora came in behind them.

"Samuel," Idelle protested, "let him go! You're killing him!"

"That's the idea," Pritchard said, ignoring her. "What's it gonna be, Strobl? Do you tell me what I want to know, or speak your last words? Either way, you're gonna talk."

John Babbit suddenly rushed into the jail. He instantly surmised what the marshal was trying to elicit from his suffocating prisoner.

"Put him down!" he said, waving a telegram he held in his hand. "He can't tell you who put the price on your head! He doesn't know!"

CHAPTER 18

Pritchard sat at his desk and ran his hands through his bristly blond hair. Only Tater, Ditch, Idelle, Eudora, and John Babbit remained in the office. After depositing the unconscious Struthers in the cell adjacent to Strobl's, the townsmen hastily left, more than happy to make their exit, given the marshal's mood. Count Strobl sat on his bunk. He was green-faced and rubbing his neck.

Tater unloaded his shotgun and replaced it in the wall rack along with Pritchard's Winchester. Pritchard's empty Colts lay on the desktop before him.

Tater leaned over and examined Struthers. "He's bleedin' mighty bad, Marshal," he said.

"Let him bleed," Pritchard said into his hands.

"I received a telegram this morning," Babbit began, "from a fellow reporter who's a friend of mine. He writes for the *Saint Louis Dispatch*. Word about what's been going on here in Atherton has traveled fast."

"I'm sure it has," Idelle said.

"My friend did some digging," Babbit continued, "and discovered there's a bounty out on you."

"A bounty?" Idelle said.

"We already guessed that much," Ditch said, "from the kind of men who've been comin' into town lately gunning for Samuel." He pointed at Struthers, in his cell. "That feller as good as told us. What we don't know is who put up the bounty, or why."

"That's what I'm getting at," Babbit said. "Nobody does. Except the person who posted it, that is."

"How is that possible?" Eudora asked.

"According to my friend," Babbit said, "ten thousand dollars in gold certificates was deposited anonymously in the Wells Fargo branch in Saint Louis. No one knows who put up the money, because it was deposited by courier into a numbered account. Nobody knows who the courier delivered the receipt to. The bounty is supposed to be paid out, no questions asked, to the person responsible for Joe Atherton's death."

Babbit placed the telegram on the desk for inspection. Pritchard read it, shaking his head. "How many times do I have to say it?" he said, almost to himself. "I ain't Joe Atherton anymore."

"Evidently," Babbit said, "there're those who disagree."

"Ten thousand dollars," Tater whistled. "That's a plumb fortune. This territory's chock-full of jaspers who'll gut you, belly button to Adam's apple, for a plugged nickel. For ten thousand dollars—"

"That's enough, Deputy Jessup," Idelle cut him off.

"As you can see," Babbit said, pointing to the telegram in Pritchard's hands, "someone, also anonymously, paid for an advertisement in the *Saint Louis Dispatch* announcing the bounty and terms for its award. It's undoubtedly the same person who put up the money."

"When did this happen?" Eudora asked.

"The newspaper containing the advertisement was published five days ago," Babbit said. "We've got to assume it's already been seen from Kansas City to Chicago, and maybe as far as Memphis and Little Rock."

"Five days," Tater said. "That's only a couple of days before Count Strobl arrived here in town."

"He told us he came from Chicago," Idelle said.

"The timing fits," Ditch agreed. "It would explain the flood of gun-toting strangers in town."

"And the unprovoked attacks on Samuel," Eudora said.

"One thing's for certain," Pritchard said. "That much money will surely draw more headhunters. Ten thousand in gold is more'n most folks see in a lifetime."

"What are we going to do?" Idelle said.

Pritchard didn't answer his sister. Instead, he produced a pistol-cleaning kit from his desk, extracted the empty cases from the pair of Colt revolvers on his desk, and set about the task of cleaning them.

Ditch silently reloaded his Henry rifle with several fresh rounds from his pocket, then checked the Colt on his hip to ensure it was loaded with five rounds.

"Is that all you two are going to do?" Idelle said. "Ready your guns?"

"Trains come in from Kansas City or Saint Louis twice a day," Pritchard said, "not to mention the stage lines. And anyone can enter town on a horse. I've got a feelin' Atherton is gonna be experiencing a population explosion of well-armed fortune seekers in the next few days."

"In that case," Ditch said, "I reckon you should give me a star and swear me in."

Pritchard looked up at his friend. "You sure about this, Ditch? This ain't your fight."

"No," Idelle said, "it isn't." Concern for her fiancé's safety framed her face. "Maybe you should take some time to think this over?"

"Nothin' to think about," Ditch said with an easy grin. "Me and Samuel fought a lot of battles together. Not countin' today, I can't begin to remember the number of times we've spilled blood, or had ours spilled, alongside each other. If you think I'm gonna cut and run now, you'd be mistaken."

"I reckon so," Pritchard said, his face finally

relaxing after the row with Strobl. He opened another desk drawer, took out a star, and handed it to Ditch.

"Raise your right hand," he said.

"Oh, shut up," Ditch chuckled, pinning on the star. "Anything you want me to swear to, you know I'm gonna do anyways."

"Marshal," Tater said from inside Struthers's cell, "I think your prisoner's expired."

Pritchard rose from his desk, entered the cell, and checked on Struthers. Tater was right; the Kansas bounty hunter was dead. "Damn," Pritchard cursed.

"Don't blame yourself," Ditch said. "He was gut-shot. Probably wouldn't have lasted the day, even if we had fetched the doctor."

"That ain't what irks me," Pritchard said. "My only regret is knocking him out and easing his sufferin'. The bastard deserved to die screamin'."

"You don't mean that," Idelle said.

"Hell, if I don't," Pritchard said. "There's a fourteen-year-old girl on death's door because of him. I aim to see no other innocent citizens come to harm on account of me."

"What do you want us to do?" Ditch asked.

Pritchard returned to his desk and issued his orders while giving his Colts a hasty cleaning.

"Tater," he said to his deputy, "go over to Tilley's Mortuary and tell Simon and his son Seth they've got another body here in the jail to add to their collection. Bring your shotgun with you, and don't take any chances. We don't know if any other pistoleros have ridden in. As soon as you're done at Tilley's, get back here as quick as you can and button up the jail."

"Will do, Marshal," Tater said. He retrieved his shotgun, loaded it, and headed out the door.

"John," Pritchard said to Babbit, "if you wouldn't mind, I'd like you to go over to the telegraph office. I need you to wire the federal marshal in Jefferson City, and the town marshals in Saint Louis, Kansas City, and any other nearby towns you can think of. Word the message as you see fit. Let them know about the bounty, if they don't know already, and what's going on here in Atherton. They'll need to be on the lookout for any bounty hunters and gunmen headin' through their jurisdictions in this direction. Have the telegraph operator bill me."

"I'll do it right away," Babbit said. "I'll also write up a story in the *Athertonian* detailing what's transpired and make sure it's printed for wide distribution. If I hurry, I can have the edition ready for delivery on the last train out tonight."

"I appreciate it," Pritchard said. He finished cleaning his revolvers and reloaded them. He replaced the Remington .44s in his hip holsters with the .45 Colts and stuffed the Remingtons back into his belt.

"Ditch," Pritchard said, "I want you to escort

Idelle and Eudora back to the hotel." He turned to the women. "Remember what happened last night," he reminded them. "You're to stay in your rooms, out of public view, and especially out of the restaurant and bar. Have your meals brought up to your rooms from the kitchen."

"I will not," Idelle refused. "I'm going to the van der Lindens' to see if I can be of help. Jennifer was one of my students."

Before becoming mayor, Idelle Pritchard had spent her teenage years as an assistant teacher at Alice and Rodney Nettles's two-room school-house.

"Very well," Pritchard said, knowing he couldn't persuade his sister otherwise. "I'll go along with you. Ditch can take Eudora home."

"How long do I have to stay confined in my room?" Eudora asked, stepping close to Pritchard and putting her hands on his chest. Ditch and Idelle cast sidelong glances at each other.

"Not long," he answered. "Just until Ditch and I can check the town and make sure there aren't any more gunmen lurking about. A few hours, at most."

"Will you come back and let me know you're okay?" Eudora asked.

Pritchard took his Winchester from the gun rack and wiped off the dust it collected when he discarded it in the street before striking Struthers. Then he replaced the four .44-40 cartridges he expended during the gunfight, and lowered the hammer.

"I'll be by later," he said to her. "But first, I'm going over to the van der Lindens' to check on little Jenny. Then I'm heading down to the station to meet the next train."

CHAPTER 19

As Pritchard strode with Idelle toward the van der Lindens' home, which was above the bakery, he encountered Benedict Houseman, Jack Stearns, and the young woman claiming to be Bonnie Shipley.

"I'd like a word with you, Marshal," Houseman announced, tipping his hat to Idelle and stepping in front of Pritchard.

"Not now," Pritchard said, brushing past them. He held Idelle's arm in his left hand and carried his Winchester in his right.

"You must listen to me," Houseman insisted, following on the big marshal's heels. "In light of the recent shooting incidents here in town, especially the gun battle fought in the streets this morning, I suggest, as a mayoral candidate—"

"I told you already," Pritchard interrupted him, "not now. I'm busy."

They reached the bakery, which was closed. The door was locked. Pritchard knocked.

"I'm merely offering," Houseman continued, "the services—"

"I don't have time," Pritchard cut him off again. "I'll be glad to converse with you when I ain't so pressed."

The bakery door opened, and Braam van der

Linden stood before them. His eyes were red, and his shoulders slumped. He motioned for Pritchard and Idelle to come inside.

Houseman started to follow, but Pritchard barred his entrance with the Winchester. After Pritchard and Idelle entered, van der Linden closed the door and relocked it, leaving Houseman, Stearns, and Shipley on the sidewalk.

Pritchard and Idelle were led upstairs to a bedroom. Inside was Jenny van der Linden, lying on the bed. Her mother, Pearl, sat beside her, holding one of her hands in both of her own. Dr. Mauldin, in his shirtsleeves, was finishing up.

Jenny was unconscious and wore a compress over her forehead. Idelle and Braam went to her.

Dr. Mauldin stepped outside the room to greet Pritchard.

"How is she?" Pritchard asked.

"It's bad," Mauldin said, "but could have been much worse. The bullet didn't go in too far; just enough to bust a rib and puncture her lung. I'm guessing it was a ricochet, by the shape of the slug I pulled out. I've inflated her lung and patched her up as best I could. The rest is up to her and God."

"Is she going to . . . ?"

"Too early to tell," Mauldin said. "She's young and strong. If infection or pneumonia doesn't set in, she's got a good chance. The next twenty-four hours will be critical."

"You do whatever you have to, Doc," Pritchard said, the torment clear in his voice. "I'll pay for anything she needs, and I'll send a rider for anything you might need to treat her that we ain't got here in Atherton."

"Don't worry," Mauldin said, "I have everything I need."

"I know, Doc," Pritchard said, "but if—"

"It wasn't your fault," Mauldin stopped him. He could see the anguish in the marshal's face. "You can't blame yourself for what happened."

"If I wasn't here," Pritchard said, "those gunmen and bounty hunters wouldn't have come to Atherton."

"Their bad deeds aren't your responsibility."

"Maybe," Pritchard said. "Maybe not."

"Speaking of gunmen," Dr. Mauldin said, "I understand you have a patient for me at the jail?"

"Not any longer," Pritchard said. "He's Simon Tilley's customer now, along with those other four gun-totin' vermin he came into town with. Can't say I'll be mournin' any of 'em."

"Just as well," Mauldin said. "I need to stay here, close to Jenny."

"I'm obliged," Pritchard said. "And you'd best understand, the van der Lindens don't pay for your services. Not a dime. You send your bill to me, you hear?"

"Whatever you say, Marshal," Mauldin said. "Can I see her?"

140

"Only for a minute. She needs to rest."

Pritchard removed his hat, set his rifle against the wall, and tiptoed into the room. Idelle, Braam, and Pearl van der Linden looked up when he came in.

"She's asleep," Idelle whispered. "She's still under the ether the doc gave her."

Pritchard nodded. "I'm powerful sorry about what happened to your daughter," he said to the van der Lindens.

"It wasn't your doing," Braam said in his thick Dutch accent. "It was the evil men with guns who came into town. You fought them, Marshal. You saved us from them."

Pritchard's heart sank, wondering if Braam van der Linden would absolve him of responsibility in his daughter's plight if he knew the "evil men with guns" came to Atherton on his account.

"I am a Christian man," Braam said as a tear tracked down his weathered cheek. "But these men, with guns, I wish them to go straight to hell."

"They're already there," Pritchard said. "I made sure of it."

"I'm going to stay," Idelle told Pritchard. "Don't worry about me. Go do what you have to do."

"Okay," Pritchard said. He stepped quietly out of the room and picked up his hat and rifle.

"You and Ditch be careful," she whispered after him.

When Pritchard exited the bakery, he found Houseman, Stearns, and Bonnie Shipley still waiting for him.

"Mr. Houseman," Pritchard said, before the attorney could speak. "I don't mean to be rude, but I simply don't have time for talk. I've got to get to the station. The next train will be here any minute." He began walking.

"That's what I'm trying to tell you," Houseman said, struggling to match the much taller marshal's pace. "It's all over town about the bounty on your head. Everybody knows why the gunfighters have been coming to Atherton, and that more are likely to arrive."

"Good for them," Pritchard said without breaking stride.

"I presume," Houseman said, "you're going to the station to turn away any more pistol-packing fortune hunters?"

"You presume correctly," Pritchard said.

"All by yourself?"

"I have a deputy," Pritchard said.

"If you're referring to Deputy Jessup," Houseman said, starting to run short of breath, "no disrespect intended, but you may as well be alone. Tater isn't exactly the gunfighting type."

"What would you suggest I do?" Pritchard said, not disclosing he'd deputized Ditch. "Not go to the station? Hide in the jail? Let a bunch of professional gunfighters and killers invade the town?"

"How about some help?" Houseman said. "Another deputy would mean more than your lone gun facing who-knows-how-many guns arriving on the next train."

Pritchard halted in his tracks as Houseman skidded to a clumsy stop. Stearns and Bonnie Shipley, who'd been lingering behind, caught up.

"Are you offering yourself as my deputy?" Pritchard asked. "No disrespect intended, Mr. Houseman, but you ain't exactly the gunfighting type. Do you even know how to use a firearm?"

"I wasn't referring to myself," Houseman said, mopping his damp brow with a handkerchief. "I was offering—"

"Me," Stearns cut him off. "I'll volunteer to be your deputy, Marshal Pritchard."

Pritchard stared at Stearns. "What's in it for you?"

"Nothing," Stearns said, "beside my civic duty. You forget, Marshal, this is my home now, too. I don't want to see it overrun with bounty killers any more than you do."

"That's mighty noble of you," Pritchard said. "You look like a man who's done gun work before."

"Some would say more than my share," Stearns said.

"All right," Pritchard said. "I accept. I ain't got time to get you a star or swear you in, but consider yourself deputized."

"Duly witnessed," Houseman said.

"Let's go," Pritchard said to his newest deputy. He resumed his journey to the depot while Stearns fell in beside him.

"I'll escort Miss Shipley back to the hotel," Houseman said.

"You do that," Stearns said.

It took several minutes to get to the outskirts of town where the train depot was located. Ditch was waiting for them near the ticket office with his Henry rifle tucked under his arm.

"What's he doin' here?" he asked, motioning to Stearns.

"He's been deputized," Pritchard said, "just like you." Stearns smiled and tipped his broad-brimmed black hat.

"I won't say we can't use the help," Ditch said. "How do you want to play this?"

"The good news," Pritchard said, "is that it shouldn't be too hard to spot any professional gunmen or bounty hunters among the regular passengers. The bad news is, when the train starts unloading, this station is going to be crawling with folks. If there's gunplay, it could get messy."

"That might be a problem," Stearns said, "after what happened to that little girl this morning."

"It ain't gonna happen again," Pritchard said.

"How do we avoid it?" Ditch asked.

"What I'd like to do," Pritchard said, "is to steer all the gun hands in my direction when they get off the train. Draw them to me, and away from innocent bystanders."

"How're you gonna accomplish that?" Stearns asked.

"I've got me an idea," Pritchard said.

CHAPTER 20

The three-fifteen from Kansas City slowed to a halt at the station with a burst of whistle and a cloud of steam. Besides Pritchard, the only others at the platform to greet the train were the ticket agent in his office and the station janitor waiting in his apron and cap with his pushcart full of brooms and cleaning supplies.

Once the passengers disembarked, it was the janitor's job to pass through each car and clean up the discarded newspapers, peanut hulls, cigar stubs, cigarette butts, and other debris accumulated during the journey. This task had to be completed in the brief time it took for the freight and livestock to be off-loaded and for the train to be restocked with water, fuel, freight, fresh livestock, and passengers before going on to Saint Louis.

Pritchard stood alone at the end of the platform. Normally the townsfolk, freighters, stock-handlers, and folks waiting to greet passengers, or board the outgoing train, would have been milling about on the platform as well. But word of the bounty, and the marshal's predicament, had already spread like wildfire throughout Atherton. The crowd awaiting this particular train, including the freight wagons and their drivers, chose to assemble well away from the platform, behind the railroad office. They were close enough to observe the proceedings, but far enough away, in theory, to avoid the fate of young Jennifer van der Linden.

Pritchard stood with his hands loosely at his sides and his thumbs resting lightly on the Colt Single Action Army .45 caliber revolvers holstered at each hip. His old pair of .44 caliber Remington New Model Army revolvers were tucked into his belt at front and back. He was facing east, the same direction as the incoming train, with the sun behind him.

Passengers began to disembark. As they did they looked bewildered, finding no loved ones or friends to greet them. Most grasped the situation when they saw the solitary, six-and-a-half-foot-tall marshal, fully armed and standing on the platform.

The townsfolk called out and waved to the arriving passengers from a distance. They hastily gathered themselves, their children, or their traveling companions and scurried for the relative safety of the assembly behind the railroad office.

Within moments, all the arriving passengers except a group of seven men had vacated the platform. These men apparently waited until all the others had gotten off the train before getting off themselves.

It was an eclectic group, who shared only one

thing in common: every man was wearing at least one pistol. One man, quite tall and heavy, was clad in buckskin breeches and wearing a fur hat. Another was wearing a denim shirt, but wore the boots, trousers, and kepi of a U.S. soldier. A third, a negro, was clad in a wide-brimmed hat and corduroy coat. Still another was wearing a tailored suit and cravat, and topped his ensemble with a bowler hat. Two sported the boots, dungarees, blouses, and weathered Stetsons of the range cowboy. At least one, of Mexican descent, was dressed in the flared pants and sombrero common to his countrymen.

The seven men stood in place, glaring at Pritchard, once they disembarked. They were waiting for an eighth man, the last to get off, to move to the head of the pack.

Pritchard immediately recognized the leader. This fellow sported an expensive, wide-brimmed, felt hat, had long hair and a sculpted beard, and wore a fancily embroidered suit along with equally fancy, hand-carved boots. He also wore twin cross-draw holsters, bearing engraved Colt revolvers with the same custom, five-and-a-half-inch barrels as Pritchard's and Ditch's guns.

The leader's most unique feature, however, were the odd-looking leather gloves he wore. They were black, quite thick, wholly inappropriate for the warm April afternoon, and extended all the way to his elbows.

"Can I get on the train now, Marshal, and get to sweepin' up?" the janitor asked.

"Help yourself," Pritchard told him. The janitor clambered on board the nearest passenger car, hauling his cart over the steps.

The leader began to walk toward Pritchard, at the far end of the platform. His men fell into step behind him.

"That's far enough," Pritchard called out. The group halted ten yards away.

The group's leader was Colonel Dexter Bennington. He was a trick shooter employed by a firearms salesmen Pritchard and Ditch encountered in Kansas last summer, at the end of their cattle drive. The blustery Bennington claimed to be a Union war hero, Indian fighter, and the finest pistol-shot in the territory.

After insulting the Confederacy and threatening to shoot Ditch and his brother, Paul, in the back, the colonel also threatened Pritchard, who was still known as Joe Atherton at the time. Pritchard agreed to accept Bennington's challenge to a shooting contest, with the prize being a brand-new, custom-barreled Colt revolver.

In the resulting duel Pritchard elected not to kill Colonel Bennington, instead shooting him through both wrists with his Remington .44s. His intent was to maim the blowhard and bully and prevent him from shooting other hapless

Southern cowboys, as was his practice, who had the misfortune of arousing his ire.

Pritchard won the Colt revolver, purchased another to match it, and left Bennington with crippled hands. As Pritchard left him, bleeding and cursing, the colonel swore, "I'll get you for this."

"Good afternoon, Joe," Bennington said.

"That ain't my name anymore, Colonel," Pritchard said.

"I heard. I'm glad to know you remember who I am."

"I remember you," Pritchard said.

"Do you remember," Bennington said, holding up his gloved hands, "what you did to me?"

"I do," Pritchard said. "What I mostly recall is letting you keep your life."

"Do you recall what I told you," Bennington continued, "the last time we met?"

"Yep," Pritchard said.

Colonel Bennington lowered his stricken hands. "You're going to die today."

"Maybe," Pritchard said. "No man who sees the sun rise is promised a sunset, that's for sure. Me livin' or dyin' this day, as opposed to any other, don't matter. What does matter is that I'm the law in this town. And in this town, we've got laws against assassins and hired bounty killers. You and your boys had best drop your guns, turn around, get back on that train, ride out, and never come back."

"Or else what?" Bennington asked.

"You'll be arrested and jailed."

"What if I resist?"

"You'll be shot down where you stand."

"Those're awfully brash words," Bennington laughed, "coming from a man with a price on his head facing eight guns all by his lonesome."

"Not brash," Pritchard said. "Just true."

"I can't leave yet," Bennington said with a malevolent smirk, "and neither can these boys. I promised three thousand dollars to whichever one gets you."

"Who gets the other seven thousand of the bounty?" Pritchard asked.

"Me, of course," Bennington said. "I paid for their train tickets."

Pritchard noticed while he and Bennington conversed, the other seven gunmen cast suspicious glances at one another. Each one was thinking about the bounty and wanted to claim it for himself before the others did. Two of the gunmen, the one in the bowler hat and one of the cowboys, began snaking their hands toward their holstered revolvers. The rest were priming to.

"Three thousand dollars seems like a king's ransom," Pritchard warned, "but last I checked, dead men don't spend money."

The lure of easy cash was too much. Bowler and the cowboy drew. Several of the other gunmen, reacting to their associates' draw, followed suit.

Two gunshots cracked the air as one. The man with the bowler was struck in the head, through his hat, from above, and dropped like a stone. The cowboy was hit from behind, between the shoulder blades, and fell dead onto his gun after barely getting it out of the holster.

Pritchard had his twin Colts out and leveled, with their hammers back, before Bennington or any of the remaining five gunmen could bring their own pistols fully from their holsters. They froze, with their hands on their still-sheathed guns, frantically searching for where the shots came from.

"You were mistaken, Colonel," Pritchard declared, "when you said I was facin' eight guns all by my lonesome. Like you, I brought friends. The next man to pull, dies."

Bennington's face twisted into a mask of loathing and rage. "You son of a bitch," he sputtered.

"You boys can either drop your guns," Pritchard said, "like I ordered, and get back on that train, or make your play and take your chances. Don't matter a whit to me."

The surviving gunmen looked at one another, shrugged, and began to unbuckle their gun belts. They lowered their pistols to the platform, turned, and headed back to the train, stepping over the corpses of their friends as they went.

"Where are you going?" Bennington yelled

after them. "Get back here! I paid for your tickets! What about the bounty?"

One by one five men, shaking their heads and muttering, reboarded the train.

Bennington stood alone, facing Pritchard. At his feet lay a pile of holstered revolvers and two bodies.

Pritchard lowered his gun's hammers and holstered both his weapons. Ditch began to climb down from the water tower, his Henry rifle slung in one hand. Jack Stearns, dressed in janitor's coveralls and cap, stepped off the train carrying Pritchard's Winchester.

"If you know what's good for you," Pritchard said to the colonel as he walked toward him, "you'll lose those guns and get on the train with your boys."

"Go to hell, Atherton," Colonel Bennington spat. He clumsily fumbled for his guns with his mutilated hands.

Pritchard, nearly twice Bennington's size and half his age, effortlessly reached out and snatched the two revolvers from the furious colonel's clumsy grasp.

"You're under arrest, Dexter," he said. "Start walking." Pritchard prodded the colonel in the direction of town with his own guns. Stearns followed.

"I'll stick around," Ditch said, "to make sure the train leaves and all these guns lyin' on the platform stay."

"I'll get word to Simon and Seth Tilley," Pritchard said to Ditch over his shoulder, "and have 'em bring their wagon down for the carcasses."

"I like your rifle," Stearns said, examining it closer. "Heard about the new Winchester model, but haven't fired one before today. It's got a shorter action than my old Winchester, and the trigger is much smoother."

"I'm obliged for your marksmanship," Pritchard said. "But in truth, I'm wonderin' why you did it. Seems to me if I'd been slain, you'd be runnin' for sheriff unopposed."

"I took an oath to be your deputy," Stearns said. "If I swear to watch a man's back, I watch his back."

"Actually," Pritchard corrected him, "you didn't take the oath yet. We didn't have time, remember?"

"Oh yeah," Stearns said. "I guess I forgot."

CHAPTER 21

It was standing room only in the town hall. What began as yet another death inquest presided over by Judge Pearson had morphed into a general citizens' meeting. The judge had barely finished pounding his gavel, after deeming the killings of a pair of gunmen by newly appointed deputy marshals Clemson and Stearns as lawful and justified, when people began to speak out.

"The war ended eight years ago!" a man shouted. "With all the gunfire lately, you'd never know it!"

"We've had shootings in Atherton every day!" called out another.

"The diner was shot up," a woman said, "with folks eating inside."

"A man was wounded in the hotel," said someone else, "and a little girl shot down walking our streets in broad daylight! Who's gonna be next?"

"Simmer down," Judge Pearson insisted, banging his gavel again. Seated next to him on one side was Acting Mayor Idelle Pritchard, and on the other Marshal Pritchard. Ditch and Eudora sat behind them.

"Everyone is aware of what's been going on in town lately," Judge Pearson said, once the crowd

155

quieted. "I'm just as concerned as any of you. But shouting at one another doesn't help us solve anything and only serves to rile everybody up. If folks can't speak calmly, and one at a time, I'm going to have to shut this meeting down."

Judge Pearson's admonition had the desired effect. The townspeople in the hall settled.

"Atherton is a quiet, family town," a woman began. "At least it was before a few days ago. I don't know what's gotten into the marshal, but he's been shooting people left and right. It's getting so decent folks are afraid to walk the streets for fear of being shot."

"It seems to me," a townsman added, "that the quality of life in Atherton has gone to hell since all these gunfighters and bounty killers started showing up. We've had two shootings down at the railroad station, alone. How long before folks stop comin' in on the train, for fear of getting shot to pieces? I've got a business to run. I can't run it in the middle of a shootin' gallery."

"They're right," another man said. "Folks are afraid to come into town. I've already noticed less customers in my shop, and it's only been a few days. Where's it gonna end? As it stands now, the only business in town that's booming is the undertaker's. Simon Tilley's got bodies stacked up like firewood."

"It's the marshal's reputation that's bringin' all these pistol-men into town," still another man added. "Everybody knows Marshal Pritchard used to be a famous Texas gunfighter. Maybe it's time we got ourselves a sheriff who wasn't so famous!"

The crowd began to murmur their agreement and grow animated again. Judge Pearson once more deployed his gavel.

"Quiet down," he barked.

"I'd like to speak," Idelle said.

"What's she gonna say?" someone in the back of the room muttered. "She's the marshal's sister, for heaven's sake." More muttering followed.

"This is what I have to say," Idelle said, rising to her feet. The room went silent. "I say you folks ought to be ashamed of yourselves. It wasn't a year ago, Burnell Shipley ran this town. He and his men took what they wanted from you and your families, whenever they wanted. The people of Atherton slaved away in poverty and shame, surviving off the scraps from Shipley's table. This went on for years. Don't any of you remember?"

Idelle glared at the crowd. Many averted their eyes.

"Bullets were flying freely then, too," she continued, "or don't any of you remember that, either? There was one difference, however: the bullets were only flying in one direction. It wasn't until my brother arrived, and started shooting back, that the course of this town, and all of our lives, changed for the better."

The silence, which had consumed the townspeople, was palpable. For once, no one wanted to look at their beautiful, twenty-one-year-old mayor.

"Samuel and my fiancé," Idelle continued, motioning to Ditch, "Dave Clemson, are both local boys, born and raised in Atherton. They took on more than a dozen gunmen, all by themselves, to rid us of Shipley. The gunmen they battled were not strangers, like the ones coming into town now, but homegrown killers from right here in Jackson County. Samuel and Ditch risked their lives to give you the freedom you didn't have the courage to get for yourselves. That battle cost Ditch's brother, Paul, his life."

Pritchard and Ditch looked at each other, remembering that fateful day. In the back of the room, Benedict Houseman, Jack Stearns, and Bonnie Shipley stood watching.

"Since then," Idelle went on, "Samuel's been your town marshal and acting sheriff. He's kept the peace. Whether it was mobs of reveling cowboys, hordes of drunken lumbermen, or rustlers, robbers, or thieves, he's taken them all on single-handed and kept us safe."

"We ain't sayin' we ain't grateful for what Marshal Pritchard's done," one of the previous speakers said. "All we're sayin' is—"

"I know exactly what you're saying," Idelle

cut the speaker off. "You're saying you want an omelet, but don't want any broken eggs."

The speaker looked down at his feet.

"I know how you all feel," Idelle said, scanning the faces in the crowd. "You're afraid. All these bounty killers and gunfighters arriving in town would frighten anyone. I'm scared, too. But getting rid of the sheepdog doesn't keep the wolves away. All it does is invite more wolves."

Idelle's eyes met Houseman's in the back of the room. "And believe me," she said, "there are wolves circling." She sat down. "I've spoken my piece."

"What are we supposed to do?" a woman said. "Nothing?"

"Something's being done," John Babbit said. Everyone turned to look at him. "On the marshal's orders, I wired the governor's office in Jefferson City for help. We've asked Governor Woodson to send a federal marshal here to Atherton."

"Fat lot of good that's gonna do," someone said. "Even if the federal marshal comes, he won't get here for days, and it'll only be just one more badge and gun. What good is one more gun going to do us? We've got a stampede of gunfighters comin' into town right now."

The crowd once more descended into bickering and argument.

"I'd like to speak," a voice from the back of the room called out. It was Benedict Houseman.

"Go on ahead," Pearson told him, once again resorting to banging his gavel to establish calm.

"My name is Benedict Houseman," he said, removing his hat and moving to the front of the room. "Many of you already know I'm a candidate for mayor in the upcoming elections."

"Who could forget?" Ditch whispered to Pritchard.

"There is no question," Houseman said, "Marshal Pritchard once did Atherton a great service. His heroism and sacrifice, during some of this town's most difficult times, cannot be disputed."

"How would he know?" Ditch whispered again. "He wasn't around."

"But times change," Houseman said. "Marshal Pritchard's brand of law enforcement was appropriate, some would even say necessary, as recently as last year. But today, as an increasingly civilized Atherton puts its lawless and violent past behind it, perhaps it is time for the citizens to ask themselves, Is Marshal Pritchard part of the solution or part of the problem?"

"That slimy son of a—"

"He's got a right to be heard," Pritchard cut his friend off. "Let him speak."

"As you're all aware," Houseman continued his speech, "Marshal Pritchard used to go by the name Smokin' Joe Atherton. While this deceptive practice raises its own questions about the marshal's integrity, one thing is indisputable: as

Joe Atherton, Marshal Pritchard was responsible for countless deaths."

Houseman glared smugly at Pritchard as he sat impassively beside the judge. "There is no way to accurately determine how many men the marshal gunned down during his infamous stint as Smokin' Joe," he said. "But if we use his tally here in Atherton, both last year and in recent days, as a yardstick, and extrapolate a similar tally over his more than ten years as a Confederate guerilla and Texas Ranger, one can only surmise a death toll numbering in the hundreds."

"That's a damned lie!" Ditch said, standing up. He was unable to contain his anger any longer.

"Is it a lie?" Houseman shot back, his own voice rising. He pointed his finger accusingly at Pritchard. "Or is it the undeniable truth?"

Houseman had the crowd's attention and knew it. He was obviously a skilled orator, reveled in the limelight, and knew how to manipulate an audience.

"The fact is, Deputy Clemson," Houseman continued his speech, "that death surrounds Marshal Pritchard. Recent events would suggest that sooner or later, wherever the marshal goes, and by whatever name he calls himself, death follows. Death to those who oppose him, death to those who ride with him, like your unfortunate brother, Paul, and death to any of the innocent bystanders who are unlucky enough to wander into the path of his guns."

"Who are you," Idelle said, "a man who until a few day ago was a stranger here in Atherton, to cast aspersions on Samuel?"

"Merely a man," Houseman answered, "who can see with his own two eyes the simple truth many of you are unwilling to admit to yourselves. Your town marshal and acting sheriff, Samuel Pritchard, is a born killer."

Houseman stuck his thumbs in his vest and turned from Idelle to again address the crowd. "It is my understanding that even Marshal Pritchard's fiancée was murdered. If he couldn't protect the life of his own beloved bride-to-be, how, I ask you, can he protect yours?"

Ditch started toward Houseman with his fists clenched and an expression of fury on his face, as the crowd erupted again into shouting and arguments. Pritchard restrained his friend, and the judge pounded his gavel on his plank-bench until he was red-faced from exertion.

"It is long past time," Houseman bellowed over the fray, "to rid this town of the scourge of the gunfighting lawman and restore Atherton to its rightful place among civilized society! The only way to stop an army of bounty killers from coming to Atherton is to eliminate their reason for coming!"

The crowd erupted into bedlam. Pritchard wordlessly stood, put on his hat, and made his way to the exit.

CHAPTER 22

The door to the marshal's office opened and Idelle, Ditch, Eudora, and Judge Pearson entered. Pritchard was leaning back in his chair with his boots on his desk, next to his holstered guns.

"Why did you walk out of the meeting?" Ditch said. "It went on for another hour."

"I heard all I cared to," Pritchard said. "Besides, it was feedin' time. I had to relieve Tater so he could get the prisoners their dinner."

"Pay no mind to what folks were saying about you," Idelle said as Pritchard rose. "They're just scared, and rattled, and their tongues got the better of their brains, that's all. They didn't mean the things they said."

"They surely did," Pritchard replied, "because they're right. If I wasn't here, there wouldn't be any gunmen in Atherton. That's a fact."

"What exactly are you saying?" Eudora asked.

"I'm saying," he said, "it's gettin' to be time I moved on."

"You don't really mean that?" Idelle said, disbelieving her ears. "Atherton is your home."

"I was run out of Atherton once before," Pritchard said, "when I was seventeen, remember? I recall the way."

"But you . . . we . . . fought for this town,"

Ditch said. "It's ours as much as any of those yellow-bellied, ungrateful fools running their mouths over at the town hall. Hell, if it wasn't for you and me, there wouldn't be any town hall. Nor any new school, nor churches, nor anything else worth a damn in Atherton because the town would still belong to Burnell Shipley."

"He's right, you know," Judge Pearson said. "Without you, the town of Atherton would be suffering under Shipley's rule to this day."

"Maybe so," Pritchard said, "but that was then, and this is now. A year ago, folks were afraid to walk the streets for fear of Shipley's hired guns. Now, they're afraid to walk the streets for fear of the guns aimed at me. Guns are guns, Judge Pearson, and bullets don't discriminate. Iffen you don't believe me, just ask Braam and Pearl van der Linden."

"You're not actually considering leaving Atherton, are you?" Idelle said, her face ashen.

"I don't much like that Houseman fellow," Pritchard said, "nor what he said tonight. But me dislikin' his words don't make 'em any less true. The sooner I'm gone, the sooner all these bounty-huntin' pistoleers will go away and leave Atherton be."

The conversation was interrupted by Tater, struggling to squeeze his bulk through the office door with a pair of trays balanced in each hand.

"It is about time our food arrived," Strobl said

from his cell across the room. "Like caged dogs we are treated!"

"Hold your horses," an out-of-breath Tater said. "I'm a-comin' with your supper. It's beef stew and corn bread tonight, fellers. Best meal I've ever had."

"You say that about every meal," Strobl said.

"That's because it's true," Tater replied.

"I heard what you said, Marshal," Dexter Bennington remarked from his cell, adjacent to Strobl's. He sat on his bunk, examining his gloved hands. "It makes no difference whether you leave or stay. Ten thousand in gold is a lot of money. Wherever you go, bounty killers will find you. There's an army of them, and it's growing. They'll hound you into your grave."

"Shut up," Ditch said to Bennington.

Idelle moved closer to Pritchard and looked up into his blue eyes. Her matching blue orbs welled with tears. "You have as much right to stay here as anyone," she said.

"Is isn't about my rights," Pritchard told his sister. "It's about innocent folks gettin' hurt because of me. My sworn duty, as town marshal and acting deputy sheriff, is to protect people from harm. I can't very well do that if I'm the cause of the harm, can I? My bein' here is what's drawin' all the gunfire."

"It's precisely because of the shootings in town that we need you," Idelle argued. "Now, more than ever, we need a lawman who can fight for us. For everyone."

"You're wrong," Pritchard said, not harshly. He put his hands on her shoulders. "I'm the magnet that's drawin' all the bullets. And the plain truth is, I can't live with any more innocent folks getting hurt or killed on account of me. I just can't. Not after what happened to Caroline."

"Caroline's death wasn't your fault," Ditch said.

"It was," Pritchard said. "If she hadn't taken up with me, she'd still be alive. I live with that every minute of every day."

Pritchard stepped away from Idelle and walked to the window. "Seeing little Jenny van der Linden, lyin' on death's door from a bullet meant for me, was like a mule kickin' out my insides. It brought back the same feelings I had after what happened to Caroline. Feelings I'd thought I'd buried. Feelings that made my decision for me. Any lingering doubts I had about leaving were erased after what I heard tonight at the town meeting."

"You're really gonna leave Atherton, Marshal?" Tater said.

"Afraid so," Pritchard said, turning from the window to face the group. "My time as a lawman here is done. I thought about staying on until the federal marshal arrives, but decided against it. Ditch and Jack Stearns can hold down the town as well as me, and besides, the quicker I depart, the quicker the bounty killers will dry up."

Pritchard unpinned his badge and tossed it on the table. "I hereby resign as town marshal of Atherton and acting sheriff of Jackson County. The judge here is my witness." Judge Pearson lowered his head and nodded.

"A touching speech," Bennington said, clapping his crippled hands. "But it fools no one. You can masquerade your cowardice as concern for the safety of innocent citizens to these idiots, but you don't fool me. You're scared, and you're scampering. Once you were Joe Atherton, then you became Samuel Pritchard, and who knows what name you'll travel under as you flee for your worthless life. You're making a run for it, Pritchard. Plain and simple. You're yellow, and you're running."

Pritchard wordlessly belted on his revolvers. Then he took the keys from Tater, opened Bennington's cell, and stepped inside.

"What are you doing?" Idelle asked.

Pritchard ignored her question. "On your feet," he said to Bennington.

"I'm comfortable right here," Bennington said with a smirk.

Pritchard grabbed the colonel, picked him up bodily, and threw him from the cell. Bennington flew across the marshal's office and came to rest against the opposite wall.

"Samuel!" Idelle gasped. He continued to ignore her. Everyone watched as Bennington struggled to stand. Pritchard opened a locked desk drawer with a key and retrieved Bennington's pair of engraved Colt revolvers, still in their holsters.

"Put 'em on," he said, tossing the guns at Bennington's feet.

"What for?" the shaken, and now nervous, Bennington said.

"Because you're about to find out what every other money-grubbing, pistol-packin', bounty killer in Missouri is going to learn the hard way."

"What's that?"

"That I don't wear a badge anymore," Pritchard grinned. "Which means I don't have to play by the rules, and follow the law, any more than they do."

Pritchard backed up from Bennington the full length of the office. Ditch extended his arms and ushered Idelle, Eudora, Tater, and Judge Pearson out of the line of fire.

"You can't shoot me," Bennington protested. "I'm a prisoner."

"Looks to me," Tater said, pointing to the open cell door, "like you just escaped."

"You called me a coward," Pritchard said, his grin fading. "I'm callin' you out. Pick up your guns and make your play. I'll even offer you the same courtesy I extended last year in Abilene. I'll let you draw first."

"This is outrageous," Bennington said. He turned to the judge. "You're an officer of the court, aren't you? Are you going to allow this?"

"Not much I can do to stop it," Judge Pearson said. "Samuel was the law a minute ago. Now he's not. As far as I can tell, legally, this is merely a personal matter between you and him."

"Samuel," Idelle said, "you can't just—"

"You want the bounty killers stopped?" Pritchard cut her off midsentence. "There's only one way to stop 'em—dead in their tracks." He returned his attention to Bennington. "Pick up your guns or die without 'em."

Bennington stooped to pick up his pistol belt. He looked for a moment at his gloved hands, then shook his head and slowly stood back up. By the time he was fully erect, he was trembling.

"I can't," Bennington said. "I don't stand a chance. You'll kill me."

"That's right," Pritchard said. He walked over and slapped Bennington, bloodying his lip. "You'd best remember that, Colonel. The next time you unbutton your lip on me I'll kill you, whether you're heeled or not. Get back in your cell."

A defeated Dexter Bennington averted his eyes from the others as he reentered his jail cell. Tater locked the door behind him.

Pritchard strode over to Strobl's cell and stared at the count through the bars. "How about you, duelist?" he asked. "You were right bold when it came to challenging the town marshal. I ain't a lawman anymore. You want to try your hand against a gunfighter, instead?"

Count Florian Strobl, of the Austrian Strobls, stared up at Pritchard from his bunk. He wiped the beef stew from his whiskers and silently shook his head.

"Samuel?" Idelle asked, her voice little more than a whisper.

"What?" Pritchard said as he recovered Bennington's guns and replaced them in the desk drawer.

"I've never seen you behave like this before," she said.

Pritchard shrugged. "I've always worn a badge before. Now I don't."

"Would you really have shot him," she asked meekly, "merely for insulting you?"

Instead of replying, Pritchard walked over to the stove, picked up the pot, and held a mug aloft.

"Coffee, anyone?" he said.

CHAPTER 23

Pritchard walked Ditch, Idelle, and Eudora back to the Atherton Arms. Judge Pearson had already made his exit. At Pritchard's request, he promised to return to the jail at eight o'clock the following morning with newspaperman John Babbit.

When the group arrived at the hotel they found Benedict Houseman, Jack Stearns, and Bonnie Shipley waiting in the lobby.

"I'd like a word, Marshal," Houseman said.

"No," Pritchard said, "you wouldn't. And I ain't the marshal anymore." He walked past the attorney and into the hotel bar, leaving Idelle, Ditch, and Eudora in the lobby.

"What did he mean by that?" Houseman asked.

"You heard him," Idelle said. "He turned in his badge."

"Why, that leaves only Deputies Clemson, Stearns, and Jessup as the law here in Atherton," Houseman said, unable to contain his pleasure.

"It would appear so," Ditch said. "Until the federal marshal arrives, anyway."

"What an interesting development," Houseman said. "This calls for a drink."

Houseman squeezed his way into the crowded tavern, with Stearns and Bonnie Shipley on his heels. Pritchard was already at the bar nursing a shot of whiskey with his hat tilted back on his head. Ditch, Idelle, and Eudora also made their way through the throng.

"Let me buy you a drink, Mr. Pritchard," Houseman said, patting Pritchard on the shoulder, "to thank you for your service and wish you the best in your future endeavors."

Pritchard downed his shot, placed his glass gently on the bar, then turned and grabbed Benedict Houseman by his lapels. He lifted the portly attorney off the ground and brought him up to eye level. The room instantly became silent. All eyes went to Pritchard.

"You all might as well know," Pritchard announced loudly to the patrons, though staring directly into Houseman's terrified eyes, "I resigned as marshal and sheriff tonight. I'll be leaving town in the morning.

"There's something else you'd better know, Mr. Houseman," Pritchard said. "And it goes for everyone. My sister and best friend live in this town. I said I was leavin' in the morning, and I aim to. But I didn't say I wasn't comin' back."

As Pritchard spoke, Jack Stearns leisurely moved in behind him. He leaned against the wall, nonchalantly, with a bored expression on his face. His right hand began to gradually meander its way toward the butt of the Smith & Wesson .44 holstered on his opposite hip.

"Anyone crosses my family, crosses me,"

Pritchard said. "I ain't a lawman anymore. You all had best remember it."

No one spoke; everyone was afraid to. Beads of sweat formed on Houseman's forehead. Stearns's fingers reached the wooden grips of his revolver.

"I'm gonna look into who you are," Pritchard said to the petrified attorney dangling in his grasp, "and I'm gonna find out who that soiled dove you're trying to pass off as Burnell Shipley's daughter is."

Jack Stearns was slowly easing his pistol from its scabbard when he felt something hard jab into his side and heard a pair of muffled *click*s. He glanced down and found the barrel of Ditch Clemson's .45 Colt pressed against his kidney.

Ditch had sidled up to Stearns unnoticed, drew his revolver, folded his arms, and pointed the barrel into his fellow deputy marshal's torso under his armpit. Anyone looking at them, which was nobody given Pritchard's attention-garnering display at the bar, would have merely seen two men standing side by side.

"Your boss gave his speech at the town meetin' earlier," Ditch whispered in Stearns's ear. "I believe it's my friend's turn to speak."

Stearns relaxed his grip on his revolver, dropped his hand to his side, and smiled innocently. Ditch kept his gun on him. Pritchard continued speaking to Houseman.

"You can bet the ranch, Mr. Big Shot, Saint

Louis Attorney," Pritchard said, "if I don't like what I find, I'll be back." He released Houseman. "For you."

Houseman fell to one knee, his now-wobbly legs temporarily unable to support his weight.

Pritchard grabbed the bottle of whiskey he'd been drinking from off the bar, pushed his hat forward on his head, and made his way to the exit. All the bar's patrons hastily parted before him. He'd almost reached the hotel's main doors when Idelle, Eudora, and Ditch caught up to him.

"Samuel," Idelle cried out. "Wait!"

"Hurry up, then," Pritchard said without breaking stride. "I've got things to do."

"Like what?" Ditch asked.

"Packing, for one thing," Pritchard replied.

"That's nonsense," Idelle said. "Everything you own fits on your saddle."

"Maybe I've got someplace to be?" Pritchard said, making his way toward the livery.

"Where on earth could you be going at this time of night?" Eudora said. "It's after dark."

"I thought I'd take a ride out to our old place and visit Ma's and Pa's graves," he said.

Thomas and Dovie Pritchard were buried side by side beneath a sycamore tree overlooking the pond on the Pritchards' property, a couple of miles outside of Atherton.

"Why don't you visit them in the morning," Idelle asked, "when you ride out?"

"Because I ain't riding out," Pritchard said. "I'm takin' the first train to Saint Louis."

"What's in Saint Louis?" Eudora asked.

"Answers," Pritchard said.

"You want some company tonight?" Ditch asked.

"Why not?" Pritchard said.

After walking Idelle and Eudora back to their rooms in the hotel, Pritchard and Ditch went down to the livery. It was an unseasonably balmy night, even for April in Missouri. Ditch sniffed the air and declared rain was on the way.

At the stable, Pritchard saddled his beloved Rusty. The twelve-year-old, chestnut-colored Morgan stood eighteen hands tall and had been broken in as a colt by Ditch and his father. Pritchard fled Missouri on Rusty at seventeen. The loyal animal had been his companion throughout the war and during his years as a Texas Ranger.

Ditch saddled one of the several mounts he kept in town. At his property outside of town, adjacent to Pritchard and Idelle's, he had over forty more horses.

Lightning flashed overhead as Pritchard and Ditch rode out into the darkness. Both remained alert to the possibility of ambush as they traveled. Soon they found themselves at the Pritchard place.

The Pritchard family home had been burned to the ground on the day Thomas Pritchard was hanged. Ditch and Idelle had begun rebuilding the house the previous autumn, but the crew had to abandon the project when the snows came. Construction had only recently resumed, and so far, only the frame had been erected. The skeletal bones of the structure loomed over Pritchard and Ditch like the decomposed carcass of a long-dead dinosaur.

They tethered their horses and walked to the sycamore tree overlooking the graves of Thomas and Dovie Pritchard. Pritchard uncorked the whiskey bottle, and both sat down with their backs against the tree.

"By the way," Pritchard said, taking a slug of liquor and handing the bottle to Ditch, "I forgot to thank you."

"What for?" Ditch said, accepting the bottle.

"For keeping Stearns in his place back at the hotel bar."

"You saw that?"

"Of course," Pritchard said. "You didn't think I'd take my eye off Jack Stearns while I was throttling his boss, did you?"

"I reckon not," Ditch said. He took a drink. "I sure can't figure that Stearns feller out."

"Me either," Pritchard said. "He saved my life back at the railroad station against Bennington's boys. Seems to me, if he'd let me catch a slug he'd have gotten in good with his boss and won my job."

"This whole situation's got me flummoxed," Ditch said. "Just when things are finally settlin' down in Atherton, we get a stampede of shooters comin' in. Professional killers and bounty hunters like Count Strobl, Dingo Struthers, and that horse's ass Colonel Dexter Bennington, to name only a few. If that ain't trouble enough, along comes this Houseman character, as slippery a critter as I've ever seen, chaperonin' a young gal he claims is the rightful heir to Shipley's money and land. Money and land that Shipley stole from the likes of honest people in town, such as your folks, and mine."

Ditch took another drink and handed the whiskey back to Pritchard. "This entire mess has Idelle fit to be tied. She's fuming like a mad bull. Lately, when she isn't working herself up over Houseman's plan to steal everything we've fought for and built, she's worryin' herself sick over you gettin' gunned down. Doc Mauldin said all the stress ain't good for her or the baby."

Pritchard whipped his head around to stare at Ditch. "The baby?" he said.

"Aw, hell," Ditch said, hitting his forehead with his palm. "I wasn't supposed to let that slip."

Pritchard stood up. "Idelle is pregnant?"

"We just found out a week ago," Ditch protested. "I'm so sorry, Pritchard. We meant to tell—"

Ditch's sentence was cut short by two giant hands that grabbed him by his coat and launched him to his feet. At more than half a foot shorter and nearly seventy-five pounds lighter than Pritchard, he was no match for his enormous friend's strength and size.

Ditch winced, covered his head with his hands, and awaited the impending blow from one of Pritchard's massive fists. Instead, he found himself being bear-hugged and swung around like a teenage girl at a barn stomp.

"I'm gonna be an uncle!" Pritchard exclaimed. "By Jupiter, I'm gonna be an uncle!"

"You ain't mad?" Ditch managed to ask, in the midst of being crushed.

"Hell, no," Pritchard said, realizing in his excitement he was suffocating his friend. He released Ditch and picked up the whiskey bottle, which had lost half its contents.

"We were gonna tell you," Ditch said, catching his breath. He took the bottle from Pritchard once more, and this time took a long, hard pull. He needed it to calm his nerves. "But with all that's been goin' on lately, we didn't want to burden you."

"Burden me?"

"That's partly it," Ditch said sheepishly. "And partly because we didn't know how you'd take the news, us bein' unmarried and all. Especially with Idelle bein' your baby sister."

"It ain't like you ain't gettin' married," Pritchard said. "Hell, June's hardly more'n a month away."

Pritchard grabbed the bottle back from Ditch and raised it up. "Here's to my niece or nephew!" He drank, and shoved the bottle again at Ditch.

"Here's to my son or daughter," Ditch said, taking another drink.

"You got any names picked out?" Pritchard asked.

"We do," Ditch said, the first signs of slurring overtaking his speech. "Iffen it's a girl, Idelle wants to name her Dovelina, after your ma."

"And if it's a boy child?" Pritchard asked.

"We decided on Samuel," Ditch said with a lopsided grin, "after Idelle's idiot brother."

CHAPTER 24

Pritchard and Ditch got to the hotel just as the rain became a downpour. It started to sprinkle during the ride back to Atherton, along with liberal doses of thunder and lightning. By the time they reached the livery, the showers began.

After returning their horses, they checked in on Tater at the jail. They found the deputy peacefully snoring away under a blanket in one of the vacant cells. Count Strobl and Colonel Bennington were fast asleep as well. Locking the door after themselves, they headed to the Atherton Arms.

Pritchard bid a tipsy Ditch good night and made his way to Eudora's room. He knocked lightly, and the door opened.

Eudora Chilton stood framed in the doorway, wearing only the sheerest of clothing. She was clad in a flimsy, translucent robe that left nothing to the imagination. She reached out, grabbed Pritchard by his neckerchief, and pulled him inside.

"I'd offer you a drink, cowboy," she said, "but it smells like you've already had one."

"I got some good news tonight," Pritchard said, removing his hat and gun belt. "First I've had in a while. Ditch and I were celebrating."

"Let me get in on the celebration," Eudora said,

steering Pritchard to the bed. She pushed him down, slipped out of her transparent nightgown, and came to rest on top of him. In another moment, both were no longer clothed.

Afterward, Pritchard and Eudora lay in each other's arms watching the room's solitary candle flicker and listening to the steady drumbeat of the rainfall outside.

"Doesn't seem fair," Eudora said, brushing a lock of hair from Pritchard's forehead and tracing the bullet scar with a forefinger.

"What doesn't?" Pritchard asked.

"Just when we're getting to know each other," she answered, "and I'm starting to cotton to you, you're leaving town."

"I won't be gone forever," he said.

"A man I met in Memphis once said those exact same words to me," Eudora said, "before he rode off. He left right after I fell in love with him."

"Did he ever come back?"

"No," Eudora said. "I had to go looking for him."

"And you found him?"

"I did," she said. "We were married. And happy for a time."

"What happened?"

"He was a traveling man. He was captured and killed by Indians in the New Mexico Territory."

"I'm sorry," Pritchard said.

"No," Eudora said, "you're not. It's polite of

181

you to say so, but you can't really be sorry. His death isn't yours to be sorry about."

"I reckon so," Pritchard admitted, before drifting off to sleep.

Pritchard awoke at dawn to a cloudless sky and sunlight streaming in through the window. Eudora was already up, dressed, and seated at the dressing table. Her back was toward him, and she was busy brushing her ginger hair.

"Good morning, Eudora," he said.

"Good morning," she replied curtly.

"You're sure rarin' to go," Pritchard remarked, rubbing his eyes.

"I've got a lot of errands to do today," she said, her voice suddenly all business. There was no trace of her soft, romantic tones from the night before.

"After breakfast," she said, "I'm scheduled to meet your sister at the Sidewinder. We're signing rental agreement papers Judge Pearson drew up for us. After that, I've got to commission a work crew to get the place ready to open. Then I've got to stock up. It'll take a couple of days for the liquor to get here from Kansas City, not to mention the piano, furniture, pool tables, and all the glassware. The sooner I order it, the sooner it'll be delivered."

"Sounds like you've got the Sidewinder practically open for business already," Pritchard said.

"I've done this before," she said. "I hope to be up and running within a week."

"Good for you," Pritchard said. "Hopefully good for Atherton, too."

He got out of bed and began to dress. A moment later he was belting on his guns, holding his hat in his large hands, and at the door.

"So long, Eudora," Pritchard said.

"Good-bye, Samuel Pritchard," she said without looking at him or getting up.

Pritchard shook his head, shrugged, and departed Eudora's hotel room.

He walked over to the jail in the bright, April sunshine. Atherton was waking up. Windows were lifting, shops were opening, and the enticing smells emitting from Perkins's Diner wafted across the town square.

At the jail he found Tater, as usual at this time of day, anxiously waiting to go to the diner. He scurried off as soon as Pritchard entered. He also found John Babbit and Judge Pearson, sipping Tater's freshly made coffee and waiting for him to arrive.

"Did you do what I asked?" Pritchard said to Babbit.

"Take a look," Babbit replied, showing Pritchard the stack of flyers he'd printed. The flyers read:

TO WHOM IT MAY CONCERN
☞In lieu of recent events, and in the interest of maintaining peace and public

safety within the Town of Atherton, Missouri, be it known that SAMUEL PRITCHARD, formerly recognized by some as "Joe Atherton," has hereby resigned as *Town Marshal* and *Acting Sheriff* of Jackson County, effectively immediately.

☞Be it further known that Samuel Pritchard has vacated the Town of Atherton, and no longer resides within town limits or in Jackson County. His whereabouts are currently unknown.

Any individuals seeking Samuel
Pritchard for nefarious purposes
are duly warned that any and all threats
to his life will be met with the harshest
possible consequences.

"The posters look fine," Pritchard said.

"I'll have them put up at the train station, stage depot, and all over town as soon as you leave," Babbit said.

"I'm obliged," Pritchard said. He removed a set of saddlebags from a hook in his room and began to pack.

"I'm sorry to report," Judge Pearson said, "that I've yet to hear anything back from my contacts in Jefferson City regarding Benedict Houseman. I'll check again this morning at the telegraph office, but likely you'll be gone by then."

"Thanks for tryin', Your Honor," Pritchard said.

It didn't take Pritchard long to pack. Despite his family's wealth, and his own healthy bank account, he lived a Spartan existence. Other than his horse and tack, everything he owned could be worn, stuffed into a saddlebag, or lashed to a saddle.

"I did, however," Pearson continued, "take the liberty of wiring the governor. If you're in the vicinity of the capital, which I know you'll pass on the way to Saint Louis, you might want to stop in and see him. Governor Woodson is expecting you."

"I don't plan on makin' any social calls," Pritchard said.

"I'd consider it a personal favor," Judge Pearson said.

"Then of course I will," Pritchard said. "You've been a good friend, and it's been an honor to serve you here in Atherton."

"What about these two?" Babbit asked, pointing to Count Strobl and Colonel Bennington. Both prisoners had awakened and were listening keenly to the conversation between the newspaperman, judge, and the former marshal.

"I almost forgot," Pritchard said. He took 120 paper dollars from his pocket and handed them to the judge. "That'll cover the count's fines. With over eighty days left to serve, I ain't sure who's gettin' punished more: him or Tater."

"What about Colonel Bennington?" Babbit said.

"That's out of my hands," Pritchard said.

"Bennington will be held for trial," Judge Pearson explained. "He brought paid killers to murder our town marshal, which will likely see him sent to the penitentiary in Jefferson City. It's been so busy lately, I haven't had a chance to seat a jury."

Pritchard shook the judge's and Babbit's hands before both men left.

He opened Count Strobl's cell door. "You're a free man, Your Highness."

"I am touched," Strobl said solemnly, "by your most generous gesture. It will not be forgotten. I realize, now, what an error I made in challenging your character and honor." He bowed. "I am indebted to you."

"As long as you don't try to smack me with any more gloves," Pritchard smiled, "we'll call it square between you and me." He patted the count on the back. "I wouldn't be in too much of a hurry to leave, if I were you. Deputy Jessup will be back any minute with your breakfast. From what I could smell on the way over, it'll be a hearty one."

Sure enough, Tater showed up carrying two large baskets. He had blueberry preserve residue smeared on his upper lip.

The last items Pritchard loaded into his saddlebags were his two Remington revolvers, ammunition for both guns, as well as cartridges for his pair of Colts and the Winchester. He shouldered the bags, picked up his rifle, and put on his hat.

"I sure wish you weren't leavin' us," Tater said. "I'm gonna miss you, Marshal."

"I'm going to miss you, too, Tater," Pritchard said. He extended his hand, and Tater shook it. "You never know when our trails will cross again."

Pritchard left the jail and started toward the livery. The workday was in full swing, and the sidewalks were bustling with lumbermen off to the mill, cattlemen heading for the stockyards, and travelers making their way to the railroad station.

He carried his saddlebags over his left shoulder and kept the Winchester in his right hand. Despite the serenity of the scene unfolding before him, he knew lurking around any corner could be someone with a gun and a hunger to become $10,000 richer.

Across the street, he saw Eudora Chilton coming out of the telegraph office. She didn't notice him and walked briskly toward the general store. He surmised she must have just placed her liquor order over the wire, as she'd mentioned earlier. He knew she could obtain delivery of anything else she needed to get the Sidewinder back in operation at the mercantile.

"Samuel!"

He turned to find Idelle and Ditch descending the hotel steps. They were holding hands, and Idelle waved to him from across the square.

When they got close, Idelle released Ditch's hand and ran into Pritchard's arms. She hugged him fiercely as tears streaked down her face. It was awkward, hugging her in return around his stuffed saddlebags and the Winchester.

"Do you have to leave this minute?" she tearfully asked. "I hoped we could have breakfast together."

"It's almost eight," Pritchard said. "The train departs in twenty minutes. I barely have time to get to the livery, saddle Rusty, and get him boarded. Besides, every minute I stay in Atherton is another minute some trigger-happy fool with dollar signs in his eyes could make a gun play. We've had enough bullets flying in Atherton lately. It's long past time for me to go."

Idelle only nodded and hugged him even tighter.

"Look after them," he admonished Ditch. "You've got two people to care for now."

Idelle gave Ditch a look of astonishment.

"It slipped out," Ditch said sheepishly. "He was going to find out sooner or later."

"You aren't disappointed, are you?" she said, looking up into her big brother's eyes.

"Of course not," he said. "Other than your lousy taste in men, you're the best little sister a feller could have. I'm right proud of you."

"We're getting married in June," she said. "You'd best be there."

"I wouldn't miss it."

"I'll walk you down to the station," Ditch offered.

"You most certainly will not," Pritchard corrected him. "You'll stay away from me, stay here with Idelle, and keep your eyes peeled and your pistol handy. If there're bounty killers about, more'n likely they'll be waitin' for me at the station."

Ditch nodded, deferring to Pritchard's irrefutable logic. "Keep your powder dry," Ditch said, shaking his lifelong friend's hand, "until our trails cross again."

"Until we cross trails," Pritchard said.

"Take care of yourself," Idelle said, now openly crying.

"Don't worry," Pritchard assured her. "Once I'm gone, all the gun hands and bounty hunters will skedaddle. Atherton will go back to bein' just another sleepy little burg on the Missouri River."

CHAPTER 25

Pritchard left Ditch comforting his weeping sister in front of the hotel and made his way down to the livery.

He'd passed the town square and was halfway to the stables when Jack Stearns slowly stepped out from around the corner of one of the shops on Main Street. He was picking his teeth with a toothpick in his left hand. The thumb of his right hand was stuck casually in his belt buckle, only inches from his holstered Smith & Wesson.

Pritchard halted and discreetly thumbed back the hammer on the Winchester. Stearns noticed.

"Didn't figure you for the runnin'-away type," Stearns said. "Looks like this morning proves me wrong."

"Never figured you for a back-shooter," Pritchard replied. "You proved me wrong last night."

"I couldn't very well let you thrash old Benedict, could I?"

"You couldn't have stopped me. Besides," Pritchard said, "I didn't thrash Houseman, I only got his attention. Iffen I'd thrashed him last night, he wouldn't be in one piece today."

"Any place special you're going?" Stearns asked.

"What do you care?"

"I don't," Stearns said. "I'm just curious."

"I believe I'll wander awhile," Pritchard said. "See where the wind takes me."

Stearns tipped his hat, turned, and started to leave.

"Hey, Jack," Pritchard called out. Stearns stopped and turned back around.

"I swore an oath," Pritchard said, "more'n ten years ago, that any man who pulled on me would die. I owed you one for what you did for me at the train station. I paid that debt last night by lettin' you live today." He lowered the Winchester's hammer. "We're square."

"Safe travels," Stearns said as he turned again and walked away.

At the stables, Pritchard found no attendant about, which wasn't unusual for that time of the morning. Once the horses had been fed, the stable manager could usually be found at either the blacksmith's forge or the leather shop, having horseshoes made or tack repaired for his customers.

Pritchard had just finished putting the bridle and saddle on Rusty and was inserting his Winchester into the scabbard, when he sensed motion behind him. He immediately sidestepped, pivoted, and drew both guns, bringing them around to bear on whoever had crept up so quietly behind him.

Eudora Chilton gasped and froze in her tracks. She dropped her handbag and parasol and stared at Pritchard with her mouth agape.

"Eudora," Pritchard said, surprised to see her. He lowered the hammers and reholstered his revolvers.

"Oh my," she exclaimed. "You nearly frightened me to death."

"That goes for both of us," he said. "What are you doing here?"

"I came to apologize."

"What for?"

"I was cold to you this morning," she said. "I owe you an apology."

"You don't owe me a thing," Pritchard said.

"Yes," she argued, "I do. Certainly, an explanation. Ever since I was young, I've hated good-byes. It's why I don't behave very well when it's time to say them. I can be especially petulant when it's someone I care about, and I'm afraid I won't ever see them again. If you haven't figured it out yet, I care about you. You didn't deserve to be treated that way. It wasn't fair, and I'm sorry."

"Forget it," Pritchard said. "I thought I'd left a bad taste in your mouth, that's all. I've found I tend to rub some folks the wrong way."

"I like the way you taste," Eudora said, stepping in, putting both arms around Pritchard's neck, and pulling him down to her.

"I like the way you say *good-bye,*" Pritchard said, bending down to kiss her.

"I know a better one," Eudora said. She pushed Pritchard back into a stall and began taking off her dress.

Pritchard and Eudora went at each other front, back, and sideways. The only thing that matched the frantic intensity of their repeated pairings was the force of their passion. At one point, during a particularly feverish moment for both of them, several of the horses in the nearby stalls began to whinny and stomp, agitated by the sounds of the couple's extremely athletic union. It wasn't until almost an hour later that they collapsed, naked and exhausted, onto a stack of hay.

"Goodness gracious," Eudora finally said, catching her breath. "It has been my experience that men of your size aren't usually quite so limber. Or insatiable."

"I make up for my lack of charm with my boyish enthusiasm," Pritchard said, rubbing a cramp out of his hamstring.

"Is that what you call it?" Eudora laughed.

"I've been told that one of my failings is I don't know when to quit."

"Whoever told you that," Eudora said, "described you perfectly."

"We'd better get dressed," Pritchard said. "The livery man could be back any minute."

"I think you missed your train," Eudora remarked as she plucked bits of straw from her hair and garments.

"There'll be another train out later this afternoon," Pritchard said. "Besides, this morning's ride was much more enjoyable than any old train."

"I'd have to agree."

Eudora glanced at the pocket watch in her bag and began to dress more hurriedly. "I'm late for my meeting at the Sidewinder with your sister and the judge," she said. "You'll forgive me if I don't linger."

"Thank you, Eudora Chilton, for sending me off with a proper good-bye."

She kissed him briefly, looked into his eyes, and said, "Good-bye, Joe Atherton."

"You mean Samuel Pritchard, don't you?"

"Of course," she said, grabbing her hat and parasol. "What's come over me? Your masculine charms must have flustered me more than I thought. Good-bye."

"Ain't you gonna ask if I'm comin' back?" Pritchard asked.

"That's why I hate good-byes," she said. "They're so final." She kissed him once more, scurried out of the stable, and was gone.

Not five minutes later, as Pritchard was buckling on his gun belt, the livery attendant returned with several bridles slung over his shoulder. He sniffed, looked around at the unsettled horses pacing in their stalls, and turned to Pritchard.

"What the heck got the horses all riled up?"

"I dunno," Pritchard said innocently. "Maybe they saw a rat?"

CHAPTER 26

Pritchard awoke to the sensation of the train abruptly slowing. The whistle blew several times, the sound of screeching metal filled the cabin, and the train began to brake so sharply that passengers were jolted back in their seats. He sat up from where he'd been slouching, raised his hat from where it rested over his eyes, and looked around.

He'd purchased his ticket, loaded Rusty on the horse car, and departed with a trainload of fellow passengers at three o'clock in the afternoon. Pritchard spent the hours between Eudora's exit and his new departure time alone in the livery. He had no desire to repeat the good-byes he'd already said, nor to explain the reason why he missed the morning train.

Pritchard sent the liveryman to Perkins's Diner to fetch him a meal and paid him extra to ensure he kept his mouth shut about the ex-marshal lounging in his stable. Then he ate, practiced with his unloaded guns, napped, and set off by train for Saint Louis, more than 250 miles away.

What would have been at least a five-day journey by horseback only a few years ago now took less than a day by rail. Even with scheduled stops in Higginsville and Boonville for more freight and passengers, Pritchard expected to arrive in Saint Louis before dawn.

He looked out the window into the darkness as the train ground to a halt. There was no station in sight.

"Why are we stopped?" several of the passengers asked.

"Don't know," the conductor said, checking his watch. "It's not even eight o'clock yet. We're still ten miles from Boonville."

Suddenly the sound of gunshots erupted. They emanated from outside, at the front of the train, near the engine. Some of the female passengers screamed. "It's a robbery!" a man shouted. Panic began to ensue.

"Quiet down!" Pritchard commanded in his deep voice. To the conductor he said, "Turn down the lights and get everybody on the floor."

"Who're you?" the conductor asked indignantly.

"Just a feller with some sense," Pritchard answered, standing up. "Do as I say."

The conductor dimmed the kerosene lamps and loudly announced, "You heard the man, get yourselves on the floor!" The passengers complied.

Pritchard had deliberately chosen the train's third passenger car to travel in. Most preferred the forward ones because the last passenger car was linked to the horse car, which tended to emit an odor common to the livestock it contained. He headed back to the rear of the car as the gunshots outside ceased.

Pritchard made his way through the passenger car's back door, clambered over the linkage, and entered the corresponding front door of the horse car. He heard men's voices barking orders, but couldn't make out exactly what they were saying.

Because of the diminished light, it took Pritchard a moment longer than it should have to locate his saddle in the darkened car and get it cinched on Rusty. Once he had his horse saddled, he withdrew his Winchester from the scabbard, patted the Morgan's neck, and said, "I know you're gettin' a little old for this stuff, but it looks like we've gotta ride together under fire once more."

Rusty gave Pritchard an injured look, as if insulted he'd been doubted because of his age. Pritchard quietly levered a round into the Winchester's chamber and cautiously slid the freight door open as silently as he could.

As soon as the big door was open, Pritchard could hear the voices arguing outside more clearly.

"Where is he?" he heard a man's rough voice demand. "Where's Atherton? You'd best tell us. Iffen we've gotta go look for him ourselves, you're catchin' a bullet."

"I don't know who you're talkin' about," another voice protested.

"He's a real big hombre," said the first voice, "as tall as a tree. He has a pistol-ball scar on his forehead and wears a two-gun rig. You can't miss him."

Pritchard peeked around the edge of the door. A nearly full moon ruled above a cloudless sky. He could easily make out at least five men, on foot, standing by the engine. Another man stood off, holding the reins of half a dozen horses. The men all had revolvers in their fists, and their neckerchiefs pulled up over their noses under their hats. They were pointing guns at the train's engineer and fireman, who held their hands high in the air.

"I've seen a passenger who looks like that," the fireman said, pointing along the train in Pritchard's direction. "I believe he's in the last car."

One of the gunmen remained at the engine, covering the two crewmen. The others, all except the one securing the horses, began to walk along the tracks toward the passenger car Pritchard had just vacated.

Pritchard looked down. He was relieved to note the train had come to rest on flat ground, and not over a ditch or gully. He recognized the terrain as river country. If what the conductor said was true about being ten miles from Boonville, the train was just west of the Missouri River.

"Here we go, Rusty," Pritchard said. "Just like

we used to do in Texas." He mounted up, took the reins, and spurred the horse off the train.

Rusty leaped to the ground from the livestock car. Pritchard bounced in the stirrups, but stayed in the saddle, and halted his horse as soon as it gained footing. The advancing gunmen looked up, startled by the sudden appearance of a horse and rider along the tracks ahead.

Their astonishment lasted for only an instant. The four gunmen began to run toward him.

Pritchard shouldered the Winchester, took aim, and fired. The closest approaching gunman, who was no more than thirty yards away, fell forward on his face. His companions immediately halted and began to fire their pistols.

Pritchard reined Rusty toward the caboose, away from the approaching gunmen, and gave him the spurs.

Shots continued to ring out behind them as Rusty sprinted toward the rear of the train. Pritchard heard and felt several bullets whiz past, an experience he and his horse had endured together too many times to recall. He looked over his shoulder, and in the bright moonlight saw the three uninjured gunmen had turned around and were running back to retrieve their horses. He breathed a sigh of relief.

Pritchard's decision to run, instead of remaining to fight, was made the instant he heard the first gunshot while still on the train. He'd faced worse odds before, and his instincts generally leaned toward meeting attackers head-on in direct combat. But the passenger cars were loaded with women and children, and any number of men who were potentially armed. If he stayed and engaged multiple gunmen in a shoot-out, the ensuing melee of gunfire would undoubtedly have resulted in innocent passengers being hurt or killed.

Just like back in Atherton, Pritchard knew he was once again a bullet magnet. He realized if he was to protect the passengers, he must lead the gunmen away from the train. This was the reason he took the shot with his Winchester instead of merely fleeing on Rusty's back; he wanted to incite the highwaymen to pursue him. He only hoped the engineer possessed the wisdom to get the train moving again, and his passengers as far from danger as possible, once the gunmen got on horseback and started after him.

Rusty was now at full gallop, and Pritchard steered him toward a stretch of open prairie that lay before them. Soon he detected the sound of hoofbeats behind him. He looked over his shoulder to see five riders, off in the distance, following in his wake.

He slowed Rusty to a halt and dismounted. While the moon overhead enabled him to see much farther than on a moonless night, it was nonetheless dark. At their current frenetic pace, and in the diminished light, Pritchard feared Rusty might trip and break a leg in an unseen hole or downed tree branch while sprinting over the unfamiliar ground.

Pritchard pulled Rusty down onto his haunches by his bridle. The riders grew more distinct as they neared, and the sounds of their horses' hoofbeats grew louder.

Laying his hand over Rusty's forehead, he pushed the horse over onto its side and pressed his head to the ground. "Stay here and lay quiet, Rusty," Pritchard reassured him. "I'll be right back."

Pritchard and Rusty had covered enough ground that he could no longer see the train. He could see the riders, however, advancing on him rapidly with their mounts at full gallop. The five horsemen were approximately one hundred yards away. He opened his saddlebag and grabbed a box of .44-40 cartridges, hastily stuffing its contents into his hip pockets.

CHAPTER 27

Pritchard jogged away from Rusty as he levered a fresh round from the Winchester's tubular magazine into the chamber, replacing the one he'd already expended. Then he inserted two more cartridges into the Winchester's loading gate to top the rifle off.

When Pritchard was ten yards from his horse, he knelt, shook out the tension from his shoulders, back, and neck, took in a deep breath, and shouldered the Winchester. He could now feel the vibration from the oncoming riders as well as hear them. He exhaled evenly through his nose, placed the rifle's front sight on the closest rider, and put his finger on the trigger.

Shots rang out. The riders were now close enough to see Pritchard, kneeling alone on the prairie, and began wildly firing their pistols at him. He wasn't concerned, despite once again hearing and feeling bullets whizzing by. His history as a Confederate guerilla and Texas Ranger taught him that accurate pistol fire from running horseback was all but impossible at anything but point-blank range, especially in the dark.

As soon as he expelled the air from his lungs, Pritchard fired. The nearest horseman toppled from his mount.

Pritchard continued to fire, expertly levering the Winchester's action from his shoulder by tilting his head between shots. Firing a round per second, he smoothly moved his front sight from rider to rider. He put three rounds into each moving target and watched as they tumbled, one by one, from their saddles. He steadily squeezed the trigger, cycled the action, and squeezed again, firing sixteen times.

Two of the approaching horses also fell under Pritchard's withering fusillade, though it wasn't his intent to injure the animals. It was simply their bad luck to be driven into a barrage of steady, accurate, rifle fire by their master's poor judgment.

The final rider crashed to the ground not ten yards from Pritchard, as the Winchester's action clicked on an empty chamber. The three uninjured horses, now without their riders, wisely galloped off.

Pritchard stood and moved as he swiftly reloaded the Winchester from the fresh rounds in his pocket. He realized if he could spot his adversary's muzzle flashes, they could spot his. He stopped when he got twenty paces from his original position. Out in the darkness, one of the downed horses was baying in pain and he could hear at least one of the men groaning.

Pritchard said nothing until his rifle was fully reloaded. He'd survived too many gunfights to be lulled into the belief that because he'd put five men on the ground they were out of the fight. Once his Winchester was recharged, Pritchard lay flat on his belly. He pointed his rifle in the general direction where the gunmen and their horses had fallen.

"You there," Pritchard called out, "lyin' in the weeds? Iffen any of you fellers ain't dead, you'd best surrender. You've lost your mounts, you're only armed with pistols, and you've been shot to hell. I've got a good rifle, plenty of cartridges, and nary a scratch. Stand up with your hands empty, over your heads, and I won't shoot no more."

In response, a pistol shot was fired at Pritchard's voice. He marked the location of the muzzle flash.

"That wasn't very charitable," Pritchard said.

"You go to hell, Atherton!"

"How many damn times do I have to say it?" Pritchard retorted, as much to himself as to the gunmen out on the prairie. "I ain't Joe Atherton no more." He fired three more times in rapid succession, aiming a few inches lower than the muzzle flash he'd marked.

Pritchard was rewarded with a short scream. He rolled onto his back, restocked the Winchester with three more cartridges from his pockets, and then rolled back over to the prone position again.

"There's no hurry, boys," Pritchard hollered.

"Take all the time you want. I ain't bleedin', and I've got nowhere else to be. I'm content to wait here all night. Got me this here fine Winchester rifle and a hankerin' to use it. Yessiree, I'm as comfortable as a frog in a bog."

"All right," an agonized voice said. "I give up."

"Then throw out your gun," Pritchard ordered, "and stand up."

"I can't," the man replied. "I've been shot through the belly, and I busted my back when I fell off my horse. I can't move."

"What about your friends?" Pritchard said.

"They're done," the voice said. "You finished 'em."

Pritchard stood and cautiously moved backward, keeping the butt of his rifle in the pocket of his shoulder and his finger on the trigger. Stepping slowly and making no sound, he navigated a wide, half circle around the general area where the gunmen and horses lay. The wounded horse continued to thrash and bay, which helped cover the noise of his movement.

It took several long minutes, but Pritchard eventually made his way to a spot behind the hidden gunmen, 180 degrees from his original position. Then he slowly began to advance.

Pritchard almost stepped on the first gunmen he encountered, lying in the shin-high scrub. He lay dead on his side with his eyes open and a bullet hole in his throat. The man was clad in a suit more appropriate for town than afield. He stepped over the body and continued advancing.

The second gunman he encountered was also dead. This one had been shot several times in the chest. He still wore his hat, a bowler, and clutched a Remington revolver in one lifeless hand. He was wearing field boots, but like the first man was attired in town clothes.

Pritchard next passed a dead horse. There was no water on the small pancake saddle it wore.

The third gunman Pritchard found he presumed was the one who'd fired the single pistol shot after shouting, "Go to hell!" He suspected this because the body was lying prone with a Colt revolver extended at arm's length. Two of his Winchester's .44-40s had decimated his face. He, too, was wearing the attire of a city denizen.

Pritchard could see the bulk of another horse ahead, and could tell this one was still moving. It was unable to stand and had stopped whinnying, but he could hear its labored breathing.

Pritchard regrettably walked around the horse, leaving it in torment. As badly as he wanted to put the suffering animal out of its misery, he couldn't risk giving away his location with a gunshot. A few silent steps later, he was glad he didn't.

Twenty feet from the writhing horse was another gunman. He was also clad, like his brethren, in the garb of a townie. But unlike the three other gunmen Pritchard had come across, this one was still alive. He was sitting with his back to Pritchard, and it appeared one of his legs was either broken or had taken a bullet. He'd tied the handkerchief, which had been over his face, around his right thigh and steadied a Colt Navy converted to fire metallic cartridges in both hands. It was aimed where Pritchard had previously been, with the hammer back.

"Say somethin'," the gunman whispered to another man Pritchard could vaguely see lying farther out in the dark. "Get him to talk again, so's I can find him."

"Don't bother," Pritchard said, pressing the muzzle of his rifle against the man's neck. "He's right here."

The man dropped his revolver and raised his hands. "Don't shoot, Joe," he pleaded.

"The name's Pritchard," Pritchard said. "Get up."

"My leg's shot," the man said. "I can't walk."

"Then hop," Pritchard said, dragging the man to his feet by the back of his collar. With one hand on the man's neck, and the barrel of his Winchester pressed against his back, Pritchard used his hostage as a shield as he pushed him toward the final gunman.

Pritchard found the last gunman on his back, looking up at them with tortured eyes. "I wasn't lyin', mister," he said, holding up his empty hands. "I can't move or feel anything below the belt. I ain't no threat."

A glance told Pritchard the man was telling the truth. He was in a town suit like all the others, and lay with a blood-soaked abdomen and his legs askew in a manner no one with the ability to feel pain could have tolerated. Clearly his spine was shattered. His holster was empty, and no pistol was about. Pritchard guessed he'd dropped it when he'd fallen from his horse.

Pritchard shoved his hostage to the ground next to his crippled companion. "I'm gonna ask you fellers some questions," he said, "and you're gonna answer 'em. But first I've got to take care of that injured horse. I can't abide an animal suffering needlessly. Stay here, don't move, and no tricks."

"Where the hell are we gonna go?" the gunman with the bandaged leg said. He sat up, stretched his good leg out, and moved closer to his friend.

Pritchard strode over to where the injured horse lay gasping and twitching. He knelt by its head and stroked its neck, calming the terrified animal. He noticed the bullet wound in its breast, and it brought back painful memories of the dozens of mortally wounded horses he'd had to put down during the war.

"I'm truly sorry," Pritchard said. "It weren't your fault you were rode by an outlaw." He stood, leveled the Winchester, and fired, ending the horse's pain.

As he was walking back to the two wounded gunmen, Pritchard levered another round into the Winchester's chamber. He'd just finished inserting another cartridge into the rifle's loading gate when he noticed the seated gunman, contrary to what he'd ordered, was moving. He was also pointing a Remington derringer at Pritchard's chest.

Pritchard instantly dropped as the tiny pistol discharged. A bullet sailed past his ear. The .41 caliber projectile was aimed at his middle, and passed Pritchard's head on his way to the ground. He rolled, came up to one knee, and fired the Winchester as the seated gunman had just finished re-cocking the minuscule weapon for a follow-up shot.

Three more times Pritchard squeezed the trigger, levered, and squeezed again. His first shot struck his target in the chest, and the next three moved progressively upward in a vertical line until the last bullet landed between his eyes. The gunman fell dead alongside his wounded partner.

Pritchard stood. This time, after refilling the rifle's magazine, he didn't lever a fresh round into the chamber. When he walked up to inspect the dead gunman, he noticed one of the pants legs of the crippled gunman had been pulled up. Obviously, the two-shot derringer had been taken from the boot of the paralyzed man.

"Thanks for the warning," Pritchard said drily. He whistled, and a moment later Rusty came walking up. Pritchard patted his horse's forehead and returned the Winchester to its scabbard.

"What are you gonna do?" the gunman asked.

Pritchard wasn't sure how much pain the man was in, due to his shattered spine, but the anguish of his hopeless plight was plain to see on his face.

"Same thing I said I was gonna do before your partner took a shot at me," Pritchard said. "I'm gonna ask questions, and you're gonna answer 'em."

"You can go to hell," the man said. "You'll get nothin' from me."

"You boys are all townies, ain't ya?" Pritchard remarked. "You're all wearin' city duds, and none of you brought any water, prog, or rifles. I'm guessin' you didn't come far. Jefferson City, maybe?"

"Like I told you," the man said, "you can go to hell."

"Okay," Pritchard said, unlimbering his canteen and taking a long drink. "You don't want to give me information, maybe you'd be willing to sell it?"

"I'm gonna die soon," the gunman said. "You ain't got nothin' that can help me."

"What's your name?" Pritchard asked. "You already know mine, because I heard your friends use it. I can at least call you by your given name while we converse."

"It's Tyler," the gunman said. "Yancy Tyler. And unless you can fix up my back and take the bullet out of my guts, you still ain't got nothin' I can use. You may as well get on your horse and ride."

"Fair enough," Pritchard said, putting a foot in the stirrup and mounting Rusty.

"You were mistaken when you said you'd die soon," Pritchard told him from horseback. "Going out by gut-shot can be a mighty slow death. I've seen it a thousand times. You could last a day or two, maybe longer. During the war I saw some gut-shot fellers last a week, and every minute they was in barkin' agony. Helluva way to die, iffen you ask me."

Yancy Tyler continued to stare up at the starlit sky and refused to look at Pritchard. But tears began to eke from the corners of his eyes.

"It ain't like you're restin' in a warm bed somewheres," Pritchard continued, "bein' comforted by a nurse. You're lyin' out on the cold prairie, in a puddle of your own blood and manure, puttin' out stench for miles. How long do you think it'll be, Yancy, with you surrounded by dead men and dead horses, before the bears, wolves, coyotes, and buzzards catch wind of your scent?"

Tyler's lower lip began to tremble. He angrily brushed away his tears with both hands.

Pritchard pointed Rusty east and started to

211

ride off. "So long, Yancy Tyler," he said over his shoulder.

"Wait!" Tyler called after him. "You can't leave me like this!"

"I believe I can," Pritchard replied.

"You just put down a shot horse," Tyler yelled, "to ease its suffering, but you won't do the same for a man? At least give me a gun so I can do it myself."

Pritchard halted Rusty and turned him back around to face Tyler. "I'd be glad to," he said. "But like I already told you, it'll cost you some answers."

"What do you want to know?"

"Who are you boys?"

"We used to work for the Quincy Detective Agency."

Pritchard, like most lawmen, was familiar with the Quincy Detective Agency, and Dominic "Cottonmouth" Quincy, the venal man who owned it. Though not as well known as the Pinkerton Agency, which was headquartered in Chicago, Quincy's outfit operated out of Saint Louis. Both served similar masters, such as banks, railroad companies, mining interests, cattle and land barons, and employed an army of hired guns.

"You don't work for Quincy anymore?"

"No," Tyler said, turning his head and spitting blood. "Me and the others went freelance a week ago. Got a better offer."

"From who?"

"You."

"Me?"

"Heard about the bounty on you," Tyler said. He had to pause to cough more blood. "Ten thousand dollars is a lot of money."

"I don't get it," Pritchard said. "Why did you have to quit the agency to go after me?"

"Company policy won't allow employees to keep any bounty money on anyone they bring in."

"That would explain why you quit the agency," Pritchard said. "Was it worth it?"

"Thought so at the time. It was better'n what Cottonmouth was payin' us."

"How'd you find me?"

"Got a juicy tip from someone," Tyler said. "He said you were leavin' Atherton by train, and for a slice of the bounty he'd tell us which one."

"What's his name?"

"Do I have to tell you? He's a friend of mine."

"Iffen you don't want to die feedin' critters, you do."

"Searcy," Tyler said. "Jim Searcy. He used to be with the Quincy Agency a long time ago."

"Never heard of him," Pritchard said.

"I told you all I know," Tyler said. "I held up my end. Don't leave me to be gnawed on by coyotes."

Pritchard dismounted and recovered the

derringer from the dead gunman's hand. He lowered the hammer and broke it open to ensure the gun still contained an unfired .41 caliber cartridge. Then he closed the gun's action and tossed it back and forth between his hands as he looked down at Yancy Tyler.

"Please, Joe?" Tyler begged. "Give me the gun. Don't leave me like this."

"By all rights I ought to," Pritchard said. "If you and your friends had your druthers, you'd be leadin' my horse into Saint Louis with my carcass slung over the saddle."

"Please?"

Pritchard didn't answer him. Instead, he leaned down and placed the derringer on Tyler's chest.

"Hey, Joe," Tyler said as Pritchard turned and headed for his horse. He pointed the gun at Pritchard and cocked it. "How do you know I won't shoot you in the back?"

"Because if you waste your only shot on me," Pritchard answered over his shoulder, "you'll be back to dyin' slow and feedin' the critters." He remounted the big Morgan and pointed him east.

"So long, Yancy Tyler," Pritchard said over his shoulder.

Rusty hadn't taken Pritchard fifty yards before he heard the shot.

CHAPTER 28

Pritchard was five miles from Boonville, just west of the railroad bridge spanning the Lamine River, when Rusty suddenly collapsed. The horse abruptly fell to its side, tossing Pritchard to the ground.

Pritchard had ridden Rusty several miles from the scene of the battle with the ex–Quincy Detective Agency men. One of their three surviving horses had followed. It wasn't uncommon for stable-broke horses to automatically follow another, and every so often Pritchard would look back and see the forlorn animal trudging along behind them.

At first, Pritchard thought Rusty stepped into a gopher hole. As he got up and dusted himself off, he realized the big Morgan was in distress. A quick examination revealed his horse's legs were unbroken, but his right rump was covered in blood he hadn't noticed earlier due to the darkness and the reddish hue of the animal's hide. He surmised Rusty must have taken a bullet during their flight from the train, and mentally kicked himself for not checking his horse more thoroughly after the gunfight.

"I'm sorry, brother," Pritchard apologized, soothing the horse. "Why didn't you tell me? If

I'd have known you were hurt, I never would have mounted you."

Pritchard quickly uncinched his saddle and bags, which were laden for travel, and lifted them off Rusty's back. "It don't help any that I'm as big as I am," Pritchard continued talking to his horse, "and you're loaded down for war. Next time, you stubborn old cuss, say somethin' to me, will ya?"

Pritchard examined the wound more closely. The hole was in the meatiest part of Rusty's butt and seemingly hadn't struck any vital organs or major blood vessels. Had that been the case, Rusty would never have made it as far as they'd gone without breaking pace. Pritchard was reassured that his beloved horse would recover, provided he dug the bullet out, cauterized the wound, infection didn't set in, and Rusty got some rest.

Pritchard filled his hat with the contents of his canteen and watered Rusty, who drank greedily. He was contemplating building a fire, when he saw a light flickering ahead in the distance through a stand of trees. Evidently someone else already had one going.

Pritchard walked out to meet the docile horse that had been trailing them. It was a good-sized, black quarter horse, sixteen hands tall, and approached him without hesitation. He took the reins, unhooked the tiny pancake saddle it wore, and tossed it away. Then he led the animal back to Rusty, and in another minute had his saddle cinched on the quarter horse's back. He gently nudged Rusty to his feet.

Rusty could stand, but Pritchard could tell he was weak and unsteady.

"C'mon," he said to both horses, taking their reins in his left hand. He put his Winchester in his right. "We don't have far to go."

Pritchard led both horses toward the light. He walked slowly, because he could tell Rusty was having a hard time. "I know you want to lay down and rest," Pritchard said to his weary horse. "Let's see if we can't get you some help up yonder."

Pritchard didn't know who the fire belonged to, but dared not make one of his own so near another's camp unannounced. Some would interpret such an act as hostile, and he wanted to avoid further hostilities if he could.

As Pritchard got closer, he could hear music. It was a stringed instrument of some kind, similar to a mandolin he once heard at a county fair. He could also hear a violin, but it didn't sound the way the violins did at the barn dances he'd attended. He stopped at the tree line and peered through the foliage at the scene before him.

There were eight, ornately decorated box wagons parked in a semicircle on the bank of the Lamine River, and at least that many tents.

A bonfire was blazing, and more than two dozen people sat on chairs and logs surrounding it.

The group comprised men, women, and children. Pritchard could smell beef cooking, and saw both a caldron and a metal rack containing steaks, over the fire. Three seated men were playing the music, one with a violin, one with something that looked to Pritchard like a guitar, but was shaped differently, and one with a wind instrument of a type he'd never before heard.

What struck Pritchard most was their appearance. The people were all fairly dark-skinned, similar to the Mexicans he'd encountered in Texas, and in the New Mexico and Arizona Territories, but shared none of their Hispanic features. Their dress was different, too. Their boots, hats, and coats were of a cut and style he'd not seen before.

Pritchard put his Winchester back into the saddle scabbard and led the two horses slowly into the camp.

"Good evening," he said.

The music stopped. Everyone in camp suddenly turned to face him. Women scurried to grab their children, and some of the men grabbed weapons, which included a single-barreled shotgun, an old Fayetteville musket, and an ax.

"Easy, now," Pritchard said. "I come in peace."

"Who are you?" a man said. He was a swarthy, broad-shouldered fellow in his fifties, with thick eyebrows and a dark mustache. By his carriage, Pritchard surmised he was the one in charge. "What do you want?"

The man's voice was deep. To Pritchard's surprise, he spoke with a British accent.

"My name's Samuel Pritchard," he answered. "I was on the train to Saint Louis and ran into some trouble. My horse caught a bullet in his hind. I was hopin' you folks would allow me to treat him at your fire, and perhaps rest a bit? I'd be glad to pay you for the privilege."

A handsome woman in her forties approached the man. She glared at Pritchard, and spoke into the man's ear in a language he'd never heard before and didn't understand. She pointed to the pistols on his hips and made a slashing motion across her throat.

"How did your horse get shot?" the man asked.

"It's a long story," Pritchard said. "Let's just say I was fleeing some fellers who didn't have my best interests at heart."

The woman continued to gesture angrily and argue with the man. The others in the crowd watched Pritchard, some in fear and some with disdain they weren't shy about displaying. Small children clung to their mothers, reflecting their parents' doubt and fright.

Pritchard noticed the men, regardless of age, were muscular, with the builds of those who'd spent their lives in manual labor, and had hard, suspicious faces. He also noticed the women, some of whom were quite young, were exotically beautiful.

The man in charge nodded to the woman, then gave her a dismissive wave. She stopped speaking and stepped back with the others.

"You must go," the man said to Pritchard. "You cannot stay here."

"I wouldn't be long," Pritchard said. "I need light to dig out the bullet, and a fire hot enough to get my knife heated red to sear the wound shut. It'll take me an hour or more to get a fire that hot going myself, and you've already got one. My animal's in pain and bleedin' bad. I'm obliged to do what I can to ease his sufferin'. Like I said, I can pay you. I'd be deeply in your debt, if you'd reconsider."

"These are your troubles," the man said gruffly, "not ours. Go."

The men with the guns, and the one with the ax, took a step toward Pritchard.

"Very well," Pritchard said, tipping his hat. "I'll thank you nonetheless, and bid you all good night." He turned around and led Rusty and the quarter horse back the way they'd come in.

CHAPTER 29

Ditch, Idelle, and Eudora Chilton sat in comfortable chairs on the big porch of the Atherton Arms Hotel. It was an unseasonably warm night, even for late April, and the full moon hung over the town as big as a nickel. Ditch was nursing a beer, while Eudora and Idelle were each enjoying a glass of wine. The dinner hour had passed, and the kitchen was closing up. Inside, it was standing room only at the hotel's small bar.

"I wouldn't have admitted it a few days ago," Idelle said, "but I'm looking forward to the Sidewinder's opening. It'll be a relief to have the hotel lobby less populated in the evenings."

"Don't worry," Ditch said. "Not long after the wedding our house will be finished. Once we move in, it won't matter how crowded the hotel gets at night."

"True," she said. "Tell me, Eudora, how soon do you anticipate opening the Sidewinder for business?"

"I'll be open in a few days," Eudora said.

"That was quick," Ditch said.

"The building itself is in fine shape," Eudora said. "What work needs to be done inside will be finished in a day or so, and the delivery of liquor and beer from Kansas City should arrive any day now. I've already hired a bartender and a couple of local gals to sling drinks. Everything else will fall into place once I open the doors."

"Congratulations," Ditch said, raising his glass. "I look forward to becoming a regular visitor."

"Not too regular, I hope," Idelle said with a smile.

"If Ditch gets too regular at the Sidewinder," Eudora said, with a smile of her own, "I'll refuse him entry."

"How will you stop me?" Ditch teased. "Call the law and have me locked up?"

Idelle's smile suddenly vanished. "Speaking of the law," she said, "what do you suppose Samuel's up to right now?"

"Hard to say," Ditch said. "If I know Samuel, he's plenty busy."

"What do you mean by that?" Eudora said.

"He made a fuss about leaving Atherton to keep folks in town safe from any bounty killers and gunfighters," he said, "but that was only part of the reason why he left. You heard what he said to Benedict Houseman last night?"

"I also saw what he did to Benedict Houseman," Idelle said. "I thought he was going to tear that man's head off."

"That was nothin'," Ditch said with a grimace. "That was Samuel givin' Houseman a polite warning, that's all. If he wanted to hurt ole

Benedict, he could have. During the war, I once saw him kill a man with one blow."

"If that was being polite," Eudora said, "I'd hate to see him riled."

"You don't know how right you are," Ditch said. "Iffen you've ever seen Samuel Pritchard with blood in his eyes, like I have, you'd know what trouble looks like. He's gonna find out what's what with Houseman and that Bonnie Shipley gal, or whatever her name is, and God help anyone who tries to get in his way."

"I just hope he's safe," Idelle said. "I know he's my big brother and can take care of himself, but I still worry about him."

"Me, too," Eudora said. "I'm not ashamed to admit it, but I've grown very fond of your brother. He's young, but he's a lot of man. You don't find his kind very often."

"I've noticed you and him having eyes for each other," Idelle said.

"I hope that hasn't offended you," Eudora said.

"Not at all," Idelle said. "It's nice to know someone else besides me cares enough about my brother to worry over him."

"I am worried," Eudora said. "Maybe even as worried as you."

"You two should save your worryin' for anyone who tries to cross him," Ditch said, draining his beer.

John Babbit and Judge Eugene Pearson walked

up the hotel steps. "Is there a place we can speak privately?" the judge asked, after greetings were exchanged.

"The hotel office," Idelle said. She led everyone into the hotel, to a room behind the main desk.

The office was empty, save for a large table and several chairs. It had once been Burnell Shipley's official office, his unofficial headquarters being the Sidewinder, and was the room where he'd coerced Dovie Pritchard into marrying him to spare her son Samuel's life. Idelle had all Shipley's personal effects and furniture burned, and rarely went into the room, believing it held too many bad memories. Tonight, it was the only place for them to meet without prying ears and eyes. Ditch lit the kerosene lamps and everyone took a seat.

"We have news," Babbit said. He motioned to Judge Pearson.

"I got a telegram from a friend of mine, an Illinois magistrate working out of the capital in Springfield," the judge began. "He responded to my query about Benedict Houseman."

"What did he say?"

"It's as bad as we thought," the judge said. "Houseman once had a law practice in Chicago specializing in probate law."

"Probate law?" Ditch asked. "What kind of law is that?"

"It's the law governing the transfer of a deceased person's property."

"That figures," Idelle said.

"It gets worse," Judge Pearson continued. "Houseman was involved in the highly questionable seizure of a number of deceased person's assets. Apparently, he has a history of filing claims against estates in probate by producing hitherto unknown heirs."

"People like Bonnie Shipley," Idelle said.

"Precisely," the judge said.

"How can he get away with that?" Ditch said.

"He knows the law," Pearson said. "Houseman can tie up the probate process with frivolous, expensive filings for so long that he eventually wears the legitimate heirs down and they settle the claim."

"You mean, he swindles the rightful heirs out of their inheritance," Eudora said, "or forces them to pay him off with a percentage to avoid losing it all in a costly legal battle?"

"That's correct," Judge Pearson said.

"He's a thief," Ditch said. "Instead of a gun, he uses a law degree."

"Again, correct."

"How come Houseman hasn't been arrested?" Idelle asked.

"Two reasons," Pearson explained. "First, he's a smart, slippery character who knows how far he can push the law before he breaks it. In most cases what he's doing, while unethical, is perfectly legal. At least no one can prove it isn't."

"And the second reason?" Idelle asked.

"Heirs that are in legal conflict with Benedict Houseman's mysterious clients have a habit of turning up dead."

Ditch and Idelle exchanged glances.

"That's right," Pearson said. "One of the defendants in a claim Houseman filed died in a highly suspicious riding accident. Another just happened to get shot dead during a street robbery. And an entire family, including children, who were in legal dispute with him over one of his dubious probate claims, perished in a fire."

"That's horrible," Idelle said.

"That dirty son of a bitch," Ditch said.

"The authorities couldn't pin any of the deaths on Houseman," Judge Pearson said, "but he certainly benefited financially from them. As a result of the bad press, and out of fear of vengeance from the rightful heirs, he was forced to flee Illinois. According to my source, Houseman was last rumored to be residing and practicing law in Saint Louis."

"Burnell Shipley spent years drinking, gambling, and whoring in Saint Louis," Idelle said. "His absences were the only time Ma and I got any peace. That can't be a coincidence."

"Unfortunately," Judge Pearson said, "Shipley's well-known sojourns to the brothels in Saint Louis not only put him in Benedict Houseman's crooked sights, but lend credibility to Bonnie Shipley's claim to be his daughter."

"This is great news," Idelle said, rubbing her forehead. "Either Houseman is going to fleece me out of everything I have, or I'm going to have a fatal 'accident' of a highly suspicious nature."

"Neither of those things are going to happen," Ditch said, taking Idelle's hand. "I won't let them. If Benedict Houseman tries to harm you, I'll—"

"That's where you might run into trouble," John Babbit said, cutting Ditch off.

"What trouble?" Idelle said.

"Not what," Babbit said. "Who. Jack Stearns, that's who."

"What about him?" Eudora asked.

"Remember when I told you after Pritchard's first inquest that I wired every newspaperman in the territory?" Babbit said. Ditch and Idelle nodded. "Yesterday, I got a response from a freelancer in Omaha. He wired me with information about a man named J. Stearns who was involved in a shooting there a few months ago."

"Is it the same person?" Idelle asked.

"I asked myself that exact question," Babbit said. "So, I sent another telegram to the Douglas County sheriff, in Nebraska. He replied this afternoon. He informed me a man named Jack Stearns gunned down a person named William T. Judson in Omaha last November."

"Stearns gunned Wichita Willie Judson?" Ditch said.

"You know him?" Babbit asked.

"Not personally," Ditch said. "I've heard the name, and heard Samuel speak of him. Judson was a rustler and stage robber out of Kansas. He was supposed to be a pretty dangerous hombre, and very handy with a gun. From what he told me, he was nobody to trifle with."

"Whoever he was," Babbit said, "Stearns collected five hundred dollars' reward for putting him down."

"So what you're telling us," Idelle said, "is that Jack Stearns is—"

"—a bounty killer," Babbit finished the sentence for her. "It sure looks that way."

CHAPTER 30

"Howdy, folks!" the man with the Henry rifle announced. He stepped into the camp along with three other men also bearing rifles. When one of the men in camp tried to grab a shotgun leaning against the wagon, another of the armed newcomers clubbed him in the skull with the butt of his rifle, knocking him out cold.

It was less than an hour after Pritchard departed the camp when the occupants found themselves again beset by intruders. Small children were once more placed behind their mothers' skirts, men stood protectively in front of their women, and everyone in camp turned to face the interlopers.

"What do you want?" the camp leader said.

"We smelled the beef cookin' a ways off," the first man said. He was old, stooped, and wore a scraggly beard over few teeth. The three men with him were much younger, but appeared just as dirty, malnourished, and disheveled. The heavy odor of moonshine liquor emanated from all of them.

"Your dinner smells mighty good," the old man went on. "Where'd you steal that calf?"

"We didn't steal it," the leader said. "We bought it in Boonville today. Before the people of Boonville chased us away."

"I heard about that," the man said, turning his head to spit a glob of tobacco juice. "Evidently they don't cotton to thieves in Boonville."

"We are not thieves."

"Hell if you ain't," the man said. He pointed his rifle at the chief. "You look too well fed for an honest man. Me and my boys here are honest men, and we're barely scratchin' out a livin'."

"What do you want?" the leader repeated.

"Impatient, ain't he, Pa?" one of the other armed men said.

"What we want, we'll take," the older man said. "Bring out your money and valuables."

"We don't have much money," the leader said. "If you leave us and hurt no one else, you are welcome to what little we possess."

"Hear that, boys?" the older man said to the others. "Iffen we don't hurt 'em, he's willin' to give us what money he's got."

"That's right generous of him," one of his sons said, "iffen you ask me." They all laughed.

The camp leader, who spoke English in a British accent, said something in a foreign language. One of the women entered a wagon and came out a moment later bearing a wooden box. She silently handed it to the chief and retreated to the fire.

The leader opened it, to reveal a small cache of paper money and coins. He set the open box on the ground and stepped back.

"There is almost eighty dollars," he said. "It is all we have. Take it, and go."

"That ain't all you have," the old man said, as one of his sons picked up the box, closed it, and tucked it under his arm. "I notice you've got women. Have 'em step forward."

"Our wives and daughters are not for sale," the leader said.

"I wasn't askin' to buy your women," the old man said with a leer. "Me and my boys just want to borrow 'em for a while." More laughter among his three sons broke out.

"We won't hurt 'em," the oldest son said, "much." They laughed even harder.

The old man suddenly stopped laughing, and his face got hard. He raised the Henry to his shoulder and aimed it directly at the leader's face. "You talk that gibberish of yours," he ordered, "and tell your women to get out front here and line up. Just the young ones, mind you; don't bother with any of the withered ones. You can either line 'em up yourself, or me and my boys'll line 'em up ourselves after I plug you. Either way, it's gettin' done."

The camp leader said nothing. He squared his shoulders, stuck out his chest, and glowered in defiance.

"I reckon he's defyin' you, Pa," one of the boys said.

"Looks like he's willin' to eat a bullet to keep his

womenfolk from gettin' soiled," another boy said.

"I'll oblige him," the old man said, thumbing back the Henry's hammer.

"*Nai!*" one of the younger women suddenly blurted. She and six others stepped forward and lined up between the old man aiming the rifle and their chief. The women ranged in age from approximately sixteen to thirty, and all were darkly beautiful.

"That's more like it," the old man said. "Tell 'em to ditch their clothes."

The leader shook his head.

"Get undressed!" the old man commanded the women. "Lose them skirts, or your boss is gonna lose his brains!" His three sons raised their rifles and swept them toward the people assembled around the fire.

The women looked at one another in anguish and shame, then slowly began to undress. The old man's sons ogled the women and cackled in anticipation.

"You picked yours out yet?" the eldest son asked his brothers. "I'm a-claimin' that one," he pointed his chin at an especially buxom woman in her late teens. "That gal with the big—"

"I wanted her," the second eldest interrupted. "You always get your choice. Ain't fair; I had my eye on her first."

"Quit arguin'," the old man said. "You can both have her; you'll just have to take turns."

"Maybe so," the eldest said, "but I'm goin' first."

"Reckon it's a mite cold out," Pritchard said, "to be sheddin' duds, ain't it?"

Everyone, including the four men wielding rifles, looked up to see Pritchard enter the encampment. The old man and his three sons swung their rifles to cover him.

"Whoa, there," Pritchard said with an easy grin. "That ain't no way to greet a guest."

"Who're you?" the old man said.

"Just a feller like you," Pritchard said, "with an empty belly who smells a meal a-cookin'. Who're you?"

"Ain't none of your business who we are," the old man said. "All you need to know, mister, is we was here first. You'd best get on your way, while the gettin' is good."

"Ain't very neighborly," Pritchard said, "tryin' to run me off. Where're your manners?"

"My manners are in this here rifle," the old man said.

"Pointin' your gun at a feller is mighty rude," Pritchard said. "How would you like it if I pointed my guns at you?"

"Why don't you just try it," the old man challenged, "and see what happens?"

"All right," Pritchard said, drawing.

Pritchard drew both revolvers at the same time and fired two shots from each Colt. It happened so fast no one saw him move before hearing the reports. None of the four men aiming rifles at him even got off a shot. All fell where they stood.

The two closest riflemen, including the old man, took headshots. The two farthest received torso hits. One of those men wasn't killed outright, and landed on his back. Pritchard finished him with a shot to the forehead as he vainly struggled to bring up his Henry rifle.

Children began to cry, and some of the women rushed over to attend to the man who'd been clubbed. Pritchard holstered his left gun and began to reload his right-hand pistol from the cartridge loops on his belt. The camp leader approached him.

"I am Manfri Pannell," he said, "the chief of this Romanichal clan. You said your name was Samuel Pritchard? I thank you, Samuel, for what you have done."

"I didn't do it for you," Pritchard said. "I don't abide men who molest womenfolk."

"Nor do I. Why did you come back?"

"I was collecting wood when I detected those fellers creepin' up on your camp. I couldn't very well build a fire of my own until I knew who they were and what they were up to, so I tracked 'em here."

Pritchard holstered his right-hand gun and reloaded his left-hand Colt. "I'll bid you good night," he said, tipping his hat, "for the second time."

"Wait," Manfri said. "Stay and dine with us."

"I cannot," Pritchard said. "I told you, my horse is in a bad way. If I don't get a fire goin' so's I can dig that bullet out of him, and quench his bleedin', he's done for."

"Vano, Danior," Manfri called out. Two husky young Romanichal men approached. "These are my sons," he said. "Go with Pritchard. Bring his animal and have Kezia tend to it."

"I won't ask you folks to do what you don't want to," Pritchard said. "That ain't my way."

"My wife was one of the women being forced to disrobe," Danior said. "It will be my honor to assist you."

"We are a people who work with animals," Manfri said. "Vano and his wife, Kezia, are the best healers you could find. They will care for your horse."

"I'd surely be obliged," Pritchard said.

CHAPTER 31

Pritchard took Vano and Danior to the place he'd tied Rusty and the quarter horse, and the three of them led the animals back to the Romanichal camp. Rusty was feverish and weak and offered no resistance when Pritchard laid him down near the fire. Vano's wife, a striking woman in her twenties, and also one of those nearly made to undress, came out of a wagon and began to examine the injured horse.

She looked at his eyes, mouth, and ears, ran her hands along his back and flanks, then carefully scrutinized the gunshot wound in his hindquarter. Pritchard knelt at Rusty's head, patting his neck and reassuring him.

"You care for this animal," Vano's wife said. It wasn't a question.

"Rusty has always taken care of me," Pritchard said. "I guess you could say we look out for each other."

"I am Kezia," she said. "I will care for your Rusty, too."

When her examination was complete, Kezia began issuing orders in her native tongue. People scrambled to comply. One man began to stoke the fire, already a glowing pile of burning coals, with more wood. Another fetched water from the river, and began to boil it in a pail over the fire. Still another retrieved a satchel from one of the wagons, and gave it to her. From it she withdrew a mortar and pestle and began to grind a mixture of herbs.

One of the men brought a large bowl and poured an entire bottle of amber liquid into it. Kezia added her herbal mixture and placed the bowl before Rusty, who eagerly lapped it up.

"It will help with the fever," Kezia explained, "and dull the senses when I cut into flesh."

"I trust you," Pritchard said.

Kezia opened a leather wallet to reveal a number of wicked-looking blades and instruments. She handed them to her husband, who selected one of the larger ones and placed it into the heart of the fire's coals. Others he placed into the boiling pail of water.

Pritchard noticed a group of Romanichal men collecting the bodies of the four men Pritchard shot dead.

"Tell 'em to dig one, deep hole, at least a quarter mile from the river," Pritchard advised Manfri. "If they bury 'em too close to the water, one day the river will rise and spit 'em back up." The Romanichal chief translated Pritchard's suggestion into Romany. The men lashed the carcasses over the backs of horses, along with shovels and pickaxes.

"You have buried men before?" Manfri asked.

"Too many to count," Pritchard said, thinking of the first grave he dug, at age seventeen. It was his father's.

"I'd recommend keeping their rifles," Pritchard went on, "and making sure you're always stocked with cartridges."

Manfri again translated Pritchard's words. They gathered the four dropped Henry rifles and placed them into a wagon before leading the horses and their dead burdens off into the darkness.

"I have never seen such skill with a gun," Manfri said, "as you displayed tonight. I realize now, when you first entered our camp, you could have taken what you wanted from us had you chosen to."

"Whyever would I do a thing like that?" Pritchard said.

"You are an honorable man," Manfri said. "We have rarely encountered such men, here in America."

"Where're you folks from?"

"Originally, our people come from many places. Our particular Romanichal clan hails from Wales. We emigrated to America a year ago, to escape persecution by the English government."

"I imagine it ain't been much different here?" Pritchard said.

"Unfortunately," Manfri said, "you are correct. Two days ago, we arrived in Boonville. One of our vardos, what you call *wagons*, needed repairs we could not do ourselves. The blacksmith at the forge in town refused to do the work for us. It was only after we explained to him that unless he fixed our vardos, we could not leave, that he agreed to complete the repairs. But he charged us an exorbitant fee, and we had no choice but to pay him."

"He had no call to do that," Pritchard said.

"Perhaps not," Manfri said, "but this is how we are often treated. While we were in town, awaiting the repairs, no one would allow us to enter their shops or restaurants. The general store wouldn't even sell us salt or grain. And all the time we waited, the townsfolk insulted us and called us vile names. Children even threw rocks at us. We finally left this morning and were lucky enough to encounter a farmer who agreed to sell us a calf for an outrageously inflated price. Our children were hungry, and we had no food, so once again we were forced to pay far more than the calf was worth. It has been the same story at almost every town since we arrived. There are over thirty of us. Without food and supplies, we cannot go on."

"Where are you heading?"

"We don't really know. We are moving west, in search of a place to settle and raise our families in peace. A place where people will not fear or revile us. So far, we have found no such place."

"You don't find such a place," Pritchard said.

"You make it. But you have to be willing to fight, and even die, to make it happen. That's just how it is."

"These are wise words," Manfri said, "from one so young."

"Take a few more words of advice," Pritchard said. "From now on in your travels, you'd best keep two men with rifles on watch at each end of your caravan or camp at all times. And as much as I enjoy good music, I wouldn't be playin' it at night in unfamiliar territory. Music alerts people of ill intent to where you are, prevents you from hearin' 'em creep up on you, and sends the message that you folks don't know how to protect yourselves iffen you're playin' music at night. You ain't in Britain anymore, where you're subjects of the crown. You're free here in America and have a right to defend yourselves and your kin. But you ain't gonna get it done playin' melodies in the dark in hostile country or protecting yourselves with a rusty bird gun, an old army musket, and an ax."

"From this day forward, Samuel, we will do as you say."

"You don't have to heed my words," Pritchard said, "but I reckon you folks will stay healthier iffen you do."

"I am ready to cut now," Kezia announced. "I will need you to calm your animal."

Pritchard lay across Rusty's neck and removed

his hat to cover the Morgan's eyes. When the bullet-scar on Pritchard's forehead was revealed, all of the Romanichals exchanged awed glances.

Vano brought over the blades he'd removed from the boiling water, and Kezia selected one. Two of the men brought a large mirror from one of the wagons, and held it at an angle that both reflected, and directed, the bonfire's light onto Rusty's injured rump.

Kezia quickly and confidently sliced into the wound. Rusty tensed, but Pritchard softly began to sing a lullaby into his horse's ear. It was a tune he picked up in Texas during his years as a Ranger.

"See those tumbleweeds a-blowin. Lord, it makes me want to cry," Pritchard soothed. "It reminds me of my daddy, and that Texas lullaby."

Within seconds the bullet was out. Kezia barked an order and Vano handed his wife a bottle. While she poured liquid from the bottle over the wound, he retrieved the instrument which had been heating in the coals, using a square of leather to protect his hand. Kezia placed a similar leather pad in her hand and accepted the red-hot blade.

"Yippi yi, little dogie, roll on, roll on," Pritchard crooned, as the sound and smell of searing flesh arose. Rusty tensed again and tried to lift his head, but Pritchard pressed him down and continued to sing.

"Yippi yi, little dogie," Pritchard sang. "Yippi yi."

Kezia stood, wiping her hands. Pritchard followed. "It is done," she said. She handed Pritchard the bloody .45 caliber bullet.

"Thank you, ma'am," Pritchard said sincerely, with his hat in hand. "I'm right grateful. I'm also in your debt."

"Your horse is a magnificent animal," she said. "He is strong and will heal. But he has lost much blood. He will not be able to travel for a day, perhaps two. He needs to rest, and to eat, and to replenish what he bled out. I am sorry, but we have no grain to feed him."

"That's all right," Pritchard said. "I'll grass him tonight, iffen he can eat. Tomorrow I'll be goin' into Boonville to fetch grain and supplies." He turned to Manfri. "I'd be honored if you'd accompany me into town."

"We are not welcome in Boonville," Manfri said.

"You will be tomorrow," Pritchard corrected him. "You talk with your people and make up a shopping list. I'll see it gets filled."

"I will go with you," Manfri said.

"Have you eaten?" Kezia asked. Pritchard shook his head.

Pritchard and Manfri were served a plate of beef, and offered a seat by the fire. Rusty, exhausted and under the effects of whatever potion Kezia administered, snored contentedly. All of the children, and most of the adults, retired to their wagons and tents.

After they ate, Pritchard realized how tired he was. It had been an eventful day. His empty dish was taken, and Manfri produced a bottle of liquor from his vardo. He poured them each a generous quantity.

Pritchard found the liquor bitter, very strong, and it tasted like nothing he'd ever had before. As they drank, the handsome woman in her forties who'd initially rejected Pritchard's request for help approached and spoke into Manfri's ear.

"My wife, Sabina, is a *drabardi*," Manfri told him.

"I'm afraid I don't know that word," Pritchard said.

"A *drabardi* is a diviner. What you would call a 'fortune-teller.' She will not allow me to accompany you into town tomorrow unless she reads you first."

" 'Reads' me?" Pritchard said. "I reckon I don't understand."

"Come," Manfri said. Pritchard stood and followed Manfri and Sabina to one of the larger vardos. Inside, there was small table and two chairs.

Sabina went inside and lit a candle and motioned for Pritchard to enter. He removed his hat and stooped to fit his six-and-a-half-foot frame into the wagon. Manfri did not enter behind Pritchard, remaining outside and closing the curtain.

Sabina lit a candle. "Give me your right hand," she said in a Welsh accent.

"I didn't know you could speak English," Pritchard said.

"When I choose to." She took Pritchard's very large, callused hand and examined both sides of it. Her own hands were warm and strong.

"You were raised on the land," Sabina observed.

"My family owned a sawmill," Pritchard said. "I grew up cutting and hauling wood."

"You are a man of great strength," she said, staring at his palm as if reading words from a page. "I do not speak merely of the body. Your spirit is very strong. You possess many passions and few doubts."

She began to trace the lines in his palm with a ringed forefinger. "You are a lonely man. You have suffered much loss."

"I'm not alone in that," Pritchard said.

"Death surrounds you," she said. "It has surrounded you for a long time. It follows you like a jilted lover." One of Sabina's eyebrows raised. "You do not fear it."

"Me and death have met before," Pritchard said, tapping the scar on his forehead with his left thumb. "We have an understanding."

Sabina continued to caress and scrutinize Pritchard's right hand. "There are dark forces circling you," she said. "Those you care for believe you are running from this darkness, but you are not. You are rushing to meet it."

"Do you see anything else?" Pritchard asked.

"Yes," Sabina said. "I see deceit. This deception is patient. It lurks, waiting to ensnare you."

"How will I recognize this treachery when I see it?" Pritchard said.

"You will not," Sabina said.

CHAPTER 32

Ditch walked toward the Atherton Arms from the marshal's office. After dining with Idelle, he'd gone down to the jail to check on Tater and his prisoner, Dexter Bennington. Judge Pearson announced his trial was scheduled to begin tomorrow, and as a result, the incarcerated former Union colonel and trick shooter was in a fouler-than-usual mood.

There was still no word on when the federal marshal would arrive, but Ditch expected him any day. Until then, he, Tater, and Jack Stearns were the only town marshals and sheriff's deputies in Jackson County.

Sharing duties with Stearns wasn't something Ditch was pleased with, but could do nothing about. According to Judge Pearson, because Pritchard swore him in, Stearns had as much claim to the job as he did.

Thankfully, things had calmed down significantly in Atherton. It had been only one day since Pritchard's resignation and departure, but already the bounty killers and gunfighters had stopped arriving. Evidently, word in the bounty hunter community traveled fast.

Ditch paid several visits to the station during the afternoon to greet arriving trains. He watched as a number of shady characters wearing guns disembarked, read the announcements posted all over the depot, then turned around, reboarded, and left. He also stopped by the stage line for the arrival of the afternoon coach from Kansas City, and the same thing occurred. A pair of men wearing pistols got off, read the poster, cursed, and got back on the next stage out.

Because Idelle wasn't feeling well at dinner, which she attributed to the pregnancy, Ditch walked her to her room and then set off to check on the jail. He spent an hour drinking coffee and chatting with Tater before heading back to his own hotel room at the Atherton Arms, down the hall from Idelle's, to turn in for the night.

Ditch was just mounting the steps to the hotel when someone bumped into him. He looked up to find Bonnie Shipley.

"Pardon me," Ditch said, stepping aside and tipping his hat.

"It was my fault," Shipley said. "I'm the one who collided with you."

"No harm done," Ditch said.

He took a moment to appraise her. He had never actually been this close to Shipley before. She wasn't much older than Idelle; perhaps in her early twenties.

The young woman was also petite, like Idelle, but had dark brown hair, in contrast to his fiancée's white-blond locks, as well as a much more hourglass figure. Her brown, intelligent eyes were the focal point of a dimpled, comely face, which contained a prominent beauty mark just above her lip.

"Perhaps you'll allow me to buy you a drink in the hotel bar to make my clumsiness up to you?"

"I don't think that'd be a good idea," Ditch said.

"You don't trust me," she said, "do you?"

"I don't know you," he said. "To be honest, I ain't even sure your name is Shipley."

"It's the only name I've ever known," she said. "What's the matter, Deputy Clemson? Are you afraid to have a drink with me?"

"I'm not afraid of you," Ditch said.

"Then you're afraid to be seen with me, is that it?"

"I ain't afraid of nothin'."

"You don't need to deny it," she said. "You're engaged, and your fiancée is carrying your baby. You wouldn't want her to catch wind of you speaking with another woman, even if it was only an innocent conversation. I understand."

"How did you know about the baby?" Ditch asked.

"There are some things," Shipley said with a wink, "a girl just knows. Things men are blind to, but other women can spot a mile away."

"I guess this town doesn't hold many secrets," Ditch said, shaking his head.

"Even if you're reluctant to be seen with me,"

Shipley went on, "and too afraid to have a drink, can you at least walk a lady to her room? A gentleman, and officer of the law, can't expect a respectable woman to march unescorted through the hotel lobby with a gauntlet of drinking men only steps away at the bar."

"Where's Houseman?" Ditch said. "Or his lapdog, Stearns? Why aren't they escorting you?"

"Benedict Houseman is my attorney, not my keeper," Shipley said. "As far as Jack Stearns goes, I prefer not to be in his company. I find him distasteful."

"We share that sentiment, at least," Ditch said.

"What do you say, Deputy? Will you walk a girl home?"

"I suppose it couldn't hurt," Ditch said. "I'm goin' thataways." He gave her a stern look. "And for the record, I ain't afraid."

"If you say so," Shipley said with an impish smile.

Before he offered, she took his arm. A number of people watched as Ditch escorted her through the lobby and up the stairs, including Jack Stearns and Benedict Houseman, who were sipping whiskey together in the hotel bar.

When they got upstairs to Shipley's room on the third floor, one floor above Ditch's and Idelle's rooms, she opened the door.

"Won't you come in and join me for just one drink?" she said. "Please?"

"I'd better not," Ditch said.

"That's right," Shipley said. "I forgot about your pregnant, jealous fiancée."

"Who said Idelle was jealous?"

"She must be, for you to be so nervous," Shipley said. "For a man with a badge and a gun, you certainly are a fraidycat. What do you think I'm going to do, bite you?"

"How many times do I have to tell you?" Ditch said. "I ain't afraid."

"Maybe you'll have to show me," Shipley said. She stepped into the room, tossed her hat and purse on a chair, and lit the lamp. "I want a drink, and I hate to drink alone. What do you say, Deputy? Are you going to be a nervous Nellie and make me drink all by myself, or continue to be a gentleman and join me for a nightcap?"

"All right," Ditch relented. "Maybe just one."

"One it is," she agreed. "You can even leave the door open, if it makes you less nervous."

"I ain't nervous," Ditch insisted, "and I ain't afraid."

There was a bottle of whiskey and two coffee mugs sitting on the dressing table. Shipley poured both half-full and handed the mug closest to the edge of the table to Ditch.

"Bottom's up," she said, and slammed the entire contents of her mug down in one gulp. Ditch winced as he watched the pretty, petite, young woman down her whiskey in a single swallow.

"Your turn, Deputy," Shipley said with a laugh, "or are you too afraid to drink, too?"

"I ain't afraid," Ditch repeated. He followed her example and chugged his whiskey in one swig. Shipley laughed as he coughed and made a sour face.

"What the hell kind of whiskey was that?" Ditch asked. "It tastes like turpentine."

"Tastes just fine to me," Shipley said. "You must have a particularly delicate constitution."

"I've got no such thing," Ditch said indignantly.

Shipley poured herself another drink and extended the bottle to Ditch. He put his hand over his mug.

"I said just one, Miss Shipley," Ditch said.

"Please, call me Bonnie." She stepped in close and took his mug. "Tell me something, Deputy Clemson," she began, "did you enjoy getting Idelle pregnant?"

"Huh?" Ditch said. His jaw dropped.

"You heard me. Was it fun? Idelle is cute enough, but awfully innocent. I can't help but think she isn't much of a sporting gal when it comes to skill in the bedroom. Did she just lay back and frown at you, or is she a more spirited woman than I give her credit for?"

"That's a . . . mighty . . . rude . . . question," Ditch said, struggling to get the words out. His head suddenly felt heavy, and thick, and he blinked several times to try and focus his rapidly failing vision. He looked down at his hands, which seemed to have swollen to the size of wagon wheels, as Bonnie Shipley stepped even closer toward him.

Ditch felt her lips on his, and tried to bring his strangely enormous hands up to push her away, but they wouldn't move. Neither would his legs. The room swayed, and his field of vision narrowed to an increasingly diminishing tunnel. Without warning he found himself on the floor, looking up at the ceiling, but didn't remember falling, or even hitting the ground. That was just before everything went dark.

CHAPTER 33

It was midmorning when Pritchard rode into Boonville on the quarter horse, with Manfri, Vano, and Danior Pannell traveling in a stripped-down vardo pulled by a pair of stout draft horses. The quarter was a bit larger than average, at sixteen hands, but much smaller than Rusty, and as a result appeared somewhat undersized beneath Pritchard's gargantuan frame.

Boonville wasn't nearly as large as Atherton, and the town square was composed of only a general store, blacksmith's forge, livery, and a few shops and businesses. People in the street glared at them as they entered. Pritchard and the three Romanichals parked in front of the store.

"I'm not so sure about this," Vano said. "The people in this town do not like us."

"They made their feelings clear yesterday," Danior said, "when they told us not to come back."

"They are right, Samuel," Manfri said. "Perhaps we should try our luck at the next town?"

"Stay here," was all Pritchard said. "I'll be right back."

Pritchard tied his horse to the hitching post and entered the general store. Behind the counter was a small, bespectacled man in his forties, who first looked inquisitively at Pritchard as he came in, then craned his neck to look past him at the trio seated out front in the wagon. When he saw Manfri, Vano, and Danior Pannell, his expression changed from curiosity to scorn.

"Can I help you?" the proprietor asked.

"I'd like to get this order filled," Pritchard said, handing over the shopping list. The shopkeeper examined it.

"Twenty bags of grain, ten bags of flour, ten pounds of salt, ten pounds of coffee," he began to read aloud. He stopped reading halfway through the list and looked up at Pritchard.

"How're you going to carry all this freight on one horse?" he asked.

"I ain't," Pritchard corrected, pointing to the vardo outside. "It's goin' into that wagon."

"No, it isn't," the proprietor said.

"Are you tellin' me you don't have these supplies in stock?" Pritchard asked.

"No," the proprietor said, "I have everything on this list in my inventory. I'm telling you I don't sell to their kind. They were told that yesterday, when they came riding into town with the rest of their unholy, Gypsy filth. Trying again today, with a big saddle tramp wearing two pistols to buy their groceries for them, doesn't intimidate me and doesn't change a thing."

"That ain't very neighborly of you," Pritchard said. "It's also insultin'."

"They're not my neighbors," the proprietor said smugly, "and I don't care whether you're insulted or not. I'd thank you to leave my store, except I'm not going to thank you for anything. Get out."

"You're an audacious little feller," Pritchard said, "I'll give you that. But for an unarmed gent to talk like you do, to an armed stranger, doesn't speak too complimentary of your brains."

"Joyce," the shopkeeper said to a woman across the room. "Go to the smith's and fetch Michael." The woman wordlessly disappeared through the back of the store.

"I've got cash money," Pritchard said, "and I'm here to conduct honest business. And you want to throw me out of your store?"

"That is correct," the proprietor said. "I'll tell you again; get out."

"Or what?"

"What?"

"You heard me," Pritchard said. "Are you gonna evict me? Because, little brother, iffen you are, you'd best get help. There ain't enough of you standin' there to do it."

The other patrons in the store had already stopped their shopping to observe the exchange between Pritchard and the proprietor. They now moved back, and one woman gathered her two children and scurried out.

"I don't take guff from range drifters in my store," the proprietor said.

"Who's givin' who guff?" Pritchard replied. "I only want to conduct a lawful transaction."

"You aren't going to conduct it here," he said. "Your size, and those pistols, don't scare me." His hand suddenly darted under the counter.

Pritchard reached out with his right hand and grabbed the shopkeeper by the throat. With his left he intercepted the Beaumont-Adams revolver as it emerged from under the counter. Like Pritchard's Remingtons, it had been converted from cap-and-ball to fire metallic cartridges. He bent back the hand holding the pistol, and the proprietor shrieked in pain. Then Pritchard snatched the gun from the proprietor's hand and shoved him roughly away.

The proprietor watched in fury as Pritchard took out the center pin, removed the cylinder, dumped the cartridges onto the floor, and then tossed the weapon's disassembled components into a nearby flour barrel.

"You just pulled a gun on me," Pritchard said. "By all rights, I could have shot you dead. Evidently, I'm in a good mood today. Fill my order, and it'll stay that way."

"I will not," the proprietor said, rubbing his throat.

"Then I'll help myself," Pritchard said. He picked up a burlap bag from a stack near the flour bin and began to scoop.

A man walked into the store from the back room with Joyce behind him.

"Michael," the proprietor said to him, pointing at Pritchard. "This man came into town with those damned Gypsies and assaulted me."

The man who entered was very big. He was an inch shorter than Pritchard's six-foot-six, but at least fifty pounds heavier, and not much of his bulk was fat. He was in his thirties, balding, had a full beard, and wore a leather apron over his barrel chest. His bare arms were as thick as most men's legs.

"Did you assault my friend?" Michael said.

"Nope," Pritchard said, still scooping flour. "I did him a favor."

"A favor?"

"Yep," Pritchard said. "He pulled a gun on me. That wasn't very courteous. I, however, was courteous. I let him keep the rest of his life."

"You're a brave man," Michael said in a very deep voice, "wearing those guns."

"I'm the same man in my birthday suit," Pritchard said.

"Prove it."

Pritchard sighed, took off his hat, and unbuckled his guns. "What a feller has to go through to get a few sundries in this town would try Job's patience," he said. He set his pistols and hat on the counter.

"If you touch those," Pritchard said to the proprietor, "or any other weapon, I will kill you." He faced the blacksmith. "Do your best, smithy. But know this is a fight I don't want."

"What you want," Michael said, removing his apron, "and what you get, Gypsy lover, are two different things."

"I'll remember you said that," Pritchard said.

Once he removed his apron, Michael ducked his head and charged at Pritchard like a bull. Pritchard sidestepped him, and as the lumbering blacksmith stumbled past he made a mental note not to underestimate the man's speed, despite his vast size.

What Michael the blacksmith didn't know, was that as a teenager Pritchard was the bare-knuckle champion of Jackson County, Missouri. By virtue of the large physique he inherited from his father, plus a youth spent doing intense physical labor at his family's sawmill, he'd developed great strength. But from his petite and graceful mother, Dovie, he inherited economy of movement and uncannily quick reflexes. These qualities, coupled with his years of daily pistol practice, were the genesis of not only his remarkable gun-handling skill, but uncommon ability in unarmed combat, as well.

Michael charged again. This time, instead of sidestepping, which he figured wouldn't work twice, Pritchard dropped and rolled. The blacksmith tripped over him, and his forward momentum sent him tumbling headlong into a wall display, collapsing the shelves and sending an entire rack of canned goods and preserve jars crashing to the ground.

Michael got up, red-faced and furious. He shook off the fruit and vegetable residue covering him and faced Pritchard again.

"You sure you want to keep doin' this?" Pritchard asked.

In response, Michael roared and lunged again. Pritchard parried the beefy, outstretched, arms and landed a three-punch combination consisting of a hook, straight punch, and uppercut. The blacksmith fell back on his heels, his nose and mouth bloodied, and tried to brace himself by grabbing a standing shelf in the middle of the store. Like the wall shelf, this display also collapsed under the weight of over three hundred pounds of thrashing man. Both plunged to the floor.

"Hey," the proprietor complained, "take it easy, Michael, will you? You're tearing up my store."

Michael again got up, more slowly this time, and gave the storekeeper a sideways look as he wiped his bloody face on the back of one fore-arm. His chest was heaving, and his eyes blazed.

"I ain't even breathin' hard yet," Pritchard said. "Give it up. It ain't gonna end how you think."

"Go to hell," Michael said, spitting blood. "I'm going to break your back."

"Listen here," Pritchard said, his voice

hardening. "I'm done playin' games. I showed courtesy to your friend by not endin' him when he pulled on me, and I've given you two free shots at knockin' me out. I'm fresh out of charity. You'll not get a third pass at me. Call it a day."

"I'll call it a day," Michael said, his voice dripping with rage, "when you're busted in half and spend the rest of your days a cripple." He charged Pritchard once more, this time with his fists clenched.

Pritchard bent down, picked up a jumbo-sized can of tomatoes, and hurled it with all his might directly at Michael's face. The heavy tin can collided with the blacksmith's forehead. Instantly knocked unconscious, the giant man fell forward on his face and landed with a *thud* that resonated throughout the store's wooden floor. Once he landed, he didn't move.

Pritchard and Ditch, like so many other American boys raised along the Missouri and countless other rivers, lakes, and ponds, spent an incalculable number of their childhood hours chucking rocks. Consequently, Pritchard's accuracy with the hurled can was only slightly less acute than with aimed bullets fired from his revolvers.

So when Pritchard suddenly picked up a smaller container of tinned beef and slung it at the proprietor, whose fingers were starting to wrap themselves around the butt of one of his

Colt revolvers holstered on the counter, it was no surprise that he scored another bull's-eye.

The tin of beef struck the proprietor directly in the chin. His head rocked back, his glasses flew off, and he fell to his rear end behind the counter.

Pritchard walked over to the counter, put on his hat, and began belting on his pistols. "I believe I told you," he said to the seated shopkeeper, "if you went for a weapon, I would kill you?"

"Do you have any idea how much paperwork I'd have to do iffen you killed him, Samuel?" a voice behind him said.

Pritchard turned around to find a tall, heavyset man in his fifties, with a pleasant face and muttonchop whiskers. He was wearing a badge and a holstered Navy Colt revolver, and grinning with his hands on his hips.

"Howdy, Bob," Pritchard said.

"Been a long time." They shook hands.

"Surely has," Pritchard said. "How's Etta?"

"She and the kids are fine," the marshal said. "Thanks for askin'."

"You know this man?" the proprietor said.

"I do," the marshal said. "What happened here?"

"I'll tell you what happened," the store proprietor said as he stood up. He was holding his apron to his bloody chin. "This man came into my store, assaulted me, tore the place up, and attacked Michael! He's knocked out cold on the floor! This fellow's a menace, and he needs to be locked up! He also needs to pay for the damages to my merchandise and my store!"

"Is that what happened?" the marshal asked Pritchard.

"Not exactly," Pritchard said.

The marshal rubbed his chin and looked around at the carnage within the store. "I think I've got a pretty good idea of what transpired here today. I happen to know Dustin, Boonville's illustrious general storekeeper, and Michael, our town's resident blacksmith and local bully, fairly well."

"I'm not sure I like your tone, Marshal Blevins," Dustin said.

"Shut up," the marshal said. He turned to Pritchard. "I'd wager Dustin insulted you and your friends outside and tried to run you out of his store. When you wouldn't be buffaloed, he sent for his friend Michael next door, a feller who never needs a reason to push someone around." He shook his head. "It looks like they both bit off more'n they could chew this time. Tell me, Samuel, did Dustin try to pull that British horse pistol he keeps under the counter on you?"

"It's in the flour bin," Pritchard said. "In pieces."

"I figured as much," the marshal said.

"Who is this man?" Dustin said. On the floor, Michael began to groan.

"Samuel Pritchard," Marshal Blevins said.

"You might have heard of him when he went by the name Joe Atherton. Until recently, he was Atherton's town marshal."

"You heard about my resignation?" Pritchard said.

"Word gets around," Blevins said. "I know all about the bounty, too. Hell, it's all over the territory. I also heard tell of all the pistol fighters Atherton's been attractin' lately. In your shoes, I'd have turned in my badge, same as you. Wouldn't want my hometown turned into a shootin' gallery on my account."

"That's what I reckoned," Pritchard said.

"This man is Joe Atherton?" Dustin said incredulously. "Smokin' Joe Atherton?"

"In the flesh," Marshal Blevins said. "Did you think he got that scar on his forehead pickin' apples?"

Dustin's face turned white. "I pulled on Smokin' Joe Atherton?"

"You're a darned fool," Blevins said to the proprietor, "and you're lucky you ain't shot full of holes."

"I go by my given name, now," Pritchard said to Dustin. "I don't use Atherton no more."

"I'm sorry for the misunderstanding," Dustin said. "If I'd have known—"

"A man in your position should treat all folks square," Marshal Blevins cut him off, "whether they're famous gunmen or not. I was off in the county chasin' a rustler yesterday, but when I got back I heard about what you and Michael done to those travelers who came into town. Leavin' folks with kids to starve out on the prairie on account of your hateful ways ain't Christian, Dustin. What you got today is proof the good Lord is payin' attention. You sell these men what they came for, and don't jack up the price, neither. You hear?"

"Yes, Marshal," Dustin said. He picked up the list Pritchard left on the counter and retreated to the back room.

"And you," Marshal Blevins nudged the groggy blacksmith on the floor with his boot, "get your oversized carcass up, get on back to your forge, and learn somethin' from this."

CHAPTER 34

Ditch groaned and slowly sat up. His vision was blurred, and his skull felt like he'd been kicked between the eyes by a government mule. It was almost a full minute before he was able to shake the cobwebs from his head and get his bearings.

"Good morning, Deputy Clemson," a voice said. "I trust you are enjoying the accommodations as well as I am?"

Ditch looked over to find the voice belonged to Colonel Dexter Bennington. Bennington was speaking from the cell adjacent to the one Ditch currently occupied.

To his alarm, Ditch found himself seated on a bunk in a cell in Atherton's town jail. The cell door was locked. If this inexplicable predicament wasn't enough for him to swallow, he also found himself wearing only his longhandle underwear and socks. Other than Bennington, there was no one else in the marshal's office.

Ditch stood up on shaky legs and rubbed his head. He recoiled in pain when he found a gash in the back of his head, which seemed to have been stitched.

"What the hell am I doin' in jail?" he asked.

"When a man wakes up where you did and asks that question," Bennington said with a mirthless chuckle, "it usually means he had quite an evening the night before."

"When did I get here?"

"You were carried in a little after midnight," Bennington said, "much to my chagrin, by Deputies Jessup and Stearns. Dr. Mauldin arrived a short time later to treat your head wound and ensure that I got absolutely no sleep whatsoever."

"I don't understand," Ditch said truthfully. "I don't remember any of that. How could this happen?"

"I'm sure your bartender knows the answer to those questions," Bennington snickered.

The door to the marshal's office opened and Tater Jessup, Judge Eugene Pearson, Benedict Houseman, and Jack Stearns entered. Tater and Stearns were each carrying a tray of food.

"Tater," Ditch said. "Let me out of this cage!"

"I'm afraid that's not possible," Stearns said.

"I'm sorry, Ditch," Tater said. "I wish I could let you out. I surely do."

"Why am I locked up?" Ditch said.

"You don't know?" Houseman asked.

"Of course I don't know," Ditch said.

"What's the last thing you remember?" Judge Pearson asked.

"I remember Miss Shipley insisting I walk her up to her room. Then I remember she kept prodding me to come inside and have a drink with her. I didn't want to, on account of how it

266

might look, but she kept wheedlin' me. She called me a fraidycat, and a nervous Nellie, and told me I was too scared of what Idelle would think."

"So you went into her room and had a drink with her?" Houseman asked.

"I did," Ditch said sheepishly. "I guess I didn't like being called a fraidycat and wanted to prove I wasn't."

"Then what happened?" Judge Pearson asked.

"That's the trouble," Ditch said. "I can't remember nothin' after that."

"Convenient," Houseman said to the others, "how his lapse of memory begins just before the assault."

"Assault?" Ditch said. "What assault?"

"See what I mean?" Houseman said.

"Will somebody please tell me what the hell is goin' on?" Ditch said.

"Last evening," Judge Pearson began, "several residents of the Atherton Arms heard a woman's screams emanating from Miss Shipley's room. Deputy Stearns happened to be in the lobby—"

"—I saw him, along with Mr. Houseman," Ditch added, "on the way up."

"—and went upstairs to investigate," Pearson continued. "Perhaps you should tell the rest of the story, Deputy Stearns, since you were there."

Stearns was leaning against the wall with his thumbs in his gun belt, a toothpick between his teeth, and a bored expression on his face.

"I found the door to Miss Shipley's room locked," he said, "and her screaming like a banshee inside. I busted it open, and found you, Deputy Clemson, in your underwear. You had her backed into one corner of the room. Her dress was torn half-off, and she was hysterical. When I tried to pull you off her, you attacked me. I had to crack you over the noggin with my pistol. But then, you know all of this already, don't you? You were there, same as I was."

"That ain't what happened," Ditch said.

"How would you know?" Houseman asked. "You can't remember, remember?"

"I know I didn't assault Miss Shipley," Ditch said. "That's a stone fact."

"She says different," Stearns said. "So do I. And so does her torn dress."

"If Bonnie Shipley's lyin' about who she really is," Ditch said, "which she is, she ain't gonna have no reservations lyin' about me attackin' her."

"Then how do you explain what Deputy Stearns saw?" Houseman asked.

Ditch looked directly at Stearns. "He's lyin', too. They set me up, the three of 'em, and I was lunkheaded enough to walk into their trap. They were all in it together, with that oily sidewinder Houseman the varmint who probably thought up the scheme."

Stearns spit out his toothpick and pushed

himself off the wall. "So, Clemson," he said, "you're calling me a liar?"

"Looks that way," Ditch said, "don't it?"

"You're lucky you're unarmed and locked in that cell," he said.

"Those're two things that can be remedied," Ditch said. "Tater, open this door and get me my gun."

"I'm afraid that isn't possible," Judge Pearson said, repeating Stearns's words. "Miss Shipley has sworn out charges against you, Ditch. For assault and attempted rape. Deputy Stearns has signed a witness statement. You're going to have to be held for trial, like anybody else."

"You don't believe her, do you, Judge?" Ditch said. "Or these other two lyin' skunks? The three of them are so crooked they could eat nails and spit out corkscrews!"

"It doesn't matter what I believe," Judge Pearson said. "Two citizens have sworn out statements of charges against you, and one of them is a deputy town marshal. I have no choice but to go forward with a trial."

"What about lettin' me out on bail until the trial?"

"I would object to granting bail," Houseman said. "Mr. Clemson is well known in these parts as not only a cattleman of great wealth, but a former Confederate guerilla. Given the seriousness of the charges he's facing, and his potential for being sentenced to the penitentiary, I believe he has both the motive and means to flee the jurisdiction and never return. And I'm not even going to mention his other potential motive for fleeing Missouri."

"What motive would that be?" Judge Pearson asked.

"Since you ask," Houseman said, "it is common knowledge there is a young, unmarried woman in town who is carrying Mr. Clemson's child. He wouldn't be the first man to shirk such responsibility."

"You son of a bitch!" Ditch howled. He attempted to grab the attorney, but was prevented from reaching him by the cell's bars. "I'll wring your fat neck! When I'm done with you, Houseman, there won't be enough left of you to snore!"

"This must be the side of Deputy Clemson Miss Shipley met last night," Houseman said, stepping back.

CHAPTER 35

"If you follow the Missouri River west," Pritchard said to Manfri, "about one hundred miles, you'll run into a town called Atherton. My little sister, Idelle, is the mayor. It's a decent, peaceable place surrounded by good land where folks with families who're willing to work are welcomed. Tell 'em Samuel Pritchard sent you."

"I cannot thank you enough for all you've done for us," Manfri said, shaking Pritchard's hand.

After Dustin filled the Romanichal's list of sundries, Pritchard paid the banged-up shop-keeper for all the supplies. To the shopping list, he added four boxes of .44 rimfire cartridges for the four Henry rifles now in the clan's possession. He also paid another ten dollars for the damages to the store and inventory. When Manfri objected and tried to pay Pritchard from the group's collective fund of eighty dollars, he just shook his head.

"Keep your cash," Pritchard told the chief. "You'll need it for seed money when you get settled. You took me in and treated Rusty's injury. I don't forget such kindness."

"We, too," Manfri said, "will not forget."

After the Romanichals left, Pritchard bought a few supplies for himself. He was loading them into his saddlebags on the quarter horse when Marshal Blevins approached.

"Iffen you don't mind me askin'," Blevins said, "where're you headed?"

"Going down to Saint Louis," Pritchard said, "with a stop in Jefferson City."

"Business?"

"Got somethin' needs doin'," Pritchard said, "though I wouldn't call it strictly business."

"Fair enough," Blevins said. "You plan on takin' the next train?"

"Nope," Pritchard said. "Tried that, and it went poorly. Which reminds me, a few miles east of here you'll find a few stray horses and a handful of carcasses in city duds that were once employees of the Quincy Detective Agency."

"Cottonmouth's boys, eh? I'm a-guessin' you had something to do with them becomin' buzzard bait?"

"I did," Pritchard said, "though I might deny it if formally asked. They waylaid me on the train out of Atherton."

"I heard about a train robbery on the line from Kansas City," Blevins said. "The telegrapher told me one of the robbers was shot dead where they stopped the train, and the other five highwaymen got away."

"It weren't no robbery," Pritchard said. "They stopped the train on account of me and that infernal bounty. I dropped the one feller there, to get the others to chase me away from the train so's no innocent folks would get shot up."

"And then you got 'em one by one, Apache style, as they chased after you?" Blevins said, grinning. "That was usin' what's under your Stetson."

"Only way I reckoned to play the hand," Pritchard said.

"I'll send some boys out to fetch 'em later," Marshal Blevins said. "We'll give 'em the burial they deserve in a hog waller somewhere."

"I'm obliged," Pritchard said.

"Don't be," Blevins said. "Pinkerton's boys ain't exactly popular in these parts, but Cottonmouth Quincy's hired guns make the Pinkerton men seem as likable as pigtailed schoolgirls in pinafore skirts. Most of them Quincy detectives are back-shootin' dry-gulchers who ain't worth the powder and ball it'd take to put 'em down."

"If the ones I met are representative of the rest of Quincy's detectives," Pritchard said, mounting the quarter and taking Rusty's reins, "I'd have to agree."

"You watch out for yourself," Blevins called after him. "You've got dollar signs on your back. Best keep an eye open, your powder dry, and your cannons handy."

"Way ahead of you," Pritchard said as they shook hands.

He rode north through Boonville to the

273

steamboat docks on the Missouri River. Jefferson City was seventy miles away by boat, which meant at least a fifteen-hour trip. He'd already tried traveling by train and found that experience wanting, so he figured he might give voyaging by steamboat a try. Rusty seemed to be getting around fine, but he didn't want to ride him, or even walk him too much, until he had his strength back.

Pritchard found two boats waiting at the docks. He bought a ticket to Jefferson City on the only one leaving that day, a three-decker paddle steamer named the *Nellie Cropp*. He boarded with Rusty and the quarter, whom he stabled in the shipboard livery, and headed for his room with his rifle and saddlebags over his shoulder. Cast-off was less than an hour away.

The boat was crowded with people, and he kept a wary eye as his friend Marshal Blevins had cautioned. He noticed a number of gamblers and people who looked to be of significant financial means, as well as more than what he expected in the way of sporting gals. It was of concern because Pritchard, who already stood out due to his height, was dressed in a manner that brought more than a few derisive glances among the more fashionably attired passengers.

"What's everybody all gussied up for?" Pritchard asked a steward, as he elbowed his way through the throng of boarding passengers.

"Ain't you heard?" the steward said. "There's

a high-stakes poker tournament gonna be held on the Texas Deck tonight. They say the pot's over fifty thousand dollars. Every card-skinner from here to Ohio is on board."

Pritchard got to his room, but not before he sent the steward to the galley to fetch a roast beef sandwich and a bottle of milk. He posted a chair under the tiny cabin's doorknob, ate, and took a much-needed nap.

Pritchard awoke several hours later to a knock on his door. It was late afternoon, and he answered the door with one of his Colts behind his back. A different steward delivered an envelope, which was addressed to Joseph Atherton.

Once the steward left, Pritchard opened it. Inside was a note written in the same flowery hand the letter was addressed. It read:

Dear Mister Atherton,

As this correspondence clearly illustrates, there are persons aboard the Nellie Cropp who are aware of both your presence on the vessel and the financial remuneration which awaits the individual who removes you from this mortal coil. You are advised to exercise great caution in what you eat or drink, and all due vigilance in your interactions with fellow passengers for the duration of your voyage.

A Concerned Friend

Pritchard was disappointed, but not surprised, that bounty killers were aware he was on the boat. If Rusty hadn't been injured, he'd be riding the backroads to Jefferson City and taking his time doing it. Regardless of who penned the note, he figured the advice its author proffered was worthy of consideration.

He made sure the chair was reinserted under the knob on his cabin door, then got busy. Pritchard cleaned his revolvers, one at a time, to ensure he always had a loaded weapon ready. Then he got to work on his Winchester, which had seen some use in the past few days. He kept a gun-cleaning kit, including a full-length rifle cleaning rod that could be disassembled into three pieces, in his saddlebags.

Once his guns were cleaned, he unloaded the revolvers, but not the Winchester, and spent a half hour practicing his drawing, aiming, and firing. Then he reloaded his pistols, restocked the cartridge loops on his belt, and washed up. Pritchard was just putting on a clean, button-front shirt when another knock on the door sounded.

This time, before opening the cabin door, Pritchard belted on his guns. Stepping as far to one side of the door as his large frame would allow in the small cabin, he drew his right-hand Colt, dislodged the chair from underneath the knob with the toe of his boot, and said, "Come on in."

As the door opened, Pritchard brought his revolver up and thumbed back the hammer. He centered the weapon's front sight in the middle of the doorframe.

When the door fully opened, Pritchard was greeted by a feminine gasp.

The person staring into the barrel of his Colt .45 was Eudora Chilton.

CHAPTER 36

Pritchard pulled Eudora into his cabin as he holstered his gun. "What in the hell are you doin' here?" he asked her.

"I thought you'd be glad to see me," Eudora said with a wounded expression.

"I ain't," he said. "This is no time to be seen in my company."

"I'd hoped you'd be pleasantly surprised," she said, taken aback by Pritchard's apparent lack of enthusiasm at finding her at his door.

Pritchard wedged the chair back under the cabin door, then turned and took Eudora by the shoulders. "I'm certainly surprised," he said, "and I'm always glad to see you. But in light of my present circumstances, I'll have to set those feelings aside."

"What circumstances?"

"Eudora," Pritchard began, "one of the reasons I left Atherton was so innocent folks wouldn't get shot to pieces in my vicinity when bounty hunters come a-callin'. If you haven't figured it out already, I like you a helluva lot more than most folks. Which means I'd like to see you get shot even less."

"That's a comfort," Eudora said. "By the way you greeted me just now, one would think I had a case of the pox."

"It ain't about likin', or not likin', you," Pritchard went on. "It's about you not catchin' a bullet. The only reason I'm on this boat is because I can't travel by rail. Some fellers already tried to cash in my chips on the train ride out of Atherton."

"Who were these men?" Eudora asked, her face alighting with concern. "Who sent them? Are you okay?"

"I'm fine," Pritchard said, "but Rusty took a bullet meant for me. I aim to see you don't suffer the same fate. Where is your cabin located?"

"It's on the other side of the boat," she said. She displayed her mischievous smile. "But I was hoping to stay with you in your cabin for the duration of the voyage to Saint Louis."

"Out of the question," Pritchard said. "You're going back to your room right away, and you'll stay clear of me for the remainder of the trip. I'm gettin' off this tub when it docks in Jefferson City tomorrow, and so are you."

"Why are you getting off in Jefferson City?"

"I've got business there," Pritchard said. "You don't. You're going to catch the next train back to Atherton. Anyhow, don't you have a business to open back there?"

"I did," Eudora said, "but my liquor shipment from Kansas City got bought out from under me. I was outbid by a Kansas saloonkeeper who was willing to pay three times what I was. Apparently,

Lawrence is expecting an army of thirsty drovers any day now. It'll be another few days, maybe even a week or more, before I can get my hands on enough whiskey to open up the Sidewinder."

"I'm sorry to hear it," Pritchard said, "but you've got to leave. Every minute you're in my company increases your chances of gettin' hurt, and I simply won't have it."

"You sure you won't risk having me around for just a little while?" Eudora asked, unbuttoning the top of her dress. "You're well armed, there's a chair under the door, and I doubt anyone's going to get the jump on you in here." She shrugged out of her dress and stood naked before him in only her boots, gloves, and hat. "Anyone but me, that is."

"Lord," Pritchard said to himself as he unbuckled his guns, "have mercy."

It was after dark by the time Pritchard pushed Eudora out of his cabin and sent her on her way. He was careful to peek through the cracked door before making her depart, and allowed her to kiss him only after ensuring the passageway was clear of passengers and no one saw them together.

Before she left, Pritchard elicited a promise from Eudora to remain in her cabin until the steamboat's arrival in Jefferson City. She reluctantly agreed to dine and breakfast alone in her room. If by some chance she did come out and encounter Pritchard, she was to act as if they were strangers and stay as far away from him as possible.

As soon as Eudora was out of sight, Pritchard put on his guns and hat and left his cabin. His intention was to first go to the livery section and check on Rusty and the quarter being stabled there, and then go to the upper deck and observe the gambling. He knew it was a long shot, but hoped he might recognize someone in the crowd or otherwise get an inkling of who had written the warning note delivered to his cabin.

To get below, to the livery, Pritchard had to first go up one flight, traverse a long passageway to a main stairwell, and then go down again two flights to the lowest deck. It was during the dinner hour, and he surmised most of the passengers were either dining, in their rooms, or up on the Texas Deck gambling.

Pritchard ducked his head as he ascended a narrow set of stairs to the deck above his cabin and began making his way to the main stairwell, which connected all the decks. He looked out across the Missouri and saw the bright moon reflecting on the brown water as the *Nellie Cropp* churned its way slowly downriver.

A young couple stepped into the passageway ahead of him, emerging from the main stairwell. The male half was a dapper fellow about Pritchard's age, with a pretty young woman several years his junior on his arm. She carried her purse in both hands, and the couple looked up at the towering Pritchard in greeting.

"Pardon me," the man said, holding up an unlit cigar with the hand not attached to the young woman's elbow. "You wouldn't happen to have a match, would you?"

"I believe I do," Pritchard said. He stopped, tipped his hat to the lady, and began to reach into his hip pocket for his box of matches. He stopped when she withdrew a Whitney .32 caliber revolver from her purse and pointed it at his face. The hammer was back, and her delicate, gloved, finger was on the trigger.

"You even twitch," the woman said, "and I'll send you straight to hell."

"How ladylike," Pritchard said.

"We got him!" the young man yelled over his shoulder. He produced a revolver of his own from under his coat and pointed it at Pritchard. His gun was a nickel-plated Remington New Model Pocket revolver, also in .32 caliber.

Another man, who'd obviously been waiting out of sight below the horizon of the stairwell, suddenly appeared from behind the couple. This fellow was older, and somewhat larger, than his younger companions, though not nearly as big as Pritchard. He also wore a fancy suit and was armed with a Colt revolver with the standard, seven-and-a-half-inch barrel.

"Go diggin' for your pistols," the man said around his mustache, "and you'll be diggin' your grave." Like the other fellow, he aimed his cocked revolver at Pritchard's belly. "You're worth the same dead as alive, Atherton, and a lot less trouble dead."

"Then why don't we just shoot him," the woman said, "and be done with it?"

"Shut up, Rowena," the big man said. "I don't take orders from no woman."

"She's got a point," the young man said. "He's supposed to be faster than a buttered bullet. Whyn't we finish him now, and spare ourselves any grief?"

"I'm givin' the orders," the big man said. "You want to carry a man that big all the way down to our cabin, go ahead and shoot. Me, I'd rather herd him." To Pritchard, he said, "Unbuckle that pistol belt and hand them guns over to Dan. The instant your fingers do anything but unhitch that buckle, you get three in the guts. *Comprende*?"

Pritchard nodded and slowly unbuckled his gun belt. He handed his pistols to the younger man, who reached out gingerly and took them with his gun held steadily at Pritchard's middle.

"Gimme your hat, too," the big man said. Pritchard removed his Stetson, and this time the woman took it and passed it behind her. "Damn," Rowena said, motioning to Pritchard's forehead with her gun barrel. "Look at that scar. It's just like they say. He's been headshot."

The big man took off his bowler and tossed it over the side of the railing, where it fluttered down into the muddy Missouri and disappeared. Then he put on Pritchard's Stetson and grinned.

"He ain't so tough now, is he?" he said, pointing his gun at Pritchard. "Not without his guns. Like a defanged rattler, that's how tough. All rattle and no bite." He adjusted his new hat on his head with the hand not holding his gun. "How do I look," he chuckled, "wearin' Smokin' Joe Atherton's hat?"

When Rowena turned her head slightly to respond to the big man's query about his appearance, Pritchard charged. Using the speed and dexterity that earned him his reputation as the deadliest gun on the frontier, he snatched Rowena's gun hand and shoved her violently sideways into Dan, who was standing next to her in the cramped passageway.

Rowena's gun went off, the bullet flying harmlessly out across the water. Dan's gun discharged as Rowena crashed into him. Since she'd been thrust between his gun and Pritchard, Dan's .32 caliber bullet entered her breastbone, the muzzle blast scorching a hole in her dress.

Pritchard continued his charge. With all his might he pushed the falling Rowena, and the off-balance Dan, backward into the big gunman. All three tumbled down the stairs.

Pritchard started to go down after them, to try and retrieve one of his revolvers, but stopped when he heard the screams. He looked to his rear and saw a woman and two small children frozen in terror behind him in the narrow hallway.

When he turned his attention back to the stairwell, Pritchard found the big gunman and his younger partner, Dan, had recovered. They were stumbling over Rowena's body and scrambling up the stairs with fury on their faces and their revolvers in their hands.

Pritchard couldn't retreat, as the terrified woman and her two hysterical children blocked the constricted passageway to his rear. Charging unarmed at the two pistol-wielding men rushing up the stairs at him was certain death. Remaining where he was standing was also out of the question. Not only was he a sitting duck, but the woman and her children were in the line of fire directly behind him.

There was only one option left. Just as Dan and his partner crested the stairs and leveled their revolvers at him, Pritchard vaulted the *Nellie Cropp*'s railing and jumped overboard.

CHAPTER 37

"Did she say why she won't come and visit me?" Ditch asked.

"Idelle didn't tell me her reasons for not comin' over to the jail," Tater said, "and I didn't ask. She is the mayor, after all. I reckon she can do what she wants."

Ditch sent Tater to the Atherton Arms that morning to obtain a fresh set of clothes and to ask Idelle to come and see him. The dutiful deputy returned a half hour later with breakfast and Ditch's clothes, but without Idelle.

The day passed. Lunch, and then dinner, was served by Tater, and still Idelle hadn't come. Not long after dark, Ditch asked Tater once again to go see if Idelle would come to the jail.

"To be perfectly honest with you," Tater said, "I got the impression Miss Idelle was pretty steamed up. Last time I went to ask if she'd come to see you, she practically slammed the door in my face."

"I wonder," Colonel Dexter Bennington taunted from the cell adjacent to Ditch's, "whatever would make a woman behave so uncordially? Maybe it has something to do with her fiancé getting caught, minus his britches, consorting with another woman in her hotel room?"

"You'd best keep your lip buttoned," Ditch said to Bennington. "You've got no call to be interjecting yourself into my personal life."

"How can I avoid it?" Bennington said. "Your sordid plight kept me awake all last night. The entire sleazy affair unfolded before me, much to the detriment of my health and slumber, when you were carried in. Quite frankly, it is my opinion that Atherton's pretty young mayor could do far better than the likes of you, Mr. Clemson. You're nothing but a squalid cowpuncher, no matter how much money you have."

"Sooner or later," Ditch said, gripping the bars and gritting his teeth, "you and me are gonna be gettin' out of these cells. When we do, I'm gonna move your ivories to the other side of your head."

"Unlikely," Bennington said. "Didn't you hear? I'll be leaving Atherton soon. Sooner than you, anyway."

"Where're you goin'?"

"The Missouri State Penitentiary," Bennington said. "My trial, if you could call it that, was yesterday. I was sentenced to ten years' hard labor. I'll be departing as soon as a federal marshal arrives to escort me to Jefferson City."

"Ten years," Ditch whistled. "That'll put a wet blanket on your campfire."

"Indeed," Bennington said. "Evidently the Honorable Judge Pearson held me responsible, and not you, your fellow deputy, or your friend

Marshal Pritchard, for the untimely deaths of the two gentlemen who accompanied me to Atherton on the train from Kansas City."

"I recollect your stiff sentence might've had something to do with you bringin' in them seven gun hands to kill Marshal Pritchard," Tater offered.

"I do recall the judge mentioning something to that effect," Bennington reluctantly agreed.

"I can't say I'm heartbroken over your new address," Ditch said. "I've got a feelin' a scalawag like you is gonna feel right at home in the stony lonesome."

"I wouldn't become too gleeful at my predicament, if I were you," Bennington said. "Your own trial is coming up. Last I heard, they don't exactly sentence rapists to short stints in the hoosegow. If I were a betting man, I'd wager you won't be far behind me on the road to Jefferson City."

The truth in Bennington's words choked off Ditch's retort. He brooded in glum silence for the next hour, until the door opened and Idelle Pritchard walked in.

"Idelle!" Ditch declared, rising from his bunk.

"I'd like a word with your prisoner," Idelle said to Tater, ignoring Ditch's greeting.

"Which one?" Tater said.

She narrowed her eyes angrily at him. "Mr. Clemson, of course."

"Help yourself," Tater said. She approached his cell.

"It's good to see you," Ditch said. "How are you?"

"I didn't come to exchange pleasantries," Idelle said coldly. "I came to tell you I spoke with Judge Pearson and the town council."

"What'd they have to say?"

"Judge Pearson told me he's going to delay your trial until he can get the federal marshal here. With my brother resigned and gone, and you . . . in here, that leaves Jack Stearns and Tater Jessup as the only law. Judge Pearson is uncomfortable with that arrangement, given Houseman's and Stearns's obvious intention to take over Atherton and Jackson County."

"I would be uncomfortable in his shoes, too," Ditch said. "What did the town council have to say?"

"As you can imagine," she said matter-of-factly, "your bid for mayor is now out of the question."

"How's that?" Ditch said. "I ain't been convicted of anything, only accused. A feller's supposed to be innocent until proven guilty in this country. Somebody ought to tell that to the town council."

"That may be true," Idelle said, "but given your current predicament, the council feels it best you withdraw your candidacy for mayor. They

289

believe, after what happened last night, you're unfit for public office. They've asked me to obtain your formal withdrawal from the mayor's race. They've also asked me to remain in office and run for mayor in your place."

"I won't withdraw," Ditch said. "I ain't gonna let Houseman take over Atherton and pilfer all we've worked for, fought for, and bled for. Not no way, not no how. Who do those councilmen think they are, declaring me unfit? I wasn't unfit last summer, when me and your brother stood alone and shot it out with more'n a dozen hired guns while they hid under their kitchen tables."

"Where was that concern for the town's welfare last night," Idelle said, "when you were alone with Bonnie Shipley in her hotel room?"

"That ain't fair," Ditch said, "and you know it."

"Fair to whom?" she said bitterly. "Fair to me? To our unborn child?" She closed her eyes and shook her head. "How could you be such a fool, Ditch?"

"Don't tell me you actually believe I tried to have my way with that prairie witch masquerading as Shipley's daughter?" he asked.

"I don't know what to believe," Idelle said.

"I'm innocent," Ditch insisted. "I was set up. That's the honest truth."

"Whether I believe you or not," she said, opening her eyes again and taking in a deep breath, "doesn't matter. What matters is that

290

because of your poor judgment I'm on my own. Samuel's gone, you're locked up, the election's only a few weeks away, and Benedict Houseman and Bonnie Shipley are fast on the way to taking everything we have."

"Hold on," Ditch said. He reached through the bars and took her by the arm. "It does matter what you believe. I have to know, Idelle. Do you believe I'm innocent, or not? I need to hear you say it."

"What do you care what I believe?"

"I care," Ditch said. "You know I care more about what you think than any person in this world. Do you believe me, or not?"

"I guess I'll have to wait for your trial, like everybody else."

Ditch released her arm. His shoulders slumped, and he returned to his bunk.

"What shall I tell the council?" Idelle asked.

"Tell 'em to go to hell," Ditch said, staring at the ground. "Tell 'em Ditch Clemson doesn't quit without a fight. Tell 'em I'm still runnin' for mayor."

"Very well," Idelle said coldly. She turned on her heels and walked out of the marshal's office.

Ditch sat dejectedly on his bunk and removed one of his boots.

"I told you she was steamed," Tater said.

Colonel Dexter Bennington walked up to the bars separating his and Ditch's cells and put his face through them as far as he could. An ear-to-ear grin spread across his features.

"Looks like you've got as many troubles in your love life as you do on your legal front," he said with a chuckle. "From what I just heard, I doubt your fiancée will be coming to visit you in the penitentiary. Who knows? Maybe she'll visit me?"

Quick as a flash, Ditch threw his boot with perfect accuracy and all his might. The boot sailed between the bars, and the heel caught Bennington squarely on the forehead.

The colonel's laughter was instantly cut short. He was knocked senseless, though not unconscious, and tumbled backward to land on his butt on his cell's floor.

"I can't believe you didn't see that comin'," Tater said to the stunned Bennington.

Idelle tried to hide her tears as she walked away from the marshal's office, but more than a few of the pedestrians she passed noticed the mayor crying into her handkerchief. Seeing Ditch locked up, despite her displeasure with the lack of judgment he displayed in getting himself into such a fix, tore at her heart.

"May I be of service, Mayor Pritchard?"

Idelle looked up to find Jack Stearns blocking her path on the sidewalk.

"What do you want?" she demanded.

"I couldn't help notice," he said, tipping his

hat, "that you appear to be in some distress. Is there anything I can do?"

"I'm fine," Idelle said, wiping her tears and putting away her handkerchief. "There is nothing you have, Deputy Stearns, that I want."

"Then allow me to escort you back to the hotel," he said. "It's late, it's dark, and it's never safe for a woman to walk alone at night." An insolent smile cracked his lips. "I'm sure Mr. Clemson would agree with me."

"You stay the hell away from me, Jack Stearns," Idelle said. "I don't like you, and I'm plenty capable of taking care of myself without your help."

"I'm certain of that," Stearns said with a smirk. "Especially since I know all about how you skull-shot a deputy named Eli Gaines here in town last summer. Heard tell how you pulled out a Jim Fisk pistol and blew his brains all over Main Street."

"You mean this pistol?" Idelle said, as she smoothly drew her gun from within her skirt. It was indeed the same four-shot, .41 caliber Colt Cloverleaf she'd used to end corrupt Chief Deputy Eli Gaines during the Battle of Atherton, as the locals had since named it. She cocked the weapon's hammer and held it steadily on Stearns's midsection.

"I see your brother isn't the only Pritchard who's handy with a gun," he said.

"No," she replied, "he is not. Now, if you'll excuse me, I'd like to be on my way."

Stearns stepped aside, and once more tipped his hat. Idelle lowered her pistol's hammer, replaced the gun in her skirt, and strode off.

Benedict Houseman approached Stearns from across the street. "What was that all about?" he asked.

"Nothing of consequence," Stearns said.

"Nothing of consequence?" Houseman argued. "I just watched Mayor Pritchard pull a gun on you!"

"Idelle Pritchard is a lot of woman," Stearns said. "She's young, and comely, which tends to make folks underestimate her grit. She's made of hard stuff, Benedict." He looked down at Houseman. "Harder stuff than you're made of, that's for sure."

"Don't get too sweet on her," Houseman said. "With her brother gone, she's the only thing standing between us and a fortune."

"Her brother said he'd be back," Stearns said. "Or did you forget?"

"I didn't forget," Houseman said. "That's what I'm paying you for."

CHAPTER 38

Pritchard dragged himself to the river's bank, struggling to keep his balance on the muddy shore. Off in the distance, he could see the lights of the *Nellie Cropp* as it continued its leisurely journey downriver.

When he hit the water, he deliberately remained under it. He knew if he surfaced the two gunmen on deck wouldn't pass up the chance to take pistol shots at him. With a nearly full moon overhead, he'd be a floating duck.

He swam as fast and as far as he could beneath the surface, to get clear of both the boat's large paddle wheel and its choppy wake. By the time Pritchard came up for air, the steamboat was fifty yards away and he was halfway to the eastern bank.

Like most kids raised on the Missouri River, Pritchard had grown up swimming in its dark waters. He had a healthy respect for the river's potential to maim and kill anyone foolish enough to attempt a crosscurrent swim, even someone as strong and experienced as he was. This was especially true in the spring, when the rains raised the frigid water levels and exponentially increased the strength of the current. But he knew the instant he jumped off the *Nellie Cropp* that the Missouri River would be much more kind to him than the two gunmen aboard the riverboat.

Pritchard caught his breath and clambered up the grade through the woods. He knew if he continued east he'd hit a main road. Sure enough, within minutes of clearing the woodline, he found himself on a well-worn coach trail.

He began walking south, paralleling the river. He guessed it was nearly eight o'clock, by the height of the moon above the horizon. Though he shivered, it was a warm night. Pritchard knew it wasn't unheard of to get snow in late April, and he was grateful for the unseasonably mild weather.

He'd gone less than a mile when he heard the rumble of hoofbeats behind him. Pritchard turned to find a pair of riders approaching. He waved them down.

"Hello," Pritchard said as the riders came to a halt. It was two young men, one in his late teens, the other a bit older. Both were mounted on fine, healthy-looking horses. The older rider pulled a Sharps rifle from his saddle scabbard and readied it across his lap.

"What can we do for you, mister?" the older rider said.

"My name's Samuel Pritchard," he said. "As you can see, I've run into a bit of bad luck."

"My name's Mark," the older rider said. "This here is my brother Luke. What troubles you?"

"I was on a riverboat and fell off. I just now swam to shore."

"Was you drunk?" Luke asked.

"Nope," Pritchard said. "Actually, I didn't fall. I jumped."

"Why would you do a darned fool thing like that?" Mark asked.

"Truth be told," Pritchard said, "a couple of fellers were fixin' to shoot me."

"You look awful familiar to me," Mark said. "I'm almost sure I've seen you before somewheres. Do I know you?"

"I don't believe we've met."

He snapped his fingers. "I know where I saw you! When I was ten years old, my pa took me and Luke to the Jackson County Fair to sell our hogs. There was this great, big, blond feller in a ring takin' on all comers in wrastlin'! You were that feller! I'll never forget you! They called you the Two-Fisted Tornado!"

"You've got a good memory," Pritchard said. "It's been eleven years since I've heard that name."

"If I remember right, nobody could beat you. Pa won twenty dollars over a two-dollar bet that you'd go undefeated, and you did."

"I have a proposition for you," Pritchard said, "if you'd like to make some more money off me?"

"What's the proposition?" Mark said.

In reply, Pritchard sat down and took off one of his boots. His boots, like his gun belt and holsters, had been custom-made in Texas before he returned to Missouri last year. Inside each boot, in a special pocket he had put in the lining, he kept one thousand dollars in one-hundred-dollar notes.

"I'd like to buy your horse," Pritchard said.

"Bingo ain't for sale," Mark said. "He's one of the fastest nags in these parts. I've been offered good money for him before, and I declined. I'm sorry, Mr. Pritchard, but it's no deal."

"How about letting me rent him?" Pritchard said.

"Huh?"

"You heard me. A good horse like your Bingo is worth at least two hundred dollars. I'll give you five hundred dollars if you let me borrow him from you."

"Five hundred dollars!" Mark and Luke looked at each other in amazement.

"I'm in a hurry, boys. I'm trying to catch a riverboat, and every minute we stand here negotiating it gets farther downriver. I'll give you five hundred dollars," he held up the notes in the moonlight, "to let me borrow your horse for a couple of hours. I'll run him a few miles south, until I get ahead of that boat, and tie him off to a tree near the riverbank where you can easily find him."

"Five hundred dollars is a powerful lot of money," Mark said. "How do I know you won't run off with my horse?"

"Because I give you my word," Pritchard said.

"Okay," Mark said, after a moment's reflection. "You've got a deal." He dismounted and handed Pritchard the reins.

"You sure about this?" Luke said to his brother. "You lose Bingo, Pa will murder us both."

"You ain't gonna lose your horse," Pritchard said, handing over the money. "Follow along behind me, and you'll soon enough find him on the river. He'll be tuckered, but he'll be there."

Pritchard mounted Bingo, a sixteen-hand buckskin, and took off south at a trot. As soon as he got a feel for the horse, he sped him up to a canter.

Pritchard guessed the road generally paralleled the river, but without the bends and curves of the river itself. He estimated the speed of the *Nellie Cropp* at well under five miles per hour, especially navigating the river at night, and knew a horse as strong as the one he was riding could easily double that rate without much difficulty.

Pritchard kept the buckskin at a canter for ten or fifteen minutes, and then slowed to a trot. After maintaining a trot for approximately the same time period, he again nudged the horse to a canter. He repeated this alternating cycle several times, knowing from his days as a Texas Ranger that a good horse, and Bingo was certainly a good horse, could keep up such a pace without difficulty for a long time. Had he run the mount full out, the animal would make a mile or two at best under Pritchard's significant weight before tiring.

Not more than an hour after beginning his ride, Pritchard spotted the lights of the *Nellie Cropp* up ahead on the river.

"Okay, Bingo," Pritchard said, "let's see what you've got left."

Pritchard reined the horse to a gallop, and off Bingo went. It was almost as if the big buckskin knew his journey was coming to its conclusion and wanted to show off what Mark had said about his speed and strength. He broke the gallop without Pritchard's urging and went into a full sprint.

Pritchard and Bingo passed the boat and continued on another quarter mile south. Then he reined Bingo to a halt and walked him to the water's edge. As the horse drank, Pritchard took another five hundred dollars from his boot, lashed it to the pommel, and tied the horse off to the branch of a big oak.

"I'm much obliged, Bingo," Pritchard said, patting the horse's neck. "You are indeed one fine animal."

Helping himself to the rope from Bingo's saddle, Pritchard waded into the chilly water.

Using a powerful breaststroke, he swam out to the center of the Missouri River.

The huge mass of the *Nellie Cropp* was headed straight for him, but fortunately at a clip not much faster than the existing current. That was the smart way for a riverboat captain to keep his ship from colliding with a log or other obstacle beneath the surface. Pritchard met the front of the boat with one hand and allowed himself to drift along the port side, hugging the hull.

The lip of the lower deck was only a couple of feet above him, and Pritchard realized he didn't need the rope. Discarding it, he reached his long arms up, grasped the edge, and pulled himself over the rail and onto the deck.

A number of passengers lounging on the deck stared in amazement as he boarded the riverboat. Pritchard didn't have a hat to tip, so he merely nodded, smiled, and headed for the nearest stairwell.

Ignoring even more curious glances as he navigated through the passageways, the dripping-wet Pritchard was soon at his room. On entering, he was relieved to find no one else had entered since he'd gone overboard.

Pritchard wasted no time. He lodged the chair under the door and retrieved his saddlebags. Inside, wrapped in an oiled cloth, were his pair of Remington New Model Army .44 conversions. The pistols had served him well during his years as a Texas Ranger. Until he'd obtained his custom-barreled Colt Single Action Army revolvers last summer, they were the guns he'd trusted with his life.

Pritchard checked the guns, then loaded them with six rounds each. Then he stripped off his wet clothes and donned a fresh pair of socks, dungarees, and button-front shirt. His trousers, belt, and boots were still damp, but there was no remedying that.

He took a moment to eat some jerky and then downed a quick shot of bourbon from the flask in his bags. Both rejuvenated him. His two nocturnal swims across the Missouri River had taken some of the starch out of him, and the food and liquor brought a little back.

Stuffing his Remingtons into his belt, and a handful of spare .44 cartridges into his hip pockets, Pritchard removed the chair from the door, exited his room, and went in search of the two men who'd tried to kill him.

CHAPTER 39

It didn't take Pritchard long to locate one of the gunmen. After leaving his room he went directly to the Texas Deck, where the poker tournament was being held. The deck was crowded, with the majority of people standing around those seated at the gambling tables.

Most of the spectators were well-dressed men and women of the moneyed class, but Pritchard saw more than a few men he could safely call professional gamblers, grifters, and gunfighters. He also saw a fair measure of ladies of the evening.

On the other side of the deck, surrounded by several eager-looking men, was Eudora Chilton. She was clad in one of her usual cleavage-enhancing gowns and looked positively stunning. It was almost impossible not to notice her.

Their eyes met, but Eudora quickly looked away. Though she'd evidently forgotten her promise to remain in her cabin, she remembered Pritchard's admonition about pretending not to know each other.

Across the room, Pritchard recognized his Stetson. It was on the head of the larger of the two gunmen who'd accosted him earlier. The man was seated at a card table in the center of the deck. His back was toward him, and he could see the big fellow was also wearing his gun belt, holsters, and dual Colt .45s.

Pritchard took a moment to adjust the Remingtons in his belt, then strode over to the table. He came around in a wide circle and stopped when he was directly opposite the man wearing his hat. He glared down at him.

All the people at the table looked up at the very large blond man with the scar on his forehead looming above them. When the gambler wearing Pritchard's hat looked up, his eyes widened, and his jaw went slack, in recognition.

"This hand is over," Pritchard said to the other gamblers at the table, as he stared straight at the big gunman. "Get clear."

It was obvious what was about to transpire. Everyone at the table immediately got up, left their cards and chips, and hastened away. The entire deck went silent. All eyes were instantly riveted on the two men, one standing and one seated, in the center of the room.

"That's my hat," Pritchard said, "and those're my guns."

"Is that so?" the man said.

"That's a fact," Pritchard said. "You can hand them over, real slow and cautious, and live, or you can keep 'em, and die. Choice is yours."

The big gunman, whose hands were still above the table, looked nervously around at the faces in the crowd. "I've never seen this man before in my life," he said, dropping his cards and slowly inching his hands toward the edge of the table.

"He's lying," Pritchard announced loudly. "He met me earlier tonight, when he and his two partners, a man and a woman, robbed me and forced me overboard."

"I saw him," a woman said, pointing to Pritchard, "go over the side." He recognized her as the woman with the two children who were behind him in the passageway. "He's telling the truth. There were men holding guns on him, and shots were fired. I reported the incident to the captain."

"I've seen him before," a man spoke up. "Less than an hour ago, I watched that fellow climb into the boat from the river. Saw it with my own two eyes."

"I saw him, too," another man piped in. "Walking the decks all wet."

"If you voluntarily return my property," Pritchard said to the seated man, "maybe I'll go easy on you. Iffen you don't, you and me are crossin' swords. That's all there is to it."

"This is ridiculous," the big man harrumphed. "This man is obviously mistaken, or drunk." He folded his arms across his chest, as a slight grin cracked Pritchard's face.

Pritchard hadn't forgotten the big man held a Cavalry Colt revolver on him earlier. The weapon was undoubtedly under his suit in a shoulder rig. He realized the man wearing his Stetson and gun belt had no intention of reaching for either of the pistols at his waist.

"What's it gonna be?" Pritchard said. "Turn over my property, or eat lead? I'm a-waitin'."

"Eat this," the man snarled, leaping to his feet.

Pritchard let him get the long-barreled Colt almost all the way out from under his arm, just to make it plain to all the onlookers his adversary drew first. Then, almost quicker than the eye could follow, his pair of Remingtons were out and leveled with the hammers back.

The big man wearing Pritchard's hat froze with his hand on his revolver and the barrel not even clear of his coat.

"Go on ahead," Pritchard smiled. "Finish your pull."

"You've got me cold," the man said, shaking his head. "If I do, you'll kill me."

"You might as well," Pritchard said. "I'm likely going to end you on general principle."

"Nope," the man said. He opened his hand, and his gun fell to the floor. He removed Pritchard's Stetson, placed it on the table, then unbuckled Pritchard's guns and set them alongside the hat.

"Shoot me if you want to, Atherton," he challenged, "but if you do, you're shooting an unarmed man."

"That's Smokin' Joe Atherton!" someone in the crowd declared. "The famous Texas man-killer!" Gasps and murmurs rumbled across the deck.

The crowd watched in rapt interest as Pritchard lowered the Remingtons' hammers and set the guns carefully on the table. Then he buckled on his gun belt, checking each gun to ensure they were still in the same loaded and unfired condition as when they'd been taken from him earlier. He stuffed the Remingtons back into his belt and then made an elaborate gesture of returning his Stetson to his head.

"What's your name?" Pritchard asked.

"Charlie Tolson," the man said.

"Where's the woman your partner shot? Rowena?"

"She expired," Tolson said. "We tossed her over the side." The crowd gasped again. Several men cursed.

"Where's your partner, Dan?"

"In room number twenty-two," Tolson said, "crying into his whiskey. He was sweet on Rowena."

"You got anything else to say?" Pritchard asked.

"Nope. And only one regret. When you jumped off the boat, I'm sorry to say, we watched ten thousand dollars float away. Other than that, Joe Atherton, you can go to hell."

Pritchard stepped around the table to within arm's length of Tolson. As he did, he glanced across the deck. Eudora was gone.

"You gonna shoot me now?" Tolson asked.

"Nope," Pritchard said as he sent his left fist,

and then his right, crashing into Tolson's jaw. The big gunman staggered backward and fell to the ground, unconscious. Pritchard picked him up by the lapels and sat him in his chair.

"Are you really Smokin' Joe Atherton?" someone asked, as Pritchard rifled his pockets.

"Not anymore," Pritchard said.

In Tolson's pockets he found a wad of cash, some poker chips, and a watch. In his cuffs he found several face cards. He tossed all the items on the card table. The men who'd been playing poker with him before Pritchard interrupted their game shook their heads and swore.

Pritchard found nothing that would verify the man's identity. He picked up a drink from the card table and threw it into Tolson's face. The big man moaned, and his head rolled from side to side.

"Wake up, Charlie," Pritchard said. He slapped him across the cheek several times until he fully woke up.

"You're not lookin' so good," Pritchard told him, "but you're in luck. I know just the thing to get you back into the peak of health." He dragged Tolson to his feet.

"What's that?" Tolson asked.

"A swim," Pritchard said. People parted before him as he dragged the struggling man across the deck to the rail.

"Don't," Tolson begged. "I can't swim."

"Next time you set out to kill a man," Pritchard

said as he launched him over the railing, "you'd best finish the job." Tolson screamed all the way down into the dark waters of the Missouri River. Once he went in, he didn't come back up.

Pritchard walked away as the mob of onlookers rushed past him to the railing. He strode down the stairs, to the deck below, where the second-floor cabins were located.

When he got to room twenty-two, he drew his right-hand gun. Standing to the side of the door, in case a bullet came through it, he called out, "Hello in there, Dan. It's the feller you and Charlie tried to waylay tonight. Got a few questions I need to ask you. Come on out, with your hands empty, and I won't have to come in and get you."

There was no response from inside the room. Pritchard tried the knob and found it unlocked. He turned the handle, pushed open the door, and rushed inside.

As soon as he opened the door, Pritchard could smell the burnt gunpowder. He could also survey the entire small cabin, identical in configuration to his own, in one glance.

Dan was lying faceup on the floor. He was fully dressed and had a small, charred hole in his cheek. Both eyes were wide-open and unseeing.

Pritchard holstered his gun, knelt, and put a hand to Dan's face. He was as warm as Pritchard was. Whoever shot him hadn't done it more than a few minutes ago.

CHAPTER 40

The *Nellie Cropp* pulled into Jefferson City well before dawn, but most passengers chose not to disembark until first light. Pritchard spent the night dozing in his room with a chair under the door and his Colts on the bed.

He'd given his boots and belt, after removing the other thousand dollars within the boot's lining, to a steward. For a dollar the steward took the wet leather items to the steamboat's boiler room and dried them out, then waxed and polished them. Two hours later the boots and belt were returned, shiny as new. Pritchard gladly tipped him an extra two dollars.

He rose before sunrise, packed his saddlebags, washed, dressed, and departed his cabin. Pritchard kept his Winchester in his left hand, and his right hand free, as he navigated the boat's passageways to the livery.

Last night on the Texas Deck, he noticed a number of professional gunmen types mixed in with the gamblers, sporting ladies, and spectators. Once the crowd discovered, during his confrontation with bounty hunter Charlie Tolson, that Pritchard was Smokin' Joe Atherton, he had no doubt there were others aboard who were licking their chops over the ten-thousand-dollar price on his head.

When Pritchard arrived at the livery deck, Rusty seemed his old self. Other than the fresh scar on his rump, the big Morgan displayed no discernible ill effects of his bullet wound. The quarter horse looked well cared for, too. Pritchard paid the livery attendant, saddled the quarter, put his Winchester in the scabbard, and led both horses down the livestock plank to the river dock.

Pritchard had no sooner left the dock, and was leading his two horses over the main thoroughfare toward town, when he heard his former alias being called out.

"Joe Atherton!"

Pritchard turned to find a man standing ten paces behind him with a double-barreled shotgun. The weapon was shouldered and pointed directly at him. He wore a straw hat and crème-colored suit, and the shotgun looked out of place for a person in his citified spring attire.

"Hey, Atherton!" another man's voice shouted. Pritchard turned back around and found another man pointing a handgun at him from the opposite direction. This man was also wearing a town suit, but topped it with a western hat. The two gunmen had him in a cross fire. Pritchard knew he could get one, but not both. The men holding the guns knew it, too. He released the horses, who continued walking.

"Hey, Clem," the man with the shotgun shouted

past Pritchard to his partner, "we're about to get ten thousand dollars richer!"

"We surely are," the other gunman agreed. Pedestrians all around Pritchard scattered in panic.

Suddenly a shot rang out. The pistoleer's head spouted a geyser of blood. He dropped his gun and fell to the street.

Pritchard wasted no time. He ducked, pivoted, drew, and fired, all at the same time. The man with the shotgun reflexively fired his weapon as Pritchard's .45 caliber bullet entered his skull. The load of buckshot sailed harmlessly over Pritchard's head and out across the Missouri River.

Pritchard stood, drew his left-hand Colt, and began to scan the vicinity for the origin of the shot that had saved his life.

A man stepped out from the shadows of an alley between two buildings. He was holding a nickel-plated Chamelot-Delvigne revolver, which was still smoking. Pritchard couldn't believe his eyes when he recognized the familiar silhouette.

"Count Strobl?" Pritchard said. "Is that you?"

"Good morning, Marshal Pritchard," Strobl said, approaching Pritchard. He wore his elegant half cape, jodhpurs, and hat, but was without his sword-cane. "Count Florian Strobl," he said, "at your service." As he spoke he bowed slightly and clicked his heels.

"Well, butter my butt and call me a biscuit,"

Pritchard said, lowering his gun's hammers and tilting back his hat with one of the Colt's barrels. "You're the last feller I expected to pull my bacon out of the fire."

"I told you I was indebted to you," Strobl said loftily, as he returned his pistol to the shoulder holster beneath his coat. Pritchard noticed another Model 1873 French Army revolver in a similar holster under his opposite arm. "A Strobl always pays his debts."

Pritchard holstered his own guns and stuck out his hand. "I'm mighty grateful," he said, "and now indebted to you."

"Nonsense," Strobl said, shaking Pritchard's hand. "We are friends now, and friends do not fret over such trivialities."

"You sent me that note aboard ship, didn't you?"

"Guilty as charged," Strobl said. "I overheard men at the card tables discussing the price on your head. I thought you should know."

"I didn't know you were a gambler," Pritchard said.

"Alas," Strobl said, "I am not. I lost every penny I had. I was forced to sell all of my luggage and personal effects to pay for my steamboat ticket. Even my sword-cane."

"All right, you two," a man's voice commanded, "put your hands up. Reach for those guns and we'll drop you."

Pritchard and Strobl looked up to find themselves surrounded by four men with pistols pointed at them. All wore badges on their chests identifying them as Jefferson City town marshals.

Pritchard raised his hands, and Strobl followed suit. "You're both under arrest," the oldest of the marshals announced. The others removed Pritchard's and Strobl's guns.

"What're the charges?" Pritchard asked.

"Those two dead men at your feet say it's murder," the marshal answered.

"It was self-defense," Pritchard said. "Those two were lyin' in wait to put the drop on me. If my friend here hadn't dealt himself in, I'd be the dead man."

"If it's like you say," the marshal said, "then you've got a case for self-defense. If not, you'll swing."

"This is ridiculous," Strobl said. "This man is a lawman, too. His name is Marshal Pritchard. He was once known as Joe Atherton."

"You're Atherton?" one of the other marshals asked.

"I don't use that name anymore," Pritchard said. "I go by my given name."

"Take off your hat," the senior marshal ordered. Pritchard complied.

"Look at that scar," another of the marshals whistled. "It looks like a bullet went straight through his noggin."

"You're Atherton, all right," the senior marshal said, holstering his gun. "We know all about the bounty on you. Got a telegram a couple of days ago that would back up your self-defense claim and explain why these two fools tried to bushwhack you."

"I resigned as town marshal," Pritchard explained. "My bein' in Atherton was drawing bounty killers like flies to a Fourth of July picnic. The town was turning into a shootin' gallery."

"Give 'em back their guns, boys," the marshal said. "The governor is expectin' you, Mr. Pritchard. Told us to see if we couldn't find you, and steer you his way. We knew you didn't come on the train, because we already checked. That's why we're here at the dock." He nudged one of the dead men at his feet with the toe of his boot. "Looks like these fellers found you first, to their detriment. Consider yourselves un-arrested."

"Thank you," Pritchard said. "I was just on my way to see the governor, on Judge Eugene Pearson's behalf."

"My men will clean up here," the marshal said. "I'll escort you to the governor's mansion."

"Can my partner come along?" Pritchard said.

"Partner?" Strobl said.

"You got anything better to do?" Pritchard asked him.

"I am currently destitute, unemployed, and without prospects," Strobl said in his Austrian accent. "I don't even have a horse to convey myself upon."

Pritchard handed the quarter horse's reins to Strobl. "You've got one now," he said. "C'mon along, Florian; what've you got to lose?"

CHAPTER 41

Pritchard and Count Strobl were led by the marshal to a livery stable near the governor's mansion. Pritchard paid for the horses' boarding and asked the attendant where he could buy a saddle. He was directed to a leathersmith's shop a block away.

The marshal then escorted them across town to Madison Street, to the new governor's mansion. It was an impressive, three-story affair on an expansive lawn within sight of the statehouse. The marshal knocked on the door and introduced Pritchard and Strobl.

"Governor Woodson's expectin 'em," the marshal said. Then he shook Pritchard's hand and made his departure.

A butler took their hats and led them through the house to a sitting area. He disappeared, leaving them to admire the paintings, and returned a moment later. "The governor will see you now."

Pritchard and Count Strobl were once more led into a large, impressive room where two men were seated across an imposing desk.

"You must be Pritchard," the taller of the men said, as he stood and shook Pritchard's hand. He was clean-shaven and had a prominent forehead and stern face. "I'm Silas Woodson." He motioned to the man with him. The other fellow was of medium height, with a mustache and graying hair. "This is Henry Ewing, Missouri's attorney general." Pritchard shook his hand, and introduced Count Strobl.

"Judge Pearson sends his regards," Pritchard said.

"Gene's a damn good man," Woodson said as they all took their seats. "Did he tell you why I wanted to see you?"

"He did not," Pritchard said, "but I reckoned it had something to do with the troubles we've been experiencing in Atherton of late, on account of a fellow named Benedict Houseman. Judge Pearson told me he'd wired you all about it."

"He did indeed," Woodson said. "And you are correct. My reason for wanting to speak with you is because of Benedict Houseman."

"I'm a-listenin'," Pritchard said.

"Until recently," Woodson began, "Benedict Houseman had a probate law practice in Chicago. He'd been fleecing people in Illinois for years out of their inheritances with sketchy legal challenges, usually based on the sudden emergence of hitherto-never-before-heard-from relatives."

"Sounds like what he's doing in Atherton," Pritchard said. "He came out of nowhere, nominated himself for mayor, and filed a claim against my sister's property and inheritance on behalf of a woman he says is the rightful daughter of Burnell Shipley."

"We're aware of Houseman's legal claim against your family," Attorney General Ewing said. "He filed it here in Jefferson City."

"I remember the Shipley affair," Governor Woodson said, shaking his head. "The town of Atherton, and especially your family, suffered terribly under that evil man."

"But you corrected that," Ewing said. "And all of Missouri breathed a sigh of relief when you brought Shipley, and his whole gang of corrupt lawmen, to justice."

"Nobody was happier than me to see Shipley get his," Pritchard said, tapping the scar on his forehead for emphasis.

"Despite the unseemly nature of his law practice," Woodson went on, "Houseman was always smart enough to keep his practice within legal boundaries, if just barely. Until a couple of years ago, that is."

"After a succession of courtroom setbacks and failed financial ventures, including significant gambling expenses," Ewing explained, "Houseman found himself broke and deeply in debt. That's when we believe he switched from being merely an unethical lawyer to a murderous one."

"What did he do?" Pritchard said.

"Some of the defendants he was suing on

behalf of his plaintiffs began ending up dead, to his and his clients' benefit. One defendant was supposedly thrown from a horse, and another was shot during a robbery. And then there was the Gerdemen fire."

"The Gerdemen fire?"

"The Gerdemens," Ewing said, "were a Chicago family about to inherit a fortune in land and mining interests from their parents' estate. Houseman showed up, as you can imagine, with a supposed long-lost, illegitimate son he claimed was sired by the deceased patriarch."

"That sounds a lot like what Houseman is claiming against us in Atherton," Pritchard said, "with a gal he's trying to pass off as Shipley's illegitimate daughter."

"Just when the court was about to deny Houseman's client's questionable claim," Ewing said, "the Gerdemens' house mysteriously caught fire. The mother, father, a servant, and their four small children perished in the blaze."

"Four kids?" Pritchard said. "That filthy bastard."

"Most foul," Strobl agreed. "Most foul, indeed."

"I couldn't agree more," Governor Woodson said.

"Unfortunately," Ewing said, "we could never pin the fire on Houseman. The court, however, denied his claim. Not only did Houseman lose his legal challenge, as a result of the loss, he descended even deeper into debt."

"Seven people murdered," Pritchard said, "and Houseman got nothin' out of it. I suppose there's some justice in that."

"Benedict Houseman had no choice but to flee Chicago," Woodson said, "to escape his debtors and those who might seek revenge for his misdeeds in Illinois."

"After receiving Judge Pearson's telegram," Ewing said, "and learning Houseman was in Atherton, we believe it likely he met Burnell Shipley in Saint Louis, probably at a gambling hall. Upon learning of Shipley's death, Houseman couldn't resist the opportunity to go back to his old tricks at your family's, and the town of Atherton's, expense."

"With what I already know about Benedict Houseman," Pritchard said, "and after what you just told me, I'd have to agree."

"I have a proposition for you," Woodson said. "We are aware of the extraordinary work you did as a lawman for the Republic of Texas, the New Mexico and Arizona Territories, and here in Missouri. The governor of Illinois, John Beveridge, has asked me to do what I can to bring Benedict Houseman to justice, given he's now a resident of our state. You can only imagine how outraged the good people of Illinois are that Benedict Houseman still breathes air as a free man."

"I am prepared to appoint you federal marshal," Ewing said, "and task you with the investigation of Benedict Houseman and his alleged criminal activities, both in the state of Missouri and elsewhere. We want Houseman brought to justice, and we will pay you top wages to see it done. Will you take on the task, Mr. Pritchard?"

Pritchard stood up. "First off," he said, "my friends call me Samuel. Secondly, you don't have to pay me a plugged nickel. Iffen Benedict Houseman is responsible for the deaths of women and children, it'll be my duty, and honor, to hound him to the hell he deserves."

Governor Woodson and Attorney General Ewing stood up, nodded to each other in satisfaction, and shook Pritchard's hand again.

"Judge Pearson told us we couldn't find a tougher, and more honest, lawman for this job," Ewing said. "I understand now why he said it."

"If you don't mind," Pritchard said, "I have one request."

"Just name it," Woodson said. "Anything you need to get the job done is yours."

"Do I have the authority to swear in a deputy?"

CHAPTER 42

"You're the first person I ever saw," Pritchard remarked, "who ate a chicken leg with a knife and fork."

"And you, unfortunately," Strobl countered, "are not the first person I have seen eating an entire chicken without one. While a guest in Atherton's jail, I routinely witnessed Deputy Jessup digest any number of things, in my estimation, which required the use of utensils. I once watched him consume an entire bowl of soup while a perfectly serviceable spoon lay untouched nearby."

"Tater's a feller," Pritchard said, "who always figured the shortest distance between victuals and his gullet was a straight line. He wouldn't be one to bother with a silverware detour unless he had to."

Pritchard and Count Strobl were having supper together in the dining car on the train to Saint Louis.

After departing the governor's mansion wearing badges identifying them as federal marshals, Pritchard and Strobl retrieved Rusty and the quarter horse and made their way to a saddlery shop. There Pritchard bought a saddle for Strobl. The Austrian selected one of minimalist design.

"That ain't much of a saddle," Pritchard chided, as Strobl cinched it on the quarter horse.

"I have noticed in America," Strobl said, "that saddles seem less suited for equestrian pursuits and more suited for carrying ridiculous amounts of weapons and baggage."

"When you're livin' out of a saddle," Pritchard said, "you need one sturdy enough to haul not just your carcass, but your necessities."

"Nonsense," Strobl said. "Carrying necessities is what servants are for."

"I don't remember having any servants," Pritchard laughed. "Not when fightin' a war, nor while rangerin'."

"That is the problem with you Americans," Strobl said loftily. "You don't know how to properly wage a gentleman's war."

"You're right about that," Pritchard conceded. "I guess I never figured war as proper, nor anyone tryin' to kill me as a gentleman."

"What is this horse's name?" Strobl asked as he mounted the quarter. "He is a fine animal."

"I don't rightly know," Pritchard admitted. "I killed the feller ridin' him before he could tell me."

"I shall call him Schatz," Strobl announced. "It is a term of endearment."

"Schatz it is," Pritchard said.

The saddlery was also a general leather shop, which meant in addition to saddles and tack the workers made shoes, boots, belts, holsters, and other items. Using the custom shoulder holsters Count Strobl was wearing as a guide, Pritchard had a double shoulder rig, fitted to his jumbo-sized frame, made for his pair of 1863 Remington New Model Army revolvers.

Pritchard paid extra for the holsters to be constructed immediately. Then he and Strobl rode across town to the railroad station, where he bought two tickets, along with livery berth for two horses, to Saint Louis on the afternoon train.

It was the first time since Rusty had been shot that Pritchard had ridden him, and he wanted to take it easy on the big Morgan. Rusty, however, seemed no worse for the incident, and almost jubilant to have Pritchard aboard again.

After they bought their train tickets, Pritchard and Strobl found a café, ate a quick lunch, and headed back to the saddlery shop, where his shoulder holsters were just being finished. Pritchard tried them on and inserted his Remingtons.

"This may take some gettin' used to," Pritchard said, shrugging his shoulders.

"While no man can dispute your skill with belt guns," Strobl told Pritchard, "wearing your pistols underneath a garment has its benefits. While your draw with shoulder holsters may not be as rapid as with belt holsters, with practice it can become very fast. Being discreetly armed prevents others from becoming offended by the open wearing of guns, and protects your weapons from the elements in inclement weather. Most importantly, having your revolvers hidden can lull an adversary into believing you are unarmed, which can be a significant tactical advantage in martial affairs."

"You seem to know a lot about this stuff," Pritchard said.

"Like you," Strobl said, "I have been a student of the pistol for a long time."

Pritchard tucked his new shoulder holsters back into his saddlebags along with his Remingtons, paid the proprietor of the leather shop, and he and Count Strobl returned to the station and boarded the train. It was an eight-hour journey to Saint Louis, and they expected to arrive not long after nightfall.

Pritchard's reservations about traveling by train were diminished somewhat by having Strobl accompanying him, especially in light of the count's saving his life. But the primary reason Pritchard elected to travel by rail was for expediency. Learning of the suspicious deaths of those opposing Houseman in his past scurrilous probate disputes from Governor Woodson and Attorney General Ewing spurred Pritchard to reach Saint Louis as fast as possible. Regardless of the heightened risk of being accosted by bounty killers on the train, or at a railroad station,

Pritchard was more determined than ever to finish his inquiry quickly and return to Atherton with all due haste.

After dinner Pritchard and Strobl sat with their backs to each other. They kept their pistols handy and occupied the last row of seats in the last passenger car, just as Pritchard had done on the train out of Atherton.

"I must thank you," Strobl said to Pritchard as the train rattled along in the darkness.

"What for?" Pritchard said. "You're the one who saved my life."

"It is a shameful state I found myself in," Strobl said. "Shunned in my homeland, feared and reviled in America, jailed, and without means in Atherton. I was 'broke,' as you Americans say, which is a disgraceful station for a Strobl. Until you gave me a chance," he rubbed the badge on his chest, "to redeem myself and restore my honor. Please know I will repay you for the meals, the horse, and the saddle. For my honor, I may never be able to fully repay you."

"Forget it," Pritchard said. "We're both drawin' wages from the governor now. Besides, keepin' you healthy is how I'll stay healthy. Don't forget, I expect you to earn your keep. Ain't been a day go by since that bounty was put on my head that somebody hasn't tried to ship me to the glue factory."

"Rest assured, Marshal Pritchard, with Count

Florian Strobl standing vigil you will be safe. I have sworn to protect you, as I would guard my own life."

"Like I told the governor," Pritchard said, "my friends call me Samuel."

"Very well, Samuel," Strobl said.

"If you don't mind me askin'," Pritchard said, "why did you leave Austria? Bein' royalty and all, I'd figure you'd want to stay in your home country."

"It is a tragic story," Strobl began, "and sadly, one of my own making. I served in the Austrian army, in the cavalry, and fought against Garibaldi in the Italian Alps. There I was wounded, and sent home to Vienna, where my family had received word that my older brother, also an army officer, had been killed by the Prussians at Königgrätz."

"I'm sorry to hear that," Pritchard said.

"My brother and I were very close. News of his death broke my parents' hearts. I subsequently became involved with his widow, as beautiful a woman as Austria has ever produced, and assumed the role of father to his young son."

"Most folks would consider that an honorable thing to do," Pritchard said.

"You may have cause to change that opinion after you hear the rest of my tale," Strobl said. "In truth, I was as happy a man at that time in my life as I have ever been. We married, and for almost a year I lived a life richer than I deserved.

I had wealth, a noble title, a son who was once merely a nephew, and was in love with the woman of every man's dreams."

"Sounds like a fairy tale come true," Pritchard said. "What happened?"

"The unimaginable," Strobl said. "One day, my brother returned."

Pritchard whistled. "That'll bust the cinch on your saddle."

"Indeed," Strobl said. "As it turned out, the news of my brother's death was obviously premature. He'd been badly wounded and captured. He was sent to a prison camp in Turin. There he languished for months, in hospital, until healthy enough to be released. When he returned home, and discovered his wife had married me . . ."

Strobl's voice trailed off. He closed his eyes and was silent for a long minute. "Forgive me," he finally said. "It has been almost seven years, and still it haunts me."

He removed his monocle and wiped his eyes with his handkerchief. They were almost fully healed and displayed only the slightest remnants of blackness. "You can imagine the turmoil my brother's return brought to our family. My parents were overjoyed, but neither he, nor I, were. His wife—my wife— was distraught beyond words. His son—my son— was confused beyond understanding. And my brother, a man who had already suffered greatly, became enraged beyond reason."

Strobl returned his monocle to his eye. "I was ordered from my home by my father. While I was away, in a fit of jealous fury, my brother attacked his wife. When his son, only eight years old, tried to intervene, my brother killed him. By the time I got word, and returned home, my brother had killed his wife, as well."

"What did you do?" Pritchard said.

"I hunted and killed my own brother," Strobl said. "I was forced to watch from a distance as he was buried, along with the woman I loved and my only nephew, who I had come to love as my own son."

"I'm truly sorry for your loss," Pritchard said.

"Thank you," Count Strobl said. "My parents, overcome with grief over the second death of their eldest son, blamed me. As I already noted, they wouldn't even allow me to attend the funeral. I fled Austria a cursed man. I traveled Europe, hoping to escape my past. But as I'm certain you know, one cannot escape his past. It is our pasts, our deeds done, that make us who we are. Is not the price on your head a remnant of your own troubled past?"

"It is," Pritchard admitted.

"Word of what befell my family followed me everywhere. Men of noble descent looked upon me with scorn and challenged me regularly. I was often attacked, just as you are now, without warning by strangers. With each successive attack I survived, I became more skilled. Soon I had a reputation as a duelist, which made men of arms desire to challenge me even more."

"It's no different in America," Pritchard said. "Once I got a reputation as a gunfighter, even before the bounty was put on my head, pistoleros started a-comin' after me. I'd hoped it would rein back after I stopped bein' Joe Atherton and returned to bein' Samuel Pritchard, but it wasn't so. They're still a-comin'."

"It would seem," Strobl said, "that in this way we are more alike than different."

"I reckon so," Pritchard said.

"So you see," Strobl said, "despite my noble title, I am a man without a home, a family, or a country."

"It ain't what we've been that matters," Pritchard said. "Only what we are now. You ain't an exiled European nobleman any longer. You're a Deputy United States Marshal, same as me, charged with investigatin' a criminal matter at the behest of the governor of the great state of Missouri."

"Deputy United States Marshal," Strobl said, rubbing his badge again. "I very much like the sound of that."

CHAPTER 43

"Here's your dinner, boys," Tater announced as he entered the jail. He had to use his ample butt to push the door open, because both of his hands were filled with baskets.

"It's about time," Bennington said. "I'm hungry."

"All that hard work you've been doin' here in jail give you an appetite?" Ditch chided.

Bennington merely glared at his fellow inmate. As a result of Ditch's hurled boot, he wore a prominent, raised, heel-shaped bruise in the center of his forehead.

"Dady Perkins made you boys pork fritters and green beans tonight," Tater said. "I already sampled some. It's mighty delicious, iffen I say so myself."

"I'm relieved to know you already ate," Bennington grunted. "When will it be our turn?"

Tater set the baskets on the desk and unlocked Ditch's cell. Ditch stepped out and began to help him unpack the contents of the baskets.

"How come he's allowed to leave his cell?" Bennington griped, pointing at Ditch.

"Because he used to be a deputy," Tater replied, sticking out his tongue at Bennington. "I know I can trust him. Besides, he ain't gonna try to escape."

"Actually," Ditch said, "that ain't entirely correct." He picked up the jail keys Tater had set on the desk.

"Huh?" Tater said, confused.

Ditch gently pushed Tater into the cell he'd just vacated. He shoved him only hard enough to herd the portly jailer inside, but not hard enough to injure him. Tater landed on his rump on the bunk. As the obese deputy struggled to regain his feet, Ditch stepped out of the cell, closed the door, and locked it with the key.

"What the heck're you doin'?" Tater howled once he was upright again. "You're the prisoner and I'm the deputy! You're the one who's supposed to be locked in here, not me!"

"I'm sorry, Tater," Ditch said as he went to the desk and retrieved his pocketknife, pistol, and gun belt. "I truly am. But Idelle is in danger. With Pritchard gone, and me locked up, she's all alone with nobody to watch over her. She's the only thing standin' between a couple of thievin' skunks stealin' her family fortune and takin' over this town. I ain't about to sit idle, locked in a cage, while my fiancée and unborn baby have an 'accident.' Not while I can do something about it."

"You gonna leave me here," Tater asked forlornly, "locked up?"

"For a while," Ditch admitted. "If there was another way, Tater, I'd do it. I'm sorry."

In the drawer below the one where he found his revolver, Ditch found Bennington's guns. They were identical to his Colt, with custom, five-and-a-half-inch barrels, two inches shorter than the Army Model, except that the colonel's Colts were ornately engraved. Like his pistol, they were unloaded. Ditch reloaded all three weapons, holstered his revolver, and stuffed Bennington's guns in his belt.

"Hey," Bennington protested, "those belong to me!"

"I'll be a-borrowin' 'em," Ditch said.

"How long do I have to stay in here?" Tater asked.

"Deputy Stearns will likely be around later on," Ditch said. "He drinks at the hotel each night after dinner with Houseman. Then he likes to come into the jail and taunt me, under the guise of checkin' in. He shouldn't be more than a couple of hours. Just sit in your cells, be quiet, and he'll be along soon enough."

"I guess I ain't got much choice," Tater shrugged.

"What if I decide to raise an alarm?" Bennington asked.

Ditch turned to face the prisoner. "You'd best listen to me, Colonel Dexter Bennington, and heed my words. I'm already mad enough to drown puppies over what Bonnie Shipley, her crooked lawyer, and their hired gun did to me. If you think I'm gonna let them three mudsills harm one hair on Idelle's head, you're even dumber than you look. Nothin' is gonna stop me from protecting the woman I love, and the child inside her. Especially a two-bit, Yankee blowhard like you. You're gonna give me your word of honor that you'll sit here in your cell and be silent."

"Why on earth would I do that?" Bennington scoffed. "Why should I conceal your escape?"

"Because iffen you don't," Ditch said, drawing his revolver, cocking the hammer, and aiming at Bennington's head, "I'll save you the trouble and raise the alarm myself, right now."

"You wouldn't dare," Bennington said.

"Why not?" Ditch said. "I'm already on the way to prison. You said so yourself. What have I got to lose?"

"You'd best do as he says," Tater spoke up. "I've known Ditch since he was knee-high to a June bug and bustin' broncs on his daddy's ranch before he could walk. Iffen Ditch tells you he's gonna do somethin', you can set your watch by it."

"I do believe," Bennington acknowledged, after staring at Ditch a moment, "you would actually shoot me."

"To protect Idelle, I'd ride into hell in a bucket of water and put a bullet into the devil himself."

"Very well," Bennington said. "I will remain silent. You have my word of honor. Not because of your threats, but because if your fiancée is indeed in peril, it is the honorable thing to do."

Ditch lowered the Colt's hammer and holstered it. "I thank you," he said.

"I sure wish Marshal Pritchard was here," Tater said.

"Me, too," Ditch said.

Ditch went to the wall-mounted gun rack and unlocked the chain that ran through the trigger guards of the weapons stacked there. He took Pritchard's Henry rifle and a box of .44 rimfire cartridges from the drawers beneath it.

"So long, fellers," Ditch said as he grabbed his hat and headed for the door. "Once again, Tater, I truly am sorry for bustin' out."

"Wait!" Tater called out from inside the cell.

"You might as well save your breath," Ditch told him. "You ain't gonna talk me out of leavin'."

"I wasn't gonna try to talk you out of escapin'," Tater said. "I can see for myself you've already done it."

"Then what do you want?"

"Iffen you don't mind," Tater asked, "before you leave, could you hand me and the colonel over them two baskets?"

CHAPTER 44

Ditch left the jail through the front door and immediately went around to the back. From there he entered the woods and began to make his way to the Atherton Arms Hotel.

Atherton was a river town, nestled on the Missouri. As a result, it was bordered on both sides by heavy woods; woods that Ditch and Pritchard had been navigating since they were small boys.

Ditch realized there was no way, even in the darkness of the late evening, that he could make it across town to the hotel without being spotted by someone who knew him. By using the forest to parallel Atherton's main street, he could easily travel undetected.

Eleven years ago, as seventeen-year-old boys, Ditch and Pritchard had evaded death at the hands of Burnell Shipley's hired guns by fleeing and hiding in those woods. And it was from those very same woods that they ambushed and killed the men who'd lynched Pritchard's father and burned the Pritchard family's home to ashes.

Soon Ditch found himself in the wooded area behind the Atherton Arms. He waited unseen until a pair of hotel maids retrieving linen from the laundry lines went back inside, then made his way to the rear kitchen door.

Just inside the door was a coatrack holding the white jackets and aprons worn by the kitchen staff. Ditch removed his hat and stashed it, along with Pritchard's Henry rifle, behind the coatrack. Then he donned a white coat, chef's hat, and an apron to cover his guns, and strolled through the kitchen with his head down.

It was the dinner hour, and the kitchen was bustling. Ditch grabbed a serving tray from a shelf. Using it as a shield to cover his face, he scurried through the kitchen, past several cooks and servers too preoccupied with their own harried tasks to notice him. A moment later he exited the kitchen and found himself in the crowded restaurant.

Benedict Houseman, Jack Stearns, and Bonnie Shipley were dining at a table in one corner. Ditch went past them unnoticed, concealing his features behind the tray, and continued out of the restaurant, through the lobby, and up the stairs.

He started to go directly to Idelle's room on the second floor, then changed his mind. He went instead up one more flight, to the third floor, where Bonnie Shipley's room was located.

Ditch waited until the hallways were clear of guests before pulling out his pocketknife and jimmying open the door to Shipley's room. Once inside, he tossed the tray and his chef's hat on the bed, shut the door, and pulled the curtains to the room's only window closed. Next, he lit the kerosene lamp, keeping the wick turned up just enough to see. The last thing he wanted was for Houseman or Stearns to go outside for a smoke, look up, and see a light in Bonnie Shipley's supposedly unoccupied room.

Ditch wasted no time. He began to systematically search her hotel room, starting with the closet, moving to the dresser, and finishing at the bed. He scored in each location.

In the closet he found a suitcase. Inside, among the toiletries and lingerie, he located a photograph. It was a formal picture of Bonnie Shipley and a young man who looked to be about her age. By her appearance, it seemed as though the photograph had been taken several years previously, when she was a bit younger. The man was seated, Shipley stood next to him, and they were holding hands. On the back was handwritten the words, *To my beloved Trudy. Love, Percy.*

He pocketed the photograph and turned his attention to the dresser. In the second drawer, beneath the clothes, Ditch found a large wad of cash. He quickly counted it and determined there was over four hundred dollars. He left the cash in place, found nothing else in the dresser, and turned his attention to the bed.

There was nothing under the pillows or mattress, but three pairs of shoes were neatly arranged under the bed. In the first and second pairs he found nothing. In the final pair, Ditch found a small medicine bottle in each shoe. Neither bottle was labeled.

Ditch uncorked the first bottle, which was almost full, and brought it to his nose. The scent that met his nostrils was laudanum. The second bottle was more than half-empty, and when he uncorked it and gave the contents a whiff, he cringed. He instantly recognized the pungent, nose-burning odor as ether.

A small amount of either one of the two liquids, or in combination, added to the drink Bonnie Shipley poured him, would have knocked him clean out. He suspected she had already staged the potions in his cup before she poured their drinks, which would explain how she didn't succumb to the effects of the concoction, yet he did.

Ditch pocketed both bottles, then dimmed the lamp. He opened the curtains, retrieved his hat and tray, and left Shipley's room, peering cautiously out through the cracked door to ensure there were no guests in the hall. He locked the door behind him, redonned the hat, and made his way downstairs to the second floor, where he and Idelle's rooms were situated. He knocked on Idelle's door.

"Who is it?" he heard her muffled voice call out from inside the room.

"Room service," he said, disguising his voice, and face, behind the tray.

"I didn't order anything," Idelle said.

He knocked again. "I have an order for Miss Idelle Pritchard," Ditch insisted.

The door opened, and an irate Idelle appeared. "There must be some mistake," she said.

Ditch pushed Idelle inside and covered her mouth before she could scream. Her eyes widened when she recognized her fiancé. He removed his hand.

"Ditch!" she exclaimed in a tone that mixed anger and bewilderment. "What the hell are you doing here?"

"Glad to know you're happy to see me," Ditch said, closing the door behind him.

"You're supposed to be in jail!" she said.

"That's exactly what Tater said," Ditch chuckled, "when I broke out. And keep your voice down."

"You're in a lot of trouble already," Idelle scolded. "Breaking yourself out of jail isn't going to make things any easier on you."

"I had to see you."

"Why?" Idelle said. "Isn't Bonnie Shipley available?"

"Give it a rest," Ditch said. "I already told you, I was set up."

"That's your story, anyhow," she said, folding her arms.

"Look," he said, producing the bottles. "I found these in Shipley's room. It's laudanum and ether."

"You broke into her room?" Idelle gasped.

"Of course," Ditch said. "How else was I going to find out what she's up to?"

Idelle's eyes narrowed. "You could have gotten those bottles from the mercantile or Dr. Mauldin's office. Are you telling me the truth? Did you really enter Bonnie Shipley's room?"

Ditch held up the photograph. "Did I get this at Doc Mauldin's?" Idelle snatched the photograph from his hands.

"Good heavens," she said, "that's—"

"Somebody named Trudy who's passin' herself off as Bonnie Shipley," Ditch finished her sentence.

Idelle suddenly grabbed him, hugged him, and began to kiss his face. "I wanted to believe you," she said between kisses, "but your story was so damned hard to swallow." She rubbed the stitches on his head. "I always knew you were telling the truth. You really were drugged and clobbered."

"I told you that all along," Ditch said. "But none of that matters now."

"I don't understand."

"You don't need to," Ditch said. "All you need to know is that we've got to get you out of here before something befalls you."

"What are you talking about?"

"Do you remember when you, me, John Babbit, and Judge Pearson discussed how some of the people defending themselves against Houseman's lawsuits ended up dead?"

"I recall the discussion," she said.

"I think you're gonna become one of those

dead people, in short order, if we don't get you clear of Atherton."

"You really think Houseman would be that brazen?"

"Face facts, Idelle," he said. "Samuel's gone, the federal marshal still hasn't shown up, and framin' me for rape wasn't a coincidence. Houseman, Shipley, and Stearns have done a right handy job of takin' out anyone who could protect you. Now all they've got to do is put you in the bone orchard, and Atherton's theirs."

"What should we do?"

"It's time to go," Ditch said. "Kansas City ain't but thirty miles away. I'll get us a buckboard. Don't bother packing. We can buy whatever we need there. Grab your coat and walk down to the livery. I'll take the woods, and meet you there. If we leave now, we can be there by morning."

"We don't need a buckboard," Idelle insisted. "I can ride."

"Not a chance," Ditch said. "I'll not have you bouncing about on horseback in the dark with our son or daughter within you. I'm gonna leave now. Wait here in your room a few minutes, to allow me time to get clear of the hotel, and then head down to the stables."

"All right," Idelle said. She hugged Ditch again. "I love you, Ditch. I always have."

"I love you, too," Ditch said. He kissed her and walked out of her room.

No sooner had Ditch stepped through the doorway, when the butt of a rifle came crashing against his head. He collapsed to the floor.

Jack Stearns stood over Idelle's unconscious fiancé. He was holding Pritchard's Henry rifle in his hands.

Idelle gasped. When she reached for her Colt Cloverleaf pistol, Stearns snaked out a hand with incredible speed and snatched it from her hand.

"I'll take that," he said. "I wouldn't want to end up like the last deputy you showed this gun to."

Idelle knelt next to Ditch and cradled his head. "He's still breathing," she said, "but he's hurt bad. Fetch Dr. Mauldin."

"If he didn't want to get thumped," Stearns said, "maybe your fiancé shouldn't have tried to escape. He's lucky I didn't shoot him."

Idelle stood and slapped Stearns across the face, hard enough to redden his cheek. "You're a coward, Jack Stearns."

Stearns rubbed his cheek, smiled, and then slapped Idelle back. She didn't wince. Then he leaned down and removed Ditch's pistols. A number of hotel guests had emerged from their rooms to investigate the commotion.

"Are you going to fetch the doctor, or shall I?" she asked calmly.

"Go ahead and fetch him," Stearns said. "Tell him he'll find his patient at the jail."

CHAPTER 45

Pritchard entered the Saint Louis branch of the Wells Fargo Bank promptly at nine o'clock, the minute the doors opened for business. He was the first customer in.

Pritchard and Strobl's train arrived in Saint Louis shortly before ten p.m. the night before, and their first stop after disembarking was a local livery stable. They fed, watered, and boarded their horses, and then, much to Count Strobl's dismay, settled in for the night in the hayloft. Pritchard didn't want to announce their presence in town by getting a hotel, so he paid the livery attendant two dollars to let them sleep above the stable.

After a fitful night of taking turns sleeping and keeping watch, Pritchard and Strobl arose, washed up in a trough, ate a breakfast of jerky and canteen water, and saddled their horses. Pritchard got directions from the livery attendant to the bank, and Strobl got directions to the offices of the *Saint Louis Dispatch*.

"May I help you, Marshal?" the guard opening the door to Wells Fargo asked, noticing Pritchard's badge.

"I'd like to see the bank manager as soon as possible," Pritchard told him. A moment later a distinguished-looking, bald, spectacled man in a starched suit emerged from behind a paneled door.

"I'm Morton Westlake, the manager of this bank," he said.

"I'm Deputy U.S. Marshal Pritchard," he said. He produced a letter from his pocket. "I'm here to conduct an investigation on behalf of Governor Woodson."

As Westlake examined the letter, his eyebrows raised. "I see," he said, returning the letter to Pritchard. "What is it you believe I can do to assist you?"

"A few weeks ago," Pritchard began, "someone anonymously deposited ten thousand dollars into your bank. On the same day, someone posted a notice in the *Saint Louis Dispatch*, offering that money, no questions asked, to whoever killed a former Texas Ranger named Joe Atherton."

"I recall hearing about that," Westlake said, shaking his head in disdain. "A very nasty business."

"I want to know who made that deposit," Pritchard said.

"Unfortunately," Westlake said, "I'm not going to be able to help you, Marshal Pritchard."

"Why not?"

"Allow me to explain," Westlake said, speaking to Pritchard as if explaining something complicated to a small child. "All information about our depositors is kept completely confidential." He smiled contemptuously. "Bank policy, you understand. Now, if you'll excuse me, I have other duties to attend to. I'm sure you can see your way out."

Westlake turned on his heels and had actually taken a step away from Pritchard, when he was grabbed by the back of his neck and jerked back around so violently his glasses flew off. He suddenly found himself face-to-face with Pritchard, his collar in the grip of a fist, and his nose inches from the huge marshal's. He stared up in terror.

The bank guard clumsily started to reach for his pistol, tucked away in a full-flap holster commonly referred to as a *widowmaker,* when one of Pritchard's pistols suddenly appeared in his hand as if by magic. The guard stopped reaching for his gun, raised his hands, smiled, and nodded. Pritchard holstered his gun.

"Allow me to explain," Pritchard repeated the bank manager's words back to him. "I don't give a whit about your bank's policies. The governor wants to know who put up the bounty on Joe Atherton, and so do I. You're going to tell me, Mr. Westlake, or I'm going to beat it out of you, and then arrest you on federal charges for obstructing my investigation." He pulled the terrified bank manager closer, until their noses almost touched.

"By the way," Pritchard said, "if it helps your recollection, I'm Joe Atherton."

If Westlake was scared before, his expression now morphed into stark horror. "I'll tell you what I know," he sputtered, his head bobbing up and down. "P-please, don't h-hurt me?"

Pritchard released him. The bank guard handed Westlake his glasses, which were cracked.

"Who put up the money?" Pritchard asked.

"I don't know," the bank manager said, trying to regain his composure. "It's the truth. The funds were delivered to the bank by a third party and deposited into a numbered account, on behalf of an anonymous client. The deposit receipt was taken by the same party. The only person who might actually know would be the depositor, who, as I just explained, was merely a third-party courier."

"Who was the courier?" Pritchard asked.

"A representative from the Quincy Detective Agency," Westlake said. "If I recall correctly, it was Mr. Quincy himself."

CHAPTER 46

Pritchard and Count Strobl met outside the offices of the *Saint Louis Dispatch*, only a block from the Wells Fargo Bank.

Before Pritchard left the bank, he served Westlake with an order from Attorney General Ewing confiscating the ten thousand dollars. The money was to be kept for the state of Missouri at Wells Fargo, which pleased the bank manager, and released to no one without the express order of the governor. Westlake was also ordered to post a notice informing the public that the bounty funds had been impounded.

Count Strobl was standing with his back to the newspaper office, smoking a cigarette and keeping a wary eye as Pritchard rode up.

"Any luck?" Pritchard asked as Strobl discarded his smoke and mounted Schatz.

"The notice advertising the bounty was purchased by—"

"A representative from the Quincy Detective Agency, right?" Pritchard finished for him.

"How did you know?"

"The same party deposited the money for the bounty," Pritchard said.

"It would seem," Strobl said, "our next

destination would be the offices of the Quincy Detective Agency. I took the liberty of obtaining their address from the staff at the newspaper office. I also took the liberty of delivering Attorney General Ewing's letter."

Like his order seizing the ten thousand dollars, Attorney General Ewing also provided a letter ordering the Saint Louis newspaper to post a public notice announcing the bounty funds had been impounded by the state of Missouri, and anyone attempting to collect them would be summarily arrested.

"Why, thank you, Deputy U.S. Marshal Strobl," Pritchard said.

"You're most welcome, Deputy U.S. Marshal Pritchard."

The headquarters of the Quincy Detective Agency was an imposing building near the waterfront. They dismounted, posted their horses, and stared at the door.

"You might want to find yourself another way in," Pritchard said. "Just in case Mr. Quincy ain't receivin' guests today."

"I was thinking the same thing," Strobl said, heading around to the back of the building. Pritchard mounted the steps and went through the front door alone.

"Good morning," Pritchard said to a very attractive young woman seated behind a desk in the lobby. Behind her were several doors. "My name is Deputy U.S. Marshal Pritchard. I'm here to see Mr. Quincy."

"I'm Mr. Quincy's secretary," she said. "Do you have an appointment?"

"Nope," Pritchard said. "Just got into town this morning."

"I'm afraid Mr. Quincy is an exceptionally busy man," she said, scanning a calendar on her desk. "He's booked solid today, and for the next several days as well. I can pencil you in for a week from Friday, if that would be suitable?"

"What would be more suitable," Pritchard said, tipping his hat back and winking, "is if you wouldn't mind telling him I'm here? We're old friends, him and me. I'm sure Dominic would make some time to see me."

The woman looked up at the extremely tall, rugged lawman. She batted her eyes, blushed, and disappeared through one of the doors behind her.

Several long minutes later, the young woman returned. Instead of coquettish, she now looked angry, and was accompanied by two burly men in suits. The horizontal straps of their shoulder holsters were visible under their coats.

"You lied to me, Marshal Pritchard," she said. "Mr. Quincy said you are no friend of his."

"He certainly knows of me," Pritchard said. "He muled ten grand to the Wells Fargo Bank to have me killed."

"I think you'd better leave," she said. She nodded to the two men, who separated and began to flank Pritchard.

"And I think you'd better tell your boyfriends there ain't no way they're gonna beat me to the pull with them shoulder guns. You might also tell 'em, the first one who tries will be leadin' the other'n straight to hell."

Both men stopped moving and glanced nervously at each other.

"I know what you boys are thinkin'," Pritchard said. "You don't want to back down in front of this pretty young gal, nor to have to report to your boss that you let me buffalo you. But both of them things are preferable to dyin' on the floor of this lobby."

Perspiration broke out on the foreheads of both men. One appeared about thirty, the other in his forties, and neither looked like the kind of man who was used to letting a stranger tell him what to do, especially in their own place of employment.

The younger man's right hand began to slowly inch upward. The older man noticed, and followed suit.

Just as it looked as if both Quincy men were going to draw, one of the doors behind them burst open and Count Strobl strode in, an 1873 Chamelot-Delvigne revolver in each hand.

The secretary gasped, and both Quincy men lowered their hands.

"Sorry I'm late," Strobl said, slightly out of breath. "This building is like a maze."

"Use your left hands, boys," Pritchard said, "and drop those guns on the desk." The men complied. He unloaded their revolvers while Strobl covered them.

"Let's go see your boss," Pritchard said. He motioned the young woman toward the door she emerged from.

The secretary led the way, followed by the unarmed Quincy men, Count Strobl and his two nickel-plated guns, and then Pritchard. They navigated a long hallway and entered a large, well-apportioned study, replete with books covering two walls, a fireplace, a number of hung photographs, and an immense desk in the center of the room. Two men, on opposite sides of the desk, stood up when the entourage entered.

"I'm terribly sorry, Mr. Quincy," the woman apologized. "These men insisted on seeing you. I tried to send them away, but as you can see, they were quite insistent. They have guns."

"And apparently no trouble relieving my men of theirs," the man behind the desk said in disgust. He was in his fifties, of medium height, with a full head of gray hair, and spoke with an Irish accent. He wore a striped suit, and had an unlit cigar in his mouth.

The other man was in his sixties, florid and balding, and also wearing an expensive-looking

353

suit. He looked in dismay at the sight of the newcomers.

"You must be Pritchard," the man behind the desk said. "I'm Dominic Quincy. If you wanted to see me, you could have made an appointment."

"I needed to speak with you before a week from Friday," Pritchard said, casting a sidelong glance at the secretary.

"I don't need to be here," the other man said.

"May my previous appointment leave?" Quincy asked. "My business with him is no concern of yours."

"He may not," Pritchard said. "Because I don't know him, and how many more men you've got stashed in this building. I don't want a stampede of 'em comin' in here to interrupt us."

"I'm sorry about this, John," Quincy said.

"This is outrageous," John said to Pritchard. "What kind of brigand are you?"

"The U.S. Marshal kind," Pritchard said. "Get up."

Count Strobl herded him, along with the secretary and two Quincy men, over to a couch in one corner of the study. "Sit down," Strobl ordered them, "keep your hands on your knees, and do not move. If you move, I will shoot you." They all complied.

"You may have me at a disadvantage now," Quincy said, standing, "but rest assured, Marshal Pritchard, I will have my day." He pointed his cigar at Pritchard like a gun. "I'll see you hang for this."

"You've already had your day, Cottonmouth," Pritchard said, as he punched Quincy in the face. The smaller man flew across the room, came to rest against the bookshelves behind him, and slid down to sit on the floor.

The woman let out a short cry, and the two Quincy men tensed on the couch. Strobl cocked both of his revolvers and shook his head at them.

Pritchard walked over to the semiconscious Quincy, picked him up, and placed him back in his giant leather chair. He checked him for weapons, then grabbed a decanter full of scotch from a shelf and tossed half the contents in his face.

Quincy sputtered awake and glared up at Pritchard through hate-filled eyes. Blood and liquor dripped down his chin.

"You put up a bounty on me," Pritchard said to him. "That forced me to kill a number of men, includin' six fellers near Boonville who once worked for your agency. It also forced me to have to resign my job, abandon my home, and leave my pregnant sister alone and at the mercy of scoundrels and thieves. That don't please me. But do you know what really makes me mad enough to kick out a stained glass church window?"

"I can't wait to hear," Quincy said.

"Seein' a fourteen-year-old girl take a bullet

meant for me," Pritchard said, "on account of you."

As Pritchard calmly spoke, he paced around the study, observing the pictures mounted on the walls. Several featured Dominic Quincy posing with an individual, or with a group of people. In some of the more formal ones he recognized prominent men, such as railroad magnates, a hotel tycoon, and a state senator.

Most of the other photographs, however, were taken outdoors. In many Quincy was in field attire, sporting pistols and a rifle, and standing or kneeling with similarly dressed men posturing over the bodies of various dead outlaws. The names of those posing with him in the pictures were sometimes listed below their images. Pritchard found more than a dozen such macabre, photographic trophies adorning the office walls.

"Look closely while you can," Quincy said as Pritchard perused the photographs. "You'll find yourself on my wall, soon enough."

"Tell me who put up the bounty?" Pritchard said. "And I'll be on my way."

"Kiss my Gaelic ass," Quincy said. "I'll take the name to my grave."

"If you won't tell me who paid you to put up the bounty," Pritchard said, "I can only assume it was you. You were the one who made the deposit and posted the newspaper notice."

"Assume whatever you like."

"Very well," Pritchard said. "You've paid to have me murdered. By rights, and the code duello, I demand satisfaction."

Across the room, Strobl smiled in approval. "I knew it," he said. "Samuel, my friend, you are a born duelist."

CHAPTER 47

"Do you have a weapon?" Pritchard asked. "If not," he took out his left-hand Colt and extended it to Quincy, "I will gladly provide you with one."

"You can't be serious?" Quincy mocked. "You're challenging me to a duel?"

"That's right," Pritchard said. "I'm givin' you a chance for a more honorable death than you orchestrated for me. Certainly better than a cur like you deserves."

"I'll not participate in such barbaric nonsense," Quincy said.

"I would be honored to be your second," Count Strobl gleefully announced from across the room.

"I'm in a helluva hurry to get back to Atherton," Pritchard said, setting the Colt on the desk in front of Quincy and stepping back three paces. "I've no time for formalities like meeting at dawn, or other such trifles. I've made you a square proposition: tell me who put you up to postin' the bounty on my head, or face me."

"I will do neither."

"Suits me," Pritchard said. "I'm gonna count to three. When I reach three, you're either gonna give me a name, or you ain't. Iffen you don't, you're catchin' a bullet. Your weapon's on the desk. Whether you decide to defend yourself is entirely up to you."

"You can go to hell."

"Only if you send me there," Pritchard said. "One."

"This is against the law," Quincy protested. "You're supposed to be a lawman."

"Payin' others to murder a man is also against the law," Pritchard said. "It didn't stop you, Cottonmouth. Two."

"You're the fastest gunfighter around!" Quincy said. "This isn't a fair duel! It's murder!"

"Hirin' men to murder me from ambuscade is your idea of fair?" Pritchard said. "Three."

In a panic, Quincy's right hand darted toward the Colt revolver only inches away on the desk. Before his fingers touched it, Pritchard's other Colt was out, cocked, and aimed at his face. The draw was so fast it was as if his gun materialized in his fist from thin air.

The two Quincy detectives seated on the couch stared in awe. The young secretary began to softly cry.

"Good-bye, Cottonmouth," Pritchard said.

Quincy pulled his hand back, slumped in his chair, lowered his head, and closed his eyes. "Go ahead and shoot," he said.

"Wait," the older of the Quincy men said from the couch. "Don't kill him. I'll tell you what he won't."

"I'm a-listenin'," Pritchard said, still aiming his revolver at Quincy's head. "Iffen you lie to me, or I tire of what you're sayin', your boss gets it."

"Mr. Quincy won't tell you who hired him to put up the bounty because it's a woman," the Quincy man said. "A woman he's in love with."

"Shut up," Quincy said, opening his eyes.

"What's her name?" Pritchard said.

"Evelyn," the Quincy man said. "Evelyn Stiles."

"Stiles?" Pritchard said. "I know that name. She wouldn't, by any chance, be any relation to a dead Confederate horseback renegade named Dalton Stiles?"

"I don't know," the man said. "I swear."

"Shut your mouth!" Quincy said.

"Where can I find this Evelyn Stiles?" Pritchard asked.

"I don't know that either," the Quincy man said. "Neither does Mr. Quincy. She left him. She departed Saint Louis a few weeks ago and hasn't been seen since. He's been a wreck since she took off. He's got half of our detectives out scouring the countryside in search of her."

"Shut up, damn you!" Quincy ordered.

"I'm only trying to save your life, Mr. Quincy," the detective said. "It's that damned woman that got you into this mess in the first place. She never loved you, sir. She played you. She used you, and the agency, to accomplish her ends. Me and all the other detectives could see right through her, and that she was up to no good. You couldn't, because you were smitten. She's the one who prompted you into putting up that bounty, and look where it's got you."

"Not another damn word!" Quincy bellowed, reaching for the Colt on the desk. This time, he didn't hesitate. He grabbed the gun, cocked it, and aimed it at his employee across the room. He was about to pull the trigger when Pritchard fired.

Pritchard's .45 bullet tore through Quincy's right elbow. He dropped the revolver on the desk, howled in agony, and fell back into his chair. Blood pumped through his fingers as he clamped his other hand around the wound.

Pritchard picked up the dropped Colt, lowered the hammer, and holstered it along with its mate. "Best tend to your boss's injury," he told the Quincy men. The younger agency man rushed to his employer's side and began to tie off the shattered arm.

Strobl holstered his revolvers. The older Quincy detective approached Pritchard.

"He was actually going to shoot me," he said, shaking his head in disbelief. "I've been his loyal employee for over ten years. He was going to shoot me, like it was nothing, just for trying to save his life."

"What did you expect," Pritchard said, "workin' for a feller who's nicknamed after a venomous snake? Of course he was gonna turn on you. Old Cottonmouth has swindled, betrayed, or sold out everybody he ever knew. If you've been ridin' for his brand for more'n ten years and don't know that by now, you're a plumb fool."

"You're right, Marshal," the man said, tightening his jaw. "But I'll be a fool no longer."

"C'mon," Pritchard told Count Strobl as he ejected the empty cartridge case from his revolver and reloaded. "We've got to get goin'. We've a train to catch."

"Before you go, Marshal," the other man in the office, John, spoke up, "I'd like to have a word with you."

"Make it quick," Pritchard said. "I'm in a hurry."

"My name is John Brody," he said. "I own railroad interests in the region, as well as a construction company in Saint Louis. My firm is one of several currently working on the Eads Bridge."

"I've heard of you," Pritchard said. "You're that crooked tycoon feller who hired Quincy's boys to smack down folks a-workin' your railroads out West."

"That is a lie," Brody said.

"If so," Pritchard said, "what're you doin' parlayin' with Cottonmouth Quincy? I'll bet

362

the governor would be interested to know what you and him were a-conspirin' about? In fact, I wouldn't be surprised to find out that you had a hand in the bounty on my head."

"I had no idea Quincy was involved in a plot to kill anyone, much less a U.S. Marshal," Brody said smugly, "or any other criminal activity. Even if I was, allegedly, involved in quelling worker rebellion on my rail lines through his detective agency, you can't prove such a charge."

"I can," the older Quincy man said. "Brody has been hiring Quincy men for the better part of the past year to brutalize and harass the workers on his railroad. There have been beatings, shootings, and even lynchings, carried out by Quincy men and paid for by Brody himself. I myself was sent to Nebraska, just a couple of months ago, on Quincy's orders to maim a preacher who was helping the rail workers organize at his church."

"Are you willing to swear in court to what you just claimed?" Pritchard asked. "It would mean testifyin' against your boss."

"A minute ago, my boss almost shot me dead," the man said, staring at Quincy in disgust. "I quit. And hell yes, I'll testify."

"The next time I see you boys," Pritchard said to Brody and Quincy, "I'll have warrants for your arrest. Don't bother runnin'. You'll just be tired when I catch you."

As they walked out, the Quincy man turned to

Pritchard. "Thank you for saving my life," he said. "My name is Ed Pickens." He extended his hand. Pritchard shook it.

"Perhaps you can demonstrate your gratitude by answerin' a few questions?" Pritchard asked.

"I'll tell you whatever I know," Pickens said.

"What do you know about a feller named Jim Searcy?" Pritchard asked him.

"Jim Searcy?" Pickens said. "How did you come by that name?"

"Half a dozen ex–Quincy Agency men tried to waylay me on a train out of Atherton a few days ago," Pritchard said. "They were after the bounty money. Once I'd downed 'em, I asked how they knew I was gonna be on that particular train. One of 'em told me, before he expired, that they'd been tipped off by another ex-Quincy man named Jim Searcy."

"Searcy used to be Quincy's right-hand man," Pickens said. "He was with him even longer than I was. Helluva gun hand. Maybe even as fast as you, Marshal. A stone killer, too."

"Why did he quit the agency?"

"He didn't quit," Pickens said. "He was fired."

"What for?" Pritchard said.

"Same thing as was his boss's downfall: a woman. A couple of years ago, he took up with a local dance hall girl named Trudy Thompson. She led him to his ruination."

"How so?"

"Trudy was a pretty young thing when Jim met her, whoring out of one of the saloons near the river. But that was only her nighttime employment. Her day job was bilking rich shannies."

"How'd she accomplish that?"

"She'd dress up real nice and attend fancy society functions. There she'd find the wealthiest and most gullible fool, get them to swoon over her, and then convince them she needed money for an operation to save her dying mother, or some other such tale of woe."

"The old, damsel-in-distress game," Pritchard said.

"Exactly," Pickens said. "When the mark showed up with the cash, she would drug him, take his money, and run."

"How did she get Searcy fired?"

"One of the men she bilked was the son of one of Quincy's wealthiest clients. When Jim learned she was about to be arrested, he tipped her off and she got away. Quincy found out and fired him."

Pritchard, Strobl, and Pickens exited the building. "Would you recognize Trudy Thompson if you saw her again?" Pritchard asked.

"Hell, yes," Pickens said. "I used to see her all the time with Jim. She's a real looker. Has dark hair, and a nice figure. She's got a mole over her lip, too. What some folks call a beauty mark."

• • •

Dominic Quincy lay grimacing in pain in a private room he kept in his offices, even though he resided with his wife in an elegant mansion in one of Saint Louis's most desirable neighborhoods, Westmoreland Place. Almost an hour had passed since Pritchard had left him incensed in his study, nursing a broken nose and a shattered arm. He was waiting for his physician to return. The doctor had gone back to his office to fetch more instruments—specifically, his bone saw.

The physician had been summoned, and arrived just after Pritchard, Strobl, and Pickens left. One look at his gunshot-ruined arm and the doctor confirmed what Quincy already knew from his experiences during the war: the arm would have to come off above the elbow.

As he lay waiting, Pritchard's words, and the words of Ed Pickens, until today one of his most reliable employees, played over and over again in his mind. What infuriated Quincy the most was that Pickens was right: any fool could see his illicit affair had adversely affected his judgment. His relationship with Evelyn Stiles had damaged his reputation, harmed his business, ruined his marriage, and now cost him his right arm.

And yet all Dominic Quincy could think of, even while awaiting the removal of his right arm, was finding her.

He also thought of Samuel Pritchard, alias Joe Atherton. The man Evelyn Stiles was obsessed with. The man who took his right arm, and was about to have him arrested, and ruin everything he'd built.

"Can I get you anything?" his young secretary asked. Before he met Evelyn, she had been the object of his affections. Now she was only a distant memory, and paid well enough to remain nothing more.

"Tell Butch to come in here," Quincy said through gritted teeth.

A moment later, the younger of the two agency men entered the room. "Get out your notebook," Quincy told him.

"Get a telegram off to our boys in Kansas City," Quincy said in his thick Irish brogue. "It's closer to Atherton. Round up as many men as you can. They can beat Pritchard home and be set up and waiting for him when he arrives. It's ten thousand dollars to whoever buries the big bastard."

"But the bounty has been pulled," Butch said, looking up from his notebook. "It's been confiscated by the state of Missouri."

"I'm not talking about the bloody bounty, you idiot," Quincy snapped. "I'm paying for this myself. The ten thousand comes out of my pocket."

"The boys will be happy to hear it," Butch said.

"Be off with you," Quincy barked. "And take

special note: I want proof of Pritchard's death. He took my arm. I want his head."

"Sir, do you really want me to put that out over the wire?"

"Don't make me tell you twice," Quincy said.

CHAPTER 48

"I brought some more cold water," Tater said, carrying a pair of heavy buckets into the jail. He set the pails near Idelle.

"Thank you, Tater," she said.

It was midmorning, and Idelle was in the jail tending to Ditch. He'd yet to regain consciousness.

Ditch had been carried to the jail the night previously by four hotel employees and placed on the bunk in his old cell. Dr. Mauldin arrived shortly thereafter. He examined him and added ten more stitches to the ones he'd put in Ditch's skull the night previously. The prognosis the doctor offered wasn't encouraging.

Mauldin told Idelle that while Ditch hadn't suffered a fractured skull, he'd sustained a severe concussion. He exhibited head-swelling and a high fever. The physician couldn't tell her when, or even if, Ditch would ever wake up. And if he did wake up, he couldn't assure her Ditch would be the same. He could be deaf, blind, crippled, or worse.

Since then, Ditch's fever had fluctuated, sometimes to a frighteningly high degree. Idelle remained at his side in his cell all night, seated in her brother's handmade chair, adding cold compresses to his head and soaking his chest with wet towels.

Tater stayed up all night with Idelle, brought in pail after pail of cold water, and went to the hotel twice for fresh towels. His normally jovial features were replaced with worry.

"It's halfway till noon," Colonel Bennington complained, "and I still haven't been fed my breakfast. If you could see fit to tear yourself away from serving the mayor for a minute, and fetch me something to eat before sundown, it would be a miracle."

"You shut your mouth," Tater said. "What you did last night was lower than a snake's belly in a wagon rut."

"I merely alerted the local citizenry to an escaped prisoner," Bennington said. "I was simply doing my civic duty, that's all."

"You're lyin' like a no-legged dog," Tater fumed. "You gave Ditch your word of honor you wouldn't raise an alarm. He no sooner left the jail, when you began squawkin' like a wet hen. You brought Deputy Stearns a-runnin', and when he got here you couldn't tattle any faster. I'm so mad at you, I could slap you to sleep, and then slap you for sleepin'."

"I couldn't care less how you feel about me," Bennington said.

"When Ditch wakes up, you'll care," Tater said. "He's gonna beat you like a rented mule."

"If Deputy Clemson wakes up," Bennington said with a smirk. "I wouldn't hold my breath on that occurring anytime soon. If ever."

"How dare you!" Idelle said, standing up.

"Spare me your indignance," Bennington said to her. "I remember how you acted toward him when you came to the jail. You weren't exactly swimming in concern for his well-being."

"You'd better hope Ditch wakes up before Samuel gets back," Idelle said, her fists clenched in rage. "Ditch will only give you a beating. My brother will put you into the ground."

"Let me tell you something, little lady—"

Bennington's sentence was cut short by the pail of frigid water Tater tossed over him through the cell bars. He gasped as the cold water chilled him speechless.

"I told you to shut your mouth," Tater said, "and I meant it. There's a pump out back, and I can fetch buckets of water all day and all night."

"You listen here, Deputy," Bennington began, "you've no right to—"

Tater set down the empty bucket, picked up the full one, and drenched the colonel again. The soaking-wet Bennington stood shivering in his cell.

"You are not to speak to Miss Idelle," Tater said. "Not one more word. Every word you say gets you another bath. Do you understand, Colonel Bennington, or do I have to wash your ears out again?"

Bennington only nodded. "I'll be right back, Miss Idelle," Tater said, glaring at Bennington. "I've got to refill these buckets. You let me know when I get back if he's opened his yap while I was gone, and I'll dunk him again. Far as that polecat's concerned, I can sling water till the cows come home."

"Thank you, Tater."

As Tater walked out, Eudora Chilton walked in. "Oh, Idelle," she said, taking the younger woman in her arms. "I just got into town on the train and heard what happened to Ditch."

Idelle and Eudora embraced. "It's been awful," Idelle said. "I wish Samuel would come home." She looked over at Ditch. "I'm scared, Eudora."

"He'll be back soon," Eudora said, "I'm sure of it." She noticed the wet Bennington, drenched and forlorn, in his cell. "What happened to him?"

"Don't ask," Idelle said.

"I'll ask," Jack Stearns said, stepping into the jail. "Who's been torturing the prisoner?"

"That's exactly what they've been doing," Bennington blurted, sensing he was safe to break his vow of silence now that Deputy Stearns was present. "Dousing me with cold water like a prairie brushfire. I haven't been fed, either."

"What Colonel Bennington has been," Idelle said, "is disrespectful and insulting. And he hasn't been fed because Tater and I were busy attending to Ditch."

"I decide who gets what in here," Stearns said. "This is a jail, not a hospital."

"I am still the mayor," Idelle said. "You work for me."

"You may not be mayor for long," Stearns said, taking off his hat. "Then you'll be nothing but another unemployed, unwed mother," he pointed his chin at Ditch, lying unconscious in his cell, "without a man."

"You bastard," Idelle said, seething. "You did this to him."

"Guilty as charged," Stearns said, looking around. "Where's my chair?"

"That's Pritchard's chair," Idelle said. "I'll thank you not to sit in it."

"It's the jail's chair, now," Stearns said, "and I'll sit where I please." He entered Ditch's cell, retrieved the chair, put it behind the desk, and sat down.

"Take a load off, why don't you?" Idelle said. "Clobbering people from behind with rifles is hard work. You're a very brave man, Jack Stearns."

"He was an armed, escaped prisoner. He got what he deserved."

"When Samuel gets back," Idelle said, "you'll get yours."

"Spare me your lectures," Stearns said. "If Pritchard comes back and tries me, I'll do to him worse than I did to your boyfriend."

"You have no call to speak to her like that," Eudora said.

"I'll speak to whoever I like, however I see fit," Stearns said. "Especially in my jail."

"I'll remember you said that," Idelle told him.

"You do that," Stearns said.

Tater came into the jail, without the buckets but with several people trailing behind him. Idelle had never seen any of them before.

"There's some folks askin' to see you," Tater said to Idelle.

"Have them come in," she said.

"It's getting crowded in here," Stearns said, standing up and grabbing his hat. He looked in irritation at the people who'd entered the jail. "And odorous. I'll be at the hotel if you need me, Deputy Jessup. Feed Bennington, will you?"

"I'll slop the prisoner," Tater said as Stearns walked out.

"I can see you're busy," Eudora said, giving Idelle another hug and a peck on the cheek, "and I've got to get over to the Sidewinder. I have a liquor shipment to pay for. I'll be back later to check in on you."

"Thank you," Idelle said as Eudora made her exit. Idelle moved Pritchard's chair back into the cell next to Ditch.

Idelle turned to the newcomers. "Welcome to Atherton," she said. "I'm the mayor here. My name is—"

"Idelle Pritchard," a man said, stepping forward. "This, we already know."

"How do you know my name?" Idelle said, puzzled.

"I am Manfri Pannell. This is my wife, Sabina. We know your name, Mayor Pritchard, because your brother, Samuel, told us all about you."

CHAPTER 49

Atherton, Missouri
May 1874

Pritchard nodded to Count Strobl as the engine began to decelerate. The train was less than a mile from the depot in Atherton, and slowly preparing to stop. The two marshals got up from the seats they'd been occupying for most of the past twenty-four hours and made their way to the livery car.

After their departure from the offices of the Quincy Detective Agency, Pritchard and Strobl located the nearest telegraph office and sent a wire to Governor Woodson. They explained the status of the Houseman investigation and what had transpired with Quincy, Brody, and former Quincy Agency man Ed Pickens, whom they left with the town marshal, swearing out a statement of charges.

Then they departed for Atherton with all haste. The 250-mile journey by rail from Saint Louis consumed an entire day.

Once in the livery car, Pritchard and Strobl saddled Rusty and Schatz, and prepared their weapons. In addition to ensuring each of his .45 Colts were up-loaded to six rounds, Pritchard donned his new shoulder holsters. Then he inserted his 1863 Remingtons into them, after verifying they were both fully loaded with six .44 caliber cartridges.

It was early afternoon. The wind was picking up, and the overcast sky promised rain. Pritchard shrugged into his duster and made sure his left pocket was stocked with .44 cartridges, his right with .45 Colt rounds, and all his guns were readily accessible.

Strobl had also donned a long coat, but his was of a European cut that appeared almost like a cape. He also traded in his fur hat for a short-brimmed Mayser. Then he made certain both of his Chamelot-Delvigne revolvers were fully loaded, close at hand under his unbuttoned jacket, and that his pockets were stuffed with the short, pointed, 11-millimeter cartridges that stoked them.

Pritchard next checked his 1873 Winchester rifle and verified it was primed with fifteen .44-40 cartridges. He left the chamber empty and handed it to Strobl, along with a box of ammunition.

"Why give this fine rifle to me?" Strobl said. "Will you not wish to employ it yourself?"

"I'm large, easy to spot, and everybody will be gunnin' for me," Pritchard said. "Nobody is expectin' you to be along, backin' my play. With the rifle you can stand off a ways, observe, and pick off some of our enemies before they even know you're in the fight. It's how Ditch and I usually fought in the past when outnumbered, and it's worked out pretty fair. We're both still breathin'. Besides," Pritchard said, "I'm better with my pistols close-up."

"It is a sound strategy," Strobl agreed, examining the rifle. "I grew up hunting in the woods along the Danube. While demonstrably skilled with revolvers, I am equally versed in the use of long weapons." He levered the Winchester's action. "I will not fail you."

"Never occurred to me you would," Pritchard said.

"You, however," Strobl said, "are more than demonstrably skilled with your revolvers." He grinned. "It is lucky for me you did not accept my challenge to a duel when we first met, and satisfied yourself with merely thumping me on the nose."

"You know, Florian," Pritchard said, "you don't have to do this. This ain't your fight."

"I will pretend you didn't say that," Strobl said.

With a blast of whistle the train came to a halt at the Atherton depot.

Pritchard opened the sliding door to the livery car. "Are you ready?" he asked the count. "I've got me a hunch things could get bloody."

"We have a saying in my country," Strobl said. "In time of war, the devil makes room in hell."

"Good luck," Pritchard said, shaking his hand.

"And to you," Strobl said, bowing his head and clicking his heels during the handshake.

By previous agreement, Pritchard proceeded from the livery car alone. He led Rusty down the ramp by the reins. There was the usual crowd milling about the station: people disembarking from the train, locals greeting arriving travelers, and working folks off-loading baggage, animals, and freight. Nothing seemed out of the ordinary, except the two men in city clothes he'd never seen before. They idled in front of the railroad office trying too hard to appear nonchalant.

"Care for a paper, mister?" Ronnie Babbit said.

"Sure," Pritchard nodded, realizing the boy knew him well, always called him Marshal Pritchard in the past when addressing him, and was obviously not using his name as a signal. Pritchard gave him a dime and accepted the folded newspaper.

Inside, was a piece of paper. Pritchard recognized newspaperman John Babbit's distinct scrawl. The message read, *Seven armed men in town. Arrived on train from Kansas City last night. Ditch hurt bad, and in jail. We're with you. J.B.*

Pritchard pocketed the note, silently thanking John Babbit and his brave young son, Ronnie. Delivering the warning, with so many potential eyes and guns watching, took courage.

Pritchard handed Ronnie a silver dollar. "Take Rusty to the livery," he said, turning over the reins. "Unsaddle him, grain and water him, and stay there. No matter what you hear in the streets, you stay in the livery. Don't you come out, you hear?"

The ten-year-old newspaper boy bobbed his head up and down and led Rusty away. Back at the train, Pritchard saw Count Strobl walking down the ramp along with Schatz. He was carrying the Winchester and whistling a Beethoven sonata.

Pritchard casually swept the skirt-flaps of his duster behind the revolvers at his belt and began walking toward town. As he walked, he opened the newspaper and held it up before him. He pretended to read, but instead used the motion to discreetly draw one of his Remingtons from the shoulder holster beneath his coat. The two men in city clothes fell into step a few paces behind him.

Pritchard left the railroad station and was on the path into Atherton when he sensed motion to his rear. He dropped the paper, pivoted, and fired, holding back the trigger and fanning the Remington's hammer three times. The muzzle blasts ignited the newspaper as it fluttered to the ground.

All three of Pritchard's bullets struck the chest of the man closest to him. He stumbled backward, his derby flew from his head, the revolver he'd been drawing fell from his fingers, and he collapsed.

His partner was somewhat slower on the draw, but had almost gotten his own revolver out from under his coat when he was struck by two more bullets fired from Pritchard's Remington .44. The first shot hit him in the chest, and the second blew off the top of his head.

The newspaper burned at his feet as Pritchard reloaded the Remington. He holstered his recharged revolver and resumed his stroll into town.

CHAPTER 50

"Did you hear those shots?" the Quincy man asked.

"I heard 'em," Stearns said. "If I had to wager, I'd bet Pritchard just stepped off the afternoon train."

Stearns, Houseman, and the senior detective from the Kansas City office of the Quincy Detective Agency were standing in front of the Atherton Arms. The trio had just finished lunch at the hotel and were enjoying after-meal cigars. The Quincy man, a tall, beefy fellow named Conrad, turned to Stearns.

"Maybe my boys at the station got him?" Conrad said.

"Unlikely," Stearns said. "Round up your men and have them meet us at the jail."

"What for?" Conrad said. "If Pritchard's coming, wouldn't it be better to spread my men throughout the town, on rooftops and in alleys?"

"Don't be an idiot," Stearns said. "This is Pritchard's hometown. He grew up here. He knows every nook and cranny. Your out-of-town detectives wouldn't stand a chance."

"Then what are we supposed to do?" Houseman said, the first tinge of panic beginning to creep into his voice. "Pritchard will be here any minute!"

"Calm down," Stearns said to Houseman, "and go back to the hotel. Fetch Bonnie and get yourselves over to the jail. And you," he said to Conrad, "do like I said. Get your men over to the jail."

"I don't work for you," Conrad said.

"Fine," Stearns said. "Do it your way, Quincy man. Sprinkle your city-slicker gun hands around town and wait for Pritchard. He'll pick your boys off, one by one, like apples from a tree. Meanwhile, I'll be forded up at the jail. It's got brick walls, a tin roof, bars on the only window, and a door three inches thick. It's the only building in town that won't burn and can't be rushed."

Conrad absorbed Stearns's words. "Okay," he conceded. "We'll do it your way."

"I figured you would," Stearns said.

"Them's was gunshots I heard, all right," Tater said. "I'm positive. Sounded like they was comin' from the train station."

"It's Samuel," Idelle said, biting her lip. "He's come home."

"Let's hope so," Tater said. "If anyone can set things right, it's Marshal Pritchard."

Idelle was in the jail, in Ditch's cell, attending to Ditch, but she wasn't alone. Kezia, the beautiful Romanichal healer, had been attending to the unconscious deputy as well.

While Idelle looked on, Kezia had given Ditch a thorough examination. She lifted his eyelids, checked inside his nose, ears, and mouth, and even studied his hands and feet.

Using her mortar and pestle, she ground a number of herbs from her satchel. At Kezia's request, Tater boiled some water on the jail stove. She mixed the herbs, along with a dark liquid from a small bottle in her bag, into the boiling water and stirred. After the concoction had cooled to approximately body temperature, Tater and Idelle helped her gently lift Ditch's head into a position where the potion could be tipped down his throat.

"You wouldn't mind pouring me a shot of that stuff, would you, pretty lady?" Colonel Bennington catcalled from the adjacent cell.

"Ignore him," Idelle said to Kezia. "He's a pig."

"We Romanichals have a saying," Kezia said. "Avoid behaving like a pig. Pigs live in filth and die on the plate."

"Describes the colonel perfectly," Idelle said.

"This remedy will need some time to take effect," Kezia said as she emptied the last of the medicine into Ditch's mouth. "He must continue to rest, so his body can absorb the spirits and heal."

"I can't thank you enough for what you're doing," Idelle said.

"There is no need to thank me," Kezia said. "What your brother did for me and my people will always be remembered."

Manfri Pannell had related to Idelle in detail what Pritchard had done, and how he had directed them to Atherton. Idelle apologized to Manfri for the current state of the town, after explaining to him what had transpired since her brother left.

After Idelle finished her explanation, Manfri ordered Kezia to remain in the jail and assist with caring for Ditch. Then he wordlessly departed without saying good-bye, where he was going, or when he would return.

The door to the jail suddenly burst open and Eudora came rushing in. She wore her hat, coat, and gloves, carried her purse, and was out of breath.

"Samuel's back," she said. "I just heard two bounty hunters were gunned down at the railroad station. Everybody's clearing the streets."

Tater snapped his fingers. "I knew them's was gunshots I heard," he said.

Idelle turned to Colonel Bennington. "Scared yet?" she asked him.

"Hah!" Bennington scoffed. "That'll be the day."

Idelle wasn't convinced. "I seem to remember you refusing to face him," she said. "I also recall him tossing you on your behind and smacking you in the chops."

Bennington grumbled under his breath and sat down on his bunk.

The door opened again, and Jack Stearns walked in. With him was a big, burly man in city clothes. Idelle had never seen him before.

Stearns barely took notice of Eudora, Kezia, and Idelle. He approached Tater.

"Have you eaten your lunch yet?" Stearns asked.

"Why no," Tater said. "I've been too busy helpin' Miss Idelle with tendin' to Ditch."

"Why don't you go eat?" Stearns said. "Perkins's Diner is just across the street."

"I can't leave now," Tater protested. "Miss Idelle and Ditch might need me."

"Go eat!" Stearns said harshly. "That's an order."

"We're both deputies," Tater said, "and I've been a deputy longer than you. I don't have to take your orders."

"You do today," Stearns said, drawing his pistol. "Go eat your lunch, Deputy Jessup."

"You'd best go ahead," Idelle said to Tater. She addressed Eudora and Kezia, "You ladies better get going, too. Don't worry about me. I'll be all right."

"You," Stearns pointed to Kezia with his gun, "may depart with Deputy Jessup. You, Miss Chilton," he said, "will stay. Pritchard is sweet on you. That's something I can use."

"I wasn't in the mood to leave yet, anyway," Eudora said, moving to stand next to Idelle. Tater tipped his hat to Idelle and Eudora and escorted Kezia out of the jail.

Conrad looked out through the open door as five men, all dressed in city suits, approached. Each was wearing a revolver in a shoulder holster under his coat. Behind them, scurrying as fast as they could without actually running, were Benedict Houseman and Bonnie Shipley. Houseman had Shipley by her elbow and was nudging her along.

"My men are here," Conrad announced. "Where do you suggest I put them?"

"There's only one way in, or out, of this building," Stearns said. "Through the front door. Post your detectives outside the jail, in front, in the street. And tell 'em to be ready."

"But they'll be exposed to Pritchard's fire out there in the open," Conrad protested as Houseman and Shipley breathlessly entered the jail. Stearns closed the siege door behind them and bolted it.

"True," Stearns admitted. "But there's five of 'em. That's a lot of guns. Maybe your boys will get lucky and nail Pritchard? Then again, maybe they won't. He's sure to get a few of them, even if they do drop him. Either way, doesn't that leave you with a bigger slice of the new bounty you said Cottonmouth Quincy put up on Pritchard's head?"

"It most certainly does," Conrad said, rubbing his whiskers. He went to the window, which still had its shutters open.

"You men take up positions in front of the jail," Conrad ordered through the window. He looked back at Stearns, smiling smugly behind him. "And be ready."

"You're a pair of real heroes," Idelle said to Stearns and Conrad. "One solitary lawman is coming to face you. Instead of going out to meet him like men, you station an army outside and cower in here behind a locked door like frightened schoolgirls."

"Shut up," Conrad said.

"It's about time someone told her to shut up," Bennington agreed, from inside his cell.

"Mr. Conrad," one of the men shouted from outside. "Something's coming!"

"What do you mean, 'Something's' coming?" Conrad replied, stepping again to the window. "You mean *Someone's* coming, don't you?"

"No, sir," the man outside said. "I meant what I said. Something's coming!"

CHAPTER 51

Two large Romanichal vardos, each hauled by a pair of big draft horses, rolled toward the jail. When they were twenty-five yards away, their drivers steered the vehicles sideways and halted them in the middle of the road. Each of the vardos' drivers then dismounted, quickly unhitched their teams, and led the animals off in the direction they'd come, leaving a wall of Gypsy wagons in the street.

"What in the hell are those contraptions?" Conrad asked, staring out the jail's window. "And what in the hell are they doing with them?"

"Clearly," Stearns said, joining Conrad at the window, "Cottonmouth doesn't pay you to think. It's a barricade, you fool. They've just put up a wall in front of us."

"You said this jailhouse is made of stone and has only one window and one door," Conrad said. "Now there's a wall in front of us? That means we're boxed in."

"You figure that out all by yourself?" Stearns said.

"Look," Conrad said, ignoring the insult and pointing out the window. "People are coming."

And they were. A group of approximately ten

townsmen began assembling behind the vardos. All but one were carrying rifles.

"Mr. Conrad," one of the men outside called out. "Are you seeing this?"

"I can see," Conrad answered through the window.

"Men with rifles," the man said. "A lot of 'em."

"My eyes work just fine," Conrad said. "Don't let those guns spook you. Stand your ground."

"That's mighty easy for you to say," the Quincy man said over his shoulder, "from inside a brick jail. We're outside in the open, with nothing but pistols, facing almost a dozen men with long arms."

"You have your orders," Conrad said. "Carry them out."

"You fellers wait here," Pritchard told the group of townsmen assembled behind the vardos. "I'm goin' out to parlay."

"You sure that's a good idea?" asked Wynn Samples, the general storekeeper. He was holding a brand-new 1873 Winchester. The weapon was one of a shipment of a dozen identical rifles he'd ordered in the wake of Pritchard's endorsement. The others had been distributed among his fellow citizens.

"Wynn's right," said Seth Tilley, the undertaker's son. He'd brought along his own Sharps rifle. "If you go out there, Marshal, those Quincy men will shoot you down. I wouldn't do it, if I were you."

"Wynn and Seth are talking sense," John Babbit said. "The telegraph operator told me the wire Quincy sent out called for his men to cut off your head, after they kill you, and ship it back to him. That ought to tell you what they have in mind."

"I've got to do something," Pritchard said. "Idelle and Ditch are inside that jail."

"Miss Chilton, Benedict Houseman, and Bonnie Shipley are also in there," Tater spoke up, "along with Deputy Stearns, Colonel Bennington, and another Quincy man. I think he's the one in charge of the others."

"Maybe we can settle this without further bloodshed?" Pritchard said. "In any case, I've got to try. You boys cover me, will you?"

"Bet on it," John Babbit said. All the men took firing positions behind the Romanichal wagons. Some knelt, others stood, and a few lay prone. Ten rifles were aimed at the five Quincy Detective Agency men posted in front of the jail.

Pritchard checked his guns one last time. "If things go south," he instructed, "I'll drop to the ground and you boys can shoot over me. Just make sure to aim clear of the window. Ditch and Idelle are inside."

"Be careful," Judge Pearson said, putting a hand on Pritchard's shoulder. He was the only man behind the vardos not bearing arms.

"I aim to do just that, Your Honor," Pritchard said. "Everyone ready?"

"We're ready, Marshal," John Babbit said over the sights of his Henry rifle.

"We are ready, too," Manfri Pannell said, aiming his recently acquired Henry rifle. Three other Romanichal men with him, including his sons Vano and Danior, were also wielding Henrys.

"You, in the jail," Pritchard shouted as he stepped out from behind the vardos barricade and began walking toward the jail. "This is Marshal Pritchard speakin'."

"What do you want?" Stearns asked.

"I want to talk to Benedict Houseman."

"I'm listening," Houseman's voice answered through the window.

Pritchard halted when he was twenty feet from the five Quincy Agency men. He made sure to remain at an angle that kept one of them directly between himself and the window, so nobody inside the jail could draw a bead on him.

Each of the Quincy detectives stood frozen. Their empty hands hovered near their pistols holstered beneath their coats. Their eyes darted nervously from one another, to Pritchard, past him to the ten rifles aimed at them, and finally behind them toward the jail door.

"You're finished, Houseman," Pritchard began. "The governor and attorney general know all about your plan to swindle this town, along with that impostor you're passin' off as Burnell Shipley's illegitimate daughter. Her real name is Trudy Thompson. She's a dance hall trollop out of Saint Louis who's wanted for larceny. You're both under arrest."

"I believe I'll oblige you to come in here and arrest me," Houseman responded.

"Hell," Pritchard said, "why would I do that? You're already in jail." The townsmen behind him broke out in laughter.

"You Quincy Agency fellers," Pritchard addressed the five men standing before him, "are here to claim an unlawful bounty. To collect, you're expected to murder a federal marshal. Since I'm that federal marshal, I take that kinda personal. You've committed no crime, as yet. Drop your guns and stand down, and you'll be allowed to walk away. Continue to do Cottonmouth Quincy's unlawful bidding, and you'll find yourselves arrested, or worse. It's the best offer you're gonna get from me. While you ponder it, you should know that I've already put eight of your fellow Quincy men into the ground; two of 'em today."

The Quincy Detective Agency men looked once more at one another. An unspoken agreement passed among them.

"What's it going to be, boys?" Pritchard said. "You can walk away, be arrested, or die where you stand. It's all the same to me."

"To hell with this," one of the Quincy men said.

"Ten thousand bucks is a lot of money," another said, "but you can't spend it from prison."

"Or from a grave," a third detective said. "We surrender, Marshal." He slowly took out his pistol and dropped it on the ground at his feet. The other four men followed suit. They all raised their hands.

"Get yourselves to the railroad station," Pritchard told them. "Board the next train out of Atherton, and don't come back."

The Quincy men complied.

"Get back here!" a voice Pritchard didn't recognize ordered from inside the jail. "Pick up those guns! Come back!"

"Sorry, Mr. Conrad," one of the men said as they walked away. "You can tell Old Cottonmouth we're done. You want to shoot it out with a U.S. Marshal and half the town of Atherton, come on out of that stone jail and do it yourself."

"You yellow sons of bitches!" Conrad howled. The door to the jail suddenly flew open, and a tall, burly man in a suit appeared in the doorway. His Colt revolver was not aimed at Pritchard, but at the backs of the departing Quincy Agency men.

Pritchard instantly drew his right-hand Colt, but before he could fire, a shot rang out. A geyser of blood erupted between the burly man's eyes. He fell forward on his face, dead before he hit the ground.

Pritchard looked back to find undertaker Simon Tilley opening the action of his smoking Sharps, waving to him from behind one of the vardos. He inserted a fresh cartridge and closed the action.

Pritchard stood his ground. The door to the jail remained propped open by the big man's body.

"You, in the jail," Pritchard repeated. "Give yourselves up or come out and face me."

"Are you offerin' me the option of goin' to the train station?" Stearns's voice asked from inside the jail.

"I'm afraid not, Jack," Pritchard answered. "Or should I call you Jim Searcy? By whatever name you call yourself, Stearns or Searcy, you ain't goin' nowhere. You're under arrest."

"What for?"

"Conspiracy to commit murder," Pritchard said. "You wired six of your Quincy Agency buddies in Jefferson City and tipped 'em to which train I was leavin' Atherton on. Just like you tipped off your girlfriend Trudy in Saint Louis when the law was closin' in on her."

"How'd you figure me out?"

"Saw your picture in Quincy's office, under the name Searcy. Same name that one of my train bushwhackers gave as the man who tipped them off by telegram. By the way, how would you like me to address you? Stearns or Searcy?"

"Stearns is fine for now," came the reply. "Like

you, Pritchard, I've changed my name a time or two."

"I'm using my real one these days," Pritchard said. "What about you?"

"To be truthful," Stearns said, "I've changed it so many times, I can't remember."

CHAPTER 52

"What'll we do now?" Houseman whimpered. His voice squeaked with fear. He'd backed himself against the wall farthest from the jail's open door and stared in terror and revulsion at the deceased Quincy detective lying half in and half out of the entryway. His large body propped the door open.

"Calm yourself, Benedict," Stearns said. He stood on one side of the doorway, with his hands on his hips, staring across the room at the woman formerly known as Bonnie Shipley. She returned his stare.

"So, your name is really Trudy?" Idelle said. "Just like we suspected." She was in Ditch's cell, along with Eudora.

"How would you know?" Thompson asked.

"Ditch found a picture of you in your room," Idelle said.

"Why, Mayor Pritchard," Thompson said. "It would seem your fiancé isn't only a rapist, but a burglar as well."

"Ditch never tried to rape you," Idelle said. "You framed him, just like he said."

"Says you," she shot back with a wicked smile. "I think he liked me. All men do. Maybe Ditch would have dumped you for a chance with me."

"That'd be a cold day in hell," Idelle said.

"Too bad we can't ask him," Thompson mocked.

An enraged Idelle started toward Thompson, but Eudora held her back.

"What's it gonna be, Stearns?" Pritchard's voice yelled from outside. "You gonna give yourself up and be arrested peaceable-like?"

"Not likely," Stearns said, still staring at Thompson.

"I'd be lyin' if I said I wasn't pleased with your answer," Pritchard said. "I heard all about how you and that hookshop gal of yours set up my friend Ditch while I was away. Also heard tell how you slugged him from behind with a rifle. To be truthful, Jack, I'm beginnin' to regret my decision to deputize you. I believe I'm gonna enjoy sinkin' a lead plumb into you."

"Maybe I won't be the one eatin' the bullet," Stearns said.

"We ain't gonna find out," Pritchard said, "unless you crawl out from behind those skirts you're hidin' under inside that jail."

"Hold your horses," Stearns said. "I'll be out directly."

"What are you doing?" Thompson said. She ran to Stearns's side. "You don't have to shoot it out with him." She pointed to Idelle. "We have his sister hostage. It's why you wouldn't let me kill her before, remember? She's our insurance policy. If I recall, we agreed to keep her alive until

Pritchard was dead in case something like this happened."

"She's making sense," Houseman said. "Pritchard is hell on wheels with those pistols of his. You've seen him shoot, yourself. You don't have a sinner's prayer against him. Trudy is right. If we use his sister as a bargaining chip, we might just have a way out of this."

"I don't need to bargain over his sister," Stearns said. "I can beat Pritchard. Speed ain't everything in a gunfight."

Stearns drew his Smith & Wesson revolver, broke open the action, and checked the load. Then he reholstered the gun and took a key from his pocket.

Since Idelle had been visiting the jail to tend to Ditch, and especially after she'd pulled her Cloverleaf pistol on him, Stearns kept the desk drawers where the pistols were stored locked. He made sure that he, and not Tater, had possession of the only key.

Stearns unlocked the desk and removed Colonel Bennington's pair of engraved Colt .45s. He loaded them and handed one to Thompson.

"In case my appointment with the marshal doesn't go in my favor," Stearns said, "head-shoot the Pritchard gal, will you, honey? And while you're at it, plug Benedict."

Thompson cocked the Colt's hammer and pointed it at Houseman. "It'll be my pleasure, darlin'," she said. Houseman gazed at her in horror.

"Get into that cell," she commanded, herding the attorney into Ditch's cell with Idelle and Eudora. The cell's door remained open, but Thompson stood just outside, guarding the entrance with her pistol.

Stearns went over to Bennington's cell. "I trust, Colonel, that you're still no friend of the Pritchards?"

"You are correct," Bennington answered.

"How would you like to square your account with the Pritchard family and avoid prison at the same time?"

"I'd like that plenty."

"Can you still shoot with those crippled hands?"

"Not fast," Bennington said, "but very accurately."

"That'll do," Stearns said, unlocking his cell door and handing over the Colt. "When I go out to meet Pritchard, you take him from the window. Can you manage that?"

"With pleasure."

"You gutless mongrels," Idelle said. "I pray Samuel guns you both."

"I'd save your prayers for yourself," Stearns said, "and your unborn child, if I were you."

"Prayers ain't going to help the mayor," Thompson said. "If her brother loses, he's dead.

If he wins, she's dead. Either way, the Pritchard family gets smaller."

Stearns drew his second pistol, the .32 caliber Smith & Wesson Model 2, from under his coat with his left hand. He cocked the gun and held it behind his back.

"Like you said," Thompson told Stearns, "speed ain't everything." Her wicked smile broadened.

Stearns went to the doorway. "I'm comin' out, Marshal," he announced. He nodded to Bennington at the window. The newly freed colonel gave him a nod in return and thumbed the hammer back on his revolver.

"Wish me luck," Stearns said to Thompson.

"You won't need luck," she said, moving close and giving him a kiss. "You've got Bennington primed to bushwhack him, and that black-eyed Susan behind your back."

Stearns kissed Thompson one final time, then stepped over Conrad's body to exit the jail.

CHAPTER 53

Ditch slowly opened one eye and took in the scene before him. His head was throbbing, and he felt extremely weak. The last thing he remembered, before everything went dark, was stepping out of Idelle's hotel room shortly after he'd busted out of jail.

He discovered he was back in jail, lying on a bunk. Standing over him, with their backs toward him, were Idelle, Eudora, and Benedict Houseman. The women were holding each other, and appeared distraught, though it was Houseman who looked about to cry. Outside the open cell door, Bonnie Shipley covered them with one of Colonel Bennington's engraved Colt revolvers.

Ditch could also see Bennington, standing back from the window. He stood in a formal, one-handed shooting stance and held one of his engraved .45s at arm's length. He appeared to be aiming it between the window's bars at a target somewhere outside the jail.

No one had yet noticed Ditch was awake. He carefully flexed his fingers and toes under his blanket to get the blood flowing, and feigned being comatose. He heard voices outside in the street, and recognized one of them as Pritchard's.

. . .

"Good afternoon, Marshal," Stearns said as he slowly walked toward Pritchard. The wind had picked up considerably, and the first droplets of rain were beginning to come down.

"Good afternoon to you, Deputy Stearns," Pritchard answered. He took two steps to his left, which put Stearns's body between himself and the window.

Stearns stopped walking when he was at the picket line of pistols dropped by the Quincy Detective Agency men before they abandoned their posts. He appeared relaxed. His right thumb was hooked casually in his belt, only an inch from the grip of the Smith & Wesson .44 in the cross-draw holster at his hip. His left hand remained out of sight behind his back.

"How're Ditch and my sister holdin' up?" Pritchard asked.

"The mayor's doin' just fine," Stearns said. "Deputy Clemson, not so much."

"By the way," Pritchard said, "you're fired."

An amused expression lit Stearns's face. "Fair enough," he chuckled. "When do I draw my severance pay?"

"I'm fixin' to cash you in right now," Pritchard said.

Stearns's amused expression faded. "I'm waitin'," he said.

Quick as a flash, Stearns brought the .32 from

behind his back. The weapon's hammer was already cocked, and the pistol came up toward Pritchard in a lightning-fast blur.

Pritchard's twin Colt .45s roared.

Before Stearns could get the barrel aligned on his intended target, two slugs entered his breastbone less than an inch apart. Pritchard had drawn, cocked, and fired both of his revolvers so smoothly and rapidly Stearns never even saw the big marshal's hands move.

Stearns dropped his gun, blinked in disbelief, and fell to his knees. He looked up at Pritchard, tried to speak, vomited blood instead, and collapsed on his face.

"What are you waiting for?" an incensed Thompson hissed at Bennington. "Shoot the big bastard!"

"I can't get a shot," he retorted. "Stearns is in the way."

Thompson had been unable to contain herself and left the prisoners she was guarding to go to the doorway and witness the showdown. As a pair of gunshots rang out as one, she watched helplessly as Jim Searcy, more recently known to her as Jack Stearns, was gunned down before her eyes.

"Now I've got you," Bennington said, closing his left eye. He steadied the front sight of his Colt revolver on Pritchard's chest as his finger began to press the trigger.

Ditch Clemson suddenly threw off his blanket and leaped to his feet. He picked up Pritchard's handmade chair, which had been placed next to his bunk by Idelle, and smashed it over Bennington's head.

The chair broke into pieces. Bennington was rendered instantly unconscious, and his engraved Colt pistol discharged harmlessly into the ceiling as he tumbled to the floor.

Ditch also fell, spent from exertion. He'd used up every vestige of his fragile strength in rising to clobber Bennington, and fainted next to the inert colonel.

"You son of a bitch," Thompson snarled. She pointed Bennington's revolver down at the defenseless Ditch. "Now you'll get yours."

A shot was fired, but not from Thompson's Colt. A bullet tore into Trudy Thompson's temple. She sank on top of Ditch.

Across the room, from inside the cell, Eudora Chilton stood holding a W. W. Marston pistol with a thin trail of smoke emanating from one of its three barrels. An astonished Idelle watched as Eudora calmly walked over and rolled Thompson's body off Ditch.

"What have you done?" a flabbergasted Houseman asked. He stepped out of the cell, unable to take his eyes off Thompson, lying on the floor.

"What do you care?" Eudora said. "You heard

the marshal. They know she ain't Shipley's daughter. Your meal ticket's gone bust."

"But she was—"

"Useless," Eudora cut the lawyer off. "Open your mouth again," she said, pointing her gun at Houseman, "and you might become useless yourself."

Thompson wasn't dead yet. The .32 rimfire caliber bullet that had entered her skull didn't finish her completely. She lay gurgling in the throes of her death rattle.

Idelle watched in disbelief as Eudora cocked her pistol again and fired another shot point-blank into Thompson's head, finishing her. Then she daintily returned the tiny gun to her handbag, bent down, and retrieved the engraved Colt .45 from Thompson's lifeless hand.

"Oh my God," Idelle uttered. She rushed out of the jail cell and knelt by Ditch. He was unconscious again, but his fever was gone, and his breathing was strong and regular.

After checking Ditch, Idelle looked down at Thompson. "Did you have to shoot her again?"

"Don't be squeamish," Eudora said, pulling back the hammer to half-cock. "I saved your fiancé, didn't I? At least for now." She expertly opened the weapon's loading gate and spun the cylinder, verifying there were still four live cartridges in the cylinder.

"You had that hideout gun in your purse all

along," Idelle said in disbelief. "You could have prevented all this?"

"What makes you think I wanted to prevent it?" Eudora said, turning the Colt on Idelle.

CHAPTER 54

"What goes in the jail?" Pritchard called out. "Who fired those shots?"

"Nothing to worry about," Eudora's voice shouted back. "Everything in here is peachy. Isn't that so, Mayor Pritchard?"

Idelle suddenly appeared in the doorway. She had to step carefully, to avoid Conrad's body. She stood rigid, with her hands down at her sides. Her face was pale, and she wore an expression of dread.

"Idelle," Pritchard said. He started toward her.

"That's far enough," Eudora's voice said. She spoke from behind Idelle, using the mayor as a shield. She kept the barrel of Colonel Bennington's Colt revolver jabbed into Idelle's side.

"Eudora's got a gun on me," Idelle said. "Ditch and Colonel Bennington are both laid out on the floor inside. Trudy Thompson is dead."

"Her name ain't Eudora Chilton," Pritchard said. "It's Evelyn Stiles. Ain't that right, Evelyn?"

"Bravo," she admitted. "The intrepid lawman finally figured out who I am. Drop those guns, Marshal, or I'll drop your sister." Pritchard slowly drew his belt guns, tossing the Colts at his feet.

"Who's Evelyn Stiles?" Idelle asked.

"If I have my facts straight," Pritchard said, "she's the wife of an outlaw named Stiles I put to justice in the New Mexico Territory about a year ago, while I was still rangerin'."

"My husband was no outlaw!" Stiles screeched. "He was a former officer in the Army of the Confederacy, and a true Southern gentleman!"

"Your husband," Pritchard said, "Major Dalton Stiles, was no gentleman. He served with Shelby's Iron Brigade during the war, same as me. When the fightin' ceased, he became a holdout and refused to surrender. In the years after the war, he turned thief, robber, rapist, and murderer. He was responsible for the deaths of hundreds of innocent folks in the Arizona and New Mexico Territories."

The group of townsmen stationed behind the vardos got up from behind their makeshift barricade and walked over to stand behind Pritchard. They formed a semicircle around him, facing the jail with their rifles in their hands.

"We can rush her, Marshal," Tater said. "She can't get all of us."

"She can get Idelle," Pritchard said. "That's good enough to hold us right here."

"You're a damned liar!" Stiles shouted angrily. "My husband was no outlaw! He was a hero of the Confederacy!"

"Tell that to the people of Las Cruces," Pritchard

409

retorted. "Your husband and his gang left twenty-six dead men, women, and children in their dust after a bank robbery there. And in Magdalena, one hundred and twenty-seven miners were sealed to their fate when your husband dynamited the entrance to a silver mine. After his mob of butchers buried all the menfolk in Magdalena, they raped their widows and made off with everything in town that wasn't nailed down. Those're just a couple of your husband's better-known exploits. That's the kind of gentleman Dalton Stiles was."

"I don't believe a word of it!"

"Believe what you wish," Pritchard said. "The governors of Texas, and the Arizona and New Mexico Territories, believed differently. That's why they sent the Texas Rangers after him."

"How'd you figure out who I was, anyway?" Stiles asked, regaining her composure.

"In truth," Pritchard said, "I'm feelin' myself a regular dolt for not figurin' you out sooner. Lookin' back, you left plenty of sign."

"Maybe you would have seen it," Stiles taunted, "if you weren't so mashed up over me?"

"I reckon you're right about that," Pritchard said. "Dallyin' in your charms fogged my thinkin', that's a fact. Just like you jumbled your boyfriend Dominic Quincy's brains."

"Cottonmouth wasn't my boyfriend," she said. "He was just another in a long line of fools I used to find you, Samuel Pritchard. Or would

410

you rather be called Joe Atherton? That's the name you were wearing when you and your fellow Rangers captured my husband. You didn't even hang him, did you? You allowed him to be scalped by savages and burned alive in Magdalena's town square."

"He got what was a-comin' to him," Pritchard said. "And my name is Pritchard, not Atherton, if you please."

"Whatever name you go by," Stiles said, "I vowed to make you suffer the way my husband suffered. I heard all about how you killed over fifty men in Mexico after the death of your beloved fiancée. You killed my husband, but I don't have to kill fifty men to avenge him. All I have to kill is you."

"I've got to hand it to you," Pritchard said, trying to keep her talking while he devised a plan. "Pirootin' with a feller who owns a detective agency is pretty savvy. You must have wanted your revenge somethin' fierce."

"Mind your tongue," Stiles cautioned. "Calling me a harlot is a sure way to see your sister and her baby die before you do. The only reason Idelle's lived this long is because you're so damned hard to kill. Benedict and Trudy wanted to arrange her 'accident' the minute they arrived in Atherton. It was Jim Searcy, believe it or not, that convinced them to let her stay above ground until you went into the dirt. And as far as pirooting, I didn't notice you balking any when I shucked my linens."

"In hindsight," Pritchard said, "I should have. I realize now that playin' the hornpipe with you in the livery was no accident. You delayed my departure and put me on a train interrupted by six bounty killers. Another sign I missed."

"You slept with her?" Idelle blurted. "With that witch?"

"I didn't think she was a witch at the time I was grindin' corn with her," Pritchard admitted. "Truth be told, I don't recall gettin' much sleep."

"How could you?" Idelle said, appalled.

"That's a mighty odd question," Pritchard said, "comin' from a gal who got herself knocked up three months before jumpin' the broom."

"Don't be too rough on your brother," Stiles said to Idelle. "I'm very hard to resist."

"I guess there's no accounting for taste," Idelle said.

"Do you remember our encounter on the *Nellie Cropp*?" Stiles goaded Pritchard. "I remember it. I'm still riding sidesaddle."

"What I remember most," Pritchard said, "is shortly after runnin' into you on that riverboat, which was no coincidence, I ran into three more bounty hunters. You were the one who shot that feller Dan in his cabin, weren't you?"

"I was," Stiles admitted. "Couldn't have him talking, could I, after he and his two partners,

Charlie and Rowena, bungled cashiering you? Is that when you finally put all the pieces together?"

"No," Pritchard said. "The truth didn't strike me until I finally met Cottonmouth Quincy himself, in Saint Louis. Incidentally, where did you come up with the ten thousand dollars for the bounty on my head?"

"My husband gave it to me," she said. "He gave me a lot of money, before you had him scalped and burned."

"How do you suppose a Southern gentleman like Dalton Stiles obtained a bankroll that swollen, if he wasn't on the owlhoot trail?"

"I don't care," Stiles said. "What I care about is seeing you facedown in the dust."

"Which is something else that vexes me," Pritchard said. "I can't cipher out why you didn't kill me yourself. You surely had me at a disadvantage enough times."

"If I did it myself," she said, "folks might have sussed it out. Besides, that was the point of the bounty. When you finally got your deserts, I was going to swoon over your grave and be thought the heart-wrenched paramour."

"And then open up the Sidewinder," Pritchard said, "and run Atherton along with Houseman and Searcy?"

"You don't catch on very quickly," Stiles said, "but you do catch on. Now you're going to catch a bullet."

"Do as you will with me," Pritchard said. "But let Idelle go. She's done you no wrong."

"Not a chance," Stiles said. "She's going to suffer, too."

"If you harm my sister, you're not gettin' out of that jail alive."

"I'll practically guarantee it," Tater said. The other townsmen nodded in agreement.

"The joke's on you, Marshal Pritchard," Stiles laughed. "Living or dying is something else I don't care about."

"She's loco," Pritchard whispered over his shoulder to Judge Pearson. "She's gonna shoot Idelle no matter what."

"What can we do?" Pearson said.

"When I make my play," Pritchard said, just loud enough for all the men to hear, "open up on the jail. Be sure to aim high, boys. Idelle was shrewd enough to let us know Ditch is on the ground."

"I'm tired of conversing," Stiles said. "It's time for you to bite soil, Pritchard. I'm a fair pistol shot, but no sharpshooter. Come closer, so I can hit you squarely. I want to look into your eyes when you die. Start walking, or little sister gets a pill."

"Okay," Pritchard said, "I'll come in." He gestured to his empty belt holsters. "You can see I'm unarmed. But I'm only comin' if you agree to let Idelle go."

"No deal," she said. "If I let your sister go, what'll keep you coming?"

"I'll keep a-comin'," Pritchard said. "You have my word."

"Hah!" she snorted. "What's that worth?"

"You've still got my friend Ditch, don't you? I'll come for him."

"Deputy Clemson isn't worth much as a hostage," Stiles said. "He's practically done for already."

"Hell, if I am," Ditch said.

CHAPTER 55

Evelyn Stiles turned and swung her gun from Idelle to Ditch. The woozy deputy was still lying in the middle of the jail floor, between the unconscious Dexter Bennington and the deceased Trudy Thompson. He'd been awake long enough to take in the gist of the conversation between Stiles and Pritchard, and to realize she was holding his fiancée and unborn child at gunpoint.

Ditch was weak as a baby, but angrier than a stick-poked beehive. And he was just strong enough to pick up the colonel's other Colt revolver, cock the hammer back, and point it in Stiles's general direction.

Evelyn Stiles and Ditch Clemson both fired at the same time. Neither of them hit what they were aiming at.

At the sound of the gunshots, Pritchard drew his Remingtons from their shoulder holsters and started running for the jail, "Get down!" he shouted to Idelle.

Idelle started to run from the jail, but she tripped on Conrad's corpse and fell flat on her face. Pritchard began firing his pistols as he ran, aiming at the doorway where Stiles had been.

Once Idelle fell, Pritchard discovered Stiles was no longer framed in the doorway. He nonetheless continued to fire, figuring if he could sling enough lead it might keep her head down. He desperately wanted to prevent the insanely vengeful woman from reemerging and drawing a bead on his sister as she lay sprawled, defenseless, on the jail's porch.

The men of Atherton came to the same conclusion. Remembering Pritchard's admonition about aiming high, ten riflemen began firing at the jail's door and window. They spread out on both sides of him, to create a corridor of fire as he sprinted toward Idelle at the door. A storm of gunfire ripped into the jail.

The bullet fired by Evelyn Stiles missed Ditch, but struck Colonel Dexter Bennington, lying unconscious on the floor next to him, between the shoulder blades. He didn't even flinch.

Ditch's shot, fired while he barely had the strength to lift the Colt revolver, thumb back the hammer, and squeeze the trigger, flew wide, grazing Stiles's arm. After he fired, he dropped the gun and collapsed into exhaustion once more.

The furious Stiles ducked around the edge of the doorway, re-cocked her revolver, and was in the process of taking careful aim at Ditch when a torrent of bullets began entering through the window and door. She was so startled by the earsplitting hail of gunfire, and the impact of countless bullets as they ricocheted throughout the interior of the jail, she accidentally fired her pistol into the floor at her own feet.

Stiles kept her back to the wall along the door's edge, re-cocked her revolver for the third time, and risked a quick glimpse around the corner.

There, only a few feet away, was Pritchard. His hands were empty. He'd taken a knee between Idelle, who was struggling to rise, and the jail door. The firing outside ceased.

Pritchard fired the twelfth, and final, round from his Remington .44s just as he reached the jail's porch. Idelle lay flat on her stomach as he'd instructed, and as common sense dictated with a barrage of bullets flying overhead.

Pritchard dropped his empty guns and was helping Idelle up, when the gunfire abruptly stopped. He realized the townsmen behind him no longer had a clear shot with him and Idelle at the jail's door.

He looked up to find Evelyn Stiles, whom he'd known intimately as Eudora Chilton, standing over him with a cocked revolver and wearing a maniacal grimace. He knelt, placed Idelle behind him, and shielded his petite sister and her unborn baby with his broad chest.

Stiles was still as fiercely beautiful as when he'd known her by another name, but now her hair was disheveled, her cheeks smudged with gunpowder residue, and there was a bloody gash on her right biceps.

"Two Pritchards for the price of one," Stiles said as she raised the revolver. With Pritchard literally kneeling at her feet, it was impossible for her to miss.

"You told me once," she said, "that you were sorry for my husband's death. Are you still sorry?"

"Not a lick," Pritchard said. "Dalton Stiles died in flames, screamin' all the way to hell."

"Good-bye, Joe," she said.

Her finger had just begun to tighten on the trigger when the .44-40 bullet entered below her nose. Her head snapped back, the revolver fell from her fingers, and she dropped straight to the floor.

Pritchard slowly stood and helped Idelle to her feet. Then he turned, looked up, and saw Count Strobl holding up his Winchester rifle in triumph from the roof of Perkins's Diner, across the street. Pritchard gave the Austrian count a return wave.

Idelle elbowed past Pritchard and high-stepped over three bodies: Conrad's, Stiles's, and Thompson's, and rushed to Ditch's side. He was groggy, but conscious.

"I'll fetch Doc Mauldin," Tater said, and scurried off.

Pritchard, followed by Judge Pearson, newspaperman John Babbit, storekeeper Wynn Samples, undertakers Simon and Seth Tilley, and the Pannells, entered the jail behind Idelle.

"He's weak," Idelle said, cradling Ditch's head, "but he's going to be all right." Ditch gave Pritchard a feeble grin.

"I don't know what you're fussin' over him for," Pritchard said to his sister. "It's only a head wound. Everyone in Jackson County knows Ditch ain't got any vital organs up there." She wrinkled her nose at him.

"Bennington is dead," Judge Pearson said. "He took one in the back."

"So is Houseman," Babbit said, pointing to the attorney, crumpled in one corner with his eyes wide open. "Looks like he took at least three or four hits during that barrage we threw down."

"Benedict Houseman sure thought he was a clever cuss," Pritchard said. "But evidently he didn't possess enough sense to duck when there're bullets a-flyin' all around him."

Undertaker Simon Tilley and his son Seth took in the carnage and started their tally.

"There's one body outside," Simon said to his son, "plus the five bodies here inside the jail."

"Don't forget the two dead men at the railroad depot," Seth said to his father.

"You're right," Simon said. "I almost forgot them."

"You two gravediggers are going to be busy," observed Wynn Samples.

"I must say, Marshal," Simon Tilley said, "from an undertaker's perspective, you're the best lawman this town's ever had."

CHAPTER 56

Atherton, Missouri
June 1874

Ditch paced inside the jail office, biting his lip.

"Would you sit down?" Pritchard said over his coffee mug. "You're nervous as a whore in church on Easter Sunday."

"The marshal's right, Ditch," Tater said. He sat on a bunk in one of the empty cells with a napkin tucked into his collar, devouring a mountainous stack of flapjacks from Perkins's Diner. "All that walkin' back and forth is interferin' with my digestion."

"Nonsense," Count Strobl said. "A herd of rampaging elephants couldn't interfere with your digestion." He was seated next to Pritchard, sipping coffee and smoking a cigarette.

"I'm a little jittery," Ditch said, "that's all. It ain't every day a feller gets hitched."

"You weren't this jittery driving a herd of cattle across five hundred miles of hostile Indian country," Pritchard laughed. "Take a seat, will ya? I didn't buy all these fancy new chairs for nothin'."

After Ditch had broken his handmade chair over Colonel Dexter Bennington's head, Pritchard gave up on making another. Instead, he purchased a half-dozen, jumbo-sized, extra-sturdy chairs from Wynn Samples. The general storekeeper jokingly promised him the new chairs were guaranteed not to break over the noggins of escaped prisoners.

It was midmorning on what was shaping up into a beautiful day, and only a few days from the start of summer. It was also less than a week after the special election. U.S. Marshal Pritchard, who was now officially the town's marshal again, as well as the Jackson County sheriff, lounged in his office. With him was Atherton's newly elected mayor, David "Ditch" Clemson, Deputy Marshal Toby "Tater" Jessup, and Florian Strobl, who'd traded in the title *Count* for the title of *Deputy Marshal*.

More than a month had passed since the Second Battle of Atherton, as it was dubbed by the locals. The dead had been buried, the bullet holes patched, and peace and order had been restored to the sleepy mill town on the Missouri River.

"Here they come," Ditch said, peering out the window. "Lord a-mighty, what a caravan!"

Rolling toward them down the street was a Romanichal vardo pulled by four draft horses. It was adorned from top to bottom with flowers, and driven by Sabina Pannell, Manfri's wife. A large procession of townspeople followed, including John Babbit and his family, Wynn Samples, the Tilleys, Braam and Pearl van der Linden and their daughter, Jenny, and many other citizens, including Manfri, his two sons, their wives, and all of their Romanichal clan. Everyone was decked out in their Sunday finest.

Seated next to Sabina in the vardo was Idelle Pritchard. Her hair had been done up, she was clad in a white dress, and holding a bouquet of flowers.

"Why the parade?" Ditch asked. "I don't see why Idelle and I can't just walk over to the town hall. Hell, it's only down the street."

"It is not the distance you travel that is important," Strobl said. "What matters most is that you journey in style."

"Gate's sprung open, boys," Pritchard said. "Time to rodeo." He stood up, straightened his string tie, and buckled on his guns. Tater and Strobl did the same.

"Weddin's sure can tire a feller out," Tater said, wiping his mouth on his sleeve despite the napkin in his collar. "Marshal Pritchard made me shave, get a haircut, starch my shirt, shine my boots, and polish my badge. He even made me take a bath!"

"We should have weddings in Atherton more regularly," Strobl said, glaring at Tater through his monocle. "Say, at least once a week?"

"What exactly are you sayin'?" Tater challenged.

"Nothing," Strobl said innocently. "Only that I'm fond of weddings."

"You ready?" Pritchard asked Ditch, putting a hand on his shoulder. "We can't keep the bride waitin'. Nor Judge Pearson, who's lookin' forward to presidin' over your vows. If you're late to your own weddin', the judge is liable to lock you up."

"If I'm late to my own weddin'," Ditch said, "it ain't bein' locked up I'll have to worry about. Your sister will hang me."

"Let's get this show on the road," Tater said impatiently. "The sooner we finish the ceremony, the sooner we can get over to the Sidewinder for the celebratin'. That's the best part."

The Sidewinder's reopening had gone forward as scheduled, with Manfri and Sabina Pannell as the new proprietors. One of Idelle Pritchard's last official acts as mayor was to authorize the loan for them to purchase the building. But instead of merely opening a saloon, the Sidewinder was now also going to be a restaurant, as well.

The vardo came to a stop in front of the jail. Strobl held open the door, and Ditch stepped out.

Manfri Pannell helped his wife down from the vardo. Ditch climbed on in her place and took the reins. He and Idelle beamed at each other.

Pritchard waved to Idelle. "I'm so happy," she said.

"I'm happy for you," Pritchard said. "Our folks would be right proud."

"See you all at the weddin'!" Ditch called out.

He prodded the team, turned the vardo around, and steered it toward the newly finished town hall, which had been decorated for the occasion.

Pritchard, Strobl, and Tater waited until everyone else in the procession started back before beginning their own stroll to the town hall. As they walked, a lone rider approached.

"Howdy," the man on horseback said. He was tall, stoop-backed, at least sixty years old, with a handlebar mustache and wearing a wide-brimmed Stetson. He wore a Colt Navy converted to fire metallic cartridges, and the badge of a U.S. Marshal.

"Good morning," Pritchard answered.

"I'm lookin' for Marshal Pritchard," the man said.

"You found him."

"I'm U.S. Marshal Buck Dellums," he said. "I've been dispatched by Governor Woodson to assist in peacekeepin' here in Atherton, at the behest of Judge Pearson."

"When, exactly," Pritchard asked, "did Governor Woodson dispatch you?"

"April," Dellums said. "Or was it early May? In truth, I don't rightly remember."

"That's better'n a month ago," Tater exclaimed.

"No offense," Pritchard said, "but you're a mite tardy."

"None taken," Dellums said. "I won't travel by train, 'cause my horse don't like it, and since I can't swim, I won't travel by boat. That leaves only one way to get where I'm goin' besides walkin'."

"Jefferson City is a five-day trip by horseback," Pritchard said, "at most."

"My horse hit a rut," Dellums explained, "and I got throwed. Put my back out. Been laid up in a farmhouse near Sedalia for weeks."

"Trouble's past," Pritchard said. "We have no need for you now."

"Just as well," Dellums said. "I'm gettin' too old for gunplay." He reined his horse around and headed out of Atherton the way he came.

"How do you like that?" Tater said.

"C'mon, fellers," Pritchard said, slapping Strobl and Tater on the backs. "Quicker we get to the weddin', the quicker we get to the beer."

"I like the sound of that," Strobl said.

"You'll like the sound of this even better," Pritchard said. "I'm buyin'."

"Are you buyin' lunch, too?" Tater asked.

"Sure," Pritchard laughed. "All you can eat."

"Yee-hah," Tater hollered.

ACKNOWLEDGMENTS

I wish to express my heartfelt gratitude to the following individuals for their support in the writing of this novel:

My friend Marc Cameron. Retired U.S. Marshal, bestselling author, martial artist, pistoleer, family man, all-around badass, and stand-up joe. If you can find a better . . . well, you can't.

My friend, and editor at Kensington Publishing, Gary Goldstein. He encouraged me to turn a lifetime love of westerns into something more tangible. The fact that he is a man of great honor, a horror film aficionado, and an absolute kick-in-the-ass doesn't hurt, either. After Gary, they broke the mold. (And then performed an exorcism on it.)

My friend, and literary agent at Trident Media Group, Scott Miller. I taught my son there are only two kinds of men in this world: those who "get it done" and everybody else. Scott always gets it done.

The Calaveras Crew: Chris the Stallion, also known as Vergon, Emperor of the Dragons (17th Level Ninja of Tongular Flippage); Lothar the Merciless; Russ the Gunfighting Urologist; Canadian Todd; Barry the Duke; Savage Ed; Rodeo Eric; Rick Boat; and the inimitable Frank

Brownell. Sidehackers all, and men to ride the river with.

The Usual Suspects, whose support is deeply appreciated. If it takes a village, ours is the "Village of the Damned."

Lastly, and most important, my wife, Denise; daughter, Brynne; and son, Owen. They are the greatest blessings ever bestowed on a fellow. I am humbled every day. Today, tomorrow, and forever. You know the rest.

ABOUT THE AUTHOR

SEAN LYNCH grew up in Iowa, served in the army as an enlisted infantryman, and spent almost three decades as a municipal police officer in the San Francisco Bay Area. During his law enforcement career, he's been a motorcycle officer, firearms instructor, S.W.A.T. team member, sex crimes investigator, and homicide detective. Learn more about Sean at www.seanlynchbooks.com.

Center Point Large Print
600 Brooks Road / PO Box 1
Thorndike, ME 04986-0001 USA

(207) 568-3717

US & Canada:
1 800 929-9108
www.centerpointlargeprint.com